Supernatural Tales

Volume One

By

Peter Buckley

This edition published in 2017

Copyright

Supernatural Tales Volume One © 2015, 2017 Peter Buckley
© 2015 P.L.J.M

Supernatural Tales Volume One is a collection of four novellas
in the Supernatural Tales series.

The Burning © 2014, Driftwood © 2014, Fields of Blood ©
2015 and The Mansion ©2015 written by Peter Buckley and
published by P.L.J.M

ISBN 978-0-9933483-0-3

To my family for all their support through the years and all those that believed in me during this journey.

Contents:

Peter Buckley

The Burning

The Burning

By

Peter Buckley

Love Cannot Die

Chapter One

They rode out of town shooting into the air, laughing and shouting. The seven horsemen had left the sheriff and his deputy lying in the dust of the town road. The local lawmen had gone to the saloon to eject the drunken group after they had shot at, beaten and scared the locals who frequented the Broken Ridge Saloon. The sheriff and his deputy had tried to ask them to move on, but the seven were used to taking what they wanted through aggression and intimidation. They had beaten, stabbed and shot the legs of the two lawmen before dragging them out into the street and made sure that a message was delivered to the cowering local people hiding in the various shops and buildings of the town. The leader of the group had walked calmly up to the two and shot each one through the head. It was just another town. They had gained a fearful reputation across the Midwest; several sheriffs and US marshals had attempted to arrest or kill them. All had failed to claim the bounty on the heads of the seven, a bounty they were proud of: fifteen thousand dollars a man, dead or alive. Many of those who had tried had ended up coming to grizzly ends at the hands of the evil posse of cowboys.

They feared no man. They were a law unto themselves; wherever they went death followed. They had been cornered in the past: they had all been shot, some had been stabbed and two of the group had been shot with arrows from a small native hunting party. They had always survived and believed they were blessed— but not by god; they had killed too many people, including preachers and pastors, to know that their luck wasn't heaven sent. The wanted posters had hung in towns for the past two years, the bounty increasing with each passing month. They had been named The Riders of Death by the townsfolk of Beavercreek, Colorado, a name that made the leader of the gang proud.

Reed McDonough was raised by his preacher father in Idaho, a man who quoted passages freely to all his church flock but behind closed doors drank heavily and ruled with a strong hand and belt. His mother had died during childbirth. It was something his father held against him, right up until the day he died at the hands of his own son. After being on the receiving end of a drunken beating, Reed had run to his room and returned with a pistol he had stolen from an unconscious drunken man the last time he and his father had gone into town. He pointed the gun at his father and pulled the trigger. The first bullet hit him in the leg, causing him to fall to his knees. The second hit him in the shoulder. The third grazed the side of his head taking his right ear with it.

He pleaded with his son; however, the sixteen year old had a profound sense of pleasure and satisfaction at seeing his father begging. He raised the gun to the bloody, sweaty, tearful man and shot him through the head. It was the making of him. He spent the following five years joining up with thieves and other likeminded murderous men until he had honed his craft and built a reputation for being a fearless, mindless killer, working his way up the food chain in the small gangs until he had his own little band of killers to follow him, each one

5

having their own modus operandi. Paul McGrub and Randolph McCaula both enjoyed slitting throats. On occasion, both men had fought with each other over who could do the final life taking cut before they both stood and enjoyed seeing their victim's life drain away. They may have argued and beat on each other, but the bond between them was too great for them to completely fall out.

Linus Moonon enjoyed torturing people with his bull whip; he got excited every time he saw the whip tear into the flesh of his victim. 'Wild' Bill Hardinger, a big strong man with a carefully groomed moustache that he worked into points at each end, enjoyed beating his victims with his fists before shooting them in the chest. Jack Borgman, like Reed, was the son of a preacher and shared his hatred of religious folk. He would single out the more devout of their victims and punish them by shooting them in the hands and feet before placing them in a crucifix position and shooting them in the heart. The final member of the posse was Wheeler Blanchard, a man who had a deep hatred for native Indians. The left side of his face was heavily scared due to a fight he had had with a Native American Brave who had cut Wheeler, blinding his eye. He wore the scar and damaged eye as a badge of honor, deciding not to wear an eye patch. He enjoyed the look on people's faces when they saw the full white orb of the dead eye that sat in his socket. He was known for his enjoyment of hangings, which were reserved for any native that crossed paths with him.

The seven were very rarely separated or alone—only when enjoying the pleasures of a town's working house did they break from one another's company, and even then, sometimes they would insist on sharing a woman or two or insist on having rooms next to each other. As a group they were unstoppable: no man could get them, but individually they knew they were vulnerable.

They rode out into the plains, heading south to the border of Utah and Arizona, looking for another unsuspecting town where they could take their fill of drink, women and enjoyment, taking death, destruction and despair with them.

Later in the day they had come across a wagon train and decided to take advantage of the free food, money and women that it carried. They killed all the men, some being tortured for hours before finally being allowed to die. Some were forced to watch as their wives were raped and their young children shot or molested. For two days they enjoyed the spoils of their capture, gorging themselves on the bread, meat and whisky. Once all was devoured or packed for their ongoing journey south, they killed all that was left of the living members of the caravan and left the bodies for the birds and wild animals that roamed the plains.

They rode for several hours until they reached a small river and paused at the banks. They were aware that they were about to enter Indian land. For Wheeler, it was a moment of excitement; the thought of killing an Indian filled his mind. Reed made it clear that all seven must keep an eye out for war parties and make sure that all guns were fully loaded.

Chapter Two

The two lovers rode next to each other, chatting happily as they passed amongst the mesas of the valley, the young native girl occasionally looking around to make sure they were not being watched. She had been warned by her father and brothers that it was forbidden for her to see the young soldier who rode alongside her in his blue uniform, yet here she was leading him through her homeland. They had been meeting like this for several months, learning each other's languages. She enjoyed telling him all the stories that she had been told as a young child about the warriors and spirits that fought and travelled amongst the great towering pillars of rock. Samuel Lewis listened intently, smiling each time their eyes met. He himself knew the risks they were both taking; he, a soldier in the US army, had been asked to protect his own kind against the savages (as it had been put to him by his superiors), yet here he was, deeply in love with the daughter of a Navajo chief. He knew if he was caught by his fellow soldiers he could be tried and hanged for being a traitor, and if she was caught, she would be killed. He dared not think about what would happen to him if he was caught by her tribesmen; he had heard horrific stories of what had happened to other soldiers that had been captured by the native Indians. He was yet to witness any of the things he had been told and found it hard to believe, after spending so much time with Little River, that such atrocities happened.

She knew if she was seen by her fellow tribe's people that her white lover would be killed; she would suffer the indignity of being cast out and shame would be brought on her family. They had met when he was on a routine patrol just outside of the town of New Haven; she was riding with others when her horse was startled by a gunshot fired by another soldier trying to scare them. The horse reared up and threw her and the other soldiers laughed and carried on riding back into town and the barracks. Samuel, however, rode over to her, jumped down from his horse, helped her up off the floor and calmed her horse. There was no speaking, just the act of kindness and a meeting of eyes and a smile. Satisfied that she was not injured and safely back on her horse, he returned to the small barracks of the town, but each day he would see her sitting on her horse at the same spot where he had helped her. On a day off from duties, he decided to approach her, and from that moment, their journey together began.

They stopped underneath one of the mesas and unfolded a blanket. They sat down together and enjoyed the little feast of bread and fruit he had brought with him. They had often done this over the summer, growing closer and closer, but today was different. In all the time that they had been meeting they had never kissed or made love; today was the day that they both felt the magic of their love, not only kissing for the first time but consummating their relationship. After they had made love, they lay together rolled in the blanket, Little River nestling her head into Samuel's chest.

'What would be my name?' she asked.

Samuel looked down at her and into her eyes. He didn't understand what she was asking, his face contorted in confusion.

Little River saw his confusion and asked again.

'If I was to have a normal lady's name, what name would I have?' she asked again.

Samuel looked at her and replied, 'You have a name—a beautiful name.'

'But by what name would you call me? Just you, no one else—a normal ladies name that you will call me.'

Samuel looked up into the clear blue sky and thought. After a while he returned his gaze back to her.

'Marie,' he answered.

Little river closed her eyes and repeated the name over and over. She smiled and hugged Samuel tighter.

'So what about me?' Samuel asked. 'What native name would I have?'

Little River sat up and looked at Samuel, 'My Father taught me to see the spirit animals of people; yours is strong and caring, you spirit animal is Bear.'

'Bear hey?' Samuel smiled, imagining a large aggressive bear.

'Not an angry bear but a gentle bear, so you would be called Gentle Bear,' Little River explained, smiling at Samuel.

'Gentle Bear? That's not very warrior like,' he said, smiling at her.

'Bear is a powerful but caring animal, with a big heart,' she replied.

'Well I'll be your Gentle Bear and you are my Marie.' He then kissed her softly.

They spent the afternoon holding each other, chasing each other playfully, and discovering the beauty of the valley and the towering mesas that surrounded them.

The couple had been watched for a while—not by Little River's tribe or Samuel's military brethren, but by seven dusty, dirty and blood-lusting men. They had watched as the two chased each other joyfully. The fact that one was a white man and the other an Indian made Reed's stomach churn; others in the group looked on from their high vantage point in disgust. As the two packed their things back onto the horses and slowly rode out from underneath the mesa where they had eaten, the seven horsemen decided that there should be no relationship between a Native American and a White man.

They moved quietly back to their horses and mounted; they knew that the two lovers would be heading towards them, so they waited until they were just about to clear the mesa they had hidden behind and then launched out. The sudden force of seven horses charging made the valley reverberate with a low rumbling, like the sound of thunder. The two lovers momentarily looked up and at each other and then saw the horsemen. The sheer sight of them forced an electrical charge to surge through their bodies as fear attacked their senses.

'Go!' Samuel shouted to Little River, kicking his heels into his horse, jerking it into action.

They both pushed low into their steeds, trying to get every last bit of speed out of them as they rode deep amongst the canyons to escape the chasing posse of men. The seven men began to gain on the two fleeing lovers; every yard gained on them brought an excited smile to the faces of the seven. Reed removed his right hand from the reins; there wasn't even a drop in speed from his horse as he reached skillfully for his gun, aiming at the blue jacket of the soldier. It was a skill he had honed over the years, a necessity needed to survive, shooting at a moving target while on a horse in full gallop. He focused, looking down the pistol he held out in front of him, feeling the rhythm of the horse's movements and then, *BANG!*

Samuel felt a thud against the upper right side of his back, then the sensation of falling, the force of the impacting projectile pushing him forward and off balance. The next sensation was his meeting with the dusty ground. He landed flat on his back, and the air in his lungs burst out in one almighty breath. He then bounced a second time before rolling to a stop in a cloud of red dust. Little River heard the bang from the gun and then the thud of a heavy object hitting the floor; she looked over her shoulder to see a cloud of dust and a ride less horse, free from its pilot, bolting off to the right. She pulled sharply on the reins, bringing her horse to a skidding halt, jumped down and sprinted to the body on the floor.

Samuel struggled to breathe amongst the dust and the failure of his lungs to draw in air; he looked up at the girl running towards him. 'No, run, get away!' Just these few words took all the energy he had, but she still ran towards him. He reached down by his side, the burning sensation emanating from his back growing with each passing second. Every little movement needed to reach for his gun was met with a growing pain and resistance to move.

The horsemen, seeing the soldier fall and the girl stop and run back to him, slowed their approach. They knew they had them. There was nowhere for them to go; they had the advantage. They reached the couple, the girl pulling on the man, trying to get him to his feet, a wet patch darkening the back of his dusty blue jacket. Reed raised his pistol once more and fired. This time the dust at the girl's feet exploded like a geyser. She let go of her lover and stumbled backwards.

The horsemen jumped down from their horses, and Linus and Wheeler ran over and grabbed the girl. Wheeler, snatching at her long dark hair, yanked her head back. 'What do you think you doin', savage?' his stale breathe invading her nose and causing her to pull away from him. He just pulled harder.

'Now what do we have here? A soldier boy and his savage girlfriend.' Reed placed his boot on Samuel's chest, forcing him into the ground. 'Did no one ever tell you that White folk and savages don't belong together?' He pushed harder into the soldier's chest, causing him to wheeze as his only good working lung struggled with the pressure of the body pushing down on him.

'You're a disgrace to the army boy!' Wild Bill shouted. 'Cavorting with the enemy is punished by death.'

All the horsemen laughed; then their attention moved to the young girl. She continued to struggle against the two men holding her. They had made a mistake. They thought that she was just another female that they could do whatever they wanted with, but she was the daughter of a Navajo chief: a great warrior. She was also the only girl in the family of five and watched and learned from her brothers how to fight and hunt, even though her father didn't like it. They had left one hand free. She reached down and slowly removed a small knife from the belt that had been hidden by the length of her blouse top.

'So savage, what we going to do with you?' Wheeler said through an evil grin.

The others laughed and then Randolph made a suggestion. 'Rather than just kill her, let's see if savages are different from White folk. Let's have some fun with her little body and then Wheeler, you can finish her.'

'Don't you touch her,' Samuel coughed as blood leaked from his mouth.

Reed looked down at the young soldier, 'It's a little late for that boy, but don't worry, we're gonna have some fun with you.'

Wheeler began to laugh along with the rest of the posse, taking his attention away from the girl. In that moment, Little River brought her free arm up, knife in hand, and caught him across the face, He screamed, let go of her hair and grabbed his face. Linus, startled by his comrade's reaction, also let go of the girls arm. She used that moment to run back to her horse; a hail of bullets flew past her. As she mounted the horse, one bullet ploughed into its rear, causing it to bolt, and Little River clung tight as it sped off. Linus grabbed Wheeler and pulled him upright, telling the moaning cowboy to show him what had happened. When he did eventually remove his blood-soaked hands, Linus's mouth dropped open and he slowly backed away.

'What? What is it?' he shouted. He noticed he sounded slightly different.

The others all looked at him, shock etched on their faces. Reed then gave him the bad news. 'Wheeler, you're missing your nose.'

'What?' Wheeler shouted, padding his face and nose area with his bloody fingers. He then looked down at his feet, and there in the red dust of the canyon lay the end of his nose. The knife had taken the flesh all the way to the bridge of his nose. What remained made him look like a skeleton with two cavernous holes. Out of sheer anger, he pulled his gun from his holster, knelt down next to the soldier and grabbed his hair, pulling his head up off the floor.

'That whore of yours has just taken my nose! I'm gonna make you pay for what she did!' He put his pistol next to his ear and fired; the following sound and shockwave shattered his eardrum, the pain freezing his brain. Even with little air in his lungs, he let out a scream. Blood poured from his ear and the pain, which had a ringing to it, forced his eyes shut.

Reed removed his boot from the chest of the young soldier and looked around, scouring the scenery. He realized that they didn't have much time before a war party descended on them. He looked for a place or something they could use on the body below him. 'Pick him up,' he commanded. 'Take him over there to that tree, get some rope and tie him to it.'

Within minutes, the group had tied Samuel to the tree. Jack Borgman insisted that they tied the soldier up in a crucifix position. He then proceeded to shoot the hands and booted feet of their capture. Samuel was toyed with for what seemed an eternity but in reality was ten minutes. All seven took it in turns to dish out their punishment. Wild Bill beat the body and face with his heavy fists, leaving it swollen blue. Linus whipped the jacket, cutting the fabric. He then proceeded to use his bullwhip to lash out, the tip cutting deep into the swollen deformed face of Samuel. Paul and Randolph took it in turns to push knives into the arms and legs of the helpless body. Wheeler then cut off the other ear, pulling open the shattered jaws and placing it in the soldier's toothless mouth. Finally, Reed stood from his rocky throne, where he had watched his gang members take it in turns to inflict their punishment. He approached the body on the tree, stood staring at it, took his gun out placed it against the forehead of Samuel and paused.

'I think I'll let you suffer.' He replaced his gun and walked away, back to his horse, and the others followed, Wheeler having stemmed the blood pouring from his wound with a neckerchief tied tight across his face holding in place some material he had ripped from the soldier's uniform. They all mounted their horses, took one last look at their work, laughed and then continued their journey south towards the state line.

Little River rode her horse hard until it finally gave in. Its heart was pushed to its limits and the wound it had suffered forced it to finally fall. She picked herself up and ran until her body gave in and forced her to stumble her way through the canyon floor until she saw the smoke of the reservation tepees and other buildings. She found her second wind and managed to run, heading for the largest hut. She burst into her father's Hogan, where he sat with her three brothers, their conversation halted by her interruption. She burst into tears, trying to explain what had happened. Her brother's initial concern deteriorated into anger when she explained that she had been with Samuel; they began shouting at her about how the White man cannot be trusted and that she was forbidden from seeing him. She persisted in her telling of how she was in love with him and that he was injured and needed help. They refused to help based on the fact that he was an untrustworthy White man. Her father, Chief Dancing Elk, then sat back in his chair. She looked at him through her tear-filled eyes; she could no longer hear the voices of her brothers telling her what was right and wrong.

'Stop!' her father commanded.

The brothers ceased their berating and looked at their father. He could see that her heart and spirit were seeking help for a man she really did love. He stood and raised his usually calm, peaceful voice.

'We cannot behave like the White man does to us. We must rise like the great eagle, above our prejudice, or we can claim to have the same values,' he said.

He ordered his three sons to get their horses. They looked at him with surprise, and he again commanded them to get their horses and find the soldier. The brothers left their father's home, shaking their heads and muttering their disagreement, but he was their father and the great tribal chief, so his word was all-important and needed to be followed. Once alone he knelt next to his daughter, pulling her head into his big barreled chest.

'Daughter, you are my greatest gift given to me, so you shall have all that you desire. Even if this chosen one of yours is a White man, your spirit is true and has led you to this man. He is welcome in my home. Take your brothers to where he is.' He pushed her out of the Hogan's door, shouting to the three mounted warriors to go with Little River to retrieve the soldier.

The eldest of the three, Fighting Bull, rode up to her and grabbed her outreached arm, hauling her up onto his horse. She wrapped her arms around his waist. He looked over his shoulder at her and asked her which way; she relayed where they had been, and he kicked hard against the sides of his horse, shouted and drove his horse forward. They then galloped out into the canyon lands towards the area where Little River and Samuel had been attacked.

They rode for thirty minutes deep into the canyons and towering mesas. Little River clung tightly to her brother, and her heart pounded with fear and worry as they approached the area she had escaped. Her feelings of worry grew to momentous proportions, and tears streamed down her face. They saw the signs of struggle, the blood-stained ground, one a dull single patch the other making a trail, which on occasion led to a little pool of crimson dust. With no immediate sign of the soldier, they spread out, looking at the ground for any track or sign that would tell them where he may be. One of the warriors steered his horse around a large rock formation; he took his gaze from the floor and lifted his head. In front of him stood the old tree with the bloodied soldier tied to it. He shouted to the others, jumped down off his horse and ran over to the body. He stood in front of the bloody soldier, disgusted by what he saw. He heard the others come up from behind the rock formation. He turned to them and shouted at his brothers to keep Little River there. The panic and seriousness in his voice startled them all, and they tried to grab Little River as she jumped off the back of the horse, but it was too late; she ran past them up to the tree. Her brother saw her charging up towards him and moved towards her, stopping her with a big hug. It was too late; she had already seen what remained of the good looking, proud young man. She collapsed to the floor, her screams echoing around the canyon.

The brother's thoughts and feelings for the White man their sister had fallen for dissipated and turned to sadness and disgust. They cut his body down from the tree, wrapping it in a beautiful woven blanket that one of the brothers carried with him, carefully lifting it up onto the back of one of the horses. Little River sat on her eldest brother's horse, hunched over and weeping. There was no desire to rush back, so they slowly headed back to the reservation village. Two of the brothers walked, leading the horses with Little River and the soldier's body on it.

Once they reached their father's Hogan, they carried the body inside and lay the woven blanket that had now gained dark red stains on the floor. Little River knelt and

21

wept uncontrollably over it, and her father walked over and rested his hand on her shoulder. He looked at his sons; all of their faces depicted anger. He turned and exited his home, and the brothers followed behind. Once outside, they relayed what they had found and the disbelief that another man could do such terrible things to another. Their father walked back over to the door, looked in at his daughter kneeling by the covered body crying, looked back at his sons and ordered them to take the body to Thunderbird Cave, where they were to create a fire and lay the body on it. He then went back inside to his daughter, helped her up and took her back to her Hogan while the brothers took the soldier's body.

Once inside Little River's home, he comforted her, telling her that those that killed her love would pay for their evil deeds. He held her close, telling her stories that he knew she enjoyed as a child. He did this until she fell asleep. He then lay her down, returned to his Hogan, gathered up his medicine bag and flute, mounted his horse and headed out towards Thunderbird Cave.

Chapter Three

Chief Dancing Elk arrived at the cave to find the brothers standing around the body. He took out a large black feather from his bag and began waving it over the body. On the second pass, he began to chant, his calling and whooping filling the cave. The brothers stood back. He then threw a silver-colored dust over the covered body; the powder glistened against the shadows of the cave. He then took a piece of wood from the fire and lit it and then touched the wood below the body, which in turn burst into flames. He removed a wooden flute and began playing. Above the cave, clouds gathered, lightening flashed within them and the wind began to groan around the canyon. The brothers felt the wind pick up and heard it whistling around the entrance. The fire around the body grew stronger and stronger. As it engulfed the body, the flames turned green and seemed to dance in time with the notes of the flute. The flames intensified, throwing shadows on the cave wall. The shadows pulsed and danced, and screams and ritual chants filled the cave. The brothers moved closer to one and other. They could feel the energy building: their skin tingled, and hair stood up on their arms and neck.

The flames began to rotate into a small fire tornado, the notes of the flute became longer and louder, winds began to blow dust into the men's faces and small red embers jumped from the fire. Then it was suddenly silent. The chief placed his flute back in his bag and walked outside. The three brothers followed their father out to the plains where he raised his hands into the dark night sky and began chanting. Lightning flashed, filling the sky, and thunder echoed amongst the mesas and canyons. He lowered his arms, and his chants slowly faded as he finished the last note. He looked at his sons, motioned with his head towards the horses, and all three turned and gathered their horses and mounted. The chief slowly got onto his horse, glanced back at the cave, and then together they rode out back towards their homes, the storm building in intensity above the cave.

In the cave, the fire raged on, growing brighter with every rumble of thunder whilst outside a dark twisting shape moved across the dusty floor. It danced around the rocks and boulders that lay on the canyon floor, heading towards the cave entrance, its spinning increasing and tightening up. It burst into the cave, expanding to its outer walls, blasting the inside with rotating winds. At the center of the room, the flames of the fire rose. From within the burning embers, a hand reached up, followed by an arm and then a head. The body pushed out from the burning coals; it gained a foot hold and stood tall, the flames licked around it, yet it was oblivious to the heat and the glowing sharp flames. It looked around at the stony room, its eyes scanning the dark areas of the cave. It then turned its attention on itself, marveling at the blue military jacket, feeling each button, holding out its arms and looking at its hands and admiring them. The figure paused and reached to the side of its head, tracing fingers lightly along his ear. Then, feeling the soft skin rolling

24

between its fingers, it smiled. The soldier then set his eyes on the entrance and leapt up out of the fire onto the floor, it landed in a three point stance, then stood up. The figure slowly turned and looked at the fire, its eyes focused on a charred blackened skull deep within the burning ashes. He then turned his attention back to the entrance. A flash of lightening lit up the doorway, followed by a crash of thunder. The figure then bounded out of the cave and disappeared into the night.

A large explosion high above the settlement woke Little River. She sat up, looked around, and saw her father sitting in a chair at the far end of the Hogan. She stood up and walked over to him, kneeling down at his feet and resting her head against his knee. She could smell the distinct aroma of smoke, a thicker, dense smell, not the same as the little fire burning in the center of the clay building she was in.

'Where have you been Father?'

Her father leaned forward, put his hand on her head and smiled at her. 'The men who did that to your soldier need to know your pain.'

She pushed back off his knee, looking at his face; the warm glow of his face had gone. A colder, more serious look peered at her. The tears began to flow, 'What have you done Father?'

The wind picked up outside, pushing open the door of the Hogan they sat in. Her father stood and walked in front of her, and she peered over his shoulder and saw a figure standing in the doorway. A flash of lightening revealed some of the figures features. Little River recognized the man at the door: it was her soldier. She pushed past her father and ran straight into the arms of her lover. She wrapped her arms around his neck, but his embrace seemed cold. She looked into his eyes, which appeared void of any emotion, dark and foreboding. Little River backed away shaking her head. The soldier looked over at Little River's father, who bowed. He then held out a knife. It was the knife that had been left embedded in his thigh. The soldier took it from him and held it up, turning it slowly as he inspected it. He then turned and walked out the door. Little River ran over to her father, begging with him to tell her what he had done.

'You are my only daughter, I want you to be happy. Once he has shown them your pain he will come back to you.'

She looked at him and shook her head. 'Will it really be him? His spirit is different.' She bowed her head, the tears streaming down her face.

'He must put right what has happened; his spirit burns within him, guiding him to those who hurt you and took his life.' He put his hand on her shoulder and squeezed. 'You shall be together again but you must not follow.'

'Why father?' she asked.

'I have seen in my dreams what happens, and you must not go,' he said with a voice that held a tone of authority.

26

Little River waited until her father was asleep before saddling her horse. Walking out beyond the community of Hogans and tepees, she mounted her horse and headed south. Tears still rolled down her face.

When the sun rose, one of the brothers entered Little River's Hogan to check up on her as his father had told him to do. He looked around the deserted room and ran over to his father's home. He threw back the animal-skin door and entered. Waking his father, he explained his finding. Little River's father ordered his son to gather the other two brothers and to track Little River, bringing her back to the safety of the reservation. Within thirty minutes, the three brothers were saddled up and packed with food and weapons, heading out to follow their sister's tracks south.

Chapter Four

The blackness of the cold night was pierced by the pinpricks of light cast by the town's buildings. The town's saloon bustled with weatherworn faces. In the corner, a group sat. They emptied shot glass after shot glass of whisky. Once the bottle ran dry, they shouted at the bartender to bring another. Whenever one of the group stood or shouted, the other people present froze, afraid that any sudden movement would result in them being singled out and used for the posse's entertainment. A woman moved from table to table and flirted with its occupants. Some of the men smiled and gently pushed her away, while the more whisky influenced grabbed and groped; she then smiled a teasing smile and pushed them away. Reed had watched her visit each table in turn but avoid the one he sat at with his posse. She had tried hard to avoid eye contact. He had had enough of the drinking and chat about their last kill; he had an urge and that urge needed satisfying.

He stood up, his eyes locked onto the woman. 'Enjoy yourself boys. I'm gonna get my enjoyment somewhere else.'

The others followed his gaze, saw the woman and grinned at each other. Reed walked over to the table where the woman was sitting on another man's knee. The man squeezed her chest excitedly, and she looked down at the wide-eyed look on his face and laughed. She then felt a tight grip on her wrist, followed by a yank. She was pulled up to her feet and into the chest of a man. She went to strike out but stopped herself when she looked up at the heavily weathered face of Reed. The man sitting down who had been enjoying his grope stood up and squared up to the other man who held the woman, his anger suddenly dampened when he realized who it was he was about to lash out at. Reed turned his head and stared at the smaller drunk man. He then put his hand on his face and pushed him back, causing the man to fall over his chair. The room fell silent before it was broken by the laughter of the drunken group in the corner. Reed looked the woman up and down.

'So where we going?' he said menacingly. Fear filled her face as she stammered her answer.

'Upstairs.' Reed pushed her towards the stairs, and she reluctantly led him away up the stairs into her room.

The others continued to drink, until finally the liquid forced two of them to make their excuses, stumble out of the saloon doors and head down the side of the building and out into a small clearing to the little wooden sheds that made the toilets for the saloon. They had learned to go in pairs so one could lookout for the other. They would wait for the other to finish their business before swapping roles to make sure they weren't surprised. Tonight it was Linus's turn to stand outside and act as lookout first, while Wheeler, still wearing his neckerchief across his nose less face, relieved himself. Out in the darkness, a figure watched, its eyes burning with a deep anger. Linus hopped up and down on the spot, desperately holding in the fluid that wanted to escape.

'Come on Wheeler! Hurry up, I gotta go,' he moaned.

'Hold ya horses boy,' came the drunken response.

The figure had closed the distance between himself and the hopping cowboy. Linus heard a sound behind him; his need to relieve himself momentarily disappeared as he pulled his gun and searched the darkness. He stood there frozen, listening and scanning the blackness. Satisfied that he could not see anything, he relaxed and re-holstered his gun. The moment his gun nestled into its holster, the figure in the darkness pounced. Linus didn't have time to react; all he could manage was an intake of breath as the figure smashed a fist into his face his world melted and joined the veil of blackness of the night as he fell unconscious to the floor. Wheeler, sitting on the wooden beam that was the toilet seat, heard a thud. He sat bolt upright, his drunken state causing his head to spin. He shook his head trying to clear it.

'Hey Linus, you messing with me?' There was no answer and no sound.

Linus came too, feeling his head being shaken from side to side. The shaking ceased when he opened his eyes. His hands were tied behind his back, and a gag had been pushed into his mouth. His hands wriggled and pulled against the tie that held them together. He used his fingers to investigate the floor he was sitting on. He recognized the dry, brittle feel of straw. The light around

30

him flickered, his vision slowly cleared of the misty view it had presented him seconds earlier and his jaw throbbed. He looked around and saw a figure sitting on a chair nearby. He strained to make out any features, but they were hidden with the shadow cast by the structure above him.

The figure stood up and moved into the light, his features made sharper by the burning torches, Linus's mouth dropped open, and his face drained of all color. The face smiling back at him was that of the young soldier they had tortured and left to die only two days earlier, but it couldn't be. The figure in front of him had no injuries. His mind tried desperately to rationalize how the soldier could be standing there. He even shook his head hoping that if it was the whisky talking. He looked down at his belt, but his whip was gone. In that moment, he felt naked. He then heard a familiar sound, the sound of leather unfurling and hitting the floor. He looked back at the soldier, tears welling up in his eyes.

Samuel drew back his arm and then threw it forward; the whip shot back and then extended at speed out in front, the crack as it reached its full extension coincided with the muffled cry of pain as the whip flicked the wide-open eye of Linus. He attempted, out of instinct, to grasp his face, but his hands were blocked by his body. Samuel then wrapped the whip around the neck of the weeping cowboy and dragged him over to a thick wooden beam, the pain emanating from his eye socket and face drowning every other sense. He was pulled up on to his feet and pushed against the beam. Samuel then withdrew the knife from Linus' belt. The smiling soldier slowly removed Linus's hands from their restraint, with his hands now free he grabbed his face. Samuel pulled them back down and positioned them in a cradling position below his belt.

'You have a message to deliver.' Samuel pushed his face close to Linus's.

Samuel slowly pushed the knife into Linus's stomach, left of his navel. Linus slowly exhaled, his head moving forward slightly, causing the two men's foreheads to touch. He found he could not create any sound; he could only find the energy to breathe and endure the pain. Samuel stared deep into the cowboy's eyes as he moved the half-sunk knife across his victims stomach, at points using a sawing motion to continue the cut. He stopped on the opposite side of Linus's bellybutton. Linus felt the warmth of his blood as it covered his cradling hands and then something soft fell into his hands.

'Don't go dropping them!' Samuel said with a patronizing smile. He then backed away from his victim, watching with satisfaction as Linus slowly shuffled to the door.

Wheeler, feeling a little vulnerable, wiped his backside quickly and yanked up his trousers, the sudden movements making him feel dizzy. 'Linus, you better not be playing with me!' he shouted, leaning against the door listening. No reply came, and there was no sound. He pulled out his gun and used the barrel to push open the door, looking through the increasing gap, checking for anyone who may be waiting. No one lay in wait; all that greeted Wheeler was the blackness of the night. He stepped out of the little wooden toilet and began moving back towards the saloon. He spun round several times in the short distance to the side of the building. He pushed his back into the wall, checking the dark areas of the walkway; a figure began to walk towards him. It staggered left then right; as it got closer, he recognized it as his partner and toilet watcher, Linus.

'Where you go? You know we don't leave anyone alone.' Wheeler vented his disappointment at his friend through his neckerchief.

Wheeler continued to moan at Linus, who wobbled closer. He noticed that Linus was holding something in his hands, something that was generating steam, the vapors rising up off of it in the cold night air. 'What you got there?' There was no answer. Wheeler moved towards his friend, then froze; the sight that greeted him sobered him. A ray of moonlight burst through the cloud and cast its glare onto the very spot that Linus now stood. In his hands was a wet-looking substance. The man's face was swollen, and blood poured from his mouth. He took two more steps and his legs buckled beneath him as he collapsed down. What he had been holding spread out in front of him but seemed to attach itself to his stomach, he lay on his back, a large dark gaping hole in his stomach. Wheeler ran to the front of the saloon and burst through the door. Everyone stopped what they were doing and looked at him and the look of terror embedded on his face. The others that he drank with stood up quickly, kicking their chairs back. They rushed over to him, and he tried to explain what he had just seen, but his words, already difficult to understand because of his lack of nose, became more muddled and confused.

'Just point you stupid idiot!' Wild Bill shouted, getting frustrated with the time it was taking for Wheeler to get his words right.

Wheeler pointed towards the corner of the room, and they all looked at the wall. Then they realized that whatever it was lay beyond the wall, and they began heading out the door. They stopped after a few steps, looked around at the fearful eyes of the people in the saloon, and Jack Borgman then pushed three of them back.

'You go get Reed. We'll take Wheeler and see what's wrong.' He then motioned to Wild Bill, who grabbed Wheeler by the shoulder of his jacket and went outside; the other three ran up the stairs to find Reed.

Jack led the way. Wheeler followed, being helped along by Wild Bill. They reached the side of the saloon and paused. Jack drew his pistol and held it up in front of him. He then inched his face around the corner of the building and looked down the alleyway. He could make out the shape of a body on the floor. He returned his head to the safety of the front of the saloon, and then turned to the other two and motioned with his head to follow. Wild Bill pulled out his pistol from its holster. Wheeler looked down at his shaky hand and drew his pistol. They moved down the alleyway, their eyes scanning all shadows and possible hiding places. Wheeler could only stare at the body lying on the floor. They reached the body of Linus, his intestines lying next to him, the silky red coils glistening in the moonlight that shone from between the gaps in the clouds

Jack kicked the body at his feet just to check if there was any life left in his younger friend; there was no response. He looked at the other two, his face screwed up with anger,

'We need to find whoever did this.'

They turned and began walking back to the saloon front. There was no slow movement this time; they walked with purpose until a sudden glint and a thud stopped Jack in his stride. The other two walked into the back of him. He pushed back against them.

'What? What's wrong?' Wild Bill asked.

Jack looked up above him. He then motioned with his hand at something on the floor. Both Wild Bill and Wheeler peered over his shoulder at the wooden floorboards. There, standing tall, was a knife stuck in the board, its blade shining in the lunar rays. He bent down, pulled it out of the wooden floor, and looked at it carefully. His eyes widened and then he continued his walk back to the saloon, the other two following closely. He burst through the doors to find the other two waiting at the foot of the stairs. 'Where's Reed?' he barked.

'He doesn't want to be disturbed,' came the reply.

'God dang it,' Wild Bill moaned.

Jack then walked back over to the table they had shared a few minutes before. He sat down and plunged the knife into its center; its handle gently waved from side to side. The others froze and stared at the blade. Randolph's' eyes bulged; he then looked at the others. 'Where did you get that?'

'As a guess, from whoever did young Linus,' Wheeler replied.

Randolph realized that Linus hadn't returned with the others, 'What happened to Linus?'

Wild Bill filled in the other two with the gory details of how they had found Linus lying with his intestines in his arms on the floor outside. Jack then asked where Randolph had left the knife. He looked at Paul, who confirmed that the knife had been left in the soldier two days ago. Wheeler finally managed to gather himself enough to join the conversation and suggested that it must have been native Indians, looking for revenge for attacking the girl who got away.

On the edge of town, a horse slowly moved within the darkness, it's rider looking at the low glow of the building's lights up ahead. The riders' ears listened intently; she had never been this close to the White man's town before. She had heard from her brothers that going there would mean death by hanging. She had already passed a tall wooden A frame, which was dimly lit by burning torches. At its center, a noose rocked back and forth in the gentle breeze. It had been put there as a warning to any native Indian. The message clear, her type were not welcome. She ignored the warnings and headed deeper into town, keeping close to the shadows amongst the dark buildings. She was here to find her lover.

A young man entered the saloon, his blue jacket flapped open as he walked; several of the men sitting at tables around the room looked at him. They were somehow drawn to the man; there was something dark about him that made them feel uneasy as he walked over to the bar. The bartender moved down the bar to the man and placed a little mat in front of him, when he looked up he noticed the blue jacket of a soldier, he moved his gaze to the face of the stranger. His welcoming smile disappeared. The face that looked back at him had numerous scars over it, the eyes appeared as if sunken deep into their sockets.

'What'll it be?' the bartender stuttered, unable to take his gaze away from the scarred face.

'You need to leave!' the soldier answered.

The bartender backed away, slowly moving back down the bar. The soldier turned around and leaned back against the bar. He stared at the table with Wild Bill and his partners. Wild Bill had a sudden desire to look up at the bar. When he did, the look of alarm on his face stopped the conversation at the table.

'What you lookin at?' Jack asked with a confused tone to his voice. When he got no answer, he and the others followed his gaze.

One by one, each of the gang members' eyes bulged when they saw the soldier standing at the bar looking at them. Samuel pushed himself off the bar, standing up straight. He began fastening his blue jacket one button at a time, starting from the bottom and working his way up. He then walked calmly out of the door. The gang snapped out of their hypnotic state and looked at each other, looking for confirmation that they had all seen the same thing.

'Go see where he's gone,' Jack said to Wheeler, Paul and Randolph, motioning with his head to the door. He then grabbed Wild Bill's arm, dragged him to his feet and began leading him towards the stairs.

'Where you going?' Randolph called, panic causing his voice to sound higher.

'We're going to get Reed. You go follow him and we'll be with you as soon as we can,' he responded.

The three walked outside, pulling their pistols out. They looked left and then right down the dark street, their eyes searching the darkness for any sign of movement. They began walking carefully, trying to make as little sound as possible. They decided to go left towards the center of town. Then they split up, Randolph remaining on the left side of the street. Wheeler crouched his body slightly and ran to the other side of the street, pinning his back against the wall of the barber shop. Paul sighed, realizing that he had not been quick enough to respond and had been left with the duty of walking down the middle of the street. He reluctantly moved out into the middle of the street; they then began moving down towards the center of town, each one straining their eyes, scanning for any sign of the soldier or movement.

Jack Borgman banged on the door, calling Reed's name. There was no answer. He tried again, hitting his fist against the door harder, and the door swung open. Standing in only his undergarments, pistol in hand, Reed stood scowling.

'What is it!' he snapped.

'Linus is dead and we've just seen the soldier.' The speed and tone in which Jack had replied unnerved Reed.

He walked back into the room and over to a chair where the rest of his clothes lay. The others followed, noticing the woman sitting on the bed. Her face was bruised, and blood flowed from a bite-shaped wound on her cheek. She covered her naked body with the bed sheet, pulling it tighter into her chest when she saw the other two men look at her smirking. Reed pulled on his trousers and sat at the end of the bed and began pulling on his boots. He looked at the two men. 'Where's the others?' he quizzed.

They explained that they had sent the other three to follow the soldier. He nodded approvingly, stood up off the bed and began pulling on his shirt, ignoring the woman who continued to cower behind the sheets behind him. He marched out the door with his two companions following close behind. As the door shut, the woman burst into tears, partly because of the pain that had been inflicted and partly out of relief that he had left.

The three cowboys moved slowly, searching the shadows with their eyes. As each break in the buildings passed, they paused and ducked their heads into the space and back again, making sure it was clear and safe to cross the gap. Wheeler moved along the windows of the hardware store. A board beneath him made a creaking sound. He paused; the last thing he wanted to do was alert someone to his location. With his attention on the wooden beam at his feet, he did not see the face watching him from the other side of the window. When he did look up again, it was too late. His ears caught the first sound of something hitting glass and then glass shattering, but that's all he caught. The next thing he was aware of was being pulled through the window frame and into the warmer interior of the shop. He landed on his face, the pain from his nasal wound exploding. He screamed in agony, grabbing his face. He felt the neckerchief holding the blooded material on his nose yanked off, and then a hand pushed past his and two fingers inserted themselves into the large black cavities that replaced his nose. His eyes widened with the pain. He was then pulled by this facial handle along the floor and into a backroom, his feet kicking backwards, trying to gain some form of purchase on the floor. He pushed himself along, trying to release some of the pressure and pain from his nose.

The other two heard the crashing of glass and the high-pitched scream of their friend. For a moment they didn't move, they just looked at each other. Then they ran to the side of the street that Wheeler had been on and saw the broken window that he had disappeared through. They pushed themselves into the wooden wall on either side of the window and took it in turns to bob their heads in and out of the windowless frame. They could only see darkness.

In the back room, Wheeler felt a slight sense of relief when his captor's fingers were removed. He rolled onto his knees, reaching for his knife that should have been in its sheath on his belt, but it wasn't there. A sudden burst of flame jumped out from within the darkness. The light from the flames revealed the scarred and tortured look of the soldier. He stood with a rope in his hand, and at the end of the rope was a noose. Wheeler began looking around him, looking for anything he could use as a weapon. He saw a rack with several pitchforks standing in it, and he reached out and snatched at one, knocking it to the floor. The soldier didn't move. Wheeler grabbed it, stood, and thrust it at the soldier, as if to scare him, but he did not flinch, Wheeler then took three steps towards the soldier and stabbed out with the pitchfork; the prongs went deep into his body. Wheeler pushed against the resistance of the soldier's body, plunging the fork deeper. He managed a small smile as he did and then let go of the

41

long handle and stumbled backwards, waiting for the soldier to fall. The soldier looked at Wheeler, and an evil smile crossed his face. He looked down at the fork sticking out of him and tossed the burning torch to the floor, small bright red hot embers jumped as it hit the wooden floor, bouncing along the wooden boards of the backroom, some coming to rest on canvas sacks. The embers burned the dry material, causing it to smoke and then catch fire; the growing fire added more light to the room, revealing more of the scars on the soldier's face. The canvas bag was soon passing its flame to its neighbor, which in turn passed it onto the dry wood of the counter that they lay against.

***

They heard the scream just as they exited the saloon. The sound of a man screaming with such intensity stopped them in their tracks. Realizing that it was one of their own, they ran in the direction that it had come from. They found the other two pinned to the hardware store wall on either side of the broken window. They pushed in behind Paul, guns drawn. They could see a light flicker from deep within the dark, and a strange crackling sound began to build from within.

Samuel pulled on the shaft of the pitchfork with his free hand, the prongs slowly inching out. No blood flowed from the holes left by the four sharp spikes. He turned the fork around and pointed it at Wheeler. Wheeler froze with fear; he didn't even have the ability to move as the soldier returned the favor and rammed the fork into Wheelers leg. He fell to the floor; his face was numb, and the tears in his eyes caused by the intruding fingers joined those of the pain of his stabbed leg. Samuel used this moment to drop the noose over the head and bloodied face of Wheeler, pulling the knot tight against his neck. He stood back, looked up at a beam high above him and threw the rope over it. Once its end had returned via the other side of the beam, Samuel pulled. Wheeler felt himself rise as the noose pulled tight against his throat. He quickly attempted to get to his feet to take away some of the tension, but it was too late, his feet left the floor, the rope cutting into his throat, stopping the air flow that his body needed to survive. his muscles tensed, causing his body to arch in mid-air as the final moments of his life began to leave his body. The flames grew around them, and Samuel stood staring at the body, the red and orange glow of the flames causing a dark shadow of Wheeler's now limp body to appear on the wall like a large black painting.

Reed led the way, stepping through the broken window frame, pistol at the ready, heading towards the increasing glow beyond the door. The others followed close behind. He could hear the sound of snapping wood and smell the burning from behind the smoke-hazed door. He turned the handle and pushed the door open; the heat from the burning room hit him in the face, forcing him to look away for a second. When he looked back into the room, his eyes were more acclimatized and could see two people; the others pushed in behind him. Wheeler's body hung from the ceiling, his legs now on fire. Just beyond him stood the soldier, staring up at him. The bright, ever-changing light from the fire painted his heavily scarred face with a gentle warm red color. His dark eyes showed no emotion; he seemed unmoved by the heat or choking smoke that filled the room. Reed shouted and fired, and the others joined him, finding a space in the door frame where they could see their target and empty their pistols into the soldier. The increasing heat and smoke caused them to blink and squint. Their normally perfect aim became erratic; the bullets not only ripped into the body of the soldier, causing him to jig around in a wild dance, but many of them hit the burning body of Wheeler, whose body began to swing and move in time to the bullets. The fire continued to grow; it reached out towards the door where Reed and the others stood. They fired until they heard the clicking sound that told them they were out of bullets and needed to reload. Satisfied that they had hit the soldier, they backed out of the doorway and back to where they had entered, back through the broken window and out into the street.

They stood in the middle of the road and watched; the fire had engulfed the downstairs rooms, burning out of control.

'Well, whoever he was he's now dead!' Wild Bill laughed.

There were shouts from people who had heard the gunfire and had come to investigate and saw the growing light of the fire. Even with a town building on fire, they still knew not to get involved, especially with the five cowboys standing outside watching it. From inside the building there was movement; they all saw it and looked at each other as if confirming what they had seen. The front door of the store, which had been locked, burst open, and standing in the burning frame stood the soldier, his body engulfed with flames; however, he and his uniform remained untouched, and he did not flail about in agony. He just stood looking at them. Reed and the others fumbled with their pistols and bullets, trying to reload quickly. The odd bullet fell to the floor as shaky hands struggled to find the holes for them.

They fired again at the burning body standing in the doorway. This time the soldier laughed as the bullets ripped through his body. Once the firing had stopped, he walked towards them. The flames that surrounded him faded and finally died out as he walked. The five men turned and ran. Jack and Reed ran back towards the saloon, Paul and Randolph ran across the street towards a large building and Wild Bill stood his ground. He was running from no man. He dropped his pistol at his feet and clenched and unclenched his fists as the soldier walked towards him. Once within range, he swung at the face of the soldier, his fist connecting. Samuel's face shot one way and then the other when a left hook hit. The clapping sound of fist on face continued for a further three strikes. Wild Bill took a step back, ready to admire his work and allow his human punching bag to fall to the floor. The soldier stood strong, turning his head to face him, and then smiled. Wild Bill suddenly froze. Fear had drained him of all strength and ability to move. With his guard down and strength sapped, Samuel shot out a hand, grabbing him around the back of the head and pulling Wild Bill towards him. The sudden pull caused him to fall to his knees. Samuel then pulled the hair on the back of his head, forcing Bill to look up at him. He then took his free hand and placed three fingers in Bill's open mouth; his thumb pushed into the soft skin under his chin and pulled. Wild bills muffled moans were drowned out by the cracking sound of his jaw snapping, the bones exploding and the sound of tearing as his jaw was ripped from his face. Samuel threw the bloody mandible to the floor, then grabbed Bill's head in two hands. His thumbs rested over the big man's eyes, which stared at him though a tear-formed veil. He then began slowly forcing his thumbs into Bill's eyes, pushing against any soft resistance. Wild Bill's body thrashed around uncontrollably. Samuel pulled his thumbs out of the now black and bloody sockets of the cowboy and let him drop to the floor, leaving him on the floor to suffer. Samuel began walking away but paused after a few steps. He turned and looked at the writhing body on the floor. Sighing, he returned to Wild Bill, picking up the cowboy's pistol and removing a single bullet from the belt. He loaded it into the chamber, pulled back on the hammer, pointed the gun at the big man on the floor and fired. Wild Bill groaned and shot into a fetal position, holding his now burning groin. The blood poured from the hole that the bullet had made. Samuel smiled nodded and threw the gun on the floor. Satisfied, he walked away.

Reed and Jack ran back into the saloon. The remaining customers looked at the pair as they fell through the door, their terrified faces causing some of the regulars to make their excuses and head towards the door, side shuffling past the two panting cowboys.

They walked over to the bar. Reed pointed his gun at the barman, who slowly backed away and exited the room via a side door. Jack walked around the back of the bar and pulled a bottle of whisky from beneath it. He placed it on the counter top in front of Reed, who just looked at it and shook his head. Reed's eyes stared into the floor, his head bowed deep in thought. Jack shrugged his shoulders and pulled out the cork from the neck of the bottle. He didn't want a shot glass; he needed more than just a shot. He lifted the bottle to his lips and took two big gulps. The burning sensation that the liquid produced forced him to close his eyes, and plant the bottle back onto the wooden top with a bang. The sound startled Reed from his deep focus. He looked at the bottle and then at his partner. Jack's eyes were beginning to water from the strength of the alcohol.

'Wowee! I needed that.' He coughed.

Reed stood up and walked to the door. Jack watched him from the safety of the bartender's side of the bar. Reed pushed the door open and stepped out. He looked down the street at the burning building and could see figures running around, some throwing water with nothing more than a bucket over the angry flames. He turned and took a step back towards the door he had just exited, but a movement out in the shadows caught his attention. He paused, took a step back and focused on the figure on the horse. The dull, ever-changing light from the burning building down the street slowly revealed the rider in brief pulses. Reed's eyes stopped straining and widened when he recognized the Navajo woman. He pushed himself against the wooded wall of the saloon deep within its shadow, his breathing slowing as if afraid that the woman would feel his exhaled air. He moved slowly down the wall, staying within its shadows, his eyes burning with anger. The fear he had felt when he saw the soldier was gone, replaced by the need and focus of wanting to capture the rider.

Little River's eyes darted between the scurrying people. She searched for her lover but could not see him. Slowly, she moved deeper into the town, staying close to the sidewalk, within the shadows of the buildings. She moved past the light of the saloon windows, her eyes watching for movement from within. She couldn't see the figure shrouded in the blackness of its shadow until it was too late. Reed burst from the shadows, ran at her and grabbed her white animal-skin jacket, pulling her off the horse. She had no time to react or cry out; she had caught the movement just as he grabbed her arm, pulling her upper body past her left leg. The momentum forced her to roll in mid-air, her legs accelerating past her upper body until she hit the dark dusty floor on her right side, the force of the landing pushing out any air that had been in her lungs. When she did manage to take a breath, it caused her to cough and choke on the dust that had been kicked up and surrounded her from her heavy landing. The horse reared up out of fright. The moment its front hooves touched down into the dusty floor, it turned and bolted back the way it had come. Little River continued to gasp for air as she was pulled across the dusty road by her hair, she clawed at the hand that had clamped around her long black hair. Reed dragged the struggling woman back across the road, yanked her up the two steps onto the sidewalk outside the saloon and then back through its doors into the bright lights of the bar. With one last heave of hair, he threw the wriggling body in front of him and drew his gun, pressing it against the now straggly hair of the woman.

Chapter Five

Paul and Randolph crashed through the large door of the building, and both fell to the floor. The fear and panic that raced through their bodies forced them back to their feet and into a run. They searched the dark room; the outline of a stagecoach loomed out of the darkness, and they both pulled at the doors and clambered inside. Randolph pushed his body into the coach floor, while Paul, realizing that his partner had beat him to the darkest space, lay on the seat and pressed his back into it. They both lay silent, their ears searching the air for any sound that may tell them that they were not alone. The concentration to do this against the pounding sound of their hearts and heavy breathing caused them to squeeze their eyes shut, screwing their faces into painful expressions. They lay there for what seemed an age but in reality was just a few minutes. Randolph was the first to break the silence.

'You think we gave him the slip?' he began, and even though whispering he feared he was too loud, getting quieter the longer he spoke. 'Paul, can you see anything?'

Paul lay motionless, his eyes searching the darkness of the carriage. He was too afraid that even moving would alert anyone to his location. 'I can't hear no one.' He responded just as silently as Randolph had. In unison they rose, slowly trying to avoid any sudden moves that could cause any sound. Once sitting up, they reached down to their holsters and felt the empty spaces where their guns usually sat.

'I don't have my gun!' Randolph whispered with an air of panic in his voice. The light sigh coming from his partner unnerved him, he knew without Paul saying that he had also lost his gun.

Their hands automatically moved from the empty holsters around to the knives resting in their sheaths. Both the men felt a sense of relief when their palms wrapped around the knife handles; these were the weapons they were more comfortable with and they both knew that no one apart from each other were more skilled as they with a blade, not even a native warrior.

Their moment of comfort was suddenly taken away when a creaking sound split the air and the silence; it sent a shockwave through their spines, causing their hearts to jump into high speed.

Samuel could feel their presence; he could hear their hearts beating and the smell of blood pumping through their bodies. He'd calmly traced their path, just like a rattlesnake tracks its bitten prey: following their smell and body heat. They had run into a stagecoach barn, where a large carriage stood. Bales of hay formed a wall behind them, stacked from floor to ceiling. The two cowboys had dropped their guns near the broken door. The soldier had picked them both up and placed them in his waistband and then proceeded to the stagecoach, where the two murderers lay hiding. He grabbed the frame of the stage, and in one aggressive surge of anger lifted it up. The sound of wood splitting and snapping as well as the thumping sound of two bodies being tossed around inside the carriage interior filled the blackness of the room. The carriage, which had become Randolph and Paul's world and hiding place, suddenly bucked and moved violently; they were thrown from their seated position into each other as the floor became the roof and the roof became the floor.

The stagecoach lurched into the air, its wheels leaving the firm ground beneath them. Before it landed, it momentarily balanced on two wheels, then rolled onto its side, and then with new-found momentum, continued onto its roof. The two cowboys hiding inside found themselves laying together, Randolph on top of Paul, but both clinging to each other, they realized that they were no longer moving and scrabbled on hands and knees out of the gapping side that once held a door. They both pushed each other out onto the straw-covered floor, rolled onto their backs and moved like crabs until the speed of movement forced their arms to buckle and their backs to crash into the floor. They both scoured the darkness, looking for any sign of the soldier.

'I can hear your hearts beating. I can smell your fear.' A voice pierced the black veil that surrounded them.

Paul shot to his feet and placed his hand on the knife handle at his side. Then he felt a thump and a strange light filled his head before he fell into unconsciousness.

Randolph trained his eyes on the direction he thought he had heard the voice come from. He slowly pushed himself up onto his feet he stared straight ahead, trying to make out any shape or movement. 'Paul, where you at?' he whispered.

There was no response. He repeated his question, but again he heard nothing. He began backing up, one hand reaching out behind him, the other gripping his knife, which he held out in front as his eyes searched the darkness.

'What's wrong?' the blackness asked, 'You feel helpless in all this darkness?' the voice teased.

'I'm not afraid of you,' Randolph shouted in defiance.

The soldier in the darkness began to laugh. Randolph moved his head left and right, trying to see anything that could tell him where the soldier or his partner were. The laughing surrounded him; it squeezed his senses. As he felt the strength in his body drain away, it made him feel claustrophobic.

'Oh I know you are afraid, I can feel it,' the soldier whispered.

Randolph shouted again, this time his voice broken and uneven. 'Where are you?'

'Let me help you,' came the reply as a burst of light exploded from the blackness, causing Randolph to cover his eyes with his knife-wielding hand and arm.

Flames leapt up around him; the straw covering the floor burst into flames, creating a circle that locked Randolph within. When he removed his arm, he could see the upturned carriage and his partner sat up against it. The room swayed with the orange and red flicker of the flames. He could not see beyond the heat and brightness of the circle, but there was no sign of the soldier. He carefully walked over to Paul, searching the flames for his captor. He knelt down in front of his partner and began to shake him until he came to. Paul's head wobbled uncontrollably as he was shaken, his eyes fighting to gain control and focus. Slowly the world came back to him. First he could see Randolph looking at him with wide eyes, his face glowing with a strange color. His mouth moved, but no sound came out. He stared at Randolph as slowly the sound began to grow. Randolph's voice grew louder and louder, each word making more sense until finally he was back; it was not only the sound of his friends voice he could hear but the crackling of the flames and the smell of burning wood and smoke. He pushed his partner away and looked around at the tall flickering flames that surrounded them; panic began to replace the lost groggy feeling that had entered the conscious world with him. He began to push himself up onto his feet. Randolph grabbed his arm and helped him in the last part of the assent and then continued to support him. They both looked around for a clear passage through the flames and out of building.

'You are going to pay for all that you have done,' the voice called from beyond the flames.

The two cowboys moved closer together, both now holding their knives out in front of them, they stared straight ahead at the flames from where the voice had come. The flames grew higher, and then a dark shape appeared within them. The shape grew darker until it formed an outline of a man. The figure stepped out from within the flames. First a leg and then a torso, the blue uniform untouched by the raging fire that had engulfed it, the soldier stared straight at them; an evil sadistic smile joined the heavy scars that adorned the face. He walked purposely towards them, a knife in his right hand.

'For all the pain you made me suffer, I will now repay.' Drool flowed from his vengeful smile as he spoke.

The two fear-filled cowboys' eyes began to well up and then started to slowly leak, tears of fear falling down their faces. They didn't move. Rooted to the spot like statues, they held out their knives, which began to quiver and shake. The soldier threw up his knife, watching it twirl in the air, and caught it by the blade. In one smooth movement, he pulled it up past his head and then threw it at the two fear-frozen cowboys. It thundered into Paul's right shoulder, the force of impact knocking him backwards. For a moment, his knife hung freely in the air before falling to the floor. He fell back against the broken carriage, slamming against it and then falling to his knees, his face screwed up in horror, his eyes wide, staring at the embedded knife. His mouth open as if to let out a scream, but no sounds came. Randolph was suddenly awoken from his fear-induced trance. He looked back at his partner, who was doubled over behind him. He let out a scream and ran towards the soldier, knife raised above his head. Samuel stopped and opened his arms out to his sides, imitating the pose of Christ on the cross. Randolph brought the knife down into the soldier's chest, using his momentum to plunge it in as deep as he could. He found himself nose to nose staring into the soldier's eyes. For a moment he smiled, but then that smile turned to worry and fear as the soldier stood there smiling back, his scarred face stained orange from the surrounding glow of the ring of fire. It began to ripple with life as scars appeared and disappeared.

Samuel stared deep into Randolph's' watery eyes; he could see the pupils of the bearded cowboy grow larger and larger as the seconds passed. He brought his hands in from their open-armed crucifixion position and placed them on either side of Randolph's face. He then began to bring his thumbs in, across the eyes, before pushing them deep into the sockets. Randolph couldn't move; he clung onto the knife that he had sunk into the soldier's chest. Even when he could feel the pressure build and the stinging of Samuel's dry thumbs pushing into his open eyes, he clung onto the knife, his grip tightening as the thumbs pushed deeper into his eye sockets; the popping sound as his eyes gave way to the probing thumbs was joined by his scream. Samuel slowly removed his thumbs from the now wet, soft squelching flesh of the sockets. Removing his grip of Randolph's head, the cowboy slowly sank to his knees, the grip on the knife momentarily remaining until finally his grip failed and he fell to the floor, screaming, his hands now holding the black and red holes that were once his eyes.

Paul sat and watched his friend slowly slide down the front of the soldier to the floor screaming; he then saw the knife that Randolph had clung onto being pulled out by the soldier, who then held it up, admiring it in the flickering light of the room. Paul looked down at the knife protruding from his shoulder then back at the soldier whose gaze now fell on him. The feeling of fear he had been struck with was replaced by a strong need to run, to escape—a deep wanting to live beyond tonight. He grasped the knife with both hands and pulled; the knife tore at his flesh as he slowly reversed its entry, tears streamed down his face and the sound of a repressed muffled screaming escaping his clenched teeth—teeth that were slowly collapsing under the pressure, bits breaking off and falling to the floor. The tip of the knife finally left the opening of the wound; it was dropped onto the dirty, straw-covered floor. He pushed himself up with his uninjured side and broke into a stumbling run around the broken carriage that he had been kneeling against and towards the tall flames of the fire wall. He had lost sight of the soldier, but he didn't care; he just wanted to get away. The sound of his friends screams filled the air, the smell of burning wood and smoke attacked his nose and his heart felt like it was going to burst from his chest, but still he moved towards the flames. He stopped just before the burning wall and turned. He could see Randolph curled up on the floor, rocking back and forth and screaming, but he could not see the soldier. He returned his gaze and his attention to the wall of flickering flames that towered above him. He searched the flames for a way through, but none revealed themselves. His mind shouted at him to jump through, but he hesitated, and that's when he saw him.

The soldier's dark shape walked towards him through the flames. A hand shot out from within the flames and grabbed his throat. Paul could feel the heat from the hand burning his flesh. The grip tightened and the scream of pain was extinguished before it escaped.

'You don't want to do that,' the soldier's voice teased from within the flames. 'I haven't finished with you.'

Paul watched as the ravaged face appeared from within the wall of flame, the scars on the soldier's face slowly reducing in number as the flames died down from around his features. He beat his fists against the outstretched arm of the soldier, trying to force him to let go of his throat. With every desperate swing of his arms, he felt what little energy he had left leave him. Then he was free of the hand that held him. The soldier stepped out of the flames and grabbed Paul by the greasy, sweat-stained, neck-length hair and pulled his head close to his.

'You cut me, you tortured me, left me to die a slow and painful death,' the soldier shouted. He then yanked hard on the cowboy's hair so that his head was pulled as far back as it would allow. Paul's eyes looked as far right as they would go, into the angry disfigured face of the soldier.

Samuel pushed the wet handful of hair sharply forward, causing Paul to stumble forward and onto the floor. He reached behind him and pulled a knife from the back of his blue trousers, he held it out at Paul, turning it slowly left and right, smiling with an evil grin that sent shivers down the scared cowboy's back. Paul began pushing backwards, kicking his legs into the ground and reaching back with his hands, trying to increase the distance between himself and the soldier. He no longer felt the pain of his open knife wound; he just needed to get away. Samuel stalked him, walking slowly and keeping the same distance throughout, teasing him with the knife, waving it back and forth. Paul's crabbing attempt to get away ended with a dull thud as he hit the moaning, rocking body of his partner Randolph. He quickly looked back at his friend and then climbed over his bloody, shaking body, pushing him away towards the oncoming soldier. Samuel looked down at Randolph's body as he stepped over him, smiling at him as he did. He then turned his attention back to the other scurrying cowboy who continued to back away like a crab. Samuel's eyes grew wider as he lifted the knife to his lips. He kissed the blade and then threw it at Paul. Paul saw the soldier's eyes grow wider and then the knife glinting as it rotated through the air towards him. He could only keep backing up; he couldn't get his body to move in any other direction apart from backwards towards the wall of flame that was getting hotter and hotter. The knife sunk deep into his right leg, forcing it to fail in its attempt to propel the body away from the stalking soldier. He bent forward, clasping the leg.

Samuel stood smiling at Paul as he rocked back and forth, clutching his leg around the embedded knife. The soldier then moved in closer.

***

Reed dragged Little River across to the bar where Jack stood. He shoved her into the wooden structure, forcing her head to bounce with a thud. Jack stood with a whisky bottle in his hand, opened mouthed.

'Now you little whore, let's see what your boyfriend will do now.' Reed's sharp words mixed with spittle and the stench of his rotten tooth breath were shouted at her from just inches away.

Jack took his knife from its leather cover and looked at Reed with excitable eyes. 'What you gonna do?' he asked Reed.

'He's gonna see his lovely savage woman slowly tortured unless he leaves us,' Reed replied.

'I want to scalp the bitch,' Jack hissed.

Reed looked at his partner, who excitedly turned his knife slowly between his right hand and the index finger of his left, the point creating a little indentation as it turned. He smiled at Jack and then looked down at the young girl, who sat slumped against the bar, holding her head, blood seeping through her fingers from a cut above her left eye caused by the collision with the wooden structure. He looked back at Jack, 'You can do what you want with the dirty whore but not yet, I want the bastard soldier to see,' he said, holding up a finger as if to control his partner's urge to begin the torture of the girl.

The smile on Jack's face fell into a look of disappointment when Reed held up his finger and told him he had to wait. Patience had never been one of his strong points. He walked around to the front of the bar and looked down at the young girl. He lifted his right leg and pushed his boot into the bloody hand, forcing her head back. She looked at him through bloodied, dirty hair. She grabbed his boot with her free hand and tried to push it off her, but he just pushed more weight to overcome her resistance.

'You are going to feel pain like you've never felt before savage,' he snarled before removing his boot.

Reed no longer felt the uneasy feeling he had felt when he saw the soldier survive the hail of bullets. He had something to hide behind and he had a bargaining tool—he realized he had an edge. He had also come to the conclusion that if he had to sacrifice his partner to survive the night and avoid death then he was happy to let Jack be the sacrificial lamb.

'Jack, let's go and get our friend's attention.' He nodded his head to the saloon floor and then the door. 'Take some chairs and tables outside and set them on fire.'

Jack looked at Reed with a look of concern. 'What about you?' he quizzed.

'I'll bring the girl outside. When he sees who we have, he'll come straight to us. Then we'll bring him in here.'

Jack's look of concern eased, and he smiled; his friend and leader had a plan and his plans have never failed them, no matter how difficult the situation had been. Satisfied with Reed's answer, Jack began dragging chairs, small tables and stools out into the middle of the dusty street. He piled them up on top of each other and poured the contents of a brandy bottle over them before striking a match and letting it fall onto the wooden items. It burst into flames, and the initial explosion of flames and burst of heat caused him to look away. Reed lurched through the doors, gun in one hand and dragging Little River by the hair with his other behind him. He pulled at her every time she fought against his grip and momentum. Reed joined Jack behind the little bonfire; he pulled the girl in closer to him and held his gun to her head.

'Soldier boy,' he shouted, 'We got somebody who wants to say hello.'

He looked at Jack, who drew his knife again and pushed it into Little River's shoulder and proceeded to slowly push it deeper, turning it as it went into her flesh. He relished the sensation of flesh resisting and then giving way; she let out a scream of pain. Satisfied she had screamed long enough and loud enough, he yanked it back out of the wound, and her scream of pain hit a high note that made Jack's eyes widen with surprise. He then smiled; in that moment he had discovered withdrawing quickly hurts more than if done slowly. They then stood, Reed tightening his grip around the fist full of hair of the young woman now slumped on her knees. The light of the fire cast dark shadows on their deep-set facial features, making their appearance more like a pair of skeletal cowboys. Their eyes scanned the dark town in front of them and waited.

***

Samuel grasped the knife handle and pulled at it. He deliberately drew it down the moaning cowboy's leg, cutting into the flesh, opening the wound by several inches. Paul sat writhing in agony, the pain stopping him from fighting off the soldier who crouched over him drawing the knife down his leg. He could only watch with wide eyes and grasp his bloody leg that began to spill like an overflowing river engorged by spring rain. The soldier then quickly withdrew it, held it above the stricken cowboy and plunged it into the thigh of the other leg. Once in, he began using a sawing motion as he opened up Paul's leg. The cowboy let out a high-pitched scream that continued for the length of the mutilation. He could feel the knife point hit the bone on the downward movement. Amongst the pain and shock, his brain registered a sound each time the knife point touched the femur: doink, doink, doink. The sound and feeling increased the closer the knife got to the thinner part of the thigh just above the knee. Blood poured out onto the straw-laden floor. He could no longer hold his legs, the pain forcing him to sit back. His bloody hands stretched out behind him acted like buttresses, supporting him. The smiling soldier stood, looked down on the man below him and admired his work as the floor around him grew darker with a thick viscous liquid. Paul's face grew whiter as his life slowly vacated his body via the two large, gaping wounds in his legs.

A scream erupted from outside; its power and energy pulled on Samuel. He felt a surge of pain from within him, and he fell to one knee, grasping his chest with his free hand. The other still clung to the bloody knife that he had used to cut into Paul's legs. The scream filled his head. It sounded like it was coming from within the same room but at the same time had a sense of distance. He stood, looked at the now barely conscious Paul and then at Randolph who continued to squirm around the floor, and walked through the wall of flames and to the wide-open doors of the building. His movement had an urgency and a purpose; his face rippled with movement as scars appeared and disappeared. The skin moved like it had been invaded by insects crawling around beneath. As he exited through the open doors, he squeezed his eyes shut, when he opened them the building exploded, sending a ball of flame and shattered wood high into the air. Pieces of wood flew past him, and a body engulfed in flames landed before him. The thud as it landed caused the flames to flatten before continuing their vertical dance on the disfigured black and blood red body. Even the body didn't break Samuel's stride as he turned and appeared from behind the building and into the street. Figures littered the floor, some crying, others getting to their feet and running away from the fires that lit the street from either side of the towns' dirt road.

Jack and Reed both jumped back when they heard and saw the huge ball of flame explode from the darkness at the end of the street. There were shouts and screams as the town folk fighting the store fire dove for cover. Seconds later, little pieces of wood and glowing embers began to fall around them; they both stood momentarily transfixed by the glowing flakes as they fell. That hypnotic moment was shattered by an explosion of wood and fire as a body fell from the sky and landed on their little bonfire of tables and chairs. They both fell backwards, but Reed's grip never let up on Little River's hair, and she found herself being yanked along the floor as he fell over. They sat up and looked at the stack of burning wood. Lying across it on his back, staring at them from upside down, were the empty eye sockets of Randolph, his flesh blackened with a red tinge where his skin had burst open, creating deep, long wounds. They scrambled to their feet and looked at each other. Jack wanted to run for the safety of the saloon and the comfort of the bottle of whisky he had left on the bar, but he knew that Reed would disapprove of his cowardice. Reed stared at the body of Randolph and then moved his gaze from the burning body and peered through the climbing flames that had burst from the new fleshy fuel. The smell and crackle of the burning flesh engulfed their senses. Little River began vomiting, and the force of the wrenching movement on her body pulled against the tight grip of her captor. Reed looked down on her and moved his boots away from the pool of sick. The smell of burning flesh didn't move him—he was used to it. Many a time he and his posse had burnt and feasted on human flesh, usually Indian flesh. Jack on the other hand found the smell harder to ignore as he stared at the burning body of his friend.

Samuel marched towards the little fire at the far end of the town, his fists clenched tight. A red glow emanated from them and his skin crawled as scar after scar appeared and disappeared on his face. A local man ran up to him and pleaded with him to help save the town by fighting the fires, but when the man looked at the soldier's face, he froze, his eyes full of tears widened with terror. The man froze to the spot as Samuel continued his march towards the little beacon flickering ahead of him. As Samuel reached the mid part of town, he saw the two cowboys standing behind the flames. His attention then went to the young woman at the feet of the larger of the two, and his anger grew and his movement quickened when he saw them move into the building opposite the fire. The dragging of his love across the floor and up the steps caused his facial features to ripple quicker with worm-like movement and his face and hands to glow with an orange hue.

***

Reed saw the figure of the soldier appear out of the ever-moving shadows caused by the fires at the far end of town. He motioned to Jack to get inside and began dragging Little River through her own pool of sick across the now hot, dusty ground up the wooden steps and back into the saloon. Jack moved quickly over to the whisky bottle he had left on the bar. He grabbed it, pulled out the cork and took a big gulp, before slamming the bottle back down and wiping his mouth. Reed dragged the girl with him over to the bar. He pushed her over towards Jack, who looked at Reed with a concerned stare.

'You take her,' he barked at Jack as he placed his gun on the bar along with another pistol and several bullets.

Jack paused briefly, contemplating his position. His inebriated inner voice increased in volume as he weighed the pros and cons of being given the girl. He reasoned that if he had the girl then he was safer than without and could do what he wanted to her to gain an upper hand with the soldier. He grabbed her hair, pulled her head back and smiled at her. Then he reached back to the bottle of whisky and took another deep gulp of the spirit. He again slammed the bottle on the surface of the bar. He reached for his knife and withdrew it from its sheath, placing the blade against the tightly pulled hair of Little River. Reed grabbed both guns, placing them into their holsters, and grabbed a lasso he had left by the table that they had sat at earlier. He then hid in a doorway just off to the right of the main doors and waited.

Out in the darkness of the upper part of the town, away from the panic and the fires, three horsemen approached, staying deep within the shadows. They could see the two cowboys and their sister at their feet. Afraid that they could be walking into an ambush of some kind, they watched and waited. They saw the cowboys head into a building, dragging Little River with them. They searched for what had made them leave their fire and could see the soldier approaching from the south part of town.

Samuel burst through the doors; the doors themselves crashed against the walls, stressing the hinges, splintering the wood. His eyes trained on Little River and Jack. Jack's eyes shot to the side of the room, tipping off Samuel to the location of the other cowboy. Just as he began to turn his head and look in the direction of Jack's telling eyes, a rope dropped over his head and was pulled tight. The lasso tightened around the soldier's neck, but he stood motionless, the rope twisting his flesh, cutting into it. A groan of effort came from the wrangler at the other end as he yanked it hard,

'Got you now boy,' Jack shouted from across the room.

Reed pulled hard on the rope again, but the soldier didn't move. It felt like he had just caught a marble statue. He yanked at it hard again but still no movement. Samuel slowly continued turning his head towards Reed, the rope cutting deeper as the flesh fought against the biting rope. Jack saw his partner struggling on the other end of the rope, and he put the knife he had been holding against the girl's head on the bar behind him and pulled out his gun. He fired two shots, and both struck the blue jacket of the soldier, the impact of each one causing the material to flutter as the bullets pushed beyond the blue barrier and into the flesh below. Samuel heard the shots and felt them hit his body, but he felt nothing but anger and rage as he stood staring at Reed, who still struggled with the rope. Jack saw the lack of response and quickly replaced his gun and reached back for his knife.

'Hey, soldier boy,' Jack shouted.

He began to slide his knife into Little River's hair and into her scalp. The knife cut deep below his fist full of hair and began to push into and under the skin. The scalp pulled away from its anchor, rolling forward like a knife collecting butter. The scream that rang out caused both Reed and Samuel to quickly turn their attention to its origin, and the rope cut deeper into the soldier's skin as he turned his head again. For a moment Reed felt the rope he was struggling to move give. He then returned his gaze back to his human steer, and yanked hard again. Samuel looked at the young girl screaming as the knife slowly cut through her scalp and then found himself pulled off balanced and on to his knees.

Jack smiled when he saw the soldier pulled to his knees. 'See boy, we hold all the cards.' He then pushed harder into the head of the girl. The blooded knife finally cutting through and, freeing itself from the flesh of Little River, she fell to the floor, her hands holding the bright red space that once was covered by flesh and hair. Jack stood up, still holding the long strands of hair and now scalp of the girl in his right hand. He put his boot onto her hands that protected her head and pushed. He smiled as he did.

'You leave us be soldier boy and you can leave with the girl alive,' Reed called.

The skin of the soldier's face rippled with life and began to glow white then red; it pulsed, as did his hands. Reed pulled hard on the rope again, but he met the unmovable force once more. Samuel placed a foot in front of him and began to rise from his knees. Reed struggled with the rope, pulling it over and over again, hoping that whatever allowed him to pull the soldier to the floor would return. Samuel stood, face and hands pulsing with light. Scars appeared and disappeared on his face, his eyes fixed on jack who had noticed his partner struggling once more. He reached down and grabbed the arm of the girl and pulled her to her feet. He held the knife against her throat as he hid behind her.

'You not getting it boy?' he shouted. 'I will kill her.'

Reed drew one of his guns and fired three bullets from close range into Samuel's head. The soldier's head jerked to the side, but no blood came from the three small holes that each of the bullets had made. Reed had expected to see the head of the soldier disintegrate from the bullets entering and then exiting the skull. Samuel straightened his head, never taking his gaze from Jack and Little River, and the bullet holes slowly closed. Reed's eyes widened and he lost control of his hands as first the pistol fell to the floor and then the rope he had being pulling tight slackened as he dropped and relaxed his arm. The rope around Samuel's neck began to smoke and then burst into flames. After a few seconds of intense flame and heat, it fell to the floor. He stepped towards Jack, who pulled Little River closer to him, forcing the knife against her exposed throat. Reed took advantage of the distraction and ran out of the doors of the saloon into the dark street. Samuel continued to walk towards Jack, who was finding it difficult to hold the knife still. It shook in his trembling hand.

'I will kill her,' he warned through a quaking voice. 'Don't you care?' he shouted as the soldier closed within eight feet of him.

Samuel's face rippled like a box full of worms. It pulsed with white and red orbs of light, his eyes black giving the illusion of having no eyes in the sockets. 'If she dies we will be together,' came the reply to Jack's question.

Realizing that he had nothing to bargain with, he raised his knife into the air and plunged it deep into Little River's chest with a shout of defiance. Little River gasped as the knife punctured her chest, her eyes fixed on Samuel. Blood escaped her mouth as she became limp in Jack's arm. He let her fall to the floor and jumped at Samuel with his knife raised above his head. He brought down the knife, aiming at the soldier's head. The downward arc of the knife was blocked by a defending arm. Jack then felt a burning sensation around his neck as Samuel grasped the cowboy by the throat, forcing him back against the bar. The bottle of whisky fell on its side and rolled towards them. Jack felt the wrist of his knife-wielding arm begin to burn, and the pain grew and grew until he could no longer hold onto the knife. It fell to the floor at his feet. In one quick movement, Samuel let go of the wrist and slapped Jack across the face. The force of the blow caused Jack's head to sharply turn to the side, a handprint branded into his face as the bottle of whisky continued its slow journey down the bar. Samuel grabbed the shirt of the cowboy with both hands and picked him up, pushing him back into the bar. The bottle rolled once more a little closer. Samuel reached out, grabbed the bottle and smashed it into the face of Jack. The bottle exploded on contact, glass splintering and burying itself into the facial features of the now-screaming cowboy, who pleaded—he even began begging.

'Please, please, have mercy, please god help me.' Jack after years of resenting any religious person had suddenly begun to ask for help.

'God can't help you,' came the reply.

Samuel picked him back up by his shirt and threw him once more against the bar. Blood poured from the open wounds that glistened with shards of green glass. He was then picked up and slammed on top of the bar, the force winding him and causing his arms to open out into a crucifixion position. Samuel held up a fist and extended his index finger. It began to glow before bursting into flames.

'Let me help you find god,' Samuel teased.

He held down Jack's right arm and pushed his burning finger into his hand. The finger began pushing

72

through the flesh of Jack's hand, and the skin surrounding the probing finger crackled as it melted. Bones snapped as the finger pushed through them. Jack screamed as the finger entered the wood of the bar beyond the cowboy's hand. Samuel slowly removed the finger, and Jack attempted to pull his hand into his body but found that he could not move the hand from where it had been melted to the wooden top of the bar. He attempted to hide his other hand but could not fight off the strength of the smiling soldier. Samuel repeated the burning finger drill with Jack's other hand, pinning him in a lying crucifixion position. Tears mixed with the flowing blood of Jack's face as he pleaded and begged for mercy. Samuel climbed up onto the bar, kneeling next to Jack's head, and slowly pulled out glass shards from the cowboys face.

'I'm not sure if you have been baptized,' he quizzed. 'Let me bless you.'

Samuel held up his flaming finger, Jack's eyes widened as the finger closed in on his forehead. He felt an initial freezing sensation as the finger touched his forehead and then the pain of the heat as it was pushed into his skin. The finger then began its slow journey down the center of his face, travelling down his forehead along his nose, melting the thin skin on its bridge revealing the bone. The finger continued down over the lips, causing them to bubble and burst. Samuel removed the finger and placed it on Jack's cheek and traced it across to the other cheek, creating a cross-shaped brand.

Jack screamed throughout, pleading with god to stop the pain. Samuel smiled.

***

Reed ran out into the dusty road, the small bonfire still burning, the body of Randolph now down to charred bones and bubbling flesh where the limbs hung outside the fire. He looked back at the saloon and began running up the middle of the road towards the outskirts of town. He had managed twenty meters when he saw the three horsemen appear out of the darkness. He skidded to a halt, and the horses continued to close in on him. The shadowy figures became clearer and clearer, and his heart sank when the three came into clear view. He felt like crying; he didn't know what to do or where to go. The three native brothers stood before him and freedom. He knew that if he continued he would be outnumbered and would be captured, but if he went back he would be facing the soldier and certain death. Two of the brothers jumped down from their horses and approached Reed. One of them held an axe in his hand. Reed, seeing the axe, began backing away. He moved side on, looking for a way of escaping his current predicament. The two brothers began to speed up their approach, and the third stayed mounted on his horse and watched. Reed began running back towards the fire. He had decided that he would leave via the other end of town, even if that meant taking on the locals fighting the fires.

On seeing Reed begin to run, Little Elk, who stood with the axe, raised it above his head and let fly at the fleeing cowboy. Reed could hear the whistling of the rotating axe as it approached through the air and then he felt the thud as it hit him in the leg, the initial impact knocking him off balance and to the floor. The pain then followed, and he looked down and saw the axe buried in his calf. The two brothers calmly walked up to Reed, who was sat clutching his leg, moaning in pain. He tried to push himself away, but the axe handle caught the dusty floor and pushed the sharp head deeper and higher up the lower leg towards his knee, tearing at the skin. The sharp pain made him wince. He still held tight to his pistol but had found that his natural instinct to fire upon any threat had deserted him. He clung to it as he rolled over and attempted to crawl away from the two brothers closing in on him. Grey Crow ran and jumped in front of Reed, blocking his path as the other brother grabbed the axe handle and yanked it out of the cowboy's blooded leg, causing an arc of blood to follow its path from the leg and back into the air. Reed screamed as the axe left his leg, leaving a deep open wound that pumped with thick red blood out onto the dusty road. He rolled over, raised the pistol, held it in the direction of the axe-wielding brother and squeezed the trigger. The two shots missed the axe-wielding native Indian by quite a distance, his shaking hand unable to focus his aim. Even so, the brother moved to the side quickly on seeing the gun being raised towards him. Grey Crow, who blocked Reed's path, kicked out at the gun-wielding arm, catching Reed's elbow with enough force to cause the elbow joint to lock out sharply. The pain from the limb forced the gun-gripping hand to open and the gun to escape the cowboy's grasp and fall onto the dusty road. Little Elk, angered by Reed's attempt to shoot him once more, raised the blooded weapon above his head. He was about to let fly at the head of Reed with the axe when Fighting Bull shouted to stop from his horse. The axe-wielding brother froze, looked back to towards his mounted brother and slowly lowered the axe. Grey Crow and Little Elk then stood over Reed, making sure that he could go nowhere and waited.

***

Jack screamed with pain. His hands ceased moving, and he tried moving his fingers but they refused. His eyes blinked wildly through thick salty tears. They rolled into the open wounds across his cheeks, adding a stinging sensation to the raw open wounds. Samuel looked down at Little River. He knelt beside her and cradled her. Her lifeless body hung limply in his arms, and blood oozed from the open chest wound. Blood stained his blue jacket as he pulled her close, pressing the wriggling skin of his cheek against hers. He moved his left arm under her knees and stood. Her head fell away from his face and hung loosely. He stood in front of Jack, who still fought to free himself from the surface of the bar. The arching position of his body caused a sharp pain down his back as he fought to lift his head up off the surface and look at the soldier standing before him.

'You're an abomination. You've lost, even if you kill me. I've killed the savage whore. You couldn't protect her.' The words that required lip contact failed to sound correctly as he shouted and spat from his bloodied, burnt, split lips. He knew he was going to die but found it in himself to remind Samuel that the woman he loved had been killed by his hand.

Samuel's face began to ripple faster, the red and white pulsing grew brighter and faster; he looked down at Little River's lifeless body in his arms and lay her back onto the floor. He stroked her chest, smearing his fingers with her blood and then stood staring at Jack. He held the bloodied hand out in front of him, out towards the cowboy. Jack fought against the pull of gravity and the pain shooting through his neck as he strained to keep his head up off the bar and his gaze on the soldier in front of him. The hand that waved in front of him began to glow and then burst into flames. Jack's eyes widened. Samuel moved the hand closer to the stricken cowboy, holding it just above the disfigured face. Jack could feel the intense heat probing the open wound. He closed his eyes tightly and began to moan. He then felt the intensity of the heat slowly disappear, first from his forehead, then his eyes and then his skinless nose.

He opened his eyes and saw the hand slowly travel down from his face and down over his chest. The burning heat followed the path of the hand, and he began kicking out with his legs as the hand travelled further down his body. The legs ceased fighting when the burning pain dug into his groin. The pain rose up into his stomach as his testicles began to burn, making him feel sick. Samuel withdrew his hand and clenched it into a fist. The flames grew stronger and brighter. He looked down at Little

River and then reached down with the flaming hand and grabbed Jack's boot. It immediately burst into flames. Jack saw the flames rise up as he felt the heat on his feet so once again began kicking out, but this time he was not trying to fight off the soldier but attempting to kick off his boot. When he realized that was not going to happen, he waved the leg around trying to put out the flame. The flame quickly ate away at the boot and engulfed his foot. The flame then slowly began feasting on the cowboy's leg, working its way up the body. Jack began screaming, the intense pain causing his already contorted body to arch more. Jack's waving of the burning leg in an attempt to put out the flames knocked against his other leg, and flames immediately jumped onto it, eating away at the trouser and then skin.

Samuel watched briefly and then knelt once more beside Little River's body, gathered her up into his arms and walked to the broken saloon doors. As he reached the open doorway, he paused and turned to see Jack's legs engulfed by flames. His screams grew louder and louder as the flames inched their way up his body.

Reed could hear the screams of his friend piercing the night sky. The three brothers looked at each other, nervousness showed in each of their faces. They all looked at the saloon doorway, and they could see the flickering of flames play with the shadows of the boardwalk out in front of the saloon. They then saw the silhouetted figure of the soldier carrying a body through the doorway. The two brothers standing over Reed backed away from the cowboy, and the eldest brother stepped down from his horse and approached Samuel. When he saw that the body he carried was Little River, he fell to his knees and sobbed. The other two brothers forgot about their prisoner and ran over to their older brother. They too fell to their knees when they saw the scalped, bloodied body of their sister. The screams from inside the saloon suddenly stopped. Samuel looked back and saw Jack's body completely engulfed by flames and motionless.

Reed used this moment to begin to slide himself along the dirty road. He pushed himself up onto his good leg and slowly hopped towards the fires at the far end of town. The three brothers looked at Little River and then to Samuel, Fighting Bull telling him that they had the cowboy who had tried to escape, pointing to the road. Little Elk looked back and saw that Reed had begun to move away. With anger raging through his body, he ran after the hopping cowboy, catching him without any problems and kicking Reed's bloodied dragging leg. He fell to the floor, clutching it and moaning with the pain. The youngest of the three brothers grabbed him by his ears and began dragging him back over to the others.

Samuel looked at Little River in his arms and then at the two brothers, and the glowing and rippling skin of his face faded. 'He has caused you pain as well as me. He will now be punished for all the pain he has brought,' he said reassuringly to the brothers.

He walked over the eldest brother's horse and lay Little River's body over it. He then turned and faced

79

Reed, who had been dumped back in the middle of the road near the now-glowing embers of the fire he and Jack had started. The blackened bones of Randolph lay atop. The brothers gathered together and mounted their horses, the eldest joining his youngest on his horse. They then watched as Samuel approached the cowboy. Reed pushed himself back to his feet and stood in front of the soldier. If he was about to die then he was going to go out on his feet and fighting—or so he thought. The closer that the soldier got, the stronger the sick sensation grew within him and the more violent the shaking of his hands. Samuel lifted his arms, palms open, as he approached. His face began to glow once more, the red and white light pulsed faster and faster and the scars on his face began to appear and disappear quicker and quicker, causing his face to ripple continuously. His eyes burned red until finally his whole body burst into flames. Reed's jaw dropped open, his eyes widened. He lost control of his bodily functions the fear gripped his every sense so much so that he didn't feel the wetness of the urine running down his leg.

As Samuel got closer, the wind began to increase, swirling around them both, the dirt and dust of the road being picked up creating a growing wall of dirt that rotated around the two men like a tornado. The twisting winds and wall of dirt tightened as Samuel got closer to Reed, who was frozen to the spot. He stared at the approaching soldier with wild wide eyes that never blinked. Samuel stopped just feet away from Reed. The twisting winds continued to tighten. They passed over

Samuel, and as they did, his flames joined the wall of dirt, creating a fire tornado that burned white. The walls of the tornado closed in around Reed. Samuel stood on the outside, his eyes fixed on the gaze of Reed. He raised his arms above his head, and the tornado squeezed Reed's body. The white hot flames and dirt began tearing at his clothes, ripping them from his body. He stood still, motionless. Fear had invaded his body and rooted it to the spot and then, bit by bit, piece by piece, Reed's skin began peeling away from his body. Finally he felt something; what he felt grew from within until finally he let out a high-pitched scream. Samuel pulled his hands into his body, and as he did, the tornado strengthened, picking Reed up from the floor and into the air. He couldn't move. The force of the rotating wall pinned his arms and legs together, and he felt every inch of flesh slowly leave his body until finally he was left red, bloodied and featureless. Samuel relaxed, and the tornado began slowing and gradually dissipating. With less energy to keep him airborne, Reed fell to the floor. He no longer screamed but lay shaking, his breathing fast like a panting dog. Samuel stood over him; the flames that once engulfed him faded, the ripples on his face slowed, and as he stood and looked at Reed, a smile briefly crept across his face.

'Kill me,' Reed rasped as he lay shaking on the floor.

'No, I want you to suffer,' came the answer

Samuel turned and walked back towards the three brothers and the horse bearing Little River's Body, He mounted the horse, and they all slowly headed out of town just as the darkness of the sky gave way to the first lighter shades of a new day.

The townsfolk had been fighting the fires for most of the night, eventually containing it enough so that other buildings didn't catch fire. They had begun their daily routines, however today was different: a group of people gathered together in the center of town, all looking down at the shaking and whimpering red, skinless body of Reed. He begged them to kill him, but they stood staring. In the saloon, the owner and a couple of regular patrons swept around a blackened skeleton that had melted itself into the bar. Outside, others gathered up the remains of another skeleton who had been found on the smoldering embers of a fire left in the middle of the road. In other parts of the town were other bodies: some burnt, others disemboweled. One had no jaw and had bled out from his groin. They were gathered and taken to the coffin maker. The local sheriff rode into town with his two deputies and a prisoner in tow. He saw the damage and bodies and began asking questions as to the previous night's events. The skinned body of Reed was taken to the Sheriff's office and laid on the floor in one of the cells. There he eventually died from his wounds. There was no funeral service, just four coffins. The bodies of Reed, Linus and Wild Bill were placed in their own and the bones of the others thrown in the fourth. The coffins were taken out beyond the town and buried in unmarked graves.

Chapter Six

They rode through the day. Not a word was spoken between any of them. They finally reached the outside of the reservation as the sun began to dip behind the mountains in the distance. They rode amongst the mesas until they came to the outskirts of their father's land. They could see a large number of people gathered, many in traditional dress, the feathers in the headdresses standing high into the early evening night. Bells jingled as some of the people wearing ankle bracelets covered in silver bells moved around. Drums were being hit with a consistent rhythm. As they approached, the people stood and bowed as the three horses passed them. Ahead, they could see their father standing in front of a large pile of wood in full headdress and animal-skin clothing, carrying his wooden flute. He slowly walked towards them. Tears ran down his face as he greeted his three sons, and then he walked towards Samuel and the body of his daughter. He looked up at the soldier sitting above him, his blue jacket darkened by the blood of his daughter. Samuel gently lowered Little River into the arms of her father, Dancing Elk. He carried his daughter's body through the crowd of people who wept and gasped at the sight of Little River and her blood stained-face and scalped head. He walked over to the large table of gathered wood and placed her body on top of it. The people gathered in a circle around them. Drums began to pound a rhythmic beat, two elders began chanting in time with the drums, and the three brothers entered the circle and stood with their father.

The chanting grew louder, along with the drums. Dancing Elk then raised his hands and all was silent. In his hand he held his flute. He put it to his lips and began to play. A slow melodic sound filled the air, and two elders joined him in the center of the circle and began chanting. The drums began their rhythmic beat once more. The clear night sky began to cloud over. The building clouds began to come to life. There was no rain, just the sound of thunder and flashes of lightening. From the circle, a burning torch was brought forward and handed to the eldest brother.

Others in the circle began chanting, and the flute playing began to build, getting louder, as did the sound of thunder. The lightening began to increase in intensity but still remained within the confines of the clouds above the circle of people. Dancing Elk played his final note, which hung in the air. He lowered the flute and took a burning torch from his son. He then touched along the wooden table's base, which immediately caught fire. He then placed it against the wood and stood back. He took hold of his eldest son's hand, who in turn grabbed his brothers until they all stood linked, heads bowed. The circle of people also linked hands. There was a large clap of thunder, and the burning table exploded with flames. Little River's body became engulfed with a wall of licking flame.

Samuel had sat on the horse throughout the ritual, staring at the body of Little River. Now that it was surrounded by flames, he slid off the horse and began walking towards the fire. He approached the circle of people who parted for him. Once within the circle, it was closed again. He walked up to Dancing Elk and the three brothers. All turned and faced him and bowed. He bowed in turn before climbing up through the flames onto the table and stood above Little River. He looked down at her body before reaching down and taking her hand. The chanting from the circle of people suddenly stopped when they saw Little River sit up, her body unharmed by the flames that raged around her and Samuel. She stood and looked into her lover's eyes. She smiled before turning and looking at her father and brothers and bowed towards them before returning her gaze to Samuel. They embraced each other, their arms holding the other tight. The flames around them began rotating tightening around the pair, increasing in speed until the two lovers were the center of a tornado of flame. Dancing Elk and his sons began backing away. The vision of the Little River and her soldier began to fade. The tornado of flames moved from the table to the dusty floor below and began moving slowly out towards the circle of people, they parted just as they did for Samuel and, once clear, closed again.

As the tornado moved out along the dusty plain, the flames began to die as more and more dust was pulled in by the winds. As it moved further away from the reservation, the dust tornado began to fade until finally it was gone.

85

Dancing Elk thanked all those who had attended the ceremony and had helped as they returned to their homes. His youngest son approached, looking confused.

'What is it that troubles you son?' he asked

'How can you be so calm father?' came the reply.

Dancing Elk exhaled and began explaining how he had seen in his dreams a man in blue protect his daughter and suffer because of his love and that both Little River and the soldier would be born of fire. He then told of visions he had had while sitting in his sweat lodge—that his daughter would become one with the earth.

'You will see your sister again.' Dancing Elk smiled.

Many years later, Fighting Bull, Grey Crow and Little Elk were riding amongst the mesas and canyons after a successful hunting trip when they saw a tornado of red dust move along the path in front of them, they sat on their horses, looked at each other and smiled. Within the turning dust they could see the figures of their sister, Little River, and her lover Samuel dancing.

Peter Buckley

DRIFTWOOD

EVIL HAS SURFACED

Driftwood

By

Peter Buckley

I

Evil can control our thoughts and actions
if we allow it.

They dragged her through the cold, damp streets of New London. The crowd grew as word spread and she passed by, all shouting and cheering with the capture of the witch. They could now celebrate their freedom from the evil that had besieged their town. For the past eight seasons, crops failed to grow, children went missing and those that were found had been discovered with no skin on their bodies or with limbs missing. Animals also disappeared. Townsfolk suffered from an illness that became known as the red plague, its name making reference to the large red welts and spots that, when burst, left their host permanently disfigured. It had been dark and wet throughout this time; the sun was always locked behind dark grey clouds.

Mary had been a well-respected member of the church. She had gone into the surrounding woods to collect herbs to help cure a local boy who had fallen ill with the red plague. A dark shadow had watched her from the murky depths of a stream in the woods. It craved a vessel to help it satisfy its bloodlust. It had taken her and began its slow invasion of her body. At first she felt ill; then she started hearing a voice—a voice that told her to harm others, even animals. Over the following six days, it grew in strength until it had consumed her mind, body and spirit. She alarmed friends and neighbors with her behavior. She was cast out of the local church because of her ranting and disturbing behavior. Several times she had stunned the parish flock by walking down the aisle naked and masturbating in the rear of the church during services. She interrupted the priest's sermon by shouting in an unearthly voice and in an unknown language. She had cursed them all when she was grabbed and cast out onto the muddy road outside the church. Her transformation from beauty to beast was complete when being caught forcing herself onto a neighbor by his wife. She proceeded to beat both husband and wife with an inhuman strength until they could no longer move due to the number of broken bones. Mary, who had become covered in their blood, laughed throughout. Their ten-year-old son had walked into the room to see Mary sitting by the couple's motionless bodies licking the blood from her hands. The son had run to another neighbor and relayed what he had seen. The neighbor arrived to find the couple on the floor barely alive—but no sign of Mary.

She had been seen late at night skulking through the town. She was once seen by a local fisherman grabbing a rat that had run from an alleyway and biting into its squirming body. Stories of her dark powers had grown over two years. According to many, she could turn into black birds, dogs, cats and once she was said to have turned into a goat.

The town priest had preached to his followers, telling of the evil that had cast a dark veil over the town and that Mary had to be caught and tried for witchcraft. Only when she had been rid of the evil inside her would the town return to its once prosperous ways. The priest had written and asked for help and support from the head of the church in Boston. Three soldiers had been dispatched to aid in the capture. They were no ordinary soldiers but soldiers of God, trained in the art of exorcism and witch hunting. It had been four years since the witchcraft trials had peaked, where hundreds of women and men suspected of witchcraft were tried and hung, drowned and burned at the stake. Many had been normal people who had only wished unwell to someone in an argument. When that person fell ill, they had been labeled witches and warlocks.

Mary had been found amongst the trees of the forest north of the town. She had been lying in a small stream, her white dress spread out around her and rippling in the flowing waters.

The priest led the procession. He clung tight to his big black leather-bound bible, his fingers pale white from the pressure of his grip. The woman screamed and spat at the baying crowd. The white dress she had put on that morning was no longer bright; it was stained with dirt, blood and urine. Her captures had enjoyed their moment of power once her hands were bound and she had been beaten to the floor. They had taken it in turns to relieve themselves on her. Three long ropes had been secured around her neck—ropes that were pulled tight. Two of the soldiers pulled from the front as she was guided through the town; the third restrained her from the rear and stopped her moving any quicker than the hunters wanted her to. The townsfolk mocked her, some threw sticks and some even threw feces that lay in the gutters of the road. They all shouted abuse at her.

She was dragged down to the small harbor that had once been a bustling hive of activity. Ships travelled from around the eastern seaboard and Europe to trade in its busy harbor, but now it lay almost empty. Only the local fishing boats moored there. Ships that did dock there left with tales of plague and death. Some left and never made landfall, with all crew dying on the journey back to their home ports. A large rowing boat lay waiting. Four local men sat, oars at the ready. Mary was shoved into the center of the boat with the three soldiers of god securing her position by pulling the ropes they held tight. The priest stood proud at the head of the boat and commanded the oarsmen to beginning rowing. They rowed out to the bay's mouth, where a small rocky island lay. On it, a large wooden cross stood, its thick wood stained green and black from years of abuse from the ever changing tides. At its base barnacles clung to the rock it was embedded in.

On reaching the rocky island, the priest stepped off and began reciting from his holy book.

'Come to the assistance of us oh lord, who was created to his likeness and whom he has redeemed at a great price from tyranny of the devil.'

Two of the oarsmen jumped out and secured the boat to two large iron pegs that protruded from the rock. The three soldiers carefully moved from the boat, keeping the growling wild woman under control. As they approached the cross, one of the men slipped, and for a brief moment, she was free to reach forward and grab one of the others by the head. Her long fingernails dug deep into his head. He screamed as a burning sensation began to infect his skull. He let go of his rope and grabbed his now bloody head. The soldier who had slipped regained his feet, saw his comrade being attacked by the wild woman and drew his knife. Using the handle end, he hit her over the head until she eventually let go. Blood poured from the wound left by the knife handle. He pulled tight on the rope again as the other rope-bearing soldier picked up the loose rope and pulled it tight, Mary slowly stood up, part guided by the tightening of the rope but also by her own strength. Laughing out loud as she did, she looked at the stricken soldier clutching his head on the rocky floor.

'Boil within until it is time to die.' Her words were sharp and attacked the soldier's ears.

The priest began reading louder, and Mary screamed. She struggled against the ropes that began to burn into the flesh of her neck. They dragged her to the large wooden cross, maneuvered her against it and then quickly used the ropes they had used to keep her under control to tie her to the structure. She spat and cursed in between the screams of pain as the priest shouted out his biblical commands. The two soldiers wound the rope tighter around her. As she got louder, so did the moans of the injured soldier. He held his head tight, rolling across the rocks. One of the oarsmen moved towards him in an attempt to help but froze when he saw the rise and fall of the soldier's head; it bubbled like a pot of boiling water. The soldier continued to roll towards the edge of the rocks until finally he dropped off the edge and disappeared into the cold dark sea that surrounded them. As his body bobbed back to the surface, the water around his now still body bubbled and steamed before the lifeless body slowly sank beneath the cold dark surface.

The soldiers tied the rope off and stood on either side of the priest as he began the last of the passages in his bible. The screaming and cursing from Mary ceased, and her head dropped and hung loose. A clap of thunder rolled above them, and for a brief moment they all looked up at the clouds above them. As they returned their gaze to Mary, they were met by her stare. The soldiers quickly turned their heads but the priest refused. He pulled out a small bottle from a side pocket on his long black coat, uncorked it and splashed some of its contents onto her face. On contact, it immediately burned the flesh and smoked.

'Demon that has taken Mary from us, you will now be released back to the fires of hell. Your fires of evil will be extinguished by the waters of the sea, releasing your curse from our lands,' he shouted.

Mary began laughing at him. Her eyes never leaving his as she tilted her head from side to side, mocking him.

'You shall pay for what you are about to do. This will not be the end priest; this is just the beginning,' she spat.

The open wound on the back of her head from the soldier's knife handle began to flow freely. As it trickled out into her thick matted hair, she rubbed the blood into the wood of the cross. The priest, disgusted by her threat, moved towards her and put his bible against her forehead, pushing her blooded head harder against the wood. He pulled away, opening his book again to the marked page he had been reading from. Balancing the book in one hand, he then began to empty the contents of his bottle onto her face. As she began screaming, he poured the holy water down into her open mouth. Her screams became gargles, and smoke rose from inside her, escaping from her mouth. He backed away from her when no more liquid fell from the bottle. Her body writhed against the ropes around her, cutting deep into her flesh. Blood oozed over the darkened threads of the rope. Her movements became wilder until her violent shaking suddenly ceased and her body fell limp.

The priest looked at the soldiers and the oarsmen and signaled for them to leave the rock island. They boarded one by one and cast off; the oarsmen soon found their rhythmic stroke. The boat moved away from the rocky island as they all stared at the cross and the woman. Her head slowly lifted, her eyes wide, staring at the men in the boat. She pushed her head back against the cross and began quietly reciting in a long lost language. Above her, clouds swirled and lightning flashed.

The priest commanded the oarsmen to cease their stroke and hold their position. He then stood at the head of the long rowing boat and waited as the tide began its slow rise. They floated there for an age, watching the slowly disappearing rock island and its lonesome inhabitant. They floated at the safe distance, all watching as the tide crept its way up over the rocky floor and slowly up the length of the cross and Mary. As the cold waters moved up her body, she screamed out in a language that none of them could understand, until finally the screaming stopped and her head disappeared below the surface; only the top of the cross was left visible. Happy that his job was done and all was safe, the priest turned to the oarsmen and told them to continue their row back into the harbor and the safety of land.

Beneath the waves, Mary stared back towards the land. Words still left her mouth, but no sound came— only bubbles as the words were formed. Her eyes began to glow a copper color that pierced the darkness of the waters around her. She then let out a silent scream that made the water explode with bubbles. The water above her head rose and began moving out away from where she was tied. It began to pick up speed as the small rise became a wave. The priest briefly turned and looked back at the area where the top of the cross protruded. What he saw made him gasp; the wave closed in on them, growing as it approached.

'Brace yourself,' he shouted.

The others in the boat looked back and immediately felt a sinking in their stomachs, and their limbs froze with fear. The wave hit the boat, throwing it over. The men fought against the cold dark water as the collapsing wave's energy came down on them. It pushed them down deeper into its depths. They finally gained control and surfaced, gasping for air. They swam over to the upturned row boat and held onto it, drawing cold air into their starved lungs. The oarsmen climbed up onto the wooden domed bottom of the boat and began helping the two soldiers up. They looked around them into the now calm dark waters, searching for the priest.

Beneath the surface, the priest struggled against an unseen force that pulled at his robes, dragging him deeper and deeper into the darkness. He kicked out and waved an arm, trying to pull against the invisible grasp and back towards the safety of the surface and the air that his body needed. Even though he was drowning and he could lose his fight to live at any moment, he never let go of his bible. His mind raced, sensing that his life was leaving him and that at any moment the water he was fighting to keep out would breach the barriers that his lips had made and fill his lungs. He closed his eyes and began reciting the Lord's Prayer in his mind. At that moment, he felt the force that was pulling him down let go, and he began rising back to the light of the surface. The priest burst from the water, gasping, coughing and thrashing around. The men on the boat all looked out towards the disturbance, and one of the soldiers jumped back into the water, went to the aid of the priest and helped him back to the safety of the upturned boat.

People in the harbor had seen the boat flip over and its passengers thrown into the water. Two boats had been launched and headed to the upturned boat's location and rescued the seven men, returning them to the safety of land. The crowd of people cheered when the priest and the others wearily walked back up the cobbled street and into the church. There they sat together and prayed until a shaft of light burst through the stained glass window above them, showering them in an array of color. They looked at each other and smiled. It had been months since they had seen the sun. They could hear cheering from the people in the streets outside. The priest ran to the bell tower and began pulling on the rope that hung from the old metal bell, causing it to swing and come to life with a clang.

'We are free of the evil,' he shouted as he pulled on the rope.

The bells rang out for hours, and the townsfolk danced and celebrated in the streets of the harbor well into the night.

Out at the rocky island, the tide slid back slowly, revealing the wooden cross and the body of Mary. Over the following twelve months, her body remained tied to the cross, being eaten away by time, animals and the elements until finally her body broke free and dispersed into the waters of the bay. The cross slowly eroded over the centuries until that too fell into New London's cold waters.

Over time, the story of the curse that befell the harbor town became a story that was shared amongst the locals. Eventually, it too became so diluted that it became more of a myth that was told by groups of teens gathered around campfires on the beaches during the spring and summer months or as part of the festivities of Halloween, when effigies of a woman in white were hung around the town.

II

When evil lives within water, it can rise again just like the tide rises and falls each day.

Jane Mellows had moved to the small picturesque harbor town with her fifteen-year old-daughter after her marriage broke down when her former husband's infidelities came to light and caused fights and continuous arguments. Trying to continue the city life had become too much of a burden, so she used part of the money from the divorce settlement to buy the small house up on the hill that over looked the town. She had converted the small box room of the three-bedroom house into a workshop and art studio where she began indulging her passion for creative arts. Some of her sculptures and art pieces had been created from old bits of wood, metal and items she found in the local area when she went for leisurely walks to gather her mind and fragile emotions. Some of her pieces had been bought by locals and used to adorn their shops or houses. On occasions, tourists would seek her out and buy items she had created after seeing pieces in town. This led to her opening a little shop in the town at the front of the harbor, where she sold her new creations. Her daughter Megan had settled in quickly, enjoying the open space that the town offered. She had always hated the cramped dark world that the city provided. She would often go with friends down to the small beach and bring back items for her mother to use on one of her pieces.

While spending the day at the small beach with her friends, sitting, chatting, enjoying the summer sun and swimming in the cold bay waters, Kira, her best friend, began telling the group a story she had heard from her father about a witch that had been tied to a cross out at

Devil's Island. Megan laughed at the mention of witches, saying it was all fantasy. Others in the group looked at her, their smiles disappearing as their facial expression changed to a more concerned look.

'You believe that story?' she giggled. 'So where's this Devil's Island?' she quizzed, poking her friend.

'It's true, look out there.' Kira pointed out towards the mouth of the bay and the small dark line of rocks that protruded from the water. 'She was tied to a large wooden cross out on that rocky island and left to drown when the tide came in.'

The others in the group slowly nodded, Megan felt the change in the group. The laughing and joking had ceased and a more serious tone had taken over.

Megan laughed again. 'You still believe in witches?' she teased sarcastically, placing her hands on her hips, trying to lighten the mood.

Two of the others supported Kira by adding to the story, which had been added to and elaborated on over time. Megan sat back down as the story grew and grew. They explained that the witch had been tied to the cross and survived for two days; not even the high tide could kill her. The local priest had returned to the island and chopped her head off.

Megan giggled, then apologized to her friends for not believing them and their witch story, explaining that she had seen loads of horror movies when she lived in the city and that to her, witches and monsters didn't exist. Her friends smiled at her and decided to lighten the mood by taking Megan to the ice cream parlor and finish their day together on a sweeter note.

Out in the dark waters of the bay, not far from the Devil's Island, the water rippled then bubbled; a dark object broke the surface and bobbed up and down. Even with the tide retreating, the large dark piece of wood remained where it had surfaced as if tied down by an invisible anchor.

As the sun dropped below the far distant horizon, the town lights began to flicker to life against the increasing darkness. Out at sea, a mist formed and crept into the bay and harbor. Locals looked out and watched it roll in. Some turned to each other and commented on how strange it was that the mist was heading inland against the breeze. The landlord of the lighthouse tavern stopped clearing the outside tables. He looked up at the flag that hung proudly from the center of the tavern front. The stars and stripes lightly flapped out to sea. He checked twice to make sure that he wasn't imagining it as the mist engulfed his feet and continued up the street. People stopped walking when they saw the mist wash past them like a knee high wave of water. As it passed them they felt the sudden drop in temperature. The mist continued up through the town, invading every road, park and open space until it hit the dense woodland of the forest that surrounded New London. There it meandered around the thick tree trunks and fallen dead trees until it came to a clearing. The mist stopped as if blocked by an invisible force and worked its way around the edge until all that was left clear was the open grass space.

The following morning, the townsfolk awoke to see the mist still blanketing the roads and streets. Jane stood at her bedroom window, looking down at the road below and the town and the white mist. She had not slept well; strange dreams had kept her from a long and restful sleep. Although tired, she had a deep desire to go out and find objects that she could use for a project; the creative urge excited her. She slowly opened Megan's bedroom door to see if she was awake. When she peered in, she could see her daughter fast asleep, her head the only visible part on show, mouth wide open and the duvet pulled up under her chin, she backed out of the doorway, closing the door as quietly as possible, wincing at the slightest creak that may wake her daughter. She went downstairs, quickly wrote a note telling Megan she had gone out and placed it on the kitchen counter. She packed her backpack with an apple, a bottle of water, pencils, charcoal (in case she wanted to take some bark rubbings), paper and her camera. She then left, stepping out into the white, knee-high mist. As she walked down the short pathway to the picket fence that separated her garden from the sidewalk, she looked down. Every step disturbed the mist. The different shapes and swirls that her movement created amazed her. Normally she would head down to the harbor or beach and search the sands and rocks for things she could use, but this morning she had a strong desire to head back beyond her house and into the forest. She had only been walking through the dark wooded area once before, and that was the first week she had moved into the house. She felt uneasy while walking there, having a sense that she was being watched. For that reason she had never gone back until this morning.

She reached the tree line, and without any hesitation walked in. The mist continued to swirl around her. She looked down at the swirling white cloud and wandered whether she was on a trail. She could have stopped, but something drove her on. She didn't care whether she was on a path or not. She walked on until she reached a clearing, she stepped out from the mist and into the open space. The warmth of the sun hitting her face as she broke free of the mist and tree wall, she continued to the center of the clearing and then stopped. She looked around her, amazed and confused as to why this circular space was free of the mist that still circled from within the tree line.

She looked down at her feet and saw that she was no longer standing on grass. She had not noticed the change in texture underfoot. The large stone surface that she now stood on seemed out of place. Perfect in shape, the grey oblong block lay level with the grass and was covered in strange symbols that had been carved into it. The symbols themselves showed the scars of erosion, with edges rounding off, and some areas of the stone were worn down so much that the symbols became blurred. She took out her charcoal and paper and began making a rubbing of the slab and its symbols. Once done, she took her camera out and proceeded to take pictures of the stone and the weird mist wall.

Megan woke, stepped out onto the cold wooden floor of her bedroom and headed downstairs. As she reached the kitchen, she looked up at the clock on the wall. It read 10:12. She called out to her mother, but no answer came. She walked over to the kitchen counter and saw the yellow piece of paper. After reading it, she decided to quickly get washed and changed and head down to the harbor, believing that she would bump into her mother, who she knew hunted along that area for her sculpture items. As she left the house, closing the door behind her, she paused and stared at the mist. She had never seen anything like this before. In the city where she had lived, there had never been a mist or fog—not that she could remember anyway. She stepped into the white mist and began her slow walk into town.

Megan walked down to the harbor but could not see her mother. There was only one way into town and she hadn't passed her on the way down. She decided to walk around to the beach area and see if she was there. She stepped down the concrete steps onto the sand, and she shivered as she walked out further, not being able to see the sand beneath her but feeling the soft sliding of it as she placed her foot down. There was no sign of her mother. Megan looked up and down the beach but could not see her. Megan decided to walk down to where she could hear the soft lapping of the waves on the sand. As she got closer to the sea edge, she caught her foot on something solid. She fell forward, reaching out with her hands. The mist obscured the sandy surface, making it difficult to judge the impending impact. She hit the sand hard, her outstretched arms not able to stop her from burying her face in the soft sand. She quickly pushed herself up, spitting a mouthful of sand out and wiping it out of her now stinging eyes. She dusted sand off her jumper and trousers and then kicked around at her feet until she found the large heavy object that she had fallen over. She knelt down next to it and attempted to wave away the mist to get a good look at it, but she caught just glimpses of it as the mist flooded her view again and again. She ran her hands over it. She could feel the damp, smooth, slimy texture of something that had been at sea for a long time. Her fingers picked up the grooves and feel of wood and also the hairy strands of a rope.

The mist rippled as Megan ran her hands over the dark object. In parts of the town, the mist began to dissipate. Out in the woods the mist wall that surrounded the clearing slowly began to retreat. It began a journey back the way it had come; first it left the woods and fields, then the upper part of town until it backed its way out of the harbor onto the beach. Suddenly Megan came face to face with the dark object as the mist disappeared out back across the bay's water. She stood and watched, amazed, at the sight of the retreating white wall of mist. She then returned her attention to the object: a large piece of wood about a meter in length and as thick her waist that was covered in green slimy algae, barnacles and rope. The grooves she could feel were various symbols that had been carved into it: two columns of strange lines and loops that ran parallel with each other for the length of the piece of wood. She ran her fingers around the symbols over and over again and then tried to move the large piece of wood but found it too heavy to lift. She dug underneath its base and tried to roll it onto its side; she managed to lift it slightly before her grip slipped and it fell back into its sandy hole. She stood and looked around. No one was on the beach. She then returned her thoughts to where her mother might have gone. Maybe she went into a shop, and while in there, I just missed her as I walked by, Megan thought to herself. She decided to head back home and see if her mother was there. She wanted to tell her about the large piece of driftwood that had washed up. A chunk of wood like that could be used in one of her mother's art pieces.

Megan rushed up the pathway and eagerly pushed her key into the front door. She pushed the door open, calling out to her mother, who appeared from the kitchen.

'Where did you go?' Megan called as she took off her jacket and hung it on the wall-mounted coat rack. Before her mother could answer, Megan had continued to tell her about the mist and the large piece of driftwood on the beach.

Megan's mother apologized and explained that she had been up to the forest and found a large stone in a clearing. She then asked her daughter more about the driftwood. Megan explained about the symbols and how it would make a stunning piece. With the rubbing of the stone and its symbols fresh in her mind, she became intrigued about the symbols on the wood her daughter had found, so she asked Megan to take her to the place on the beach where she had fallen over the large piece of driftwood.

'What, now?' Megan asked.

Megan's mother nodded, grabbing the car keys from the side in the kitchen. They drove down into town, parking the car in the car park near the beach. They walked out onto the beach hand in hand. The tide had receded, leaving the large dark piece of wood sticking out against the golden sand. Megan began pulling her along the beach, eager to show her. They spent a moment of silence just standing over the old weathered wood.

Deep within the old piece of wood, an ancient evil stirred. Its liquid form began its journey, travelling along fault lines and cracks. It stopped just below the surface, attaching itself to the sharpest pieces of wood and splinters.

Jane's' eyes focused on the symbols. They looked familiar. She thought back to the stone and was sure that a few of the symbols were the same. The more she concentrated on them, the more hypnotic they became. They seemed to be calling to her. At one point some, of the symbols seemed to float up off the surface of the wood.

'So, what you think?' Megan asked.

110

When there was no response from her mother, she looked up from the wood and saw her standing, eyes wide, staring down at it, mouth open. 'You ok? Mum, mum!'

The symbols stopped moving and the sound of her daughter's voice grew louder. She blinked as she came out of her trance, looking at Megan and smiling.

'What was that sweetie?'

'You ok mum?' Megan asked again.

'Yeah fine my dear, let's try and get it back to the car,' Jane said.

They then dug the sand away from the wood's edges and attempted to lift it. They both prepared themselves for the struggle of moving something heavy but were both shocked when the large piece of wood lifted easily. They looked at each other with surprise.

'I couldn't move this earlier,' Megan said.

'Let's get this to the car quickly,' came her mother's response.

Jane found a deep desire to get the wood back home, where she could inspect the symbols more closely. Once they had moved the large piece of wood from the beach and into the trunk of the car, Megan asked if they could go to the ice cream parlor, but her mother didn't hear the request. She just drove up out of town and back home. She didn't even notice Megan's angry demeanor when she pulled up, got out of the car, opened the trunk and began sliding the wood out.

'Come on Megan, give me a hand,' she called.

Megan slowly opened her door and walked round to her mother. She grabbed the end of the wood and they carried it up the steps and into the house. Megan was about to lower her end down to the floor when her mother shouted at her.

'Don't put it down. I want it upstairs now,' she snapped as she began pulling the wood and Megan towards the stairs.

'What's the rush?' Megan groaned as she struggled to maintain her grip of the wood with her mother pulling away from her.

They carried the wood into the small converted bedroom and placed it on the floor. Megan stood up straight, put her hands on her hips and blew a cheek full of air through her pouted lips, glad that the job was finally done. She then walked out the door turned to wait for her mother, only to be met by the door being slammed in her face. Shocked by her mother's actions, she screamed at the door.

'What's wrong with you?!'

No answer came, so out of frustration, she kicked the bottom of the door before shouting that she was going back out. She expected at least a response, but again there was no comeback to her outburst. She kicked the door one last time and marched downstairs and out the front door, slamming it in the process.

Inside the room, Megan's mother stroked the piece of wood, transfixed by its symbols and texture. For that moment there was nothing more important. As she ran her hands around each of the engraved symbols, she caught her finger on something sharp. The sudden painful sensation awoke her from her dreamy state. She looked at her finger and saw a large splinter embedded in her index finger. She pulled at it with her other hand's finger and thumb and winced as it slowly retreated from the flesh it had become imbedded in. The moment it cleared, the finger began seeping blood from the little hole it had created. She stood, holding her finger, looking for something to cover the now red digit. She mumbled to herself as she gave up looking for something to help stem the blood, opened the bedroom door and headed to the bathroom. Once there, she ran the tap on the sink and placed her finger under it. The sharp pain as the water flowed over and into the wound made her wince once more. She massaged the finger as watery blood escaped the small hole. She had had splinters before but none had bled so much. She held her finger closer to her face and inspected it. She caught a dark shape beyond the finger reflected in the mirror. Initially, she didn't think much of it; her brain had made the decision that it was her reflection. When she did focus past the finger and at the mirror, her mouth fell open. Her eyes widened and she gasped. Behind her, a dark, blurred shape hung in the air.

It reacted to her actions by suddenly disappearing. Jane's heartbeat increased. She could feel her heart pounding as if it was banging against her ribs trying to get out. The room began to spin, and she could no longer focus on any one thing. The sound of the running water from the tap grew louder and louder, then disappeared altogether as everything went black.

III

There is a world that lies between this and the next where evil awaits to be shown a way in.

The dark misty shape reappeared and hung over Jane's body as she lay on the bathroom floor. It slowly lowered and began to swirl around her body until finally it found the open wound in her finger and began to enter her body via the bloody doorway. Her body jerked several times as the mist forced itself in. Once it had completely entered, Jane sat up. Her eyes still closed, she reached up and grabbed the side of the sink and pulled herself to her feet. The reflection in the mirror smiled but with closed eyes. A shaking hand grasped the tap and turned it until the water stopped flowing. She then turned and walked out of the bathroom and into her bedroom and stood at the window looking down at the town.

Megan had walked back into town and bought herself a large edible wafer cup of chocolate ice cream. She was so angry about her mother's behavior that she indulged in covering it with several different toppings. Normally she would avoid this indulgence, worried that the extra sweet particles would add to her calorie count and begin to add to her weight. She sat on her own at one of the small tables outside the ice cream parlor and stared up at the now clear blue sky. The warm summer sun eased her mood, and the events and the strange behavior of her mother ran through her head. She questioned herself; what had she done to upset her mother to the point that she would ignore her? She couldn't remember saying or doing anything wrong. Once she had finished her ice cream, she headed back home. She found herself walking slower than normal back up the hill towards the house. As she approached, she noticed her mother standing in the bedroom window. She waved but got no response. Maybe she can't see me, she thought. After she crossed the street, she waved again but nothing: no smile, no wave and no form of acknowledgement. She paused at the picket fence that separated the garden from the sidewalk and stared up. Something didn't look right. She stared for a few seconds, straining her eyes, trying to identify the one thing that looked out of place. Her mouth dropped open slightly and her eyes widened as she realized that the one thing that was out of place was that her mother was standing at the window with her eyes closed. Megan shook her head. The confused look on her face remained as she walked up the pathway and up the porch steps. She took out her keys from her pocket and looked at them in her hand and then at the door. She tried the handle and pushed. The door opened, and she smiled to herself. Coming from the city, she had always locked the door and needed the key to get in; since moving here she had not really used the key. It had taken her this long to realize this small change in her behavior. She stepped in through the doorway and closed the door. Megan walked through the hallway and up the stairs and knocked on her mother's bedroom door. There was no answer, so she slowly turned the handle and pushed it open.

'Mum, you alright?' she called as she pushed open the door.

Once open, she could see that her mother was no longer standing at the window but lying on her bed. Megan looked at the window and then at her mother, who lay in a fetal position on the bed. Megan put her hand to her face in puzzlement.

'Mum,' she called, but slightly louder in an attempt to wake her.

There was no movement from her mother, only the rise and fall of her shoulder. Megan walked over to the bed, lowered herself onto its edge and gently shook her mother's shoulder while calling her name. When she didn't respond to the first call, Megan called again in a much firmer tone and shook her mother's shoulder more aggressively.

Jane slowly opened her eyes, trying to focus on her surroundings and her daughter's voice, which became louder and louder with every second that she was awake. She rolled onto her back and looked up at her daughter and then without moving her head searched her surroundings with her eyes. She tried to make sense of what was going on and what had happened. She thought back to the last thing she remembered. She raised her hand to her head and slowly massaged her forehead and around her eyes. None of this made sense; she didn't recall lying down.

Megan noticed the look of confusion and asked what was wrong.

'How did I get here?' Jane she asked. 'What's going on?'

'Don't you remember? You shut yourself in your studio room and wouldn't talk to me,' Megan replied.

Jane shook her head and then felt the growing throb of her finger. She pulled her hand away from her forehead and held it out in front of her. The swollen blue and purple bruised index finger came into focus.

'I remember getting home and taking the wood from the beach upstairs,' Jane replied, fighting to remember. 'I don't remember anything else and where I've done this.' She showed her finger to Megan.

Megan held her mother's hand and inspected the finger. The skin around the little hole was red and swollen with the outer rim of the redness tinted with blue and purple. Jane slowly sat up and spun herself around, her legs dropping over the side of the bed and her feet landing on the floor.

'When I got home you were standing at the window,' Megan explained.

Jane looked at her with astonishment and shook her head. Megan nodded back at her.

'What's going on?' Jane asked.

Jane slowly stood up and they both left the bedroom, Megan telling her mother what had happened when they had returned home as they made their way downstairs. Megan hoped what she was saying would help jog her mother's memory. They sat in the kitchen and tried to figure out what had happened in the missing hours between the slamming of the studio room door and Megan waking her up. No matter how much she tried, Jane couldn't remember anything.

Next door a dog began to bark, and the golden retriever ran up and down the fence that separated Jane's garden and William Jacobs's garden. Jane had met him when she first moved in. She introduced herself but got a very frosty response. She learned from others in the road that he was a very opinionated loner. Others in the street had said he was in his mid-forties, but Jane had a feeling he was older. He was a successful businessman—what kind of business no one seemed to know, but he was rude and aggressive to all that tried to engage in any conversation with him. His dog had never really barked like this. Jane and Megan had often watched from the back bedroom as the dog, named Duke, happily ran after balls and other items thrown out into the garden by William. It had always seemed a happy dog, but today something was different.

The barking continued into the early evening. When William returned home, he shouted at the dog and even tried to stop it running up and along the fence but had been surprised when Duke attempted to bite him before continuing to charge up and down barking. William had looked at the fence and the house next door, looking for whatever had made his dog act this way. Not seeing anything, he decided to march next door to complain about whatever they were doing to make Duke act the way he was. He pounded on the front door with his big fists. He then turned his back to the door put his hands on his hips and cursed as Duke continued to bark in the background. Jane had barely opened the door before William began shouting at her, accusing her of upsetting his dog. He waved a finger at Jane, who took a step back and held the door, closing it slightly to create a barrier between her and the red-faced man. She pleaded her innocence, but William wouldn't accept what she was saying. He didn't believe that she had no idea why Duke had begun to act in such a strange way.

'Well if it's not you, then maybe it's that daughter of yours,' he snapped.

On hearing this accusation, Jane fired back, telling him that he had no right to accuse her or her daughter and that he should leave her property before she called the police. William continued to stand with his hands on his hips.

'I don't care what you say, one of you is messing with my dog and I want it to stop,' he shouted before hitting Jane with a verbal low blow. 'This neighborhood was a nice place to live until you lowered its tone.'

Jane's mouth dropped open. She couldn't believe what he had just said. She could feel the fear and worry of the aggressive man being replaced by anger. She wanted to lash out, but even this angry, she still worried that he might hit her back. She turned her back on him and slammed the door in his face. He stood there momentarily before walking back to his house and Duke, who continued to bark. The dog's barks had become more broken as his vocal chords began to tear and bleed.

Jane walked back into the kitchen where Megan sat with a look of shock and surprise on her face. 'What was that all about?' she asked.

Her mother sat back down next to her and held her forehead again as a dull ache began to grow from within her skull. Megan saw her mother's pained expression and took her hand and led her back upstairs, telling her mother to get some sleep because she was obviously not well. She pulled back the duvet and her mother climbed on the bed still fully clothed. The thought of undressing never registered. Megan drew the cover back up and over her mother before kissing her cheek and leaving the room, closing the door slowly and as quietly as she could. She then went back downstairs and turned the television on. She sat on the sofa, picked up the remote from its pocket located on the side of the arm of the chair and began to flick through the channels. It wasn't long before she also fell asleep. She woke a few hours later, turned the TV off and headed up to her room.

William stomped around his house, angered at the exchange between him and Jane a few hours earlier and the continuing strange behavior of his dog Duke, who, now exhausted, no longer ran up and down but walked up and down the length of the fence, releasing a whimpering cough rather than a bark. Every time he attempted a bark, blood left his mouth and fell to the floor.

122

Duke's behavior had continued into the night. William had twice attempted to stop Duke, even attempting to bribe him with a steak, but nothing worked. William had had enough. There was obviously something wrong with his beloved companion, and something had to be done to stop his behavior. He went to the front room and picked up the phone and was about to call his friend, who happened to be a vet and ask his opinion of what to do, when all went silent. The sudden calm made William stop dialing, and he put the phone down. He then walked back through the house to the open back door. As he reached the door, a sudden thud made him jump. Rolling towards him along the wooden decking was the bloody head of Duke. The sight of Duke's head, mouth open, tongue hanging out and with wide eyes caused him to stumble backwards, catching his lower leg on a small coffee table and falling over. He hit the floor with a heavy thud, the back of his head bouncing off the wooden boards. He grabbed his head that now rang from the impact. His eyes closed tightly as he attempted to deal with the pain.

As the thumping sensation and the buzzing in his head dissipated, he opened his eyes and saw Jane standing above him, hands behind her back, eyes closed and a large grin stretched across her face.

'What the fuck are you doing here?' he groaned.

Jane didn't say anything, she just continued to stand over him with an evil grin. She brought her hands into view and revealed a pair of garden shears, stained with blood and golden fur. On seeing the blood-stained garden implement, William found the strength to pick himself up off the floor and back away. He looked around him, searching for something to use as a weapon against the crazy woman in front of him. He fumbled with various small objects: ash trays, books and a snow globe, but none of them were big enough or worthy enough for him to use. He quickly looked over his shoulder and at the pool table that sat in the center of the room. He could see the cue resting on it and made a dash for it. He grabbed the cue and held it up like a baseball player preparing to hit a home run and shouted at the woman.

'Get the fuck out of here or I'll fucking kill you, you psycho bitch.'

Jane just continued to grin at him. She then began opening and closing the shears; the metallic slicing sound cut through the silence of the night. Throughout, her eyes remained closed. William moved to his side and was astounded when Jane's head followed him. He moved again, and again she followed him. He felt the strong grip of fear take hold each time the woman's grinning face and head followed him and his movements, even with eyes closed. He swung the pool cue, hoping to see her eyes flicker open and react to the movement, but nothing happened; she didn't move and her eyes stayed shut. She took a couple of steps towards him and snapped the shears shut. He swung at her and caught her across the head. The force of the blow caused the pool cue to shatter into three pieces. He staggered back, still gripping the now shorter thin cue end. She just stood in front of him snapping the shears together. The grin still etched on her face and a large red welt caused by impact of the pool cue stretching from her cheek to her ear. He looked down at the remains of the cue in his hands and then back at Jane, and the panic grew within him. He found he could not move, he was rooted to the spot by the heavy sensation of fear.

Jane jabbed out the open shears and caught William in the face, the blades slicing into the flesh of his cheeks, making his open mouth form a large bloody smile that reached both ears. He began to inhale a large amount of air just prior to the exhale and scream of pain. Before the scream could escape, Jane had closed the gap and was on him. She no longer held the garden shears; they had been dropped the moment she saw her opportunity to grab him. She pressed her open mouth against his. When the scream did escape, he found that the sound and air was being sucked from him. He tried pushing her away but struggled against her strength. He then felt the sudden rush of a liquid entering his bloody mouth, throat and then lungs. He gasped and tried to fight the fluid invading him. He managed to gulp and could taste the strong flavor of salt. His eyes widened as the water continued into him. He struggled against the woman who held him and tried to shake her deadly kiss off him by moving his head in all directions. No matter what he did, she matched his movement and continued to pass the cold liquid from her into him. Only when his body went limp did she remove her mouth and let him go. His body fell backwards, rigid and straight; there was no collapsing or bending, just a toppling movement to the wooden floor. Water erupted from his gaping mouth on impact. She stood over him, her eyes still closed, slowly tilting her head from side to side as she admired her work. Jane then turned and walked over to the bloody head of Duke. She picked it up and returned to the body of William. She placed the head on the man's chest and positioned his arms as if he was petting the dog. She then stood back again, as if to admire her work, before picking up the crimson stained shears, snapping them together twice.

IV

Spirits walk among us; they are the voices
we hear when we are at our weakest.

Megan was awoken by the sound of sirens and screeching tires. Voices chattered away, some more pronounced and authoritative than others. She climbed out of her bed and walked over to the curtains that were shielding her and her room from the early morning sunlight. She drew them back, wincing against the strong light that invaded her eyes. When her eyes had become accustomed to the sharp daylight, she could see four police cars, an ambulance and a large black van parked outside her house and next door. Police officers stood guard outside a blue and white tape that had been stretched around the front garden of the house next door to prevent anyone entering the area. She watched as a police officer walked down the path and to the front door. He disappeared out of view and then the doorbell rang. Megan quickly ran across her room, out the door and to her mother's room. She burst in, calling her mother, excited by what she had seen. The view that greeted her made her freeze. Her mother was not there, but the bed was covered in what seemed to be blood. Red stains covered the sheets and a metallic smell hung in the air.

Her head raced with thoughts. What had happened next door? Where was her mother? And where had all this blood come from? She then heard a cough. Megan walked down the hall and to the bathroom door. She could hear the sound of the water spraying from the showerhead. She knocked on the door and waited for a response.

'I'm in the shower. I'll be out in a bit.' Came the response.

Megan jumped when the sound of the doorbell rang out again, its high-pitched ding dong sound echoing around the house.

'Can you get that honey?' Megan's mother shouted from inside the bathroom.

Megan went downstairs. The vision of the crimson-stained sheets filled her head, and knowing that it was the police at the door made her heart race. She approached the front door and could see the head and hat of the police officer through the small windows on the top of the door. She took a deep breath, unlocked the door and opened it.

'Good morning miss, are your parents in?' the officer said.

The officer she had seen walk down the pathway had been joined by another, who stood behind the left shoulder of the officer asking her where her parents were.

'Erm, my mum is in, but she is in the shower at the moment,' she replied.

'Oh, ok, could you tell her that the police need to speak to her. We will wait here until she is dressed,' the second officer said with an air of aggression.

Megan nodded and slowly closed the door. As soon as the door was closed, she ran back upstairs to the bathroom. The door was open and the steam-filled room was empty. She then looked down the hall and saw her mother's bedroom door open. Megan walked quickly and entered to find her mother removing the bed sheets, calmly singing to herself.

'Mum what's that?' Megan pointed to the red-stained sheets her mother now held.

'What this?' She looked down at the red marks on the white sheets. 'Its paint my dear.'

'It doesn't look like paint,' Megan said. 'Oh, and there are two police officers waiting outside wanting to speak to you.'

Jane continued to calmly remove the last of the stained bed sheets, smiled and nodded at Megan and carried them downstairs and into the kitchen, where she pushed them into the washing machine. She added the detergent and started the machine. Jane then walked out and over to the front door and opened it.

'Good morning Ma'am, can we come in?' one of the officers asked.

Jane stood back, opened the door as wide as it would go and beckoned the two officers in. Megan joined her mother as she sat on the sofa in the front room, eager to find out what had happened next door.

Over the next thirty minutes, the two officers asked questions related to the argument between her and the man next door, which had been seen by several others in the street. In a small town like this, people were quick to share gossip, so they were happy to tell officers what they had seen from behind their curtains. They had relayed what they could recall about the argument and the words that had been exchanged. Megan supported her mother by explaining to the two officers what had happened and what had been said. The urge to want to know what had happened forced Megan to ask the officers. The more aggressive, grumpy-looking officer replied with a very political, non-revealing answer.

'We are investigating an incident next door,' he said, looking down at Megan. His low and heavy brow suggested he was having a bad morning and was tired of being asked the same question.

The two officers concluded their questioning of both Jane and Megan. The more polite of the two thanked them for their help while the other just nodded and left. Jane stood at the door and watched as they walked over to an unmarked car and begin to speak to its driver. They referred to their notepads and even pointed towards Jane's house.

Megan sat and began to run things through her head. There was something different, something odd, about her mother's behavior, but she couldn't put her finger on what. The stained sheets that her mother had said was from paint didn't feel right either. The red stains didn't look like paint. There was a metallic smell to the room when she entered and that is not a normal paint smell.

Jane walked past the front room where Megan still sat, went upstairs and into her art studio room, closed the door behind her and looked at the large piece of wood on the floor. She immediately began organizing her various tools and began cutting into the wood. She used a saw to cut the piece of wood in two, separating the two lines of symbols. She turned the two pieces of wood onto their sides and cut them down so that the final thickness of the wood was about one and a half inches. She then sanded down the surfaces she had cut but left the symbols side untouched.

Outside, the man in the unmarked car sat looking over reports of the crime scene. There was a knock on his car window. He looked up and saw Dr. Johnson, who had just finished taking photos and completing his preliminary report of the body at the scene. He had given the all clear to his assistant to remove the body. The body of William Jacobs was placed in a large, thick plastic black body bag and loaded into the big black van. The detective got out of his car and began asking the doctor what he had found. The doctor in turn handed an initial findings report to him.

'Are you sure that that's the cause of death?' the detective queried.

Doctor Johnson removed his round-rimmed spectacles and began cleaning them with a white handkerchief, 'As strange as it sounds, and with all that blood and damage to the body, I believe he died from drowning,' he answered.

The detective scratched his head and again asked the doctor if he was sure. The doctor explained that he could not say for definite; he could only say what the evidence was suggesting and wouldn't know for sure until he had done an autopsy. The detective thanked the doctor and asked him to let him know as soon as he knew for sure.

An old Volkswagen beetle pulled up outside Jane's house. The detective who had just waved off the doctor saw it and briskly walked over and greeted the tall thin man that climbed out. 'Thank you for coming, father.'

'That's ok Mike. I'm not sure how I can help you, but I will have a look.' The tall man bent down and reached back into his car, leaned on the seat and reached across to the passenger side seat and picked up a large black-covered bible.

'I must warn you, it is a horrific sight in there. I have never seen anything like it in my twenty years as a cop.' the detective said as he led the priest through the front door.

The first thing that hit Father Harris's senses was the smell, a strong metallic smell, and then his vision was invaded by the sight of three walls of the back room smeared with blood. 'Oh lord,' he exclaimed.

'Father, this is what I need your help with.' The detective turned and pointed to a large canvas painting on the wall behind him. The painting of a snow-covered forest had been changed. It's pure, beautiful, clean landscape had been dirtied by dark red symbols.

133

'The symbols have been drawn with the victim's fingers. We believe each one was cut off and used like a pen. We found them all on the floor below the painting,' the detective explained.

The priest moved closer and looked at the strange swirls and loops of the symbols and then opened his bible. He flicked through it until he reached a number of loose pages. He began comparing what was on one of the pieces of paper to what was on the painting.

He quickly closed the book again and shook his head, 'These symbols have not be used or seen for over three hundred years.'

'What are they? What do they mean?' the detective asked.

The priest began to talk of old tales of witches and demons and how stories passed down from his father and his grandfather talked of a demon cursing the land and possessing a local woman. The symbols that were written on the wall were from that time. The symbols warned of death and destruction to all those who oppose.

'Father, are you expecting me to believe in witches and demons?'

'There are things in this world that science cannot explain. Why did you ask me up here today?' the priest asked.

'Because I have seen that symbol in the church.' The detective pointed to a symbol of two interlinked rings over a cross.

The priest explained that the symbol represented consecrated ground or trapping of evil with the energy of pure and good. Other parts of the writings or symbols he did not know but agreed to look through the churches archives to see if he could find any clues to what the message said. The detective thanked the priest for his help and escorted him back to his car. As they walked, they discussed how someone may have come across the symbols and whether the person who had done the atrocity had any real idea of what they meant. The priest pointed out that if the detective had recognized the one from church then nothing stopped others for seeing and using them too. As for the understanding of what they mean, the priest paused and explained that even he, with all his knowledge, didn't know what they meant, but that symbolism had been used throughout the town's history.

'I have seen similar symbols around town,' Father Harris said.

The detective paused and asked what the priest meant by seeing them in the local area. The priest revealed that there were a number of places around the town that had similar markings.

'Do you have any idea how many places, and their locations?' the detective asked as the priest dropped into the driver's seat of his car.

'I know of three. I will get back to you with a translation of what was written in there.' Nodding back towards the dead man's house, 'and the locations of all the places that have the same symbolism,' the priest responded.

For over five hours, the police and the detective spoke to people, took photos and continued their investigation next door.

Jane had locked herself away, sawing, sanding, cutting, hammering and gluing until finally her piece was finished. What was going to be a sculpture took on a life of its own and became a large mirror. The frame itself was cut from the large piece of driftwood. The symbols running along the top and bottom of the frame, on the outer parts of the frame, were two little shelves that were artistically supported by old worn branches that twisted and turned until they met the underneath of the shelf. She stood back and admired what she had done. She stroked the frame, smiling as she did. The strange vibrating that emanated from it did not worry her but excited her.

The mirror pulsed with an energy that Jane found irresistible. The ancient evil that had begun to grow within her stared at itself in the mirror. More and more of its dark power flowed into her, the refection that looked back at her was no longer her face but that of a disfigured, brown, leathery skinned, sharp-toothed figure. The demon played with the long brown hair that surrounded its face and then ran its hands over the breasts of its human vessel, smiling as it did.

'Mum, what are we going to eat? I'm getting hungry,' Megan called from the other side of the door.

The smile on the demon's face dropped and it scowled. Jane turned towards the door and unlocked it. She opened the door and pushed past Megan, who stood at the entrance. Jane said nothing, just headed down the stairs and into the kitchen. Megan stood motionless, shocked by her mother's actions. She looked into the studio and noticed the mirror propped up on the workbench, she walked up to it and looked at herself in it. The reflection seem strange, as if the glass that had been used was somehow warped and causing her reflection to be twisted and out of shape. Megan reached out her hand and was about to touch the symbols when a voice from behind made her jump.

'Don't touch!' Jane shouted,

Megan turned and saw her mother standing at the door with her coat on and holding her handbag.

'You scared me,' she said to her mother, holding her chest and its now fast-beating heart with her right hand.

'You want to eat? Well let's go,' Jane snapped.

Megan looked at her mother with a concerned look and slowly moved past her and headed downstairs, picking up her coat as she walked past the coat hooks at the bottom. Her mother followed her down, waiting by the front door as her daughter put on her coat. Jane held the front door open. Megan walked past her mother, looking at her as she squeezed past. As their eyes met, Megan noticed the color of her mother's eyes. She had always told her mother about how she wished she had her blue eyes. The eyes that looked back at her were no longer blue but a dark brown.

'Mum are you wearing contacts?' Megan asked.

'Hurry up,' Jane said as she turned her head away and pulled the door shut.

Megan tried to look at her mother's eyes again but found that her mother was evading her. Jane kept her head down and searched in her handbag. After a brief rummage around, she pulled out a pair of sunglasses and placed them on her face before looking up at Megan.

'Come on, come on, you said you were hungry,' Jane said, pushing Megan towards the sidewalk.

Megan's frustration with her mother's behavior and suspicions of something not being right played on her mind all the way into town. She tried several times to walk alongside her mother and look behind the glasses to see if what she saw earlier was real and not just some optical illusion. Megan tried to make conversation but only got a nod or shake of the head.

As they entered the town, Jane slowed. Megan found herself walking out in front, stopping and waiting for her mother to catch up. As they reached the church, Jane stopped. Megan had carried on for several steps before realizing that her mother had stopped.

'Mum, what you looking at?'

Jane didn't respond. Her facial expression changed from the emotionless deadpan one she had carried since leaving the house to a look of disgust. Megan stared, confusion etched on her face. It then turned to shock as she saw her mother breathe in from deep within her throat and nasal cavity and spit a large green blob of phlegm at the church door. The large slimy mass of mucus stuck to the door. It then slowly travelled down the thick wooden entrance like a slug leaving a silvery trail as it moved.

'Mum! What are you doing?' Megan exclaimed, holding back her shout, enough as not to raise attention to herself and her mother.

Jane calmly turned and continued her walk through town. She didn't even acknowledge Megan or her shocked expression. Megan, for a moment, was speechless. She couldn't believe what she had just seen. She caught up with her mother and attempted to get an answer as to why she had just spat at the church, but no explanation came. Nothing came, not even a single word, Jane just continued her walk until she finally reached the Harbor Tavern and stopped outside. Megan looked at her, still struggling to comprehend what had just happened. Jane then removed her glasses and looked at Megan. Her bright blue eyes stared back at her daughter, as did the usual big, welcoming smile. Megan shook her head; confusion engulfed her and her brain began to shout and scream, '*What is going on?*' The question weighed heavy on her mind.

'You hungry?' Jane asked.

'Erm I guess so,' Megan responded in a confused tone.

Jane walked in through the door of the tavern, and the strong smell of beer and food filled the room. Philippa, the manageress who was working behind the bar, looked up from the glass she was filling with beer and smiled.

'Hey, nice to see you two,' she called.

Jane and Megan had been regulars since moving into the area. Enjoying the food and friendly atmosphere, Megan had fallen in love with the special hot wings that they made. She had never tasted anything so sweet, juicy and as hot. It was the one food item on the menu she had to have each time they ate there. Her mother always gave her the same disgusting look. Being a vegetarian, she had always asked her daughter how she could eat the body of another living thing. The answer was always the same: 'Because it tastes so nice.'

They sat at their usual table near the back of the tavern where they could do what they enjoyed doing together: people watching. Being relatively new to the town, they still enjoyed and marveled at the strange habits of the locals that came and went. They looked through the menu even though it had not changed since they first ate there. Megan went for her usual sweet spicy hot wings with fries. Her mother looked up from her menu and rolled her eyes. She then got up and walked over to the bar and placed her order with Philippa, who made polite conversation as she did with all her locals.

Philippa's husband Gary squeezed past her and began serving a customer at the end of the bar. Gary and Philippa had been married for twenty years. They had been high school sweethearts and had never felt the urge to leave New London. The tavern had been in Gary's family since it was built shortly after the first ship of pilgrims dropped anchor in the bay.

Jane smiled and chatted happily while placing the order and waiting for her and Megan's drinks to be poured; when Gary walked by and smiled at her to acknowledge her customer, Jane's demeanor altered. Philippa stopped midsentence, her jolly smile turned into a look of confusion. Did she just see that? She was sure that Jane's eyes had changed color. She wasn't sure, but something was very different, and it happened in that moment. No, she was imagining it. Maybe she had never noticed before and at that precise moment in time, her brain actually noticed the woman's eye color. Philippa smiled politely and placed the two long glasses of Coke on the bar.

Outside, a flock of seagulls flew towards the harbor. They flew out of the ever-increasing darkness of the early evening and into the light of the town. They began to gather above the tavern, flying in an ever-tightening circle. More and more seagulls arrived and joined the spinning vortex of white feathers. People below stopped and looked up, amazed at the sight of the gathering birds and their strange behavior. An old man left the tavern and saw all the people standing around looking up. He followed their stares and looked up above him. The tornado of white continued to rotate, he quickly went back into the tavern and told the others he had been drinking with to come and look at the strange anomaly outside. Others in the tavern saw the group walk out and caught their reaction as they looked up before the door closed. Intrigued, they too went outside to look.

Jane sat back down with her daughter and placed her drink in front of her, Megan had seen the others walk out and then walk back in, all chatting loudly about something they had never seen before.

'I wonder what they are all excited about?' she said, pointing to the crowd.

Jane didn't respond. She just looked at her drink and began mouthing something, Megan noticed the movement and asked what she was saying. Jane didn't answer, she just continued to mouth words. The food was brought over by a young girl. She had served Megan and Jane several times before and smiled at Megan as she slid the hot plate from her apron-covered hands onto the table. Megan looked down at the chicken wings in front of her and, out of habit and hunger, licked her lips. The girl turned and walked over to the bar and collected the other plate of food that waited for her. A large steak, cooked just enough to darken the outer part of it but not enough to hide the blood that was escaping, was placed in front of Jane. The girl thanked them, asked if there was anything else that they needed and then left when no answer was given. Megan sat mouth open wide; a shocked look covered her face.

'What is that?' Megan asked.

Jane shrugged her shoulders, picked up the sharp steak knife and the fork and began to cut into the bloody steak.

'Mum, why are you eating that? Why are you all of a sudden wanting to eat meat?' Megan quizzed, shocked by the sudden change in behavior.

Jane continued to cut into the steak until she had cut a small piece off and put it in her mouth. She chewed loudly which made Megan feel a little queasy.

V

There must be evil if there is to be good in the world. They are like brother and sister, black and white, light and dark.

Megan, still confused and concerned, began poking her own food. She didn't feel so hungry now. With the strange behavior her mother was demonstrating and the loud chewing, she began slowly nibbling on one of the chicken wings. There was something different about the taste of the chicken; it wasn't as sweet as usual. In fact, it had a sour aftertaste.

'These don't taste right mum,' she said.

Megan used the strange tasting wings as an excuse to move away from the loud chomping of her mother as she decided to take the plate over to Philippa. She placed the plate on the bar and explained that the wings didn't taste right. Philippa apologized and explained that several of the people who had received food in the last thirty minutes had returned their food, saying that it tasted odd. Philippa asked how Megan's Mum was finding her steak. Megan turned and they both looked over to Jane, who continued to cut into the steak and place the bloody meat into her mouth.

'She seems to be eating it but I don't quite understand how,' Megan replied.

Philippa asked what Megan meant. When she explained that her mother was and as far as she could remember had been vegetarian until today and this meal, Philippa asked if everything was ok with them both. Megan shrugged her shoulders looked back to her mother then to Philippa and shrugged again.

'It's been a strange day.' Megan sighed.

Megan looked back to her mother. Concern weighed heavy on her shoulders, and her young mind searched for answers but could not come up with anything. She was afraid of going back to the table. Not only did the loud slopping and chewing sound of her mother make her feel ill, but her mother's strange behavior frightened her. It was as if her loving, caring mother had woken up this morning and was a completely different person.

***

The priest exited the church with a large leather-bound book tucked under his arm. He pulled the door behind him and turned to lock it. A light above the door illuminated the doorway. His eyes automatically focused on the large slimy blob of phlegm that had slid part the way down the door, leaving a glistening trail behind it.

'What on earth?' he exclaimed.

He reached into his inside jacket pocket and pulled out a few sheets of tissue. He had always made sure that he had a small packet of tissues on him. In his line of work, he was guaranteed to meet people that needed comfort and support, which usually meant dealing with tears and runny noses. He took the tissues and wiped the unwelcome blob of mucus from the door. He looked around him for a bin to place it in. He saw a small wall mounted bin attached to cake shop on the corner and walked over to it, placing the tissues in.

He heard seagulls calling—not the usual cawing of one or two that the harbor town had become accustomed to, but a machine gun effect of lots of seagulls screeching and calling. He looked up and saw the huge cyclone of white birds. The large number and the speed with which they were flying also added another sound: the sound of wind against feathers and flapping wings. It made an unnatural, eerie humming.

He stood and watched, transfixed by the strange phenomenon, as did many around him, and those directly underneath outside the tavern. The calling stopped, and all that was left was the strange flapping and rushing sound of wind. The feathered tornado then changed shape as the birds flew up and looped over and dove straight down, building speed.

Inside the tavern, Jane continued to cut into her bloody steak. Megan still stood at the bar, not wanting to go and sit back with her mother, who's strange behavior had finally reached the point where Megan could feel the deep saddened lump in her throat begin to create emotional tremors on her chin. She then heard a strange sound, and she looked over at the door. Another person had gone outside and joined the others in looking up at something. Philippa had also looked over and asked her husband what was going on. He shrugged his shoulders and continued to fill glasses for the waiting customers. There was then a thud and then another and another. The people who had gone outside suddenly burst back through the door, cursing and shouting to close the doors, Philippa shouted across the bar and asked what was going on.

'They've gone crazy!' a man shouted.

'What's gone crazy?' Philippa asked in a confused tone.

Another man shouted the answer to her question amongst more thuds and bangs, 'The birds.'

Outside, the seagulls dove down. Some bounced off the roof of the tavern, their necks snapping on impact, feathers flying from their bodies. Others turned and began sweeping into the face of the building. The first window to be penetrated by the feathered missiles was the upstairs bedroom window. Others followed, shattering the frame. Others ploughed into the walls. Feathers and blood began to stain the outside of the tavern. The mass of kamikaze birds worked their way down the building until finally they crashed through the windows of the bar area.

The people inside had already begun to move away from the windows and door as the banging and thudding sound grew louder. With each loud bang, people began to react nervously by pulling their head down into their shoulders in rhythm to the loud thuds. When the birds finally penetrated the windows of the bar area, people screamed and ran in all directions, covering their heads against the threat of being hit by sharp beaks and heavy white bodies. Megan dropped down onto her knees and covered her head. She could hear the screams of people as they ran around the room and the sound of tables and chairs being knocked over and bodies hitting the wooden floor. She lifted her head forward while still covering it with her hands to see where her mother was. To her shock and horror she was still sitting at the table tucking into her steak. Her facial expression was the same calm emotionless one she had worn since sitting back at the table. Megan looked around her and saw people fighting off seagulls with their arms, waving them around like they were directing a plane to land. She turned her body around, still on her knees until she was facing the open door of the bar. The top was still down, but the door had been left open and she could see into the area behind the bar where Philippa and her husband had been working. She saw a mass of birds piled on top of each other covered in blood. They pecked down on something and cawed excitedly. As she looked harder she could see the arm and leg of a man, Philippa's' husband.

Philippa was on the floor propped up against the inside of the bar, her body twitching. Megan shuffled towards her but stopped when she saw Philippa face. Her eyes were gone and her face was a mass of bloody scratches. Where her throat should have been, a large seagull hung, its head buried in her throat. It had hit her so hard that its beak and head had pierced her trachea. Megan backed away quickly, tears running down her face.

Outside, the priest and a few others ran towards the now-shattered door. They burst in and froze. The room was covered in blood and feathers. The chaos of the room halted their momentum. Birds still flew wildly around, hitting people who in turn screamed and ran into objects and other people, knocking them over only for them to get back up and be knocked down by either another person or bird. The priest looked around the room and saw Jane sitting at her table calmly and untouched. The birds seemed to be avoiding her, and she didn't seemed to be alarmed or frightened about what was going on around her. Others ran in to grab people and drag them out. The priest noticed Megan curled up on the floor near the bar and ran over, ducking and swatting at the few birds that continued to fly around. He grabbed her and pulled her to her feet. He took his jacket off, covered her head and guided her across the floor and out of the tavern into the dark clear night sky. The priest removed his jacket from Megan's head and held either side of her head, looking at her to see if she was injured in any way.

'Are you ok? Do you have any injuries?' he asked with a sense of panic and concern in his voice.

'She's fine,' a voice replied.

He quickly looked to where the answer had come from and saw Jane standing, coat draped over one arm and handbag in the other hand. Megan looked up at her through tear-filled eyes. Her fear-filled body shook uncontrollably. The images of Philippa and her husband clung to her mind's eye like flypaper. Her mother's calm, unconcerned behavior scared her even more, and she gripped the priest arm.

'The emergency services are on their way and I think she needs to be checked over to make sure she is not injured,' the priest stuttered.

Jane's facial expression grew angry. She reached out to take Megan's arm, but she moved away. Jane looked at her daughter with wide eyes and again reached out and grabbed her arm, pulling her away from the priest and to her side.

'I really do think she needs to be checked out before you leave,' he said again.

Jane looked at the priest and smiled: not a thankful smile but a sinister smile, dropping her head down and looking up from below her eyebrows.

'You need to look after yourself priest,' Jane whispered.

The sirens and lights of the police cars and ambulances filled the area around the tavern. Emergency personnel took it in turns to venture into the tavern and rescue people from the chaotic scenes of the bar.

Those who had been rescued sat outside and had their injuries tended to. Police took statements from those that witnessed the bizarre event. Detective Michael Dickson pulled up. He had been looking over the evidence from the earlier crime scene and had overheard the conversations across the radio about a bizarre wildlife event that had left people injured. He saw Father Harris and headed over to him.

'So father, do you have any views on what happened here?' he asked, tucking his shirt into his trousers.

'Hi Mike. No idea, it's been a strange day,' he answered.

Detective Dickson walked over to the tavern and stood next to the senior officer, who was barking out orders at some of the emergency people who ran by him.

'What happened here then Jack?' Dickson asked.

'Oh, hey Mike, some crazy flock of birds went Alfred Hitchcock.'

'Do you mind if I have a look?' Dickson asked.

'Be my guest, just don't touch the birds. We got a specialist coming down who has said no one should have contact with the birds and glove up when dealing with people who were there.'

Detective Dickson put his hands deep into his trouser pockets and then stepped past what was left of the front door, stooping down to avoid the last remaining part of the door that hung precariously by its hinge. Parts of bird and feathers stuck to it and it flapped in the gentle breeze that blew around the harbor. He stepped over the blood-stained bodies of the birds that covered the floor. He made his way over to the bar area where a group of police and paramedics were gathered deep in conversation. He pushed his way to the front of the group until he came to the sight that had caught their attention.

Propped up against the bar sat Philippa and the throat-embedded seagull. Blood covered her face, and two dark red and black holes stared at him that once held the woman's eyes. He then looked to the other body. The large amount of birds that had covered him had been removed and his fleshless face, throat and chest had been exposed.

'What the fuck happened here?' he asked with eyes wide with disbelief of what he was seeing.

'Beats the shit out of us.'

He looked around the room. There were no other bodies, only these two; others who had been present at the time of the bird attack had suffered cuts and bruises from collisions and falling over, but there had been no other fatalities.

'Why these two?' he asked out loud, returning his gaze to the bloody mess of the faceless body.

He returned outside and took a deep breath of the cool night air, Father Harris Joined him and pointed out something at the foot of the tavern door.

'Does that look familiar?' he asked.

Detective Dickson walked back towards the door and bent down. He examined a stone that didn't fit the look of rest of the building. Its shape and size as well as color seemed out of place. He ran his hand over the shape that had been carved into it, He had never noticed the stone or sign before, Like many in the town, he had spent most if not all of his life in the small harbor town, growing up locally and only leaving to become a police officer and then returning when the chance came.

He looked up at Father Harris, a look of disbelief and confusion written across his face. The priest asked him to follow him back to the church where he wanted to show him something he found while looking into the symbols of the murder.

They walked quickly back towards the church, where they were greeted by another large slimy slug like phlegm ball sliding down the door. He explained that he had already cleaned one off earlier.

'Someone sure doesn't like the church door,' the detective joked.

Father Harris unlocked the door and entered. He flicked a switch on the wall and a light burst into life. It illuminated the entrance the detective was now standing in. The priest walked into the darkness and flicked several switches. The main church hall lights came on. He looked at the detective and encouraged him to follow him down some side stairs and into a small room filled with books and scrolls. There on a table was a large dust-covered book. The priest opened it up. The sheer size and weight of it as it dropped open created a large bang, which echoed not just around the room but seemed to travel around the church.

The two men hunched over the book, the priest running his fingers along the lines of beautifully written letters and words. He then turned the page to reveal two pages full of symbols. Next to the strange shapes, a language was written that the detective could not understand or recognize.

'Here,' the priest said, pointing at a passage. 'The symbol outside of the tavern represents protection.'

'Are you sure? Because it obviously didn't work,' the detective pointed out.

'Yes. The other symbols this morning make reference to protection,' the priest continued.

The detective looked at the priest. 'What do you mean?'

'From what I have been able to decipher so far, the message this morning says: Time has released me and there can be no hiding or protection. My time has come again.' The priest turned and looked at the detective. 'That's as far as I have got.'

'Who's being released?' the detective asked.

The priest shrugged his shoulders and suggested that it may be someone who had researched the same language and might be using it as a calling card. The detective then asked him about the events of the evening and what he thought might have caused it. The priest paused for a moment and then began explaining about the woman he had seen who had been oblivious and at ease with the chaos that surrounded her. The detective asked for a description and jotted it down in his little black book. He asked if he had seen her before. Father Harris tried to remember where he had seen her. His eyes looked into the distance of the room, and he pressed two fingers against his mouth as he tried to recall her name, when he couldn't, he explained that she was the woman who sold pieces of art in a local shop. The detective suddenly knew who he was talking about and said her name, to which the Father Harris nodded. Detective Dickson quizzed Father Harris further about what he had seen in the tavern and where the woman and her daughter had disappeared to.

'Can you keep looking into the symbols and let me know what you find?' the detective asked.

Father Harris nodded. He turned off the light in the room and they went back upstairs into the main hall of the church, shutting the lights off as they walked to the door. The heavyset doors were securely locked and the slug of phlegm was wiped off the door once again with a few sheets of Father Harris's tissues. He then headed back to the tavern to see if any further assistance could be given. Detective Dickson walked back to his car and decided to pay a visit to the missing woman and her daughter.

Megan pulled and pulled but found her mother's grip so tight that each time she yanked away she lost her balance and fell back towards her mother.

'Mum, let me go,' she shouted, tears still streaming down her face.

There was no answer from her mother, just a steely gaze that focused ahead as she continued her walk back up the hill towards home. Megan pleaded with her mother to let her go, but the grip around her arm never eased. The anger and fear of what had happened during the evening coupled with the events of the morning and the day before erupted from within her.

'What's wrong with you mum?' she screamed.

The sound of the young girl's scream reverberated around the street. Jane stopped, and Megan saw the sudden change as if a wave had washed through her body. She had suddenly relaxed her grip, her posture sank slightly and her facial expression changed to one of confusion.

'Megan. What, where are we?' she asked, her voice trembling with the fear that she was completely unaware of where she was.

'What do you mean, where are we?' Megan snapped back.

Jane looked around her, searching for clues to her location. She rubbed her head and eyes with her hands. The sensation of complete helplessness became so over powering, tears began cascading from her eyes. Megan's anger subsided enough for her to see that her mother was distressed. She took her mother's hands and began to talk to her in a soft, caring voice.

'Mum, come on let's get back and try and figure out what is going on.'

Megan held her mother's arm tight against her body. Nestling her head into her mum's shoulder, she helped guide her home.

There was a police car outside the house next door, and the blue and white tape still surrounded the house and its garden. The two officers sitting in the car watched as the two women approached and crossed the road to the pathway leading to the front door. Just as they reached the front door of the dark house, a car pulled up and parked over the road. The driver did not get out; he just turned the engine off and watched as the two females entered the house. One of the officers got out of the car and walked over to the newly parked car and its occupant. He knocked on the window and asked for the window to be lowered. The window slowly opened. The officer bent down and looked into the dark interior of the car. Detective Dickson smiled back at him, holding up his identification.

'Sorry sir, just checking,' the officer said.

'That's alright. You did the right thing. Anything to report?' Dickson asked.

'No sir, it's been pretty quiet. Only the next door neighbors coming back and a few dog walkers,' he replied.

'Well, carry on. I'm just going to stay here for a while and watch, see if I can notice anything strange,' Dickson said firmly, before slowly winding up his window.

The officer returned to his car and filled his partner in with who was in the car.

The lights went on in each room as they entered. Megan sat her mother down on the sofa in the front room and took the coat and handbag that her mother had carried under her arm and threw them onto the small leather chair opposite. She then sat next to her mother and hugged her. She looked up at her daughter through tear-filled eyes.

'What's happening to me?' she asked her daughter.

Megan shrugged her shoulders and wiped away her own tears as they flowed. The last time she had seen her mother this upset was during the period of her parent's separation. They sat up chatting for an hour, like they had done when they first moved to the town. They laughed about past mishaps and Megan's early years. They avoided the events of the evening. Megan was desperate to talk about it and her mother's behavior, but she realized that at that moment it was best left. She didn't want to ruin the moment. Jane also didn't want to talk about the events of the day, realizing that her strange behavior had had a straining effect on her daughter. They retired together to their bedrooms, shutting the lights off downstairs as they went through the house. The lights for the journey upstairs were flicked on and then off as they became redundant for the journey. They said their goodnights, hugged and kissed each other on the cheek and entered their rooms. Megan slid into her bed and lay staring up at her ceiling. She was exhausted—mentally exhausted—but afraid to close her eyes knowing that the eyeless face of Philippa was waiting for her the moment she closed her eyelids. She rolled to her side, reached up to the bedside lamp and turned it on. She usually found sleeping with any form of light on difficult. When she moved to New London, she had to get her mother to buy darker curtains to block out the light from the street lamp opposite the house. Tonight the light was a welcome friend.

VI

Where water runs deep within the earth,
evil that is buried can once again be freed.

Jane lay on her bed, still clothed. She had no energy to get undressed. Even though she was completely exhausted, she didn't want to sleep. She was worried that if she fell asleep she wouldn't have control over her actions. She lay there fighting the urge to close her eyes, but even though she felt like she was winning the battle, her eyes slowly closed.

In the studio room, the mirror vibrated with an energy. The mirror rippled from its center as if someone had dropped a stone into a pool. The ripples spread across the mirror, and the frame didn't stop their continued expansion. The air around the mirror rippled with a force, and the air in the room moved in a wave like motion. The wave of energy flowed through the door and into the hall. It travelled through the walls and into Jane's room. The wave flowed over her sleeping body and finally faded. Jane sat up, her eyes still closed.

Outside, Detective Dickson sat in his car. He periodically looked up from reading of files and making notes from the dim light of a small flashlight which he lay on the passenger seat. He looked up and scanned the building and its dark shadowy areas and then returned to his notes and pictures of the murder that had happened not far from where he sat. He had begun to write down his thoughts and ideas of what might have happened in the house and what caused someone to attack not only the home owner, but also decapitate the dog. He had received the call from Doctor Johnson earlier in the evening, just before the bird attack. The cause of death had been confirmed, but that didn't stop the detective questioning the finding: drowning. He found it a strange cause of death bearing in mind the savagery of the attack, but more brain straining was the type of water found in his lungs: sea water. This confused him immensely. Had the murderer taken the water with him? The amount that was found in the victim's body surely someone must have seen someone carrying a large container of liquid. He scratched his head and turned back to the house he was watching. He scanned the downstairs windows carefully: no lights, no movement. He then looked up at the bedroom windows. In the smaller of the two there was still a light glow escaping from behind the dark curtain. He moved his gaze across to the larger window. He suddenly took a gasp of air and moved his head back away from the car window. He slowly moved his head back to the driver's side window and looked up. Standing at the large bedroom window was the mother. She seemed to be looking at him, or he thought she was.

Jane stood at the window. Her eyes were closed, but her face looked towards the car parked over the road. Whatever controlled her could see the detective sitting in the car and looking at her. A smile broke onto her face before she turned and walked away from the window and out of the bedroom. She walked down the stairs and towards the front door barefoot. Whatever was in control had made sure that she was not wearing anything that could wake her daughter. Jane slowly opened the door, trying to avoid any sound. She pulled the door behind her but did not close it properly. The sound the catch snapping into the lock's brass hole would surely create enough noise to alert Megan. She then walked calmly down the garden path, looking at the police car parked next door. She didn't fear being seen by the two officers because she could feel that they were both asleep. They were both into the tenth hour of their twelve-hour shift, and the boredom and lack of any form of stimulation had forced them both to drift into a light sleep. Jane then turned at the start of the sidewalk and walked away from the police car and past the car where the detective sat hiding in the darkness of the car. As she walked past, she smiled and then continued down the street.

Detective Dickson pushed himself into his seat and slid down so that his profile could not be seen. He had seen the woman walk out the door and towards him. He had quickly looked at the police car to see if one of the officers had left his car to intercept her as she left her property, but there was no movement from the patrol car. He could see her across the street as she walked past. His eyes widened when he saw her look at the car and smile. The smile and behavior was strange, but that she did it with her eyes closed throughout made him feel uneasy. He waited low in his seat until she was further down the street and then slowly exited his car. He pushed the door slowly against the body of the car just to close it enough to hold the door. He then crossed the street, keeping low and moving into the shadows. He kept his distance, watching the woman as she continued to walk down the shrub-lined street. He pressed himself against walls and bushes as he went, making sure he could always see her.

Jane stopped outside a large house with a large iron gate. She placed her hand on the lock, and fluid began to flow from her hand. It entered the lock, immediately causing it to rust. As the fluid continued to flow, the lock became a darker brown as the iron oxide began to break down the structure of the metal until it fell from the gate. She pushed the gate open and walked up the winding driveway to the beautifully decorated, frosted-glass front door. Jane looked at the lock and once again proceeded to flood the internal locking mechanism with water just like the gate before. There was a snapping sound as the internal arms broke. She pushed the door and entered.

Outside, the detective had reached the gate. He looked at the rusted lock on the floor then up at the drive leading towards the house. He patted himself down and then silently cursed. He had left his gun in the glove compartment of the car. In his adrenalin-fuelled excitement and concern, he had forgotten all about it. He looked around him for something he could use as a weapon, but the well-groomed hedges and grass held no such objects he could utilize. He slowly moved his way up the driveway, still keeping to the shadowy areas the best he could.

Inside, Jane had ascended the stairs and now stood at the foot of the bed of Linda Macgregor, the woman who lived there. She lay in the center of huge oval-shaped bed covered by silk sheets. Her husband had been a sailor who had lost his life at sea when his fishing boat sank in heavy seas, taking all hands. The life insurance pay out enabled her to enjoy her days doing what she wanted, not that it made a difference. Her family had always lived in the town and generation after generation had continued to build and rent out properties. She had been the only female born since her ancestors landed in the bay. She had sold many of the buildings off and lived comfortably off the profits as well as the few buildings she still rented to townsfolk for their businesses, one of whom happened to be Jane. Linda had a son who she had brought up on her own. He went to the local school and was known for being a bully and a spoiled brat who very rarely got punished because of the power his mother held in the town.

Jane slowly moved onto the bed like a prowling cat, positioning herself above Linda. Jane then clamped her hands down on the woman's forehead and jaw, forcing her head into her pillow and opening her mouth. The sudden force and surprise woke Linda, who attempted to scream. Before a sound could leave her mouth, Jane had covered the gapping mouth with her own. She bit down on Linda's tongue and pulled back away from her. The pink muscle extended out of her mouth as it was pulled. Linda could only moan from deep within her throat as the tongue was pulled further and further out. She kicked and punched the woman holding her head down. She connected with a few feeble, side-fisted punches, and her legs kicked the sides of Jane, but nothing made her relinquish the tongue. Linda could feel the pull and then the tearing of the flesh as the tongue came away from its anchoring. Blood spurted out of her mouth as it did, and as the tongue moved away from its usual home, it oozed blood over Linda's face and Jane's hand that was holding the jaw open by the chin. Linda continued to kick and punch. Her scream became a louder painful moan and gurgle, the best she could do with the pain that attacked her nervous system and the now continuous flow of blood travelling down her throat.

Jane moved her head to the side and spat the tongue out. It bounced off the satin sheets and fell to the floor. She then returned to face Linda and once gain covered the now bloody open mouth. Her back arched as if straining when vomiting. Fluid burst from her mouth as if a fire hydrant had been turned on, and the water it had held back had finally escaped with enormous pressure. The liquid flowed continuously as it entered Linda and joined the blood as it flowed into her lungs. Linda's' flailing arms and legs slowed and then finally stopped as they fell limp on the bed.

Detective Dickson had reached the front door and slowly entered. He paused, trying to see what was in front of him, not wanting to alarm the woman and tip her off that he was in the house. He walked carefully through the hall and into the large open space that he imagined was the living room since he could make out a large seating area and T.V. With no one in the room, he backtracked to the hall and began his slow and quiet journey up the curving staircase, sliding his back against the wall and looking up ahead of him.

Jane had sensed the presence of the man as he entered. Her smile returned to her blood-stained face, but

167

her eyes remained closed. She slid off the bed and picked up the tongue that lay on the floor. She placed it in her mouth, holding it in between her teeth. She then picked up the body of Linda. There was no straining against the weight of the fluid-filled body; it was lifted with ease and then carried out of the bedroom to the top of the staircase. Below, the detective had reached the halfway point. He froze when he saw the woman appear at the top of the stairs. At that moment, he was unable to move, struck by terror. The woman stood, her eyes closed but still looking at him, holding a limp body of a woman. He could feel his body begin to shake, but could still not move. Jane spat the tongue out onto the floor and began laughing and then lifted the body high above her head and threw it down at the detective. As the body began its flight path towards him, Detective Dickson found the strength to fight against the fear that had rooted him to the spot. He began moving to the other side of the staircase, he crashed against the banister as the body of the woman bounced off the steps in front of him. Fluid ejected from the woman's mouth as she crashed to the surface. Dickson tried to maintain his balance against the banister, but a face full of the liquid thrown up from the body caused him to lean back, and that was enough for him to topple backwards over the banister. He clawed at the wooden handrail as he fell but it was too late. He fell to the hard floor below, landing flat on his back. All the air in his lungs escaped at once with a rasping sharp breath. His head then created a slightly higher-pitched thud and all went black. Jane bent down and picked the tongue back up off the floor and headed down the hall.

John Macgregor had been woken by a loud banging sound. He sat up and listened. All was quiet. He was sure that he did not dream the loud noise and decided to see if his mother was ok. He pulled the duvet off himself and stepped onto the cold floor. He walked to his bedroom door, turned the handle and pulled the door open. The figure standing in front of him smiled. The woman's face was stained with blood, and her eyes were closed. His body reacted by bolting upright, and he took a deep breath in and froze. The woman standing in the doorway reached out and placed a hand on his shoulder. She then began to push him back into his room and towards his bed. He tried to shout for his mother but no sound came from his open mouth. He attempted to hit the woman, but the moment he began moving his arms towards her, she clamped her hand deeper into the flesh of his shoulder, stopping his brief fight back.

Jane pushed the boy back onto his bed and held him down by kneeling on his legs and maintaining a strong grip of his shoulder. With her other hand, she pushed the boys mothers tongue into his mouth. As the bloody piece of muscle filled his mouth, the metallic stale taste of the blood and flesh attacked his senses and he began to wretch. He tried in vain to spit it out, but the size of it made it difficult to maneuver it into a position that he could force it out. With her hand now free, Jane held out her index finger and drew it down the front of his T-shirt. Her fingernail cut through the fabric like a hot knife moves through butter. Once she had travelled the length of the T-shirt, she peeled each half to the side, revealing the boy's chest and stomach. His chest rose and fell quickly as his panic and fear caused his heart to race and breathing to increase. He looked up at the bloody smile, and tears ran down his face, taking the same path, never deviating, flowing like a river into his ears. Jane looked at the boy and then back to her index finger that was extended in front of his face, the nail began to turn black. It was then pushed into the flesh where the throat meets the chest. The boy's skin sizzled as the nail burned its way into skin and fat. He managed a muffled moan, a moan that never ceased as the nailed moved down his chest, past his sternum onto his stomach and all the way down to his bellybutton. His head was attacked by the sensations of the burning pain from the nail as it cut its way down his body. He could hear the sound of his flesh as it crackled and the smell of his burning flesh filled his nose.

With the cut completed, Jane took her hand and dug the ends of the fingers into the open wound. She wriggled her fingers until they were underneath the skin and then pulled sharply away as if attempting to remove body hair with waxing strips, the skin and fat made a similar sound as it separated from the muscle. The boy's body arched as it tried to stay with its skin. His moan became more of a gasping for air. Jane put the bloody hand on his other shoulder and repeated the action of ripping his skin from his body with the other hand. With his body completely void of the two large flaps of skin and fat that still attached to his body that now lay flat out by his sides resembling wings, Jane let go of the shoulder and sat up and admired the crimson mess below her. The boy's breathing was short and sharp. Tears continued to flow from his eyes. The only sound escaping his mouth was a muffled whimpering.

Jane held up her blooded right hand. She placed her index finger into her mouth and sucked on it. She then proceeded to suck and lick the other blood-soaked fingers, enjoying the taste that covered them. Once she was satisfied that she had extracted all she could from them, she licked her lips and pushed the fingers tight together. She turned her hand so that the tips of the fingers were touching the bloody muscle of the boy's chest, just above his heart, pushing enough to find a gap between the ribs and then pushed down hard. The hand sunk into the muscle past the ribs and into the boys heart. A final gasp came from the boy as he was finally allowed to escape the pain he was in. Jane began to move her hand in a sawing motion, continuously stabbing at the heart, soaking her hand with the blood that had been present in the chambers of the heart at the moment the boy's life force left him.

Jane climbed off the boy and walked over to a poster-covered wall. There, she began drawing symbols with her blood-stained hands. She would return to the boy's body several times and push her hand into the ever increasing cavernous hole in his chest to cover her hand with more blood before returning to the wall and continuing her bloody artwork.

171

Manuela arrived at the house at the same time every day. She travelled the twenty miles by catching three different buses. She could not afford to live any closer on the poor wage that she was paid by Linda Macgregor. Even if her boss was a millionaire, she didn't like parting with money. Today was different. The gate that welcomed her was already open. The lock was rusted and on the floor. She stood looking at it, playing with the keys for it in her fingers. She shrugged her shoulders and walked up to the house. As she got closer, she could see the front door was open. Seeing it open made her slow her approach. This was not normal. The lady of the house and her son were never up when she arrived.

She stepped in through the open doorway and into the hall. She screamed when she saw the body of Linda Macgregor lying at the bottom of the stairs. Blood covered her face and a pool of a dark-colored liquid surrounded the body. Her arms and legs were twisted in abnormal directions that added to the shock of the scene. Manuela fell to her knees and continued to scream. Tears began running down her cheeks as she continued to stare at the mangled body at the bottom of the stairs. Out of the corner of her eye she saw an arm, the body it belonged to was being hidden by the ark of the staircase. She pushed herself up onto her feet and slowly approached. The arm became an upper body of a middle-aged man. His jacket lay open, and next to him was a black wallet that itself was open, showing his identity and police badge. She could see his chest move up and down slightly, but still approached with caution. She bent down and shook him.

'Mr. Police man, Mr. Police man.' She said as she shook him harder.

Detective Dickson moaned. His eyes flickered and he tried to lift his head. He felt a shooting pain and then his head began to throb. He relaxed his neck and placed his head back down. The moment it touched the floor he winced again.

'You should not move,' the woman standing over him said.

He lifted up an arm and pointed towards her. 'Call police, send help. Officer down.' He then placed the arm across his eyes.

Manuela ran into the front room, looking at the body at the bottom of the stairs as she passed it. She picked up the receiver and pressed the buttons before holding it to her ear. The calm voice on the other end asked her to repeat her story and details, trying to get an idea of what the woman on the end of the line needed. Manuela's strong Spanish accent being shouted hysterically down the phone made it difficult to understand. When she mentioned the words of the detective, 'officer down.' The calm voice changed, asking for the address over and over until she received the information.

'Oh lord! John,' she shouted down the phone.

Manuela dropped the phone and ran to the stairs. She stopped at the body of her employer and slowly stepped over it. Once clear of the human obstacle, she continued to quickly make her way up the stairs and down the hall to John Macgregor's room. She pushed the door open and screamed.

Detective Dickson heard the scream. It sent a shiver down his spine, and a shot of adrenaline engulfed his body. He pushed himself onto his front and came face to face with the little puddle of blood left by the wound on the back of his head. He reached back and touched the tender area. The damp, matted patch of hair surrounded a large gash in the back of his head. He could feel the walls of the deep cut. He withdrew his hand and looked at it. He could hear the woman's crying and her gibbering but didn't have the strength to get up any further than his knees. He stayed in that position and tried to remember what had happened. He strained his sore head, trying to remember, but nothing. He couldn't remember anything apart from following the woman down the street to the house and walking up the driveway. His attention was then drawn to the sound of sirens. The familiar wail of a police car in the distance became a comfort. He felt stronger as the sound got closer.

The house buzzed with activity. Manuela had been carried out by medics who attempted to calm her hysterical state. Detective Dickson sat in an ambulance been assessed and questioned by a fellow officer. He waved his arms in protest at the officer who was trying to take his statement. He moaned at the paramedic to hurry up. He was not happy at being held back, away from whatever had happened upstairs. He had seen two police officers run outside and vomit in a bush next to the front door. The forensic officer berated them, worried that they may have contaminated the crime scene. Something terrible had happened in that house and he needed to know.

'Ok detective, I suggest you get one of the officers to drive you home and that you see your doctor as soon as possible. If you feel any dizziness or nausea, get yourself to a hospital. Definitely do not go into work for a few days,' the paramedic said.

'That's not going to happen,' he shot back before slowly stepping out of the back of the ambulance and heading back into the house.

VII

Evil always looks for a door; a door into our world.

Megan was awoken by banging. She sat up and listened to the sound: *bang, bang, bang*. The sound had a faultless timing. She slid out of bed and followed the sound. It led her downstairs and into the front room. There, hammering a nail into the wall, was her mother.

'Mum what you doing?' she asked.

There was no answer, just more banging as the hammer hit the nail deeper into the wall. Once it had reached a depth that satisfied her, she turned and looked at Megan and smiled.

'I don't want to sell this I want to put it up,' Jane said.

She bent down and picked up the mirror and began hooking the wire on its reverse onto the nail. Once done, she stood back and admired it. Not satisfied with its slight odd angle, she returned her hands to it and moved it, touching each side gently until she was finally satisfied with its position. Megan watched as her mother then began to run her hands over the frame. The longer she did this the more it became a stroking motion.

'Did you sleep well dear?' Jane asked Megan.

'Out like a light, what about you mum?' Megan asked.

Jane looked over her shoulder at Megan. 'I slept like a log.'

The look on her face gave away something. Megan had seen that look before, usually when her mother was

177

trying to hide something. She turned and headed back upstairs. On the way down the corridor to her room, she paused at her mother's bedroom door and silently opened it just enough to squeeze her head in. Her eyes widened when she saw the wall above the bed headboard. The large red shape stood out against the white of the wall. The ends of the shape faded into several handprints. The pillows below were also covered in red handprints. Megan closed the door and headed into her room, scampering around picking up items of clothing that she had left on the floor. Once dressed, she quickly washed and made her excuses as she passed her mother on her way to the front door. Her mother still stood in front of the mirror.

***

Detective Dickson had decided that he had to confront the woman he had followed the night before. He had asked the patrol officer to drop him off at his car. He exited the patrol car and stood by his own until the police car had disappeared down the hill. He then removed the bandage that covered his head, pulled open the car door, leaned in and removed his gun from the glove compartment and walked over to the police car stationed outside the house next door. He knocked on the window, which was wound down by one of the officers. He explained that he had a lead on the murder and needed immediate backup. The officer in the seat opposite reached for the radio. Before he could make the call, Dickson urged them to follow him now and that there was no time to call it in; they had to move immediately.

178

The two officers got out of the car and followed Dickson. As they reached the steps of the front porch, the young girl who he had seen enter with the woman the previous night ran into him. He grabbed her arms and looked into her startled eyes.

'Hey, careful there miss,' he said.

Megan struggled to free herself but noticed the two police officers and relaxed a little.

'Is your mum in?' Dickson asked. He realized that the girl was frightened of something and it wasn't him. She kept looking back towards the house nervously.

Megan was momentarily stuck for what to say and do. She didn't want to get her mum in trouble but at the same time what she had just seen and her mother's behavior over the last few days concerned her enough to want her to say something, but not to the police.

'She may be in the shower,' she stuttered.

'What's the rush?' Dickson asked, still holding onto her Megan's arms.

'I'm meeting friends and I'm a little late,' she said.

She pulled her arms free, pushed past the detective and the two officers and ran down the drive way and across the street.

Dickson raised his finger to the doorbell, pressed it and then knocked on the door. The two officers looked at

179

each other and raised an eyebrow in surprise. Both the officers began to feel uneasy by his behavior. Dickson raised himself onto his tiptoes and peered in through the glass, straining to see past the frosted glass of the door.

The doorbells ring and the sudden heavy knocking woke Jane from her hypnotic state. She moved through the front room and to the front door. She could see a face pressed against the glass of the door, a face she recognized from somewhere but could not place. She opened the door and was greeted by a detective's shield being held in front of her face. She refocused her vision and saw the man staring at her with an angry expression. Behind him stood two police officers, who both smiled and tipped their hats.

'Do you mind if we come in?!' Dickson snapped.

Jane looked at him with surprise. 'Excuse me?' she replied.

'We need to discuss your whereabouts early this morning.'

Jane's expression of surprise changed to confusion, but she stood to the side and invited the three men in, pointing them in the direction of the living room. As she closed the door and turned to the three men walking down the small hall and into the room on their right, Jane's eyes closed for a second. When they reopened, they were dark brown in color. She walked into the living room and sat down on the sofa in front of the men.

Detective Dickson stood with his hands on his hips, his face like thunder as he looked at her. He began to remember moments from the early hours.

'Do you remember where you were between the hours of midnight and 2 am?' Dickson asked. There was a sharpness to his tone.

'Of course I remember, but you also know where I was,' Jane teased.

The two uniformed police officers again looked at each other, their faces a combination of shock and surprise.

'Oh I know where you were because I followed you,' Dickson shot back.

Jane began to laugh and shrugged her shoulders, 'I know you followed me, I watched you hide in your car and I could smell your fear when that bitch's body landed at your feet.'

The two officers reached for their side arms. Detective Dickson smiled back at her and looked at one of the officers. Raising his eyebrows and nodding in the woman's direction, he asked for one of them to handcuff her. Dickson's cell phone vibrated in his pocket. The soft buzzing sound broke the uneasy silence that had descended on the room after the woman's confession.

'Cuff her and take her to the car,' Dickson ordered as he removed the vibrating phone.

He looked down at the display screen, which lit up with the name of Father Harris, Dickson pressed the green accept button and placed the phone to his ear. He exchanged a hello before asking the priest on the other end to hold for a second. He then covered the cell phone with his free hand and looked at the two officers.

'Cuff her and get her in the car. I can't bare being in the same room as that psycho,' he said, nodding towards Jane. He then walked back to the front door and continued his phone call.

Father Harris relayed what he had found out about the symbols, their meaning and the locations of the other buildings that had the same inter-linked circles over a cross etched somewhere on its structure.

'The symbol is meant to be a protective sign against evil. The tavern belonged to a family that have always lived in the local area since the town's birth. The other place, as you know, is the church, which belonged to one of my ancestors. There is also a boat house that belongs to a Mr. Brabbings located just off the harbor.' He paused as he looked at the notebook he had written the information on. 'Oh, the old lighthouse which belongs to old Jerry Simmons, who's family have always looked after it, even before they converted it into the bed and breakfast and a house up on the hill.'

Detective Dickson interrupted him before father Harris could relay the address and its occupants.

'Don't tell me, 117 North Shore Road and a Mrs. Macgregor,' he said.

There was a further pause and then confirmation; 'Yes how did you know?' Father Harris asked.

Detective Dickson explained what he had seen and that he and two officers had just arrested the woman from the tavern.

'Mike,' Father Harris said in a concerned voice. 'There is more to it than just some crazy woman on a killing spree.'

Father Harris read an account from an old journal that belonged to the priest who conducted an exorcism on a young woman centuries ago. Detective Dickson continued to listen as he walked down the path of the house and stopped where the white picket fence met the sidewalk. He did not hear the sounds of suffering and struggle coming from within the house.

Inside the house, Jane knelt over one of the officer's bodies, her hand clamped on his face. He lay unconscious on the floor after being hit by her open hand. The impact of the blow to his head hit with such weight and force that he just collapsed to the floor. Blood escaped from where her fingers were pushing deeper into his flesh. The sound of snapping bone then echoed around the room as her grip pushed past the bony surface of the officer's cheek and forehead. The other officer lay on the floor; a clear liquid ran from his ears, nose and mouth from where she had grabbed his head, covered his mouth with hers and vomited the liquid into him until his body ceased to struggle. He was the first to die. He had had no time to react to the woman half his size incapacitating his partner with one blow. Before his partner had hit the floor, she was locked onto him her mouth closing over his.

Jane stood and stared back into the mirror on the wall. She tilted her head one way, then the other, as if admiring her own beauty, but the reflection that looked back was one of a grotesque deformed face.

'Are you trying to tell me that the woman who we've just arrested may be possessed?' Dickson scoffed.

'What I'm trying to say is that there are other possible forces at work here. Don't discount them,' Father Harris replied.

'One other thing. You need to be careful, you may be—' Father Harris began.

Dickson stood with the phone to his right ear and slowly massaged his aching forehead with his other hand. He looked back at the house and saw Jane standing at the window staring at him.

'What the?' he said, his words laced with confusion and shock.

The voice on the other end began asking what was wrong. Dickson said he had to go, hung up and headed towards the front door of the house.

'Shit,' Father Harris said before looking up at the statue of Christ above the altar and apologizing. He heard the door at the front of the church creak as it was pushed open. The sudden burst of sunlight hid the person that had walked in. He walked towards the entrance and finally saw the young girl he had helped the night before as her body blocked the beams of light.

'Hello, how are you doing?' he asked, smiling at her.

'I may need your help, but you'll probably think I'm being stupid. I, I don't know.' She stuttered as she approached him.

'Come and sit.' He said presenting an opening to the pew next to him. Megan squeezed in and sat down. Father Harris crouched at its entrance and looked at her. He could see the anguish etched on her face.

'Tell me what's wrong,' he said.

Megan began explaining about how her mother had begun to act strangely and that she was worried that she may be sick. She talked about the next door neighbor and how he had shouted at her mother before he was found dead the next morning. She talked about the incident with the birds the evening before and how she watched as her mother sat calmly amongst the chaos and continued to eat meat when she had been vegetarian since her teens. Father Harris nodded and smiled reassuringly as Megan unloaded her worries about her mother. She then mentioned the symbol that had been painted above the bed, and Father Harris stopped her at the description of the interlocking circles and cross.

'Is that the first time you've seen that symbol,' he asked.

Megan thought for a second, then continued to explain about the piece of driftwood that they had found. She also described the rubbing that her mother had done on the same morning, somewhere in the woods above the town.

It was at that moment that Father Harris remembered about his friend Detective Dickson. He was up at the house and had arrested Megan's mother, but the ending of their phone conversation didn't seem right.

'Was your mum acting strange when you left this morning?' he asked Megan.

'She had put up the mirror that she had made from the piece of driftwood we found. She was sort of acting weird,' Megan replied.

'What do you mean by weird?' Father Harris asked.

'Well she stood staring at herself in the mirror and stroking the frame?' Megan stroked the air in front of her as she described her mother's actions.

Father Harris stood up and grabbed Megan's hand and began pulling her to her feet. She pulled back her arm in surprise at the sudden action of the priest.

'What's wrong,' she asked with a hint of panic in her voice.

'Sorry, we need to get to the house now,' he said, moving towards the door and pulling Megan with him.

'Why?'

'I'll explain on the way,' he said, finally letting go and walking with speed to the church door.

***

Detective Dickson marched through the front door and into the living room. He froze as his searching eyes met the sight of the police officer with his head covered in blood, the shape of his face deformed. He looked around for the other officer but could only see a large pool of liquid on the floor. An inner voice began screaming at him to get out of the house, but he found a deep desire to continue looking for the officer and the woman. He drew his gun from its holster and held it out in front of him. The years of training with the weapon and constant scenario testing kicking in. He slowly stepped over the body, his head turning as he searched his surroundings. He moved over to a wall and pressed his back against it so that the whole room lay in front of him. He slid along the wall, the gun still held out in front as he moved towards the door and the hallway. His senses suddenly heightened; he could smell the blood on the floor and the slight aroma of the sea. His ears picked up on the slightest sound around him; a creek from one of the floorboards sounded like an explosion. He moved to the foot of the stairs and looked up past his gun, which was aimed at the top, the memory of the night before playing like a movie in his head. There was no sign of the officer or woman. He paused at the bottom and his ears strained, listening, trying to find some form of sound that would warn him to the whereabouts of the woman and the officer.

Out of the stillness of the house, a dripping sound suddenly began. Detective Dickson listened to its ever-increasing pace before realizing the sound was coming from behind him, back in the living room. He turned and, with his gun leading the way, he moved into the doorway of the living room and searched with his eyes, looking for where the sound of the dripping water was coming from. The dripping sound had begun to gain speed and strength. He looked over to the wall where the mirror had been mounted and saw water flowing from the glass, or rather what he thought was glass. The glass moved or rippled like raindrops falling into a small puddle. Water flowed out over the wooden frame, travelled around the strange symbols that were carved into it and then continued to the edge of the frame before falling to the floor below. He stopped and searched the room, making sure he was alone. Only the bloody, deformed body of the officer was present. He then moved closer to the mirror, watching as the ripples bounced around within the frame.

From within the mirror something watched. The woman and the creature within her floated effortlessly amongst the swirling water. It smiled as it observed the detective slowly approaching.

Detective Dickson stood in front of the mirror. He looked intensely at it, trying to see if there was still a plate of glass below the water, he questioned within his mind as to whether the mirror itself was a special water feature, just like the ones he had seen in the city hotels and offices that he had visited while working his beat, like the artistic features that circulated water down a free standing sculpture with a flat glass surface. He moved his gun up to the water and pushed it in. He expected the gun to hit a solid surface and make a clunking sound as the metal of his gun clashed with the glass beyond the water, but it continued to disappear until the water was touching his finger that rested on the trigger. He withdrew the gun quickly. Water dripped from its end. He looked at the mirror with confusion, no longer worried about being surprised by the woman in the house. The bizarre mirror now encapsulated him. He pushed the gun into the water once again, but this time he moved the gun in a large circle covering the space within the wooden frame, just to make sure that he hadn't pushed the gun into the hole that may have been used allow the water to flow. The gun moved within the water freely. He withdrew it again, stared harder at the rippling water and lowered the water-soaked gun, he then raised his left hand up to the mirror and slowly moved it towards the water.

The woman and her demonic controller moved closer to the surface and the reaching hand of the detective it had been watching. The demonic creature chuckled to itself when it watched the gun nozzle invade its watery world and then retract only to be pushed in again and swirled around. A deep dark instinct within the creature told it that the man on the other side was another of the few that it had to exact a long-awaited revenge upon on. It began reaching towards the surface and the hand of the detective.

Detective Dickson's hand closed in on the rippling water within the mirrors frame. He paused just above the surface. An inner voice screamed for him to stop, but another louder, inquisitive voice told him he needed to know how far back it was before he could touch the glass. A sudden sound of footsteps stopped his hand from entering the water.

'Don't touch the water,' Father Harris shouted from the living room entrance.

Father Harris had driven with Megan back to the house, explaining his findings of the symbols to her, telling her of the evil that had befell the town centuries ago and what the symbols represented. In turn Megan had retold every strange behavior or event that had happened since the day she found the driftwood. They had rushed in to the house and found Dickson with his gun drawn, held down by his side and his free hand about to touch the mirror. Megan gasped when she noticed the body of the officer on the floor and its bloody,, deformed face. Father Harris' focus was on his friend and didn't notice the body until Megan gasped and held her open mouth with both hands. When he saw the body, he could no longer hold back his horror and anger.

'What the fuck.' The words escaped before he could stop them. The sound of the holy man swearing stunned Megan. Her attention moved from the body back to the priest; even Dickson looked surprised.

Detective Dickson lowered his hand away from the mirror and stared over at his friend and the girl.

'What's going on?' he asked.

'I tried to tell you over the phone but you hung up,' Father Harris said.

'Tell me what?' Dickson asked, looking more confused than he already was.

'The people who have been killed are linked, and you also share that link,' he explained.

'What?' Dickson said, shocked.

'Where's my Mum?' Megan shouted at Dickson.

'I don't know,' He responded.

Dickson then pointed at the mirror and asked Megan how the mirror water feature worked. She looked at him then the mirror and back at him. The confusion on her face and the shrug of her shoulders told him that what was happening with the mirror was not normal. He looked back at the mirror and began backing away.

Father Harris looked behind him and down the hall towards the kitchen. He noticed a large piece of paper on the kitchen counter. Its ends were curled over, enabling him to see part of the dark color and lighter areas of the rubbing and the different symbols that had been picked out. He stepped back out of the living room and began walking towards the paper. Dickson watched him disappear from sight. He looked at Megan and then back at the mirror. The water within the frame continued to ripple from the center out towards the frame edge. Megan peered at the mirror. The circular ripples transfixed her.

'So you've never seen this before?' Dickson asked, looking at Megan while gesturing to the mirror with his gun.

Megan just shook her head.

Father Harris reappeared at the doorway holding the large rubbing out in front of him. 'Where was this taken from?' he asked, briefly looking up at Megan and then back at the piece of paper.

Megan looked over at him, and confusion covered her face. The body lying on the floor and its distorted face caught her attention once more as she looked over at the priest and the piece of paper he was looking at. She felt a cold shiver move up through her spine as the bloodied head of the police officer once more attacked her mind. She forced herself to block out the vision and focused on the rubbing now being closely inspected against the sunlight that flooded the room.

'My mum did that up in the woods when she went for a walk,' she explained.

'The symbols are very similar to what I have in the books and scrolls, but I've never seen some of these,' Father Harris said.

An explosion of water erupted from the mirror, showering the room with spray. All three gasped and squinted against the water droplets attacking their faces as they looked at the horizontal geyser. A pair of arms appeared and reached out towards the startled Dickson. A distorted face appeared out of the head of water, and it smiled through sharp, fang-like teeth. The arms continued to reach towards him, the sharp nailed fingers biting down through his shirt and into his shoulders. As the water spout and its passenger returned to the mirror, Dickson found himself being pulled up off the floor and into the mirror.

He fought against the pain of the fingers pushing deeper into the muscle of his shoulder and spread his arms out as far as he could, grabbing the frame of the mirror. The hands that grasped his shoulders let go and caught his head. He felt the nails dig into the back of his head as he resisted against them. His head began to penetrate the water of the mirror. He could feel the coldness of the liquid as it moved over his face. He closed his eyes, partly due to the water creeping over them and partly as he strained against the pulling hands. Out of pure instinct, he took a lung full of air, just as the water engulfed his head. He opened his eyes and stared into the disfigured face of a creature that was attempting to pull him deeper within the watery world he was now a part of.

The mouth of the creature snapped at him, and at that moment all he could think was piranha. He continued to push with his arms, trying to push himself back into the dry world behind him outside the mirror. He began to feel his lungs starting to ache as the oxygen he had taken in ran low. He then felt the fingers that grasped his head begin to pull away from him, digging into the soft flesh of his face. The water around him began to turn red as the sharp nails of the demon's hands ripped chunks of flesh from his cheeks and jaw. He could no longer keep his mouth closed, and he began to scream or attempt to scream against the sudden inflow of water into his lungs.

The watery world around him and the evil face smiling at him began to fade into a blur as his body began to succumb to the effects of drowning. His grip against the outside of the mirror and his resistance to the pulling demon began to fade, and he could feel the coldness of the water move down his body. He then felt a new sensation; something was grabbing his legs and pulling the other way. He could feel the warmth of the sun-drenched air of the room and then the hard wooden floor as he hit it. The sudden impact of his body hitting the floor and the rush of oxygen caused him to convulse and then expel the salt-rich liquid from his body.

For what seemed minutes, both Megan and Father Harris stood frozen to the spot as the detective stuck out of the mirror up on the wall like a hunting trophy, only this one kicked and wriggled and fought against the mirror. They both came to at the same time and grabbed a leg each and pulled. Whatever was on the other side was not willing to let go without a fight, so Father Harris grabbed the flailing detective by his belt, put a foot against the wall for leverage and pulled, when the force pulling the detective finally let go, the sudden release forced them all to fall backwards and onto the floor, Detective Dickson crashing down hard onto the wooden floor.

Father Harris and Megan sat up quickly and scrambled to their feet. They took an armpit each and lifted the spluttering detective to his knees before pulling him away from the wall and the mirror. There was another large explosion of water from the mirror as a pair of police uniformed legs flew out onto the sofa, the shoes and belt still in place. The lumbar vertebrae that protruded up from the trousers looked like a chewed dog bone. Megan and Father Harris looked at the legs that sat on the sofa in a normal sitting position, they exchanged a glance and then began pulling the slumped detective quickly to the front door, pulling it open and dragging him towards the road. Once they had reached the sidewalk, Father Harris and Megan sat the detective against the white picket fence. Father Harris began to walk back towards the house, and Megan shouted to him.

'Where you going?'

He looked back at her. 'I need that rubbing,' he shouted back before breaking into a jog back to the front door.

Father Harris paused as he reached the door. He took a deep breath and pushed it open. He could hear the sound of water droplets crashing down against the floor, the continuous un-rhythmical patter of droplets on wood. He stepped towards the opening to the living room and again paused. He pushed his back into the wall just inches from the large arch opening into the room.

'I can smell you priest,' a voice hissed.

A cold feeling ran the length of his spine and his eyes widened upon hearing the voice. He looked down at the floor and could see the edge of the paper rubbing. He slid down the wall until he was crouching and leaned towards the large piece of paper. He stretched his arm as far as it would go, trying to avoid exposing his head or body to the room where the voice had come from.

'You need to try harder than that,' the voice teased.

Father Harris moved his upper body towards the corner of paper he could see. His forehead broke free of the protection from the wall that separated the living room and the hallway he was crouched in. He had to reach further than he thought, slightly twisting his body so that he could get a firm hold of the paper and drag it towards him and the safety of the hallway. As he twisted his body, he caught a movement in his peripheral vision.

He turned his head slightly and moved his eyes so that he could see what was moving.

The distorted face of Megan's mother smiled at him, her head appearing out of the mirror like a hunter's trophy. He quickly turned his attention back to the rubbing and grasped at it. Once in his hand, he stood and ran to the door. He could hear laughter coming from the living room and then one final message before he broke free of the house.

'Your time is short, priest.'

Father Harris ran towards Megan, who stood on the sidewalk outside of the house, supporting the now standing but wobbly detective. 'What did you see?' she quizzed.

'We need to get to the church,' he shouted, grabbing Dickson's free arm and placing it over his shoulder to help Megan move the dazed and confused man to the car.

Once they reached the car, Megan let go of the detective and opened the rear door. Father Harris helped Dickson lower himself into the back and shut the door. He then grabbed the drivers handle and yanked at it. The urgency to get away from the house and the high level of adrenalin that flowed around his body caused him to almost rip the car door hand off. Megan climbed into the passenger seat and struggled with the simple task of putting on the seat belt, yanking at it forcing it to lock. Even when she tried to do it slowly, she found herself still pulling too fast. In the end, she just left it to slide back to its normal position against the side of the door and sat nervously rubbing her thighs. Father Harris dropped into the seat next to her and fumbled with the keys. He forced the key into the ignition and fired up the engine. He hadn't even closed his door when he put it in gear and began moving off with the door closing from the cars momentum.

The car swung into the small parking space next to the church. The tires screeched as they bounced and skidded from the stress of locking wheels on the dry cobbled street as Father Harris pushed hard on the brake. He turned the key in the ignition, cutting the engine. Before it even stopped purring, he pushed open the door and got out, pulling open the rear door and reaching in to grab the rubbing and help Detective Dickson out of the back. Megan jumped out of the passenger side and ran around to help Dickson clear of the car. Once out, they part carried him into the church. Dickson had begun to gain a little more control over his aching wet body, but his head continued to throb. Father Harris fumbled for his keys, struggling to put the key in the lock of the church side door. His hand shook uncontrollably. He paused for a second, took a deep breath and slowly slid the key into the lock and turned. As soon as the door was opened, they all bundled in through the small door frame. Megan hit her shoulder on the frame, momentarily knocking her off balance.

'You ok?' Father Harris asked.

'Yes I'm fine, let's just get in,' she responded. The urgency to escape the outside world to the safety of the church was evident in her voice.

They moved quickly down into the depths of the church, where Father Harris had been searching through the old dusty books and scrolls. They lay all over a large oak table, and he brushed two of the books and several scrolls off the table and onto the floor. Megan helped Dickson down onto a chair tucked away in the corner of the room and joined Father Harris as he unfurled the rubbing across the surface of the table. He hunched over and looked intently at the large piece of paper in front of him with the symbols. Megan watched him run his fingers over the rubbing. He suddenly stood up, walked over to a shelf and waved his hand in front of the spines of the books sitting on it. He stopped and grabbed a large brown book, pulling it out from the tight space in between all the others pushing against it from either side. Dust fell to the floor as it slid from its place. Once free from the shelf, he returned to the rubbing and the table. Placing the book on top, he opened it up and flicked through the pages until he saw a symbol that matched that of the rubbing.

He then held his hands to his face and pushed them back over his sweaty head as he released a massive sigh.

'What's wrong?' Megan asked.

He took his hands away from his head and looked at her before releasing all the air held in his puffed-out cheeks. 'The symbols on the rubbing and the driftwood that the mirror is made from are binding symbols.'

'Binding symbols?' Megan said, confused.

'The rubbing was taken from something that was binding that evil entity to the earth, trapping it. The driftwood symbols were copies, but not exact, so it didn't trap the evil correctly,' he explained.

'What about my Mum? How can we get it out of her?' Megan said, raising her voice.

Father Harris looked at her. 'The origin of the symbols is Native American. We need to find someone who can tell us what the symbols actually say and how we can help her.'

A voice broke the momentary silence. 'Jack Red Leaf.' Detective Dickson said.

'Who?' Father Harris asked, looking over at his friend sitting in the corner.

'Jack Red Leaf. He is the only Native American around here. He lives up in the woods,' he explained.

'I need to see him,' Father Harris exclaimed.

Detective Dickson sat back in the chair, wiping the bloody scars on his face, 'What about the others?'

'What others?' Father Harris asked.

'You said that there were others that have a connection to those already killed.'

'Oh yes, well there is you, me, Brabbings who lives in the harbor and the Simmons family who own the Lighthouse,' Father Harris recalled.

Detective Dickson pushed himself to his feet, using one hand to steady himself against the wall and said, 'You go see Red Leaf and I'll go to the others.'

'What about me? Megan said, 'You can't hold yourself up at the moment. I will help you.'

He shook his head, but Megan was already by his side. 'Where's your phone? I'll get some officers to call in to the lighthouse.'

Father Harris nodded and rolled the rubbing, tucked it under his arm and aided Megan with helping the detective up the stairs and back to the main hall. Once there, Father Harris went into a small room off to the side and returned with a phone and handed it to the detective. Detective Dickson sat at one of the pews with Megan standing next to him and began slowly pressing the keypad of the phone. He then held it up to his ear and waited for a reply. When someone answered on the other end, he began explaining who he was and that he needed a couple of officers to head up to the lighthouse. Father Harris and Megan watched as his face changed from one of concentration to one of defeat. His shoulders dropped when hearing the other person on the other end explain about the bloody scene at the Brabbings house.

'Detective, all officers are attending the house. There's blood all over the place, the whole family have been slaughtered, and old man Brabbings was found without his head sitting in front of the T.V. From what I can gather, they can't find the head,' the voice on the other end explained.

'I need a car to pick me up from the church now,' Dickson snapped. 'I don't care if it's you that has to pick me up, but I want a car now.'

He then took the phone away from his ear, looked down at the pad and poked the button with the red phone on it to end the call.

'Brabbings is dead,' he said, looking up at Father Harris.

Megan began to cry hysterically, collapsing on to her knees at the feet of the two men. 'I just want my mum back,' she repeated through her tears.

Father Harris knelt beside her, pulled her into his shoulder and looked at Detective Dickson, who sat with his head hung low over his lap with his eyes closed.

'We will find a way to get her back. You must have faith in that,' Father Harris said to her.

Detective Dickson pushed himself up from the pew, leaving the phone lying on the seat. He slowly headed to the door. Father Harris watched him carefully, half expecting him to collapse and be left in the dilemma of having to leave the sobbing girl on the floor and rush to help his friend. Dickson made it to the door just as a fist began thumping against it. He reached up and undid a bolt situated at the top of the old wooden door and pulled. Both doors opened to reveal a young police officer. The officer introduced himself as officer Michaels. He stuttered in his introduction when he saw the deep gashes on Dickson's face. He then saw the sobbing girl and Father Harris on the floor in the main hall in front of him. His introduction ceased when Dickson ordered him to help the girl to the car. Dickson himself continued his unsteady walk to the waiting car.

Officer Michaels crouched next to Megan and helped Father Harris pick her up and back on to her feet. They then walked out of the church. Once clear of the doors, Father Harris pulled them back until they locked together. He had no time or any desire to lock them. Once Megan had been placed in the car, Father Harris turned to Dickson, who sat in the passenger seat and said that he would meet them back at the church in a couple of hours and that they should bring the Simmons family back with them to the safety of the church. Dickson nodded and then pointed forward. Officer Michaels put the car into gear and pulled off. Father Harris looked down at the rubbing in his hands and jogged to his own car.

VIII

Water can flow, water can trickle. Water can crash and run. Water gives life and water can bring death.

The lighthouse itself no longer needed to shine its light across the bay; a new unmanned lighthouse had been built further out in the dark waters of the bay. The Simmons family had always owned the lighthouse, ever since it was first completed and its naked flamed light warned ships of the dangers of the rocky entrance to the harbor town. Throughout the years, extra buildings were added to its structure, enabling the family to earn extra money by renting out rooms until finally, with the new lighthouse built, the old light was turned off and it became the most popular romantic getaway and bed and breakfast establishment in the state, as voted by a tourist magazine. The lamp of the lighthouse was fired up on special occasions, most notably the town's anniversary, Independence Day and for some unknown reason, Halloween.

The police car approached the lighthouse, and the driver and passenger immediately noticed the light, its strong linear beam blinking out across the bay. They looked at each other with confused expressions before looking back up the road that led to the small parking lot out front. The officer pulled into one of the parking bays and turned the engine off. A rumble of thunder rolled across the dark sky above.

'Strange, there were no storms or rain forecast today,' the young officer said.

Dickson looked at him, sighed, raised an eyebrow and responded, 'You really believe the weather forecasters?'

Dickson pushed open the car door and immediately felt the wind push against it. The younger officer also found it a challenge to exit the car. Megan knocked on the rear window and mouthed to Dickson to open the door. He looked at her and paused. He then pulled the rear door open.

'Megan, I think it's best if you stay in the car,' he said calmly.

'No,' she said sharply.

'Listen, the officer and I are going to get the Simmons family and then they will come with us back to the church. We won't be gone long,' he said, reassuring her with a small smile.

Before Megan could say anything else, he had closed the door and joined the officer at the front of the car. They both looked up at the sky. The dark clouds above the lighthouse swirled round as if being stirred from above by a giant spoon. They looked at each other and then the front door. The officer pushed down on his hat to make sure he didn't lose it in the strengthening wind and stepped forward. They managed ten meters before the sound of exploding glass filled the air. Glass rained down on them from above. Dickson grabbed the young officer's arm and pulled him towards the door, they both hit the wall by the door and shielded their heads with their arms. Megan screamed and naturally covered her head with her arms as the glass crashed onto the car. Large pieces shattered as they hit the hood and roof, and the windshield began to crack in places, creating web-like patterns. When the rain of glass had finished, Dickson fumbled inside of his coat, his fingers wrapping themselves like snakes around the butt of his gun. He pulled it out and readjusted his grip as he pushed his shoulder against the wall of the lighthouse. They both looked out at the floor around them. Large pieces of glass embedded themselves in the grass and dirt footpath. Dickson pushed the officer in front of him, shielding himself from the door.

'You get the door and I'll back you up,' he shouted at the young officer, who still held onto his hat but turned with wide, scared eyes to Dickson.

'You want me to go first?' he stuttered.

Dickson nodded at him and pushed him in front of the door, 'Knock and identify yourself.'

The officer gently knocked against the thick wooden door and feebly called.

'Police, open up please.'

Dickson sighed, and his shoulders sank as he observed the young officer's actions.

'For fucks sake,' he exclaimed before pushing the officer out of the way. 'You want to do something, do it yourself.'

He pounded the door and shouted as loud as he could.

Megan heard the detective's assertive voice and pushed her face against the Perspex wall that separated the front of the car from the rear seats where she sat. She noticed that he had his gun drawn and that the other officer was removing his own pistol. She began to feel her heart beating against her chest, getting faster and faster along with her breathing as anxiety began to grip her. She then jumped as a bright flash followed by a huge explosion of sound filled her world.

A scream came from behind the door that the two law men stood in front of. Dickson grabbed the handle, turned it and pushed it open. As soon as his hand left the handle and the door began to open, he held his gun out in front of him, both hands supporting the firearm. With the door wide open, he moved forward slowly, his eyes darting around the room in front of him. His ears fought against the sound of the wind and claps of thunder outside and strained to listen for any other sound that could help him locate the person who had screamed or anything else inside the lighthouse. The young officer followed the detective in through the front door. The gun he held out in front of him shook uncontrollably, his eyes wide and non-blinking.

Chairs and tables of the room were strewn all over the red carpeted floor. The bar that was also used to check in was covered with broken glass from the wall of spirits behind it. Only the tops of each of the bottles remained in their supporting brackets. The smell of vodka and whisky filled the room as the two liquids flowed together along the bar and onto the floor. An archway to the left of the bar was surrounded by bloody handprints. The young officer moved over to the bar and slowly maneuvered around it, gun leading the way until he came to the bar entrance. The floor behind the bar was covered with broken bottles and liquid. The smell of all the spirits, wines and beers attacked his senses. It burned his nasal passage and made his wide eyes sting. He did not see the dark bloody shape of the young woman's body jammed under the bar behind the bar entrance door.

'Anything over there?' Dickson called.

The officer looked back at him and shook his head. Dickson moved through the bloody archway to the foot of a spiral staircase that disappeared around a corner, bloody handprints smudged up along the wall led the way. Paintings that once hung on the wall now lay broken and bloody on the stairs. Dickson looked back to the archway and the officer who stood beneath it, looking at the red-stained handprints. He nodded in the direction of the top of the last step they could see. The young man took a deep breath and nodded in return. Together they began ascending the staircase.

***

One floor above, in the lighthouse living room, a woman and young boy cowered in a corner. The woman was holding out a broom, fighting off the wild swinging arms of the crazy blood-stained woman who had entered the lighthouse only fifteen minutes earlier asking if she could have a room. The wild woman had then proceeded to attack the boy's older sister. The daughter's mother had come running down the stairs into the bar reception area after hearing her daughter scream. She ran through the archway to see the wild woman laughing to herself as she repeatedly jabbed her blood soaked fingers in and out of the eye sockets of the girl.

The mother had screamed and lunged at the woman, trying to separate her daughter from the woman, but was knocked back against the wall near the archway by the swatting hand of the woman. The crazy woman had then twisted the neck of the young girl violently to the left while smiling at the dazed mother. The woman's son had heard the scream from the lantern room, where he had been working with his father painting the guard rails on the outside of the lighthouse. They had seen the woman arrive and had thought nothing of it until they heard the scream. The son being younger and fitter darted through the glass door and down the metal steps that led from the lantern room down into the living quarters of the lighthouse. His father followed behind, gingerly moving down the steeper steps. The son had found his mother crawling up the steps leading away from the archway, her face soaked with tears and blood from where she had hit her forehead against the wall. He shouted at her to tell him what had happened but could not get any words from his hysterical mother. His father had joined him on the stairs and agreed to take his wife upstairs into the living space while the son went to see where his sister was.

The son had reached the part of the stairs where he could see the archway and froze. Standing in the archway patting her blood-soaked hands on the walls of the arch was the woman that he and his father had seen arrive minutes earlier, she looked at him but her eyes remained shut and smiled and then licked one of her bloodied fingers moaning with ecstasy as the metallic taste of the blood engulfed her taste buds.

The young man turned and ran back up the stairs he had just come down. He soon caught up with his father and mother in the living room.

'We got to get out,' he shouted.

'What you mean? What's wrong? Where's Pam?' his father shot back.

The son's face, pale with fear and breathless, scared the old man. He had never seen his son look so lost and scared before. His wife gave out a high-pitched scream, her eyes fixed wide looking at the entrance to the room. The son looked over his shoulder and saw what had caused his mother to react with such a blood-curdling scream. The wild woman with a hand covered in blood and one tucked behind her back now stood in the doorway, grinning through blood-stained lips and teeth. He ran over to his father and mother, pulling the hysterical woman's head into his chest.

'What do you want?' the old man shouted.

The woman looked at him, her grin fading as she clenched her teeth together. The muscles in her face flexed as her expression changed to one of anger before answering his question.

'I want those that are descended from the bastards that tried to enslave me.'

The old man let go of his wife's arm and stood in front of both his wife and son. 'I don't know what you are talking about. Please leave us alone.'

She then brought the hand that had been hidden behind her back forward. The head that hung from her clenched fist swung gently. The bloody, wide-eyed face of the man stared blankly at the old man.

'Oh my god,' the old man exclaimed.

The woman began moving towards them. A wind began to build within the room; magazines and papers that sat on a coffee table began to flutter around, and the wind continued to grow with every step that the woman took towards the old man and his cowering wife and son. Pictures and paintings that adorned the walls of the room began falling to the floor and sliding around with the magazines as the wind continued to flow around the room. The father squinted against the growing wind and looked over his shoulder at his wife and son.

'Stay here. I will try and get her to follow me up to the next level. When she leaves, get out of here and find help.'

His wife reached out a hand and grabbed his arm. Her head shook from side to side. Her mouth quivered as a combination of tears and snot oozed over her lips. Mr. Simmons took hold of her hand, pulled it off his arm and smiled at her, patting her hand. He looked back at the woman closing in and slid himself along the wall to the doorway.

'Come on bitch,' he shouted against the strengthening wind.

She paused her approach as the old man moved towards the doorway. She watched him from underneath an evil brow, her evil grin never slipping. She slowly looked at the mother and son holding each other and then back towards Mr. Simmons.

'No one leaves.' She laughed.

She then pointed a finger over towards the door that led downstairs back to the bar/reception area and gently waggled it. The door slowly closed. She then began to follow Mr. Simmons, who had disappeared through the doorway and up the stairs that led to the upper floors. He pushed open the door and moved himself down the small corridor, past the bedroom door. He paused at its opening and looked back, seeing the head-carrying woman reach the top of the stairs. He took a deep breath and continued to the next door, pulling it open and beginning his climb up the next set of stairs. His legs felt heavy with fatigue and fear, causing him to catch his right foot on the third step. Stumbling forward, he reached out his hands in an attempt to not only catch himself but also to protect himself. His left palm struck the lip of the wooden step and slid over its round edge. The weight and force of the fall caused his hand to slide into the wall of the next step and bend awkwardly. A new sound joined the pounding of his heart and the wind that seemed to be chasing him up the stairs; the snapping sound that came from the over-stressed hand preceded the sharp pain that shot down his arm. He winced and groaned, pushing himself back to his feet, and with his other hand he continued his climb, this time much slower as he cradled his limp hand.

He came to another door, turned the handle with his strong hand and pushed the door open. He again looked back before moving into the small corridor that led to a set of metal steps and an open hatch. He moved into the corridor and ran to the steps, hauling himself up through the hatch and into the lamp room. He moved around the wooden floor of the room until he was on the far side of the lamp. The multi-pieced round lamp allowed him to see the entrance he had just come through and through which the woman who had attacked his family would come. He pressed his back against the thick-glassed wall that separated him and the dark grey windy outside world. He felt a sudden cold feeling on his upper back, a feeling that soon became a cold wet sensation that travelled down his back and onto his hand that pressed against the glass. He took his gaze away from the entrance and looked over his shoulder at the glass. Water cascaded down the panes of glass. He looked around the room, focusing on the windowed wall of the lamp room.

Water freely flowed down the glass like a large water feature. It streamed down and onto the wooden floor. He stepped forward away from the glass he had been leaning against and looked back towards the entrance. The large lamp suddenly burst into life and began to slowly move, Mr. Simmons raised his hand and shielded his eyes as the beam of light passed in front of him. He could feel the heat from the light as it passed. An object flew from the open entrance way, crashing against the window of the room. A smudge of red stained the window where the object hit the glass. The deep red stain on the glass was soon swamped and mixed with the flowing waters, making that area of the glass wall look like a red waterfall. The object bounced along the floor and came to a rest at old man Simmons feet. The disfigured face of Mr. Brabbings looked up at him with the wide-eyed, open-mouthed, fear-frozen expression of his last moments.

Mr. Simmons stared down at the head, his own eyes wide and unable to move. All ability to control his body and move away from the bloody mass at his feet had escaped him and had left him rooted to the spot. Even the passing bright light and heat from the lamp could not move him.

A high-pitched cackle broke the spell over him. He looked up and saw the contorted face of the woman standing six feet away. He wanted to run. His mind screamed at him to move away, to increase the distance between them, but his body refused to listen. He stood, unable to move, as the woman stepped closer.

'You will pay for what you did to me,' she hissed.

Simmons managed a broken, fear-ridden response, hoping in some way to make the woman understand he didn't know her or what had happened to her.

'I, I don't know what you mean. I've never met you before.'

'Your blood runs with that of those that tried to destroy me,' she snapped back.

Before he could respond, she had suddenly closed the gap between them. Within a blink of an eye, she had reached out and grabbed his head. She buried her disfigured sharp nailed fingers into his scalp and locked her open mouth over his. Dark water dribbled down his chin, escaping the seal between her lips and his as the dark water erupted from within the woman and engulfed his mouth, throat and lungs. His body had finally started to move. His arms swung wildly at the woman's arms and head, attempting to break the link between them. His struggling and fight soon began to wane as his life ebbed away. The moment his arms fell limp, she removed her lips from his face and released her grip from the back of his head. Mr. Simmons's body fell to the floor with a splash as it landed in the pooling water. The water that cascaded from the glass walls stopped flowing the moment the old man's body became limp. The beast within Jane looked down at the body at her feet. It was not content with drowning its victim; it wanted to play with the body. It wanted to be creative with the lifeless man, but there were others to be dealt with before she could have fun.

The aroma of fear filled her senses. She looked down at the entrance and remembered the remaining family members locked in the room below. Just as she was about to descend back into the body of the lighthouse, she caught a glimpse of an approaching vehicle. She moved over to the glass and peered down at the two men now getting out of the car. One put on a hat that matched the colors of his police uniform; the other man bent down and spoke to someone in the car.

Anger began to burn deep within the beast. The man now joining the officer was the detective that she had tried to kill earlier. Her failure to kill him made Jane's body shake. The glass that formed the lighthouse lamp room began to vibrate. The glass panels began to warp like a piece of plywood being used as a musical instrument, the vibrations in the glass becoming stronger. The beast grunted and turned quickly away and headed down the room entrance. At the same time, the glass exploded out, showering the people and the car below.

***

Detective Dickson arrived at a closed door. His left hand shook as he reached up and slowly turned the handle and pushed. The door didn't move. He put his ear to the wooden barrier and listened.

'What can you hear?' the young officer asked.

Dickson closed his eyes and sighed with frustration. He looked back at the officer positioned below him on the staircase.

'If you didn't speak I could hear a lot more,' he said sarcastically.

He then returned his ear to the wooden door. The muffled sounds of crying, bumping and banging emanating from the room beyond the door filled his head. His mind painted pictures of what may lay beyond. A scream and then a shout scared him. He withdrew his head and grabbed the handle again, turning it but this time using his shoulder and body weight to attempt to move the door. He barged the door three times before it moved. A gust of wind blew through the gap of the open door, forcing Dickson to instinctively close his eyes. He shoved the door again and forced it open enough for him to step up and squeeze his body through. The young officer moved up to the step that Dickson had just vacated and followed him into the room.

Dickson looked over to the corner where he could see Megan's mother lashing out with a deformed hand at a woman and younger man who clung to each other behind an upturned sofa. He raised his gun at Jane only to be knocked to his knees by a flying painting in a heavy wooden frame that had been thrown around the room by the strengthening wind. His gun shot from his hand as he reached to stop himself being knocked flat on his face by the object. He felt a hand grab his shirt and jacket and haul him back to his feet. The young officer had seen the detective get hit and fall to the floor. He had himself just avoided a china vase that flew past him and shattered against the open door. Once back to his feet, he grabbed the other officer's gun and aimed at Jane. He fought against the wind and objects flying around him and fired. BANG, BANG. The two bullets flew past Jane and embedded themselves in the wall.

Jane turned her head and scowled at the two lawmen. She raised her hand above her head and brought it down across her body. A bright flash caused the two men, the son and mother in the room to wince and close their eyes. The sound of exploding wood and stone attacked their ears as a bolt of lightning hit the side of the lighthouse, causing the wall and window near where the lawmen stood to implode. The young officer took the full force of the wall and glass projectiles, slamming him against the door he had just entered. His neck snapped back against the frame of the door, breaking it instantly. Any chance of him surviving disappeared when the large pieces of rock and glass smashed into his chest and face, peeling the skin from his face in the process. Dickson found himself covered by the masonry and glass on the floor.

Jane took one last swipe at the mother cowering behind the sofa and caught her face with the talon-like fingers. The nails on the ends of the fingers dug into the flesh of the woman's cheeks; two fingers sunk beneath the cheek bones and anchored there. When the probing fingers were wrenched back, the sucking sound of muscle and flesh separating from the face and the cracking of bone as her cheek snapped away filled her son's ears. She screamed; the stress of the unprovoked attack on her family had already raised her already high blood pressure higher than it had ever been. Her heart beat pounded away at her chest. The pain and shock being too much for her already stressed heart caused it to finally give up. She then fell silent. Jane held up the bloody mess in her hand into the circling wind. Bit by bit it left the deformed hand and joined other objects being blown around the room.

Dickson pushed the rubble off him as he stood up. He still held onto the gun with his right hand, and he waved it in the direction of the possessed woman and fired. He no longer cared about anyone else; he just wanted to kill her. Two more bullets embedded themselves in the wall above Jane. He focused against the wind and objects rotating in the room. He was then hit by something soft, cold and wet. His face began to drip with some form of liquid. He reached up and removed what had hit him and briefly looked at whatever it was he held in his left hand: the red bloody mass of flesh hung loose in his palm. Dickson quickly shook his hand free of the old woman's flesh and fired the pistol again. One of the bullets hit a small stool that flew past, the impact of the bullet changing its flight path, forcing it into the wall. The other bullet ploughed into the shoulder of the possessed Jane. The beast snarled at the detective.

The young man holding his mother looked at her lifeless body and shook it. He no longer felt the wind blowing around him or cared about the wild woman who had just ripped half of his mother's face away. Tears streamed down his face as he knelt next to her, hoping that she would respond. The next thing he felt was his hair being pulled. He reached up and tried to pry open the hands that held him. The force of the pull yanked him to his feet. He then came face to face with the distorted face of the woman who had attacked his mother. Her brown eyes seemed to glow. The sharp fang-like teeth grinned at him. Her heavy and warm breath carried a strong smell of sea water and fish that attacked his senses.

Out of anger, he let go of her hands that held his hair and, clenching his right fist, threw it as hard as he could at her face. The fist crashed into the grinning teeth of the woman who held him. She didn't flinch; her grip didn't change. She just stood looking at him and then began laughing. He retracted his fist and winced as the pain of his sliced fist hit his nervous system and the hand began to ooze blood. The sharp teeth of the woman had done their damage. He looked at his fist and could see the wide-open wounds of his fingers just below the knuckles of his fist. The first two knuckles were open and the tendon and joint showing. He tried to open his fist but found that the damage to his hand stopped him.

Dickson pulled back on the trigger again but nothing happened. He tried again, but again nothing happened. A flash caused him to flinch. He pulled out the empty bullet cartridge from the butt of the gun and sighed. He looked at the young police officer and his deformed face and rubble-covered body and out of frustration shouted at him. 'Seriously?' A small cushion hit him in the face, followed by a mug, which exploded on impact against the side of his already bloodied and cut head. He swore and grabbed his head with his left hand, forgetting he was holding the gun cartridge. He threw it to the floor and then returned his hand back to his head. Feeling a lump and wetness around it, he withdrew it so he could see it. Fresh blood covered his already blood-stained hand. He looked at Jane who held the younger Simmons family member. He looked down at the empty gun in his hand, thought for a second and then did the only thing that he could. The pistol flew from his hand, spinning in the air towards the woman at the other end of the room. The strong circling winds changed its direction slightly in the favor of the detective, and the butt of the gun ploughed into the temple of the possessed Jane. Her head snapped sideways and her grip on the young man's hair eased enough for him to break free.

Through the wind and crashing objects of the room Dickson shouted at the young man, 'Move!'

He looked at his hand then the woman before looking over at Dickson and then moved quickly over to him, ducking and weaving around the moving objects in the room. He reached the space by the door where Dickson stood, still playing with the bloody lump on his head. They both looked at Jane, who had recovered from the blow and was staring at them. She raised her hands level with her head and then clapped them together. The circling wind in the room suddenly dropped and then blasted straight at Dickson and the younger Simmons. The blast of wind blew both the men off their feet and pinned them against the wall behind them. The rubble

222

that covered the young dead police officer was thrown off his body by the blast; he too was then pushed up onto the detective and man on the wall, his limp head and neck knocking against Dickson's head and face. At one point, Dickson found himself nose to nose with the bloody disfigured face of the young officer.

Jane calmly walked towards the two men pinned against the wall and grinned at them. She moved over to the young Mr. Simmons and placed her hand around his throat and opened her mouth wide. He looked deep within her mouth. It wasn't the sharp fanged teeth that made his eyes grow wide with horror; it was the dark fluid that seemed to crash around her mouth like a stormy sea. It did not fall from her mouth but seemed to be held back by some invisible force. She closed her mouth over his and he felt the cold salty taste of sea water as the stormy sea within the woman's mouth erupted into his. He tried to move and fight the intruding fluid but found he had no strength against its onslaught of his lungs. His eyes began to roll, his pupils looking up towards the ceiling until finally he too succumbed to death.

Dickson watched from his pinned position. He fought against the wind that held him there and the weight of the police officer's dead body. He managed to push his head off the wall, straining all the muscles in his neck to do so. He couldn't fight against the invisible force for long; his head slammed back against the wall with a thump. He pushed his arm forward quickly as if to try and surprise the force holding him there, to his surprise he managed to move his arm out in front of him until again he could no longer hold his limb against the pressure of the invisible force. His hand shot back and smacked him in the face. He didn't care about the stinging sensation from the slapping from his open hand. He had achieved what he wanted to. He smiled and mumbled to himself in defiance, 'Get to my mouth now bitch.'

Jane stood back and admired her work. She clapped her hands and the wind and invisible force stopped. The body of the young Mr. Simmons crashed to the floor, dark water spouting from his mouth. Dickson fell the short distance to the rubble-filled floor. The sudden drop caught him out and his heels slid out in front of him, causing him to slide down the wall and land on his backside, legs spread out in front of him. Through it all he still managed to hold his hand over his face.

She looked down at him, her face contorted and angry. 'You are going to suffer,' she hissed. She reached out and grabbed his head with both hands and yanked him to his feet. Even with the sensation of having his neck stretch, he still maintained his hand position. Jane moved in closer, going nose to nose with the detective. The smell of fish and seawater broke through his protective hand and attacked his senses. She opened her mouth wide, the fangs dripping with saliva. She was about to bite down on the hand that hid the detectives mouth but a voice stopped her.

'Mom!' Megan stood at the door; tears covered her face. 'Mom, please,' she pleaded.

Jane closed her mouth and looked at the girl. For a moment she didn't move, and her distorted facial features softened. Megan then saw the reflective glow of the brown eyes fade and turn light blue.

'Help me,' her mother whispered.

The eyes blinked and were back to the demonic brown. Dickson used this pause to push himself off the wall and towards Megan. He grabbed her arm and began pulling her back through the door and down the stairs.

'No, my mom,' she shouted at him as he pulled her with him back down towards the archway that led to the bar reception area.

He looked at her and then back up the stairs beyond her. He could feel the wind increase, 'That's not your mother,' he shouted at her, pulling her into the bar area and across the floor to the doorway.

'You can't escape me,' a voice screamed from the stairway.

Dickson pulled Megan back towards the car. The rain fell heavily, and the lightening pulsed above them. The little dirt pathway had become muddy and puddle engulfed. He fumbled in his pocket for the car keys. As he approached the car, he let Megan's arm go and ran to the front of the car. He pushed his foot into the ground to change direction but the ground gave way. Detective Dickson slid momentarily and then his legs left his upper body behind. He flopped onto his side, water and mud splashing into his face. His trouser leg concertinaed up, and mud filled the open hole of his trouser leg. He felt the sudden wetness against his side as the watery ground soaked through his shirt.

Megan saw Dickson quickly disappear. She gingerly slowed herself down and moved around the car to see him picking himself up. She helped him back to his feet. 'Go, get in the car,' he shouted.

She headed back to the passenger side of the car. Dickson brushed off shards of muddy glass and scrambled to the car door and yanked at the handle. The door shot open from a combination of the wind and his forceful pull. Megan dropped into the passenger seat and hauled the car door shut.

'I thought I told you to stay in the car,' Dickson said as he pushed the keys in and turned the ignition.

She just looked at him in disbelief. He grabbed the gear leaver and placed the car into drive and stamped his foot on the accelerator. Wheels spun in the muddy ground, causing the car to slide sideways as it pulled away. Dickson fought with the steering wheel until he finally had control of the car.

'How did you get out any way,' he asked.

'After the lightning struck the lighthouse, do you really think I was going to stay in the car?' she said through tear-filled eyes, her mind filled with the vision and voice of her mother trapped within her possessed body.

Dickson could feel the coldness of a breeze against his neck. He looked over his shoulder and could see the rear passenger side window; fragmented pieces of the glass clung to the upper frame of the door seal. He returned his focus to the cracked windshield and shrugged his shoulders.

Back at the lighthouse, the beast stood at the doorway and watched as the police car disappeared down the hill towards town. The fanged teeth ground back and forth as Jane's Jaw tensed in anger. She then looked up at the dark and flashing sky. She raised up her forefinger to her lips and kissed it with a "shhhh" sound. The thunder booming overhead suddenly died, leaving the continuing pulse of lightening to flash silently within the clouds. Jane then began to walk slowly down the path. The glass covered floor snapped and crunched with every step.

IX

We must learn from the past to help us. To ignore our history is to give life to evil.

Look into the flames of the past; it will be amongst the embers that a future shall be born.

Father Harris drove up the steep road towards Jack Red Leaf's house. Tall pine trees stood close together on either side like soldiers standing to attention. The trees finally gave way to a circular opening. An old wooden fence held back the trees from encroaching. A disheveled-looking wooden house stood in the center of the clearing, and a rocking chair sat on the decking of the porch. It moved back and forth with a constant slow pace. Its occupant watched the car approach and stop just before the steps of the porch.

Jack Red Leaf had lived at the edge of town for what some locals rumored to be a hundred years, yet he looked like a man in his early fifties. Grey hair intertwined with his long black ponytail. He still carried a large hunting knife that nestled against his hip. He was the last of his kind. He had watched as his family and friends had moved on looking for somewhere better—somewhere that they would be accepted. His ancestors were the first Native Americans to encounter the stranded foreigners, their ship stranded amongst the rocks of the bay. For six years the Native American tribe and the stranded visitors lived in harmony, helping each other, sharing each other's beliefs and knowledge. Over time, more and more foreigners and devout religious leaders arrived and, becoming all powerful within the small town, condemned all non-Catholics. They began to force the Native Americans out of the bay area and into the surrounding hills and forests.

Father Harris pushed open the car door and stepped out. He clutched the rubbing in his left hand.

'Hey Jack, we need your help,' he called as he shut the car door and quickly walked towards the porch where Jack Red Leaf sat.

Jack looked at Father Harris, noticing the urgency in his voice and walk. He slowly stood up, his large frame looming over Father Harris, who stopped at the foot of the steps.

'Who is we?' Jack asked.

'Well, I'm asking for your help that could save a mother and daughter and the local police who need help with catching a serial killer,' he replied.

'What would I know?' Jack asked, folding his arms.

Father Harris unraveled the large piece of paper and held it up in front of Jack. 'I was hoping you could tell me about these symbols?'

Jack looked down at the piece of paper and the outline of the symbols. His arms unfolded and his hands clasped each other as a look of concern broke out across his face.

'Where did you get this?' he asked sharply.

'Like I said, a mother and daughter are in trouble—trouble in the spiritual way,' Father Harris responded.

Jack turned and walked over to the front door. He looked over his shoulder at the religious man still standing at the foot of the steps with the piece of paper still held up in front of him. 'You better come in, Father.'

Father Harris quickly moved up the steps and followed the large man into the house. Once inside, he paused. The weather-worn ragged outside of the house didn't complement the cleanliness of the living space inside. Native American artifacts adorned each wall. He was suddenly awoken from his brief trance by a deep cough. He looked over to a door where Jack stood shaking his head.

'Come this way,' he said.

Father Harris nodded and followed Jack through the doorway and into a circular room that had a stone fire pit in the center. Small animal skins were placed on the floor around the centerpiece-like seats.

Jack sat down on one of the animal skins, picked up a large dark feather that lay on the edge of the fire pit and began to chant. Father Harris looked at the large Native for guidance but none came; he moved slowly over to Jack and waited. Jack's chanting began to die down. He then moved both arms above his head and then quickly threw them down towards the dark fire pit. The sound of air rushing through the feather caught Father Harris's attention and then he jumped as the fire pit burst into flames.

'What? How?' he stammered, staring at Jack.

Jack looked up at him. 'Don't be afraid; all that you see and feel is good earth magic.' He said, 'Now sit.'

Father Harris immediately sat down on an animal skin next to Jack, his eyes never leaving the big man.

'I have seen many signs over the last few days that have concerned me,' Jack said slowly, his eyes looking deep into the flames of the pit. 'Father, tell me what you have witnessed.'

Father Harris began his long story of events. At times, he found his voice and emotions difficult to control as vision after vision of death and evil filled his mind.

'The paper you hold in your hands is a copy of a stone tablet that was used to trap an evil spirit,' Jack began.

Father Harris unraveled the paper and explained that he had looked through the church archives and found that the symbols had been used during an exorcism of a local girl.

Jack turned and looked at the priest, his dark eyes causing the religious man to stop talking.

'It will be too difficult to explain all to you, so you need to see for yourself who and what you are dealing with. I want you to look into the flames; look deep within the fire. Let the past come to you and show you what you need to know.'

Father Harris looked at Jack with surprise. 'You want me to stare at the fire and see what?' he said, almost laughing.

'You have come to me, holy man, for answers,' he snapped. 'What you seek is from a place between the living world and the world of the great spirits.'

Father Harris sat up, the sharp heavy tone of the big man's voice making him feel uneasy. He took a deep breath and looked at the flames of the fire pit. His mind told him he was stupid and that coming here for help was a waste of time. He sighed heavily and his shoulders sank. It was then that the ever-changing and dancing of the flames caught his attention. The flames seemed to pulse; the licking hot spires of red, orange and white had a sound. He concentrated harder, straining his ears to make out the sound of the fire. The room around him disappeared as he became more and more focused on the fire. The sound he could hear began to build, and a low hum that filled his head. He blinked, and in that moment, his surroundings had changed. He found himself standing in a dense forest. He could hear the whistles and chirps of different birds and the running of a stream in front of him. The smell of fresh woodland air ran deep within him. He blinked and turned around quickly, his eyes searching. He began to panic, and then he felt a heavy hand grab his shoulder. The electric shock of fear and surprise shot from his anus to his head. He turned and saw the large figure of Jack standing next to him. The feeling of not being alone swept over him like a cold wave.

'Where are we?' he asked with wide eyes.

'Where we are has not changed. When we are is at the beginning,' Jack said.

'I don't understand. Can you stop speaking Yoda and in riddles and tell me what is going on?' Father Harris complained.

Jack looked down at the smaller man and raised an eyebrow out of disgust. 'You need to know what has been released on the world. Then you must see its beginnings.'

Jack then nodded and motioned over to the trees beyond the stream. Father Harris turned his head and saw a dark shape move amongst the trees. The shape broke free of the tree line and fell into the stream, water splashing high above the fallen figure. Father Harris turned and watched as the figure stood up, looked behind him and struggled out of the stream onto the small bank. The priest could see that the figure was an old man dressed as a dark bird. As he struggled and moved his arms, they flapped like wings, and the moans and gasps he made as he struggled added to the look, making him sound like a crow. The man's face was covered in a dark paint.

Father Harris looked back at Jack. 'Who is that and can he see us?' he asked.

Jack shook his head. 'He cannot see or hear us. What you are seeing is the ripples of what was.'

234

Father Harris looked back at the old man. He was now kneeling down on the bank of the stream, his hands raised above his head. The air around them began to vibrate with the strange sounds of the old man's chants.

'The man you see is called Black Feather. He was the medicine man of the Paungraset tribe. He was cast out for using dark magic. Crops and food began to die and become poisonous. He had tortured and killed a young girl in one of his evil ceremonies,' Jack explained.

Father Harris watched as Black Feather reached into a bag on his side and pulled out a hand full of hair. The dark fist full of long hair swung in the breeze, weighted down by chunks of bloody skin. Black Feather plunged the hair into the stream, his fist punching into the stream bed. He opened his fist and rubbed the hair into the mud and swirling waters of the stream. He looked up at the darkening skies above him and again began to chant.

Father Harris looked back at Jack. His expression begged for explanation, and the large native didn't disappoint.

'Black Feather, angry over his exile, used his magic to summon an evil spirit,' he said, looking at the feathered old man. 'He thought he would have control of the spirit and use it to punish those that cast him out, but the spirit was a young and impatient childish spirit with a compulsive temper.' He pointed back at Black Feather.

Father Harris returned his gaze to see a pair of skinny arms and long-nailed fingers reach out of the water and clasp Black Feather on either side of the head. The hands then returned back into the stream. Black Feather stood and walked towards Father Harris and Jack. As he approached, the priest shifted nervously, trying to avoid the old man dressed in black feathers walking into him. He watched as Black Feather walked past him and straight through Jack. Father Harris's mouth dropped open with surprise. Jack looked at him and again answered the unasked question.

'What you see are ripples in time. We are not of this time, neither you or I, are here.'

Father Harris looked back at the stream. He blinked wildly as the trees in front of him began to become blurred. They waved in the breeze faster and faster. The sound of the birds, running water and the leaves disappeared as time began to speed up. The priest and Jack watched as native hunter after native hunter appeared out from the deep forest and were pulled down into the stream by the evil skinny arms, just like watching a movie in fast forward. The seasons came and went in front of their eyes until life began to slow down and settled at a speed that allowed the sounds of the forest to once again fill their ears.

'This is what you need to understand Father,' Jack said in his deep voice.

Father Harris looked at him and then back to the stream. From out of the tree line a young girl walked. Her long dark hair flowed like a waterfall over her shoulders and down her back. A single feather stood tall from the back of her head, held there by a leather headband. She wandered slowly towards the stream and knelt beside it. Father Harris looked nervously at Jack. He had an urge to shout at the girl, even though he knew she couldn't hear him. He watched as she calmly washed water over her face. No skinny hands came out of the stream; there was no dragging of the girl into the world below the streams surface. He looked back at Jack, a smile of relief beginning creep across his face. The big Native American looked back at him, his serious expression never changing. He pointed back towards the girl.

Father Harris looked back at the young girl. She was standing with her back to him and the stream. She looked back towards the trees that she had emerged from. Below her a pair of skinny arms appeared from the stream, the arms bent at the bony elbows and the hands pressed into the muddy bank of the stream. A head emerged, its brown leathery skin slowly rising behind the girl. The shoulders that the head and neck attached to silently continued the elevating of the body from the stream. The bony outline of the vertebrae and shoulder blades moved beneath the thin brown leathery skin. Father Harris could feel his heart pound as he watched the beast step up onto the bank and stand upright behind the young Native American girl who seemed oblivious to the creature behind her. The naked leathery skinned creature towered over her; it then reached out a pointy fingered hand and rested it on the girls shoulder. The girl turned quickly and

237

stared into the stomach of the beast. She then raised her head until she finally looked into the large brown eyes of the beast, who smiled with a fang-filled mouth. The girls eyes widened further and her mouth opened wide. The scream that grew within her and moved up through her throat and mouth, ready to explode like a volcano, was stopped by a hand that covered her mouth. The scream became a muffled moan. She could feel the bones of the creature's hand press against her lips and face. She reached up and grabbed the hand and arm and attempted to pull it off her mouth, but no matter how much she pulled, clawed or struggled, the hand was clamped down hard.

The creature brought its free hand up to its mouth and drew its forefinger across the sharp edges of its fanged teeth. A black liquid began to flow from the gash the teeth had made. The beast smiled at the girl as it held the dripping finger over her head, three large drops of black liquid fell onto her forehead. Her wide eyes naturally looked up. She could not see the droplets but she could feel their cold movements as they began to run down, merging as one large droplet as they travelled, beginning to snake down in between her eye brows and down the side of her nose and into her eye. She could feel the black liquid as its coldness moved onto her eye. She saw the dark shadow as it began to spread across her vision. She struggled again but found that the large hand across her mouth held her in place no matter what she did. The black liquid swirled around her right eye until it finally found an entrance. It moved quickly as it attacked the tear duct and disappeared into the girl's body. She could feel the cold liquid probing its way down within her face. At times, it burnt as it invaded her muscles and capillaries. At others points, it was cold. Her muffled moans continued as she fought the pain of the probing alien liquid as it travelled deeper into her body.

Father Harris held his right hand over his mouth as he watched. The horror of seeing a young girl taken over caused him a deep sadness. His eyes widened as he saw the tall bony creature begin to disintegrate. First the feet crumbled and blew away in the small breeze, then the legs followed until finally the head and arms blew away. The girl fell to her knees sobbing and then she stood, looked towards the priest and his big Native American companion and smiled. The smile was a mischievous smile. Father Harris looked at Jack.

'Did she just smile at us,' he asked, looking up at the big man.

Jack looked concerned and began to wave his feather and once again began chanting.

Father Harris looked back at the girl who was gone. He noticed the trees and bushes that surrounded them becoming blurred. He expected to see seasons pass quickly as he had earlier but this time all the colors of the forest began to melt together and then swirl. He began looking around himself and noticed the swirl of color at his feet. He lifted his feet, trying to figure out what he was standing on, but he felt the hardness of ground. The swirling seemed to happen below whatever he was standing on. The deep green began to get lighter and then became a light brown. The swirling began to slow and he could make out shapes forming in front of him. There was no longer the thick forest but a brown clearing. On the clearing stood tepees, animal skin structures and brown mud hut buildings.

'The evil spirit you just saw take the young girl exacted the revenge of Black Feather. She returned to her village and began killing all that lived there,' Jack began explaining.

Father Harris looked at Jack and saw the pain in his face. He then looked at the village that had appeared in front of him. He could now see the sides of the buildings and floor of each of the openings smothered in blood. Bodies lay around on the floor. Some had limbs missing, and others had a black liquid oozing from their mouths. Father Harris felt his stomach begin to tighten as he saw two young boys laying together, arrows embedded in their eyes. The sick feeling grew stronger as they entered a tepee and saw a woman, her stomach wide open and her unborn child exposed to the world, still connected to its mother by its umbilical cord. Even this innocent unborn human had had its light of life extinguished before it even had a chance to burn properly.

'Nearly all my people were killed by the evil spirit,' Jack began as he guided Father Harris around the settlement. 'It took a small band of warriors to trick and capture the possessed girl.'

The settlement they walked around seemed to vibrate as time once again sped up. Father Harris watched more murders and then the capture of the girl. Time once again slowed down at the point where the possessed girl was tied to a post in a hole that had been dug in the dirt.

'The great medicine man took a young warrior's knife and cast a spell on it. The young warrior was then told to get into the hole and cut a releasing symbol into the girls shoulder.' Jack began narrating what was happening in front of them.

The young native warrior jumped down into the hole. The girl hissed and spat at him. She screamed at him but he showed no fear. Above him, others encircled the hole and began to chant.

'The young warrior cut the symbol into the girls shoulder. This released her from the hold of the evil spirit,' Jack continued.

The young warrior drew the open circle on the shoulder of the girl with the knife tip. He then returned it to the flesh in the center of the bloody shape and carved a wavy line from the middle out through the opening of the circle. A bright light began to emanate from the symbol. It grew brighter and brighter until finally it was so bright all had to look away, even Father Harris and Jack. When the light faded, Father Harris gasped. In the hole, tied to the post was the beast. Slumped in the arms of the warrior was the girl. The girl was quickly hauled out of the hole by others, followed by the young warrior.

'Could it not escape the rope?' The priest asked.

'The rope was covered in salt and earth,' Jack answered quickly.

The medicine man called to a group of men who lifted a large stone slab up and slowly carried it over to the hole. The beast tied to the post hissed and screamed at the men gathered around. When it saw the slab being slowly maneuvered into a position over the hole it began to beg and plead. The men lowered the slab down over the hole and then backed away quickly. The medicine man took the knife from the young warrior and knelt down next to the stone slab and began scratching at it.

Father Harris looked carefully at the slab. It was covered with symbols—the same symbols as the rubbing he had taken from the kitchen back at the mother and daughters house.

'Now that the young girl was free, an imprisoning stone was used to hold the evil spirit, to entrap it so that it could never get free,' Jack began.

Father Harris looked at him and then the stone and the medicine man completing the last symbol and then back at Jack.

'So if it was trapped, how was it released or how did it manage to escape?' Father Harris asked.

Jack waved the feather again and the world around them began to vibrate as season after season flew by.

They watched as the open area amongst the trees that held the native community became empty. The natives all left, and the area became grassy but nothing more grew there. Eventually time stopped and they were standing looking down at the stone slab, it looked weatherworn; some of the symbols had faded.

'So how did it get free?' Father Harris asked again.

'That is why we are here, so you can understand,' he replied.

Out from among the trees three men walked. They were dressed all in black. The man who led the way clung to a large book. Jack and Father Harris watched as the men approached the slab. The leader tripped up on the edge of the stone and fell forward. The large book he clung to flew out in front of him as he let it go mid fall and used his arms to cushion his fall. The others rushed to him and helped him back to his feet.

Father Harris looked at the book on the floor. It was one of the most beautiful bibles he had ever seen, but he was sure he had seen it before. He moved closer to it just as one of the men picked it up and began to wipe it with his sleeve.

'I know who this is,' he said to Jack. 'This is the first priest of the town. He arrived five years after the first settlers. He was the one who commissioned the building of the town church.'

He watched as the priest stood over the stone slab. His eyes grew wide and he began shouting at it, calling it demonic and blasphemous. He then began looking around him. He shouted at the others to find a rock so that the devil's stone could be destroyed. One of the men found a large stone and carried it back over to the ranting priest. The priest took the stone and raised it above his head. He called on the others to pray and began throwing the stone down onto the slab at his feet. He continued hitting the slab with the rock for several minutes before fatigue set in and made him stop. Sweat dripped from his nose and chin, and his chest burned as he gasped for air. Feeling better from his venting of his anger and feeling like he had done the lord's work and beat the devil out of the symbol-covered stone, the men left.

Jack and Father Harris moved closer to the stone slab and inspected the damage. They could not see any. The only damage they could see was the little chunks of stone that had broken off the large rock that had been used to try and smash the slab.

'It's not broken,' Father Harris said.

Jack shook his head. 'Look closer,' he replied.

Father Harris knelt down and looked closely at the stone slab. It was then he saw the crack. It ran through the final symbol: two circles interlinked with a cross, a cross that was more a plus sign than a crucifix.

'That symbol holds the evil spirit in; it traps it in the earth,' Jack began. 'With that seal broken, it is free to escape and find its power.'

'What is its power?' Father Harris asked.

'Have you not seen it? Have you not seen from where it was born?' Jack asked angrily.

'Water,' the priest replied.

Pieces of the puzzle suddenly fell into place, Father Harris could now see the big picture: the history of the town, the story of Mary and the possession. The symbolism that was used by people as a form of protection in the past and the truth that it never held any form of safety. The symbols on the slab are the true symbols that can trap the evil beast. The ones that were used on the cross that Mary was tied to and then carved into buildings of those who had helped strand her there were misunderstood and written wrong.

'Can we move forward to when the beast resurfaced in the town?' he asked Jack.

Jack nodded and waved the large feather again. The colors of their surroundings began to merge and swirl. When they stopped, Father Harris and Jack were standing back amongst the trees by the stream. A young woman was kneeling down and picking up flowers. The stream ran its unchanged course nearby. They watched as the skinny brown figure dragged itself from the water and approached the woman. Just like they had seen with the young Native American girl, the beast grabbed the woman and let black droplets fall from its finger onto the cheek of the struggling woman. Just as before, once the black liquid entered the woman, the beast disintegrated.

'That is Mary,' Father Harris said.

Jack waved the feather; the green of the trees and grass began to turn brown and then red before the orange flickering of flames filled Father Harris' view. He was back in the small circular room, the fire still burning strong, Jack sat next to him.

'I need to see more,' he said urgently.

'That is all I can show you,' Jack replied.

'But I need to know why they used the symbols on the cross and buildings,' Father Harris argued back.

Jack looked at him, his inner voice fighting with his conscience. Should he tell him the mistake he made or tell the priest only parts and protect himself?

'What is it Jack?' Father Harris asked. 'Do you need to tell me something?'

Jack shook his head.

'I pride myself on knowing when people are hiding something,' Father Harris said. 'If it's something I need to know then please tell me.'

Jack looked at the priest and then bowed his head. 'This is my fault,' he said.

Confusion attacked Father Harris.

'I became angry by how the people of the town, and especially the priest, began treating my people, so when he came to me for help I lied to him about the symbols. The woman you just saw had drawn various symbols on the church floor in her own blood. He had recognized them from the stone slab. He had tried a normal exorcism and it had not worked, so he asked me for help in understanding the symbols,' Jack explained.

'How could you do that?' Father Harris barked.

'How? You didn't watch your family and friends beaten and treated like slaves and second-class citizens by the same people that they helped.' Jack became angry, his voice booming as he argued back.

'I began telling the story of Black Feather, and he started calling my people heathens, devil worshippers and red-skinned devils. Why would I help him if all he could do was speak of my people in such a disrespectful way?' Jack snapped.

Father Harris was about to explain that back in those days they knew no better but stopped, something Jack had said didn't make sense.

'Wait, wait, wait, what do you mean you began telling him, don't you mean your ancestor?'

Jack sighed heavily. 'No, I told him. I was the young warrior boy who was tasked with cutting the young girl with the knife. Because I was chosen, I am bound to the evil spirit until it finally leaves this world,' Jack explained.

Father Harris grew angry. 'I'm here for your help; I am not here for you to make fun of me.'

Jack looked at him, his face full of rage. 'I am telling you the truth Father. It is because of my own selfishness and anger that this evil spirit is free again.' He sighed and again bowed his head before continuing; 'I have lived with the guilt for so long it has weighed heavy on my shoulders. I have been waiting for it to rise again.'

Father Harris could see the pain that the big man held within. He reached over and placed a hand on his shoulder. Jack turned his head and looked at Father Harris.

'We all make mistakes; that's what makes us human,' he said calmly. 'Now let's end this evil once and for all.'

Jack attempted a small smile and then sat up, 'We need the knife.'

'Where is it?' Father Harris asked eagerly.

'It was buried by the medicine man. He realized that if any evil got to it and destroyed it then there would be no chance of ever using it again,' Jack began. 'I will seek the help of the great spirits to help me locate it. You must try and trap the woman that holds the beast.'

Father Harris was about to ask how but was once again beaten by Jack's answer.

'You must take rope and cover it in salt and dirt and then attempt to wrap it around the woman,' Jack said.

Father Harris's mind began working hard trying to think where he could get rope. He then laughed at himself. *Fishing town with a harbor you fool, there'll be rope everywhere*, he said to himself.

Jack looked at him as he spoke to himself. He then sharply nodded his head towards the door. Father Harris nodded and stood. His legs felt tight and heavy after kneeling down for so long. He shook them and then headed out the small room back towards the front door. He paused as he grasped the door handle; he could hear the high pitched chants of Jack escaping the small room. He looked back and saw a red glow coming from the room and knew that Jack was once again on a journey into another realm or world. He took a deep breath, turned the round doorknob, pulled the door and exited Jack's house. He ran down the steps of the porch and over to the driver's side door of his car. He took one last look at the house, noticing that the chimney was void of any smoke, shook his head and got in the car. He then sat, his mind full of visions and questions. It was at that moment he began to question his faith and his religion.

In the circular fire room, Jack waved his feather over his face and arms. He looked deep into the flames and stopped chanting.

'Oh great spirits, show me where I may find the blade that can cure the evil of this land,' he said in his a deep strong voice.

The flames of the fire seemed to rise and fall in unison. He blinked, and when his eyes opened he was standing at the edge of the tree line looking down on the bay. There was no town, just a grassy hillside that led down to the sea. He felt a cold breeze against his arm as a figure in a wolf headdress walked by. He recognized the man as the medicine man who chose him as the savior of his tribe. The medicine man stopped about twenty meters in front of Jack and then turned. He looked at Jack and beckoned him forward. Jack followed the medicine man down the slope until he finally stopped. He looked at Jack and looked towards the floor. Jack hurried over to the man and looked down at where he was looking. At his feet was a large stone. On the stone's face was a star-shaped carving, a star that resembled the Star of David.

'Beneath this stone lies what you seek young Red Leaf,' a voice said.

Jack looked at the Medicine man, his face partly covered by the head of the wolf. His lips did not move, yet Jack knew that the man was talking to him.

'The stone is a sacred stone; no evil can touch the ground below it,' the voice said; again, no movement came from the medicine man's lips.

Jack looked around him, 'But great spirit, where is this place?' he asked.

The medicine man's body began to shake as time sped up. Seasons came and went, and Jack saw the ship arrive in the bay during a storm and run aground. He witnessed the birth of the town and the interactions between his people and the foreigners. Buildings began to take shape, growing like plants before his eyes as the town of New London grew. A priest walked towards them. He clutched a large black leather book. Three men in robes followed behind him, as did some of the townsfolk. Time began to slow down until the people were moving at normal speed. The priest stopped by the stone and looked at it.

'A sign from God almighty,' he exclaimed. 'This is where he wants us to build our church to him. This blessed stone shall be the center of the church.' The people gathered with him all cheered.

Time sped up once more as the medicine man began to shake. Other stones joined the one with the symbol and then wooden beams were set up as walls, and a roof was constructed quickly. The people moving around constructing the church were blurred by the speed of time.

Jack looked at the medicine man, who continued to shake. 'Great Spirit, you don't need to show me more; I know where to find the stone,' he said.

The voice of the medicine man came again. 'You need to see that all is not as easy. Evil still walked the earth, in some form.'

Time slowed once more. The medicine man pointed a skeletal hand to the sky. Jack found himself staring at the tissue less appendage. He then looked at the man's face. The skin clung to the bones of the man's cheeks; the medicine man was aging.

'Look to the sky and not onto me,' the voice shouted.

Jack suddenly looked up beyond the hand. The moon was full and a deep red color. He looked back at the medicine man, who had walked over to the door of the church. The bony hand beckoned him over. He then joined the medicine man by walking through the closed door of the church and into the aisle of the building. Around them, candles burned, their light fighting against the darkness. Shadows clung to corners, and the room suffered from a heavy gloominess. Jack could make out the center stone and its symbol. He walked over to it and pointed to it.

'It is here great spirit,' he said triumphantly.

The medicine man pointed back to the door they had just passed through. Jack looked and then froze. A dark figure covered in feathers appeared and slowly walked towards the stone. As it moved, it waved its arms up and down like a bird.

'Black Feather,' Jack whispered.

He watched as Black Feather began whispering words and waving his feather-covered arms in the air. He then began using his forefinger to draw a matching Star of David on each of the surrounding stones. He moved around the room, and not even pews and altars stopped him marking the stones beneath. His spectral hand and finger reached beyond the solid mass of wood and stone.

Once finished, the figure of Black Feather stood and walked back through the large door of the church.

Jack looked down and then to the medicine man, who was now a thin skeletal figure. His clothes and wolf head draped over his bones.

Jack was about to ask the medicine man a question when he was suddenly back in his room, the warmth of the fire caressing his skin.

He stood, took a deep breath and headed out of his house.

X

Water never stops flowing; it always finds
a way to continue its journey.

Father Harris drove down the tree-lined roads back towards the town and the church, his mind full of visions of death and evil. Several times he had to pull the steering wheel hard to the left or right as the car struggled to take the corner with the speed he was going, he found it hard to concentrate on the road ahead, constantly drifting off into a daydream or nightmare with the continued barrage of bloody images that attacked his mind.

'Wow, relax. Focus or you'll end up dead and not able to help anyone,' he said out loud.

He reached the top of the hill and the first signs of life as he drove past house after house. Their uniformed white picket fences and white fronts made him feel like he was back in the normal world, and he found the images in his head began to disappear. He drove more slowly as he weaved his way down through the roads towards the church. He noticed people walking slowly up and down the footpaths. He wondered if they knew what was happening in their town or if they were still blissfully unaware of the evil that walked amongst them.

As he approached the church, he noticed the police car parked outside, its rear side window smashed. He pulled up behind it, pulled on the door handle and shoved it open. In his rush to exit the car he fell over. A couple walking by looked at him with concern and asked if he needed help, he looked over to them and shook his head, picked himself up and ran around the car into the large wooden doors at speed, his arms outstretched and ready.

The couple looked at each other, made a comment and continued their walk into the harbor area.

The church doors burst open. Megan and Detective Dickson reacted by crouching down into the wooden benches that they were sitting in. Dickson pointed his gun at the figure that burst through; the sudden release of light into the hall only allowed the black outline of the figure to be seen. Once Father Harris had taken a few more steps in, he came into focus and both Megan and Dickson let out huge sighs of relief.

'Where's the others,' Father Harris asked, expecting to see the other officer and the Simmons family sitting in front of him.

Detective Dickson bowed his head and then slowly shook it. He didn't have the energy to explain, his head still hurt and he was finding any movement beginning to become painful. Every joint in his body ached.

Megan looked at the sweaty priest. 'What did you find out?' she asked.

'I think I know how to save your mother,' he responded.

Megan felt the warmth of a smile of anticipation grow within her. For that moment in time, the words 'I know how to save your mother,' were the biggest and most important things in her short life.

'Jack Red Leaf showed me the origins of what we are dealing with. I understand why it is killing and he has told me what I need to catch the thing so we can try and save your mother,' he said quickly.

Detective Dickson pushed himself up, using the wooden back of the pew. The tiredness, the exhaustion and fatigue were clear in his speech, face and how he now held himself. His shoulders hung low and forward.

'So how we do this then?' he said with another big sigh.

Father Harris looked at his friend. He had never seen him look so down and tired.

'We need some rope that has been covered with salt and dirt,' he answered.

Dickson's eyes widened and his mouth dropped open in disbelief. 'We need what?'

'If we can get Megan's mother and tie her with it, the demon that is possessing her will be unable to do anything,' the priest answered.

'I will get the rope,' Megan said excitedly.

Father Harris and Dickson turned and looked at Megan, who just nodded and ran out the doors before either of the men could say anything to stop her.

'Then what?' Dickson asked.

Father Harris looked at him and paused. He really didn't know what they would do next. He was hoping that Jack Red Leaf would uphold his part and help.

'Let's just try and catch her,' he answered.

Megan ran into the street and down to the harbor. She knew that she could find or rather steal some rope to use; she didn't care if she was seen. She had the sudden urge to do what was needed and no one was going to stop her. She ran past people going about their business. On a few occasions, she caught them as she squeezed past them in the narrowing streets; they huffed and made comments of how rude and dangerous it was that a young girl was running around like that. She ran into the harbor area, her eyes scouring the small ships and huts that filled the watery front. She attempted twice to pull off a wound up piece of rope that lay on the harbor side only for it to be tied to a boat. She kicked at it, frustrated by the fact that someone had bothered to wind the rope around into a neat circle even though it was tied at both ends. Her head jerked around almost robotically as she searched for a length of rope that wasn't attached to anything. She let out a 'Ha' when she saw the looped and tied rope hanging from one of the small tourist fishing huts. She ran over to it. The owner was chatting to a couple of men, showing them his leaflet when Megan ran up and grabbed the rope. He heard her heavy braking footsteps and turned to see her with the rope in her hands. He looked at her and didn't move or say anything. He was shocked by the audacity of a young girl stealing something in front of him. He then found his voice, 'What you doing?' he said with a loud confused voice.

Megan shot him a focused look and ran back the way she had come from. The fisherman looked at the two men now holding his leaflet and then back at the disappearing girl. 'Wait here,' he said to the two men and ran after her.

Megan found it difficult to run holding the heavy rope, and it wasn't long before she felt the heaviness of a hand on her shoulder. The hand grabbed the material of her jumper and pulled tight. She found herself suddenly falling backwards as her legs continued but her upper body was stopped. She struggled, holding the heavy rope against her body with one arm and scratching at the rough skinned hand with the other. She didn't feel her nails bend and break as she dug them in and pulled, but she heard the moan as the man let go. She struggled to her feet, still clinging to the rope, just as she gained her feet and balance, another hand grabbed her, this time by the hair and pulled her hard. She fell into the heavyset chest and thick jumper of the fisherman, the wool of his jumper scratching her face, the rope she had clung to falling from her grip.

'You little bitch,' he shouted at her.

She struggled again but an arm grabbed her around her chest. As the hand passed her face, she could see the bloody ooze out of the large scratch marks on the back of it. She then heard a click and she was free once more. The arm and hand holding her hair was gone. She grabbed the rope off the floor and then looked up to see Detective Dickson standing in front of her, his gun drawn and aimed at the fisherman.

'Police, Just let the girl go,' he said.

'That bitch has just stolen my rope and done this,' the fisherman said angrily, holding up his bloody hand for the gun-wielding man to see.

'All I see is a grown man grabbing a scared looking girl,' Dickson replied. 'And I'm sure all these people around here will say exactly the same thing.'

The fisherman looked around and saw several people staring at him. Some shook their heads in disgust while others shouted at him to leave the girl alone.

'But she—' he started before the policeman cut him off with a shake of his head and a "shhh."

Detective Dickson looked at Megan and told her to carry on. She quickly got back into her stride as she ran off up the small street to the church. The fisherman shook his head and turned away and headed back towards his shack and—he hoped—the two customers he had left. Dickson put his pistol back into its holster. He looked at the large jar of white powder he held in his hands and shook his head. He was about turn and walk back towards the church when he heard shouts and screams. He looked up towards the harbor and the boats moored there and noticed the masts rocking backwards and forwards violently. The bells on the boats rang out.

His eyes caught the wide eyed look of the fisherman he had just interacted with. His mouth also hung wide open. Fishing boats crashed against each other and people ran into shops and up the small hill towards him. The fisherman stood motionless on the spot.

The boats rose as the water began to rise. It crept over the harbor wall and began to fill the footpath. It seemed to have a life of its own as it snaked towards the fisherman. The blackness of it seemed unearthly. The fisherman stood and watched as the black water surrounded him. It began to rise up his boots. He could feel the coldness of the water but yet he could not move. His legs refused to budge. He began to look around and shout for help. People looked at him as they ran from the rising water. Some of the locals who had taken refuge in shops watched from behind the glass of the doors and windows with hands over shocked and fearful faces.

The water began to slow its advancement up the fisherman. He was now ankle deep in black, cold water. Noticing it had stopped rising, he let out a sigh of relief. Detective Dickson watched as all of a sudden the fisherman disappeared below the water. One moment he was standing, the next he was gone. He disappeared as if being pulled down. A local man ran out into the shallow black water to where the fisherman had been, stood and peered down into the ankle deep water. He circled round and round, shouting as he moved, and then he too was gone. There were screams from people hiding in shops and standing clear of the water.

The water began to bubble in the area where the two men had disappeared and then one by one the two men's bodies surfaced. Their faces looked up at the darkening skies, their skin was red and blistered, and their eyes were no longer in their sockets. The water began to bubble once more, the intensity of the bubbling growing. Large bubbles popped and spluttered as if superheated by a volcano fissure. The water then began to move once more. It started its meander up the road towards Dickson.

Dickson began to back up. He wanted to turn and run but was transfixed by the movement of the black oily water. The sudden burst of adrenalin running through his body masked any form of pain or fatigue he felt moments earlier.

'Dickson!' a shout from behind him caused him to snap out of his hypnotic state. He looked round and saw Father Harris running towards him.

'Move it, damn you, move!' he shouted.

Dickson began to turn and increase his speed up the small hill in the road towards the priest who had stopped, but he held out his hand and waved the detective up the slight incline. He had covered twenty meters when he had a sudden urge to turn and look behind him. The sight of the black liquid gaining on him even though he was moving uphill forced a sudden electrical charge of fear to shoot up his spine. His speed increased and he was soon moving up the hill with Father Harris alongside him.

As they entered the church doorway, Megan was waiting. She had unraveled the rope and had stretched it out along the church aisle. Detective Dickson fumbled with the large glass jar of salt. His sweaty palms made it difficult to grip the lid and body. He cradled it against his body and wiped his right hand against his trousers and grabbed the lid again. As he strained, the jar moved up his arm and body that gripped it. It then popped up out of its human vice and fell to the floor, Dickson gasped, as did Megan, who had been watching him struggle. The jar hit the stone floor of the church and exploded, the salt inside spread out like a mini lava flow.

'Shit!' Dickson shouted.

Father Harris appeared from a side door carrying a small bucket full of dirt. His heavily stained hands suggested he had dragged and scooped the soil into the bucket by hand.

'What happened?' he shouted.

He then saw the white powder on the floor, 'That's ok, just start rubbing handfuls into the rope.'

Megan crouched down over the pile of salt, scooped up a handful and then began rubbing it into the rope. Father Harris began smothering the dirt from his bucket onto the rope from the other end, Detective Dickson looked at the large door and then at the salt at his feet. He grabbed a handful and joined the other two in covering the rope.

Outside, the black water began pooling outside the church. People who had run away up the hill from the encroaching water stopped and watched it as it began to gather in an ever-enlarging pool outside the church. The tail end of the water pulled away from the high water at the harbor and moved like a snake's tail up to the growing pool, people who had taken refuge in the surrounding shops re-emerged and began to follow the water as it moved up the hill. Several ran to the two bodies lying on the cobbles of the quayside. A woman ran over to the body of the man who had gone to see where the fisherman had gone and screamed. She knelt, holding the bright red blistered man's head in her lap as she rocked backwards and forwards.

The sound of a siren pierced the air as a police car rounded a corner and headed towards the pool of water. The officers in the car were heading to the harbor where they had been directed to attend an incident involving two men. They saw the dark pool of water and thought nothing about it. The car ploughed into the liquid. Spray shot up from the front wheels and covered the shops and buildings nearby, then bang, the sound of crunching metal filled the air as the car stopped like it had hit a solid wall. The two officers shot forward in their seat. The seatbelt they were wearing tightened as their bodies accelerated forward. The strong material cut into their chests and neck. The sound of breaking bones filled their heads as collar bones and ribs snapped. The car shot into the air, the back end cart wheeling over the crushed front. There were more screams and shouts from people watching and hiding in the shops as the car flew through the air and hit a pet shop store front. The large window exploded, and cages and wooden hutches flew in all directions. The owner and two female customers could do nothing. The speed of the car as it crashed into the shop left them with no time to move. The car landed on the two women and slid into the store owner and then into a wall, the impact of car against the wall chopping him in half. Birds freed from their cages from the impact flew out of the window.

Inside the church, the trio salting and dirtying of the rope suddenly stopped when they heard a sudden crash outside. They all looked at each other and then returned to what they were doing, only this time with more urgency.

'Holy shit,' Dickson said out loud.

Father Harris and Megan both looked up at him and then to what he was looking at. The dark water that had followed them up the hill was now flowing slowly under the door and beginning to gather on the inside of the church entrance.

XI

There is no darker soul than that of the
blackest crow.

The pool of water grew as more and more of the dark liquid crept under the door and gathered on the stone step in front of the three occupants of the church. Father Harris grabbed Megan and dragged her down to the lectern at the chancel end of the church. Even though she was being dragged forcibly by the religious man, she could not take her eyes off the dark massing of water. Detective Dickson grabbed the end of the rope and ran to join the other two now standing behind the wooden lectern.

'Now what?' he said, looking at the wide fearful eyes of the priest and girl.

In unison they both slowly turned their heads and looked at him with blank expressions. His shoulders dropped further when no answer came.

The pool of water flowed off the step and into the aisle of the church. It didn't travel any further; it just grew. More and more water flowed into the church from under the door and filtered into the small pool at the foot of the step in the aisle. The floor of the church began to vibrate. Father Harris and Detective Dickson looked down at their feet and then at each other. The priest then looked at the stained-glass windows. They too vibrated, or rather stretched in and out of their frames. An ear-piercing sound grew around them, its pitch getting higher and higher. It forced them to cover their ears against the painful attack. The stained-glass windows began to warp quicker until finally they gave in. Colored glass exploded into the church, and the small pieces of glass showered the benches and floor. Pieces cut into the protecting hands of the three cowering people behind the large wooden lectern.

'Fucking hell!' Father Harris shouted.

Megan and Dickson suddenly became distracted from the pain of the cut flesh of their hands and face and looked at the priest. Shock and surprise filled their eyes. Father Harris looked at the two sets of wide eyes looking at him. He began to feel the anger grow within him.

He looked over at the large dark pool of water which had begun to bubble, gritted his teeth, grabbed a bible that lay at his feet and walked with a new-found purpose towards the water. He opened the bible and began reading out passages. His mind was racing. It was full of cascading thoughts and doubts that were somehow appearing in visions and sounds deep within his subconscious that seemed to be coexisting with a conscious part of him that was determined to meet the evil head on with his physical ability to read and cast it out, using the holy book he was reading from. His approach seemed to be taking an age; the thoughts and inner fighting going on seemed to defy time. He even found himself questioning what he was doing. Megan shouted at him to stop but he could only hear the angry voice in his head telling him to confront the evil with his faith. Detective Dickson left Megan and ran towards the ranting priest. He threw an arm around the priest's chest and dug his hand into the jacket of the man. He then began pulling him back towards the safety of the lectern.

The priest fought back against the detective. He pulled at the restraining arm with a free hand while the other held up the book in front of him. He still tried to read the blurred words as the book waved in front of him.

From within the dark liquid something stirred. The evil had heard the priest's outburst and smiled. As the religious passages were being shouted the beast began to laugh. It could feel, even taste, the holy man's fear and doubt. Then from the safety of its watery world it rose. First the un-kept dark hair of Jane appeared, followed by her grinning face. Megan's mother rose from the dark pool of liquid just as if she was on a theatre's stage lift.

She stepped forward out of the water and began walking down the aisle towards them. As she did, the large wooden benches on either side of her exploded into the air and crashed back down onto the stone floor. Some landed upside down while others shattered and splintered on impact.

'I have you both now,' she hissed.

Detective Dickson let go of the priest and drew his gun. He raised it towards the oncoming woman and began to squeeze the trigger. Megan thrust out her hand at Dickson's arm, and the impact forced the gun-holding hand and its trigger finger to jerk. The gun went off, the bullet flew past Jane and ricocheted off the wall above the door with a ping. Dickson shot an angry look at Megan, who just looked at him with surprise and a shaking head. He looked around for something to protect himself with. With nothing of worth at hand, he grabbed the bible from Father Harris's hand and threw it at Jane. The book hit her on the head and bounced off to the side, landing on the floor. She stopped and looked at it and smiled.

'You have lost your faith; it cannot help you.' She laughed.

Father Harris looked down at his now empty hands and then at the detective. 'What the fuck did you do that for?' he shouted at Dickson. He then grabbed the lawman around the throat with both hands and began to throttle him.

Megan began shouting at the priest to stop. She grabbed his hands and began to aid the detective in trying to pry the tightening hands away from his throat. Father Harris's grip tightened further and Dickson found himself struggling to inhale any oxygen. Out of desperation, he raised the hand that still held the gun and hit him across the side of the head. The impact stunned the priest and he let go of the detective, who coughed and began sucking in a large mouth full of air.

The beast within Jane began to laugh. It was beginning to enjoy watching the two men fight and argue with each other. It raised a hand above its head and stretched out its fingers. It then brought the hand down quickly. A bright flash startled the two men and Megan as a bolt of lightning struck the large open space of the window frame. Stone exploded into the church, wooden benches shattered under the impact of the large stones landing on them, and small broken bits of stone and dust covered the now crouching three.

Megan screamed at her mother. 'Stop! Please stop!'

Jane stopped her approach and for a second, and the evil grin disappeared before she raised her hand above her head again. Once more when she brought her hand down a lightning bolt erupted out of the dark skies above. This time the bolt invaded the internal structure of the church and struck the stone altar and a sculpture of Jesus Christ on the cross. The altar split in half and collapsed in on itself. The sculpture fell forward and shattered on the floor in front of it. The head of Christ broke into three pieces, and the wooden crown of thorns bounced along the floor and stopped at Jane's feet.

'You fucking evil bitch,' Father Harris shouted, his anger uncontrollable.

He ran at Jane and her demonic possessor, leaping off the top of the three steps of the Chancel like a wrestler, hitting Jane with a cross-body check. Instead of falling backwards, she just caught him and smiled as she slammed his body into the stone floor below her. The sudden impact against his back forced out all the air in his lungs, and he found it difficult to get any air back in as he gasped and choked.

Jane raised both hands above her head and threw them down to her sides. Dickson and Megan prepared themselves for the sudden bright flash of lightening, but it did not come. Instead, the pool of dark water by the door began to rise up. Just like forcing millions of gallons through a sluice gate of a dam, water burst forward and crashed into all the wooden benches and stones on the floor, its force throwing them up into the walls either side and into the side doors that ran into other rooms. The confessional disintegrated as the water devoured it. More of the damaged wall collapsed into the church as the water crashed against the walls. It headed down towards Jane and the priest who still lay at her feet, and then, just as it was about to engulf them, it stopped. It looked like it was being held back by an invisible wall. Jane threw her arms out to her sides and the wall of water reversed its journey, destroying more of the internal structures and statues of the church, it headed back into the small pool it had escaped from until there was only small puddles and a wet film surrounding the church hall. Benches, wood, broken statues, dark felted material and stone lay strewn across the floor. Rain began to pour in through the open windows and large holes in the wall. The rain grew stronger and stronger, its coldness causing Megan and Dickson to shiver as it began to wash the dust and rubble off their faces.

Jane bent down and picked up the crown of thorns that had landed at her feet. Father Harris had rolled over and was now sucking in large amounts of air into his lungs while on his hands and knees. Jane dug her talon-like fingernails into his hair and scalp, his gasping for air changing to one of gasping in pain. She pulled his head back until he was on his knees and then pushed the thorny crown down over his head. The wooden thorns tore into the flesh of his forehead.

'When I'm finished with you and your holy building the only praying you are going to be doing will be for death.' She giggled as she pushed the crown further into his bleeding flesh.

Dickson picked up an end of the rope and wrapped it around his fist and ran over to his friend and the woman. The rope trailed behind him as he went. He had no intention of trying to wrap it around her. He had a sudden need to attack her with it. He reached the woman and swung the roped hand, his fist made contact with her face. She groaned as she was sent backwards and onto the floor, and smoke rose from her face. He looked at the fist and then at the priest on the floor. He grabbed him by the arm and helped him up before pushing him behind him. Father Harris pushed the crown up off his head. The tearing of his flesh and pain as the sharp wooden needle like thorns exited his head made him feel faint. Once it was clear of his now bloody and matted hair, he dropped it the floor. Dickson looked at Jane, who had managed to pick herself up off the floor and was cursing him through fanged teeth. He managed a smile and looked back at his fist covered with the rope and then back at her. He nodded a cocky nod.

'Yeah bitch, let's see how you do now.' He smirked.

The beast within Jane grew angry. *How did he know?* It thought. Jane's arms raised once more and the heavens above began to rumble. Dickson suddenly didn't feel so cocky. Her arms came down and another bolt of bright light exploded into the church, Dickson found himself flying through the air. His flight was suddenly interrupted by the yank of rope that was wrapped around his hand; the other end had become trapped under a large piece of stone by the lectern and it had snapped tight. He then felt the cold wet surface of the stone floor as his body thudded into it.

Megan ran over to Dickson, who lay groaning, the rope still wrapped around his fist. She helped him up to his feet while watching her mother, who still stood where the aisle was once signified by the rows of benches and pews that were now scattered all over the floor.

The church doors suddenly burst open and in ran Jack Red Leaf. He stumbled over a pile of broken wood and stone on the step. He could see the large puddle below the step and tried in vain to gain his balance before falling face first into the black liquid. He disappeared with a splash into the world below its surface. Megan and Dickson watched as he disappeared and then looked at each other. Dickson could only come out with a witty comment; he didn't know why and it was certainly not the time or place for humor, but his words just escaped his mouth.

'Great entrance,' he said. Megan just looked at him.

Father Harris had suddenly felt lifted when he saw Jack burst through the door. The sensation disappeared quickly the moment Jack vanished into the water. The sense of helplessness and pain returned with a vengeance.

The beast within Jane had caught only a glimpse of the large built man with long hair falling into the pool so thought nothing of it; it was just another man trying to help who had succumbed to its watery realm.

Beneath the water's surface, Jack struggled to control his movements. He had never been one for water or swimming. The darkness of the world he floated in was full of death and destruction: wood, stone and bodies floated around him. An arm passed by, as did the lower limbs of a man. He could no longer hold his breath and gave in struggling to hold his it.

He expected the waters to begin to invade his body but it didn't. He knew he was connected to the evil spirit and that he could not die until the spirit did but thought the evil in its own watery world would try to exact some kind of pain and punishment. He looked around him looking for the way out. His eyes searched the darkness for the slightest ray of light. When he could not see any, he reached into his shirt and squeezed the small medicine bag that hung on a leather strap around his neck. He closed his eyes and began concentrating on the energy pulsing from the small bag. When he opened his eyes again amongst the death and broken bodies that surrounded him, he could see a little pin prick of light. He began to swim, or rather pull himself, towards the light the best he could. His stroke and movement resembled that of a half front doggie paddle and half breast stroke. The light grew brighter and wider until finally he thrust his arms out into the light.

The water of the pool exploded as two arms appeared and reinforced themselves against the stones on either side. The arms then pushed against the solid surface and a head and body began to rise from the waters.

Megan and Dickson looked over to the pool when they heard the splash, as did Father Harris, and his heart leapt once more. Jane turned towards the water, confusion on her distorted, fanged face.

The man placed a knee on the stones and then a foot. When he stood, dark water flowed from him like a hundred small waterfalls. He looked at the woman in front of him, and the beast within her shouted.

'You!'

At that moment, Megan and the two men witnessed the real identity of the evil that possessed her mother.

As Jane's body stood still, the evil spirit appeared to lunge at Jack Red Leaf. The further away it got from Jane, the more solid its appearance became. A small silvery, winding water thread connected them both.

The spirit had recognized the man standing in front of it as its spiritual nemesis, and out of complete rage and anger left its vessel to attack him. Jack stood firm and held his medicine bag once more. The evil spirit collided with Jack, and a bright blue light exploded from between them. Jack didn't move but the deformed, brown-skinned spirit screamed and shot back to the body of Jane as if attached to a stressed bungee cord. Jane flew back into the three steps below the broken alter. The steps cracked as she smashed into them.

'Mum,' Megan shouted.

Jane stood and screamed, and the floor began to vibrate violently. The stones at her feet began to rattle against each other. She raised her hands and the pool of water behind Jack exploded up again. The wave of water knocked the big Native American up into the air. It carried him down the church hall. What was left of the benches and statues once again became part of the crashing wave that flew down the church towards Jane. The waters swamped the hall, and Megan and Dickson were knocked off their feet and carried with the wave, crashing against the walls and other objects in the water. Father Harris ran to the back of the chancel where the statue of Christ once stood. He clambered up what was left of the foundation of the statue, trying to get above the oncoming wave. The waters washed over Jane and flowed into the chancel. It pushed up and pinned the priest against the wall before quickly receding. As quick as it had attacked the church, it disappeared back into the small pool at the foot of the step. The pool then began snaking its way out the door before disappearing amongst the cracks in the footpath and road outside.

Jack Red Leaf picked himself up off the damp oily floor. He looked around at the destruction that had been caused by the water. He looked down at the warped floor and the Star of David marked stones. He pictured where he had watched the church grow up around the one stone that identified where the dagger lay that they needed to help Megan's mother. He looked around him trying to match up his vision with what he was seeing. There was something different; the church was a different shape. He couldn't pinpoint the center of the church. Father Harris climbed down from where he had been pinned by the waters and walked over to the large man. He held out his hand while holding his wet handkerchief against the bloody wounds on his forehead. Jack held up his hand in a stopping position. The priest did stop and dropped his own hand. Jack continued to look around the church; his head darted from side to side, a look of confusion etched on his face.

'The church is larger than it was when it was first built,' he said, half pointing out his observation and half asking Father Harris if he was right.

Father Harris looked around and then back at Jack. 'The church has been added to. It was also burned down and rebuilt over time,' he answered.

'But the floor?' he began. 'Is the floor the same?'

Father Harris looked down at the stones, all with the star cut into them and shrugged and nodded. 'Why?'

'The dagger that was used to save the young girl was buried beneath a stone that had that symbol on it. The church was built around the stone. That stone was its center.'

Father Harris looked at all the symbol-embossed stones and then looked up at Jack. He was about to point out that there were more than one when the big man stopped him with the explanation.

'Black Feather's last trick was to hide it from everyone in plain sight.'

Father Harris opened his mouth wide in an understanding sound and nod of his head.

Detective Dickson picked himself up off the floor. His body creaked with every movement. He was still holding onto Megan, who sat against the wall looking at the two men standing in the middle of the church hall. Dickson helped her up and they both walked over to the big Native American and the priest, who was deep in concentration. He looked up briefly at Megan and Dickson and quickly introduced Jack to them. He then disappeared out of a side door. Jack looked at Megan and began asking her what she remembered when she noticed the difference in her mother. She began telling him all that she could remember. Even then she was sure that she had missed something—something important. She wasn't sure but there was something she couldn't remember. Jack explained about the dagger and that it could help save her mother and that they needed the rope. Dickson looked back over to the corner of the chancel where the rope was trapped. He left Megan with Jack and walked slowly over to it and began to gather it up.

Father Harris burst back into the church hall. There was a lot of banging and clanging of metal on stone as he struggled through the door with the shovels and a sledge hammer. He dragged them over to Jack and Megan and dropped them at their feet. He picked one up and looked up at Jack.

'The stone we need must be somewhere in this area. We'll just have to dig them up until we find it,' he said as he pushed the blade of the shovel in between two stones and began to pry them apart. Jack bent down, picked up a shovel and handed it to Megan.

'You help Father Harris,' he said to her.

He then picked up the sledge hammer and began pounding the stones. Some cracked, while others sank further into the soft ground below. Detective Dickson joined them and placed the rope on the floor. He then took the shovel from Megan and took over counter levering the heavy stones out of place. Megan stood back and watched as the three men began opening up a hole in the church floor. With every stone removed, a small hole was dug, looking for the dagger.

Outside, more sirens and shouts could be heard through the large holes in the church wall and empty window frames. An ambulance and two police cars had shut the road on either side of the church. They were too busy dealing with the damage to the pet store nearby to notice any banging or the damage to the church.

The wind began to grow stronger and then the rain began to lash down once more. Two officers who had been helping the ambulance crew with the crashed police car and bodies in the store quickly ran back to their car to grab their waterproof jackets. On the way back to the store, one of them noticed a strange sound coming from above. He looked up and squinted against the heavy raindrops bouncing off his face. Today had been a strange day and he'd seen more death and destruction in the last five hours than he had in twenty years of working a city beat. He called over to his colleague, who was about to step into the store.

'Hey Gibbs, you seen anything like that before?' he said, looking up.

Officer Gibbs stopped, stepped back a few paces so he could see beyond the building's roof overhang and stood with his mouth open. Rain fell into his blinking eyes and his gapping mouth. He saw what his partner had been looking at and then shook his head.

Above them crows had gathered and began circling. They called loudly to each other and chattered away, the sound of their wings growing louder as the circling black wave of feathers slowly descended. Locals who had witnessed or heard of the attack of seagulls days earlier began to seek shelter or move away from the cordoned off accident.

The crows broke free from their tight circle and dove at the street below. The two officers looking up at them ran for cover in the pet store. The crows looked as if they were about to crash into the cobbled street but at the last minute pulled up and headed to the large hole in the church.

Within the church the three men pulled at stones, searching the soft muddy ground below them. Megan stood and listened. She could hear the sound of the crows calling and then the swooshing sound of wings over the beating sound of the rain against the stone floor and the roof.

'Can you hear that?' she asked out loud.

Jack Red Leaf stopped pulling at the stones and listened. His eyes widened, and he quickly got to his feet. He could hear the beating of wings and he could feel the air around them thicken. It felt heavy, and breathing became difficult. He looked down at the two men struggling to move a stone, and he could see them gasping for air as they pulled at it.

'You need to find that dagger, and quick,' he said, looking to the large hole in the church wall and the falling droplets of water and the darkness outside.

Dickson and Father Harris paused briefly and began to suck in large mouthfuls of air, they looked up at Jack.

'Whatever you see, you must focus your efforts and find that dagger,' the big Native American said.

The two heavy-breathing men and Megan looked at him with confused faces. The confusion suddenly turned to horror as the mass of black-feathered birds exploded into the church through the hole in the wall. Megan screamed and was pulled down to her knees by Detective Dickson. All three looked at the stone that had been putting up a fight and began kicking it with their feet. It began to move, a few centimeters at first, and then it began to tip to the side as one end began to rise against the pounding from the feet of the three desperate people taking it in turns to kick at it.

The crows flew around the church hall, and Jack took a few steps away from the others. He tightened his grip around his medicine bag and tugged at it. The leather strap snapped with a dull twang. His body tensed as he watched the birds begin to tighten their circular flight in the large room. It tightened until it resembled a black tornado above the broken altar. The black mass continued to spin, getting faster and faster. The towering rotating black spout began to blur and shrink until finally the black mass became a human-sized dark shadow.

'You are not welcome here,' Jack shouted, holding his arm out in front of him, the medicine bag held tightly in his fist.

Father Harris quickly looked up from kicking the now freely movable stone and looked at the black shadowy figure just as it became soluble.

'Black Feather,' he gasped.

'What?' Dickson shouted as he grabbed the stone and began to pull at it. This stone was larger than the others, and it was buried deeper than the others. He was hoping that this was the one; he didn't have the energy to continue to push, pull, kick and pry stones. His inner voice spoke to him as he pulled: *It would be disappointing if after all this effort this stone wasn't the right one.*

Black Feather scuttled towards the three people sitting on the floor amongst a number of dislodged stones, the whites of his eyes standing out like stars in the night sky against his blackened features. His arms flapped up and down as he moved. Jack quickly put himself between the dark spirit of the medicine man and the others.

'You are not welcome here,' he repeated.

The lips of Black Feather moved, but no sounds came out. He smiled a toothless smile as dribble cascaded over his lips and down his chin.

Although there was no sound coming from him, Jack could hear Black Feather's words in his head. He shook his head and answered back.

'You cannot harm them and we shall find it and destroy your creation.'

The voice filled Jack's head again. This time it was filled with anger and malice. 'The land I was cast from is cursed, and the spirit shall always be part of it. You cannot kill something that is so ancient. It is part of the land.'

Jack moved towards the black figure and swung his fist with the medicine bag in it at the smaller man. His fist connected with a loud snap. Black Feather didn't flinch, he just smiled his toothless smile and raised a feathered arm. The feather-covered arm connected with Jack's chest. Even though the movement was slow, the moment it hit, Jack found himself being thrown across the church hall, landing on a pile of broken wood that was once a bench.

Father Harris and Detective Dickson began to haul the deeply embedded stone back and forth. With every movement it became a little more detached from the muddy earth.

Megan looked up at the closing figure of Black Feather. She began shouting at the two men who were struggling with the stone. All of a sudden the stone came free and fell against the hole they had dug to try and remove it. Dickson reached down and scrambled at its base. He felt something soft and wet, and he pushed his hands further into the mud and returned with an object covered in a wet and muddy bag of some sort. He held it up in the air, happy that the painful and strength-sapping search was over. Megan grabbed the bag and began searching for its opening. Once found she plunged her had in and grabbed the hard edge of the object within, she withdrew it quickly; not even the realization that she was holding the blade tightly and it had cut into her hand registered. She grabbed the handle with her other hand and held it up in front of her and Black Feather who was now just feet from the hole the dagger had come from.

Black Feather stopped and covered his face with his feathered arms as if the dagger was a blinding light. Megan stood up and moved towards him, stabbing the dagger below his arms into his body. Black Feather's arms opened out wide the moment the point of the dagger penetrated his body. He screamed, the sound of which changed from a human scream into a high pitched call of a crow. There was a bright light that caused all four of the church occupants to blink. When they opened their eyes, Black Feather was gone. Laying on the floor where he had stood was a solitary crow.

Outside, the rain stopped and the dark clouds quickly dissipated. The church doors burst open, and sunlight filled the church hall. Rays of light pierced the empty window frames and holes in the church walls. The two officers who had shouldered the door open stood wide eyed, surveying the damage and chaos of the church. When they noticed the young girl standing holding a large dagger in hand they raised their pistols.

'Police, drop the knife,' they shouted in unison.

Father Harris stood up from his knees and waved his arms in the air. 'It's alright officers, please lower your weapons,' he called.

Detective Dickson joined the priest, calling to the two armed officers who were still pointing their guns at Megan.

'Officers, this is Detective Dickson, lower your weapons.'

The officers looked at each other and then back at the waving priest and the dagger-holding girl. 'We need to see ID and you need to show yourself,' they called.

Dickson realized that they had a point; he was sitting on the side of the hole that had been created by digging and moving the large stone and was behind the waving priest. He pushed himself back and rolled over up onto his knees. The cold, wet, hard surface of the church floor pushed against his bruised legs. He groaned as stood and gently waved at the two officers. They both squinted against the bright haze caused by the sun. They looked at the bloodied, dirt-covered detective and lowered their guns.

Jack Red Leaf slowly pushed himself up against the wall, using it to steady himself. Megan looked at him and then the dagger in her hand. She then felt the searing pain. It burnt as she moved her fingers and opened her hand. The hand that had pulled the dagger out of its bag dripped with blood, and the large open wound ran the width of her palm. She felt suddenly sick; the sight of her hand covered in flowing blood and the pain that went with it attacked her senses and consciousness. Jack saw her wobble and moved quickly to grab her. He pulled a large blue handkerchief from his denim shirt pocket and proceeded to fold it into her palm. He helped her hand to close over it, stemming the blood flow. 'Father, we need a first aid box.'

Father Harris looked at Jack holding the now pale-looking Megan and nodded. 'Please everyone, come with me.' He then led them from the church hall into a small side room that had a sink and cupboards. He opened the white doors above the draining board and pulled out a green first aid box. He pulled out a bandage for Megan before running the tap onto a cloth and cleaning his own wounds. Dickson stood at the doorway and spoke to the two officers who eagerly questioned him about what he was doing and telling him what they had witnessed outside.

'Get on the radio or get back to the office and call the commissioner and tell him we need help: FBI, National Guard, I don't care who, but we need help,' he said to the two officers who quickly left.

He then joined the others in the room. 'So what happens now?' he asked.

Jack looked at him and then at the dagger that had been placed on the countertop by the sink. 'To have any chance of helping the girl's mother, we must trap her and place a symbol on her body. Only then will she be separated from the evil spirit.'

'Then what?' Father Harris asked abruptly.

Jack looked at him carefully. There was something different about the priest.

'Your faith is important, do not let your faith wane,' Jack said.

Father Harris scoffed, 'Faith? After all I have seen over the last few days, you want me to keep my faith?'

'It doesn't matter what you've seen or heard; it is your faith that makes you strong,' Jack answered.

Father Harris just looked at him. He was struggling with believing all he had been taught by the church and what he thought was right and wrong; his faith was shattered.

Detective Dickson lifted a finger and placed it to his forehead as he ran something he recalled through his head. 'When you appeared, the evil thing seemed to jump out of the woman's body and attack you,' he said.

Jack nodded. 'It remembered me, and its hatred caused it to momentarily appear outside its host vessel.'

Dickson placed the finger on his forehead to his dry cut lips and then pointed at Jack. 'If we try and separate the two, by getting the beast to do the same thing and then trap the girl's mother with the rope, won't that separate them?' he quizzed.

Jack screwed his face up and rocked his head from side to side as he contemplated what the detective had just said. He then answered, 'It may help to separate them enough so that the symbol can be placed on her body. The symbol must be used to separate them completely.

'So where do we go now. Do we just wait?' Dickson then asked.

Jack shook his head and looked at Megan. 'We must return to where the spirit first revealed itself.'

Megan looked up at him, sighed deeply and nodded. She knew that it was time to return to the house. Jack placed a comforting hand on her shoulder and smiled. He could feel the guilt of his previous actions eating away at him and he felt responsible for her. Father Harris took a deep breath. His mind became filled with the memories of what he witnessed at the house. With these memories and visions in his head, his shattered faith took another blow.

'Father, could you please bring the rope that you prepared?' Jack said as he picked up the dagger and returned it to its wet and dirty cloth bag.

The priest walked out of the room and gathered up the rope. Dickson watched him carefully. He too had noticed something different about his friend. It had been the first time he had heard the religious man use bad language and that worried him.

They exited the small room and found Father Harris standing in the church hall, looking at the devastation around him. 'Father, it is time to go,' Jack called.

XII

There are those that allow their desires to become the evil voice they hear.

The two officers pulled up outside the old library building that had become the police station. The outside stone carvings still had the words 'Library' above the large wooden doors. They hurried into the office space to find a senior officer they could speak to and relay Detective Dickson's message too. The last remaining senior officer stood at the front of his desk, hunched over slightly as he spoke slowly into the telephone handset. He nodded and wrote down information on a notepad that lay on his desk. Gibbs noticed the name plate on the desk: Detective White.

The moment the handset moved away from his ear and was replaced on its body, Officer Gibbs began to relay the message. The senior officer continued to write on the notepad, not looking up at the two officers but just nodding as the message was completed.

'So Detective Dickson wants help does he?' Detective White sarcastically replied. 'He should get help alright—help into custody for withholding information.'

The two officers looked at each other, confusion on their faces. 'What do you mean sir?' Gibbs's partner asked.

'He has been holding back the identity of the killer. The lighthouse was another massacre. They had CCTV set up in the bar area and it captured the killer at work and then Detective Dickson coming and going, leaving a man down and not calling it in,' the senior officer snapped.

The two officers looked at each other before Gibbs responded. 'We didn't know sir, we were attending the crash at the pet store when all hell broke loose. The church got struck by lightning, and a large flock of crows attacked the church. When we went in we saw Detective Dickson with the priest and a young girl who was holding a large dagger.'

'And you didn't think to take the weapon off the girl and bring her in? For all you know she could be involved in the killings,' White barked.

The two officers bowed their heads slightly as the shouting senior officer continued to release his anger and frustrations onto them.

'We found a few prints. The same prints were at each of the victims locations. So it's safe to say that the person doing all the killings is the same person, and that shit of a detective is trying to solve it all on his own. He obviously wants to receive all the recognition. Well, he ain't gonna get this one on his own,' he shouted.

Gibbs looked up at the now red-faced detective. His rant had left him breathless after delivering his speech without a breath.

'Who is the suspect?' Gibbs asked.

'The killer? It's a woman who has only been part of the town for a little while. She moved here with her daughter from the city,' he said. 'There is no question about it, she is the killer. The cheeky bitch killed her next door neighbor. He was the first to die. Her name is Jane Mellows, and she should not be approached unarmed.'

He walked around his desk, grabbed his jacket and turned to face the two officers.

'I'm going to the house now. I want you two to come with me as backup.'

The two officers nodded and followed him out of the office and into the parking area of the station. He pointed to their car as he walked over to his own and climbed in. The two officers jogged over to the car they had left just moments earlier and climbed back into the still-warm seats.

XIII

Faith and belief may be tested and tried by evil.

Jack Red Leaf pulled up outside the house. Megan looked at it through the rear passenger window. It had been so warm and welcoming when they first moved in. Her mother had been so much happier since leaving the city. Now the house she looked at had a darkness about it. The police barrier next door didn't really help. The white picket fence looked grey and warped. She pulled the rear door handle and stepped out of the car. The air was cold and damp. She looked up and saw the gathering dark clouds that seemed to slowly rotate above the house.

There were two police cars outside: the one left behind by the first shift and now a second. As soon as Father Harris pulled up, an officer got out and stared at the car. The officer relayed what he was seeing to someone in the passenger seat who sat with the car radio to his lips.

Detective Dickson pushed the front passenger door open and pulled himself out of the car. He groaned as he did. His body ached all over, and his head throbbed from all the bruises and cuts he had sustained. He leaned on the roof of the car and looked at the house. Father Harris popped into view from the rear passenger side. He too looked up at the house and then at Dickson. His body language suggested exhaustion. Lastly, Jack Red Leaf climbed out of the driver's seat and rested his right elbow on the roof of the car. His left hand clung to the dirty bag that contained the dagger. He looked at all three of the cars' passengers and could sense their fear.

Father Harris looked at the police car and the officer standing by the open driver's door. He then looked at Dickson, who sighed heavily and began his walk over to the officer. He waved and smiled as he approached. He looked carefully, hoping that the officer would be someone he knew, but unfortunately, noticing the darkness and precision-pressed uniform, he realized it was a new officer who he had not met yet. The officer in return nodded and then closed the door and approached him.

'Can I help you?' the officer said, holding up a hand to tell the approaching dirt-covered man to stop.

'Hi officer,' Dickson began, fumbling in his pocket for his ID. 'Detective Dickson, what's going on here?' he asked.

The officer looked carefully at the identification being held in front of him. He had already turned a reporter away who had tried to use the excuse of being a detective to gain access to the house and murder scene.

'What can I help you with detective?' the young officer replied, looking at the man's disheveled and dirty appearance.

'Oh nothing, just checking to see how things were going up here, especially with all the other crazy things going on in town and to say we—' He paused briefly and waved his hand back towards the car he had just left, 'we are just bringing the young daughter from next door back home after she was caught up in the accident. The Father and the other fellow are here also to help settle some of the neighbors' worries.'

The officer looked past Dickson at the others standing by the car. 'That's ok, we've been asked to check all comings and goings, especially after the other two officers disappeared.'

Dickson felt his face and neck begin to heat up. He was sure the other officer could see the redness in his face.

'You mean the other officers aren't helping out somewhere else?' Dickson quickly asked.

The young officer shook his head. 'We've checked, called the dispatch office and there is no response from them.'

'Oh right,' Dickson said. 'Well you keep doing your fine job and I will get on with escorting the girl home.'

With that, Dickson smiled and nodded at the officer and turned. As he walked back, he took several large breaths. He returned to the car and resumed his position against it.

The young officer opened the police car door and joined his colleague, who handed him the radio. 'Dispatch, notify Detective White that Detective Dickson and the girl have turned up at the house.'

'Detective, you go with Megan and the rope. Enter through the front, and Father Harris and myself will enter through the back,' Jack said.

Dickson looked at Jack and then Megan. He leaned into the car and spoke silently to the big Native American. 'I don't think it is a good idea to take the youngster with us.'

Jack moved closer to Dickson. 'She is the one who can give us the edge; her mother is still in there and if Megan being there gives us even a couple of seconds then we need to use her.'

Dickson's brow pushed down hard over his eyes when he heard the words, 'need to use her.' he shook his head in disbelief, but Jack nodded.

Jack looked at the nervous-looking priest and signaled to him to follow with a side nod of his head. Father Harris took a deep breath and blew out heavily, his cheeks puffing out as he forced it out. He then followed the big man across the road and up the pathway of a neighboring house. He then stopped at the door and looked at the priest, who looked at him confused.

'What? Don't we want the house next door?' he asked, pointing to house beyond the small fence.

'We need to get around back. You know these people, and I'm sure they will let you in and out back so we can get access,' Jack said.

'What if no one's home?' Harris replied.

Jack sighed and knocked on the door. 'Then we'll climb over the side gate,' he said.

'Why not do that anyway?' the priest moaned.

'I don't feel like being shot at for trespassing, especially with the cops watching,' Jack replied and then nudged Harris as the door opened.

'Oh hello,' he began. 'I, erm, we, were wondering if we could get access to your back garden. We are worried about the lady next door. She had a fall this morning and we can't seem to get an answer. Her daughter is a wee bit worried.' He pointed to the car where Megan and Dickson stood. 'So would like to see if we can get in through the back.'

The woman stood with the majority of her body behind the door and only half her face looked through the gap. She smiled at Father Harris, who she had met several times before, but looked the big Native American up and down, noticing the dirty clothed object in his hand. He didn't flinch, he just looked at her, emotionless.

She looked past Father Harris and over the road at Megan. 'Oh dear, I hope she is alright. Of course Father. Does Megan want to stay here while you see?' the woman asked.

'Why thank you. Megan's ok waiting by the car. We did ask if she wanted to come but she said she wanted to wait by the car,' Father Harris replied.

The woman pulled the door open, invited the two men in and showed them through. Jack noticed the purple flowery wallpaper and rolled his eyes. Cat ornaments and pictures filled the shelves and small tables of the living room. *Bloody suburban fools*, he thought to himself.

Father Harris carried on with the chit chat he had become used to when visiting local parishioners, until they reached the sliding doors that led to the back garden. He pulled it open and ushered Jack through. He then turned to the woman and thanked her for her help and that he was sure there was nothing to worry about. She looked at him and nodded. The moment the two men had stepped off the wooden decking, she moved quickly upstairs and into the back bedroom and stood watching from behind the white net curtains.

'For a man of the cloth, you sure can spin a yarn Father,' Jack said as they approached the fence.

The priest looked at the big Native American and smiled sarcastically.

'Lying has been the least of the things I have done this week,' he said.

Jack placed his right hand on the top of the fence and peered over. Father Harris looked back up at the house and noticed the curtains move slightly. 'Don't make this look like a siege, we have a curtain twitcher watching,' he said to Jack, who stopped peering over the fence and looked at him confused. He had never heard the phrase 'curtain twitcher.' The priest realized that it was his opportunity to answer the confused look of the man before he managed to ask what it was, just like Jack had done to him several times, and he enjoyed every second of his explanation.

'The old woman is watching from the back bedroom. She keeps getting too close to the curtains while trying not to be seen.'

Jack moved his eyes up to the bedroom window and saw the curtain move slightly. He then huffed in disgust.

Detective Dickson looked at Megan, smiled and then ducked back into the car to retrieve the rope that had been placed in the passenger seat. He popped back into view and sighed heavily. His whole body ached; every movement sent pain signals firing into his brain.

'Ready?' he asked Megan.

She nodded and joined him as he began walking across the road, grabbing his arm.

'Please don't hurt my Mum,' she said to Dickson as they approached the house.

Dickson paused at the foot of the steps leading to the front door, looked at Megan and said. 'Sweetheart I will do what I can to save your mother.'

They ascended the steps and approached the front door, Dickson held Megan back as he tried the door with his free hand. The door slowly opened. He only put a little pressure on it to see if it was open, but the door kept going. Both Megan and Dickson looked at each other with worry and concern. Dickson unfurled some of the rope and handed some of it to Megan.

'If your Mum tries to attack, hit her with the rope; it should keep her away,' he said to her.

They entered the hallway, and a strong, pungent smell attacked their noses. Dickson had experienced the smell of decomposing human flesh before, but Megan was having trouble not being sick. He removed a dirty handkerchief from his pocket and handed it to her.

'Hold this to your face. It will help,' he said.

She looked at the dirty, blood-stained piece of material and then at him with surprised eyes. 'No I will be fine. You keep that,' she said, pushing it away.

He placed it back in his pocket as they moved into the front room. The sight of the police officer's body on the floor and the half body still in the room made Megan wretch. Dickson grabbed her hand and held it tight. Water still flowed down the walls, its constant dripping filling the room with its rhythmic pace. They both looked at the mirror and its rippling water; it mesmerized both of them. The beauty of rippling water was in one sense very calming but in another frightening.

***

Outside, Jack and Father Harris began, slowly and as quietly as they could, to clamber over the fence. Jack made the climb look effortless, but the priest somehow managed to get himself caught on a splintered piece of fence and required the aid of the big man to lift him up so he could free himself enough to complete the descent onto the other side.

'I haven't climbed anything in some twenty years,' he began. 'I guess you climb all the time?' he said, brushing himself down.

Jack looked at him in anger and disbelief. 'You think because I am a Native American that I am a good climber and therefore have to climb every day?'

Father Harris looked up from the brushing of his trousers into the angry face of Jack. He then realized how what he said may have been misinterpreted. 'Oh I didn't mean it like that,' he said.

Jack turned away and headed towards the back door, Father Harris found himself wondering whether he really did mean it in a racial way.

Jack pushed his back against the wall next to the back door and turned the handle. The door opened with a slight click. Father Harris looked at him and then the door as it swung open slowly. Jack waved the priest in. Father Harris looked at him with surprise and shook his head and then pointed at Jack and the door.

304

Jack sighed and screwed up his face before whispering to the priest that he had to go first because the evil spirit needed to reveal itself, and to do that, they needed those that it wanted revenge on. He pressed a finger into the priest's chest. Father Harris looked down at the jabbing finger and thought back to his own findings. Both he and the detective were related to a former townsperson who had helped try and kill the evil.

His shoulders dropped, as did his head as he entered through the back door and into the kitchen area. A strong smell attacked his senses. It was a smell he had experienced before; it was a smell that sent pictures of a member of his church being found after several weeks left alone after passing away: the smell of death. Jack followed, keeping a small distance between him and the priest.

**

Father Harris slowly walked down the hallway and into the living room, where he found Megan and Detective Dickson staring at the mirror. They both held tight to the rope and didn't notice the priest as he entered the room. He looked at the dripping mirror and the bodies in the room and 'pssst' at them through clenched teeth. Both suddenly turned their heads and looked at the priest in surprise.

He joined them standing behind the sofa looking at the mirror and its hypnotic swirls and ripples.

'Where is it?' he asked, leaning over to Dickson.

'I am here priest,' a voice hissed.

They all looked around, trying to see where the voice had come from but could see nothing. Megan then noticed the water within the mirror begin to bubble. She gripped the rope tighter, as did Dickson. The waters continued to bubble more and more until a head appeared. The face of Jane looked distorted and scarred. Her eyes seemed wider and much larger than normal. The eyes themselves were a shiny brown that seemed to be sunk deep into their sockets. Hands then appeared either side of the head and gripped the mirror's wooden frame. The fingers were bony with long sharp nails. The beast then began to pull itself out of the watery world of the mirror as if coming out of a manhole. It climbed out and placed its feet on either side of the frame and then lowered itself down over the fireplace onto the wooden beams of the floor. It looked at all three and grinned. The sharp, fang-like teeth glistened with saliva.

It was then that Jack appeared at the open doorway. The beast turned and looked at him, and once again its anger exploded and it lunged for him, just like before its spiritual form leapt from its human host. The same watery connective stringy membrane connected it to Jane. Jack shouted 'Now!' and Detective Dickson and Megan climbed over the sofa and wrapped the rope around the woman's body.

The beast grabbed the big Native American and they fell to the floor, its sharp teeth snapping at him. He held its head and fangs away from him with one hand while he pushed the dagger over towards the priest with his other hand. The sound of something heavy rolling across a wooden-beamed floor caught the beast's attention. It watched the bag roll to the foot of the priest. When he reached down and pulled out the dagger, the beast's eyes widened. Jack used his now free arm to grab the now struggling beast by the back of its bony neck. It squirmed and kicked. Realizing that the dagger had been found and was about to be used, it tried to withdraw back to its host body but found that it couldn't return. It twisted its head and looked back towards Jane to see Megan and Dickson standing on either side with the rope wrapped tight around the woman's body and arms. It looked back at Jack below it and began scratching and kicking him; its claw-like fingers dug into the flesh of his shoulders and face. He groaned as two talon-like fingers plunged into his forehead and drew down his face. As they moved into his eye socket, one of the fingernails gouged a large chunk from his eyeball before moving into the soft flesh of his cheek. He tightened his grip around the beast's neck and face, trying to roll over, but found the flailing body stopped him from moving.

'Cut the symbol into her,' Jack shouted, just as another set of talons invaded his mouth and pulled, tearing his lips and cheek wide open.

Father Harris just stood there unable to move, watching the large man struggle on the floor with the brown, skinny demon. Dickson shouted at him, but he didn't hear. Megan let go of the rope, and it slipped slightly. She moved quickly to the priest and grabbed the dagger from him. Even this didn't awaken him from his trance-like state. She moved back to her mother and stood looking at Dickson for guidance. He looked at her confusingly.

'What do I do?' she shouted.

Dickson shook his head and then looked at the priest. Father Harris knew what had to happen next because Jack had told him.

'Hold this rope around your mother,' he shouted at her as he let go and ran to the priest.

He slapped Father Harris hard cross the face, hoping that this would wake him up, but he continued to stare at the fight on the floor by the door. Dickson stood in front of him, blocking the view of the beast and Jack fighting. Father Harris blinked and then looked at Dickson wide eyed.

'What do we do with the dagger?' he shouted at the priest.

Father Harris looked over at Jane and Megan, who held the dagger in one hand and was trying to hold onto the rope with the other. He began to move towards her. Out of the corner of his eye, he saw the fight on the floor. He was about to turn and look but Dickson grabbed him and ushered him over to Jane quickly.

Jack held tight to the beast. Even with his flesh being ripped from his face and upper body, his gripped never loosened. The beast knew that he could not kill the man below him but wanted to escape back to the protection of its human vessel. The rope that stopped it returning had begun to slip. If it could make the rope touch the floor, which was wet with the oily water from the mirror, then it could escape the grip and go back to the body of the woman. It closed its eyes and concentrated.

Outside, the rotating clouds began to flash with life. The wind began to pick up and then a bright light pulsed as a lightning bolt struck the house.

***

Detective White pulled up outside the house just as the bolt struck. The two officers who had been sitting in their car burst out of either side of it and ran to the front of the house. A large hole had been blown into its roof and a large crack had appeared down the front of the house.

'What the hell was that?' he shouted as he got out of his car.

Officer Gibbs and his partner skidded to a halt against the curb next to Detective White. They climbed out and joined the other two officers and the detective. They heard screams and drew their weapons instinctively, Gibbs was about to lead the way down the path to the front door when Detective White grabbed his shoulder and stopped him.

'You go in when I say, officer,' he snapped.

'But—' Gibbs started before being cut off by the detective again.

'In there you have a mass murderer and a cop who has been hiding evidence who may be part of it. When we go in we take no chances,' he said.

***

The explosion caused the house to shudder violently, knocking Megan, Dickson and the priest off their feet. With Megan on the floor, there was no one holding the rope, and it slid down her body onto the wet floor. The beast could feel the pull of the watery umbilical cord and felt a surge of strength that enabled it to pull Jack's hands off from around its neck. It then began to crawl towards Jane, who had begun to vibrate violently as if having a seizure. The shaking grew with every move that the evil spirit made towards her.

Father Harris was the first to get to his feet and grab the dagger. He shouted to Dickson to hold Jane still. Megan joined him and held her mother's arms still. She looked towards Jack, who had rolled over and was crawling after the beast and began screaming at it. Father Harris grabbed Jane's hand and pulled her to the floor with the help of Megan. Pulling her hand open, he rested his knee on her wrist to stop the hand flopping around and brought the dagger's point down into her palm. The beast saw what was happening and screamed. It began to crawl quicker towards them. It suddenly felt a tug on its leg and looked back to see the fleshless face of the big

Native American holding on to it. It kicked with its free leg and foot but could not dislodge the human anchor. It screamed again and looked back to see the priest begin to move the dagger's point around the hand of its human vessel.

Father Harris finished cutting the symbol into Jane's palm and sat back. The watery umbilical cord that joined her with the beast exploded. The beast screamed, and with one last stamp on Jack's deformed face, broke free. It got to its feet and leapt the last bit of distance between it and the priest, who sat still holding the dagger. He gasped as the beast buried its claws into his chest. Blood spurted up over Dickson and Megan, who both froze with fear and shock. Father Harris screamed as the demonic beast stabbed at his chest with its hands. His ribs snapped and splintered, and a large hole soon began to appear in his chest where the fingers and hands had continuously plunged in and out of his chest. Megan was the first to react from her fear driven stiffness. She grabbed the dagger from the dying priest's hand and raised it over her head. The beast saw her movement and shot to its feet. It hissed at her as she stood, the knife still held above her head. Dickson dove at its legs, rugby tackling it. As it fell, it dug a clawed hand into his upper back. He moaned as it pushed its hand in further. He could feel the fingers sink deep into his back until they hit bone. He moaned more when it withdrew them, blood splattering Megan and her mother, who still lay on the floor. The beast broke free from Dickson's hold and stood. It squared off with Megan. It raised its hand and brought it down to its side and another bolt of lightning hit the house, again sending Megan to the floor as the house shifted on its foundations. Large cracks began to appear in the walls as plaster separated under the stress and movement of the house.

The beast began to raise its hand once more. This time, water began to flow freely from the mirror like a waterfall. The dark oily water began to cover the floor. Jane moved, pushing herself up onto her hands and knees, looking at Megan who was struggling to get to her feet. She still gripped the dagger and was using it to help herself up. Jane looked up and saw the beast standing over her. She had spent the last several days as a prisoner in her own body, watching as an evil entity used her to kill and destroy. At times it had felt like she was watching the world from behind windows that were her eyes. Her anger continued to grow within her and she found a new strength that surged within her.

The beast was about to lower the arm when Jack clamped his arms around it once more.

'We are joined. You cannot kill me,' he shouted at it as he held it tight.

Jane grasped the dagger from Megan's hand, causing her daughter to lose balance once more and fall to the floor. She pushed herself to her feet and moved toward the beast and its bloody human clamp. With anger burning within her, she walked into the beast, the knife held out in front of her in the bloody, symbol-scarred hand. The knife sunk deep within its ribcage. Lights pulsed from beyond the brown leathery skin, and a dark liquid began to flow from its surprised eyes. Jane stepped back, still clutching the dagger in her hand. She then plunged it in two more times. Each time it entered the beast's body, a dark oily liquid squirted from its wounds and over Jane and the wall behind her. The black liquid landed on the mirror and ran into the rippling water.

The demonic beast's struggling began to lighten, as did Jack's grip. The beast fell to the floor next to Dickson, who rolled away from it out of instinct. The pain from his bloody back momentarily disappearing. It soon returned, forcing him to wince and quickly get to his knees to relieve the pressure off his back. Jack stood, his face torn to shreds. One eye looked at the beast on the floor and then at Jane. It was finally over for him. The beast was dead. He could finally rest. Megan got to her feet and hugged her mother. Tears ran down both their faces. They turned and looked at Jack as he began to fade from view until he was no more. He was gone. The water had stopped flowing and the mirror had returned to its normal state: a plain old mirror within an artistic frame. Jane looked down at the dagger in her hand. It was covered in the same black liquid that she was covered in.

Dickson stood and looked around the floor. The beast had gone. All that was left was the oily water that covered the floor and the body of Father Harris, his chest open to the elements.

Dickson looked at Jane and Megan and smiled. 'I don't know about you but I could sleep for a week,' he said.

Megan hugged her mother tighter just as a shout made them all jump.

Detective White burst into the room, his eyes quickly scanning his surroundings. He saw the bodies of the police officers and Father Harris at the feet of the woman and daughter. Blood covered the room and the two females in the room. He saw the dagger in the woman's hand. He watched in slow motion as she began to raise it. He didn't care if she was surrendering; she was a threat and his trophy for promotion and bragging rights. He fired twice as he moved, his aim affected by the massive amount of adrenaline shooting through him. The first bullet hit the knife-wielding woman in the head, the force knocking her off her feet. The second bullet hit the young girl in the back. She gasped several times and then fell forward onto the body of her mother.

Detective Dickson screamed at the officers entering the room. He moved towards detective White, knocking the gun out of his hand and forcing him to fall backwards. Dickson fell on top of him and began to lash out at him.

'You fucking idiot! What have you done?' he shouted.

White struggled with the man on top and shouted for assistance from the others to get him off. Two officers pulled Dickson up off him and held him up as he continued to fight and kick out.

'What do you think you are doing Dickson? I've just killed the mass murderer,' White began to taunt.

'Quick, get an ambulance,' Officer Gibbs shouted. 'The girl is still breathing.'

White looked at the officers and didn't move. 'She could well be in on all the murders. Don't do anything until I tell you,' he said to Gibbs's partner and the other two officers.

Gibbs looked at his partner in disbelief and urged him to get help. When the officer began to radio for help, Detective White looked at Gibbs and began threatening him.

'You are going pay for this you—you fucking brown-nosing, scum-sucking asshole,' Dickson said.

White walked over to Jane, pulled out a handkerchief from his jacket pocket and picked up the dagger. He held it up and looked at it as if admiring a gold coin.

The sound of a siren began to get closer and closer until finally it stopped. A medical team came over to the girl, who still lay on her mother, guided by Gibbs's partner. They quickly assessed her, applied a dressing to the bullet wound that was seeping blood and attached a drip. They then removed her from the scene.

Dickson was led out in handcuffs and attended to by a second ambulance crew that had parked outside the old woman's house next door. The woman no longer stood behind the safety of her curtains. She stood outside her front door stroking her cat, watching all the hustle and bustle, listening to all the chatter going on amongst all the uniformed people. Other people from the neighborhood had begun to gather in the now bright sunshine on the hill, standing behind the police tape that stretched in a large arc around the house and garden, out across the road and around the car that once belonged to Father Harris.

Beyond the growing number of people, a large framed figure slowly moved. He looked across at the house and the man standing on top of the steps.

Detective White stood on the top of the steps at the front of the house and began orchestrating the team of officers and forensic specialists. He smiled throughout. He loved having so much power and control. He handed the dagger to a blue-gloved forensic officer, who placed it into a plastic bag, carried it to a large black van and placed it in a drawer, he then slid the van door shut before heading back into the shattered house.

Dickson was helped out of the ambulance by the escorting police officer and taken over to a waiting police car. Due to the injury to his back, his hands had been handcuffed in front of him. As he walked to the car, he looked at the gathering crowd and noticed the large man. The moment he saw him, his heart sank. Dickson began to look around at the scene, causing the officer to grab him by the arm and push him along to the car.

'Stop struggling Dickson,' the officer moaned.

Dickinson's mind began to race. What had gone wrong? What did they not do? Where is it? At times, some of these questions formed words that he spoke out loud.

'What was that Dickson?' the officer asked.

'I need to speak to White,' Dickson shouted at the officer.

The young officer looked at Dickson with suspicion and then over to detective White, who still stood on top of the steps of the house looking proud of himself. 'I don't think he will want to speak to you until later when he interviews you.'

Dickson was then pushed into the back seat of the police car. He continued to ask to see Detective White but was refused. The police car left the scene and headed to the station, Dickson looked at the tall man as they drove past and pushed his hands against the window. The man looked at him and nodded.

As the day went on, more and more of the locals who had gathered to watch and see if they could catch a glimpse of the dead or dying got bored and moved on. Detective White had remained commanding from the steps of the house. Other detectives and senior officers had come and gone, shaking his hand on a good job, boosting his ego and self-important status even more.

By the time the sun had begun its slow decent, the number of officers had reduced, and only two had been stationed in front of the house on guard. The forensic team still worked in the house, occasionally returning to the van with various artifacts and placing them in various drawers and returning to the crime scene inside the house. White and the two guarding officers failed to notice the large man move under the police tape and sneak to the black van. After a few seconds he had managed to return to the safety of the other side of the tape. Beneath his dusty tasseled jacket he held a plastic bag with an object in it.

Just as the sun set, the last of the forensic team packed their equipment away in the van and left the scene. Detective White couldn't resist one last look at the murder scene. He walked into the front room, where instead of bodies, white tape outlined their final position. He looked around, proud of himself. 'Well, I knew you could do it Frank,' he said to himself out loud. He turned and began to walk through the doorway to the hall when he heard a noise. The sound of dripping water got louder and more frequent. At first his mind suggested a burst pipe—good reasoning since the house had been damaged so badly from the reported lightning strikes, but the dripping was behind him. He surely would have noticed it seconds earlier.

He turned out of curiosity and followed the sound of the dripping until he saw the black-stained mirror. He blinked to make sure what he was seeing was real and not some sort of hallucination, but it still remained. The mirror itself rippled like water; the blackened frame was wet with a cascading dark liquid. He moved closer, squinting as he concentrated his gaze. His eyes widened and bulged as a pair of hands shot out and grabbed his head. He tried to let out a shout for help, but the hands dragged him into the dark watery world of the mirror before a single sound could leave his lips.

XIV

The sun will always return after the dark stormy clouds have been blown away.

The police department waited for several hours for Detective White to come to lead the interview of Detective Dickson, but he never came. They sent officers to his house but he was not there. They checked with the two guarding officers, who were the last to see him up at the murder scene, and they both stated that they had seen him go into the house but not come out. Other senior officers tried to interview Dickson, but without Detective White's notes and evidence, they had nothing apart from Dickson's insistence that White had murdered an innocent person. Even stranger was that the weapon that they thought had been used—the large dagger that had been recovered—had vanished. Detective Dickson was released 48 hours after being arrested. No charges were filed against him, but he was suspended from duty for withholding information that could lead to the capture of a murderer.

On his release, he headed up to the house, cutting open the police tape that had been put up to seal the door. Other tape that surrounding the house also stated that the building was to be demolished due to structural damage. He sliced through the tape and entered the now dusty hallway into the front room. In his hands he held a white sheet and a piece of rope. He looked at the wall where the mirror had been, but it was gone. He moved quickly from room to room, each time being met by nothing. Everything had gone: books, paintings, tables, chairs, all gone. The clean paint outlines on walls were the only things that adorned the walls. He ran from the house, jumped into his car and drove up into the tree-lined road of the forest area until he came to the old wooden house that belonged to Jack Red Leaf.

He stepped out of his car and approached the house only to be grabbed from behind by the big Native American.

'Jesus,' Dickson shouted, the sudden scare making his heart pound.

'Where is the girl?' Jack asked.

Dickson shook his head. 'She didn't make it.'

'What do we do now? The evil is still here because you are still here,' Dickson said.

Jack looked at him with a mask of sadness on his face. 'It seems that I am destined never to rest.'

Jack then explained that he had taken the dagger and buried it where only he could find it.

Dickson explained about his search for the mirror that was a doorway into this world. Jack put a hand on his shoulder and told him that he must leave the town and get as far away as possible. Dickson nodded and returned to his car. As the car drove away, Jack sighed and returned to his chair on the porch of his house. It was time to wait and watch as the world drifted by—waiting until the next time.

Dickson quickly packed. He had arranged to move into a friend's apartment in the city of Boston, where he would try and start a new life. He had said his goodbyes to those who still trusted him down at the police station and then left his hometown for the last time.

He moved into the small apartment in a high rise just on the outskirts of the city. He decided to work for himself, starting his own private investigation company. He was finally happy working how he wanted to. In the two months he had been operating he had not stopped working, but he was happy.

On returning to his apartment one Friday night, he noticed a removal truck parked outside and several big men struggling with a large sofa. He smiled as he watched them behave like Laurel and Hardy in attempting to get it through the door. As he exited the lift of his floor, he noticed boxes and sheet covered objects piled up against the wall of an apartment two doors down from his. A woman appeared and grabbed a box and attempted to drag it through the open door. Dickson moved down the hall quickly and began to help her move it.

'Oh thank you,' she said, staring at the scars on his face.

'Hey, anything for a neighbor,' he replied.

Once the box was in, they introduced each other and chatted for a while. She explained she was an art collector and painter, finally getting her big break in the city. Her daughter walked past them. Headphones covered her ears, so she didn't hear or even acknowledge her mother or the strange man chatting in the doorway.

'Well welcome. If you need anything don't be afraid to ask,' Dickson said cheerfully and walked the short distance to his own apartment.

The mother and daughter spent the early evening emptying box after box and beginning to arrange the apartment how they wanted. The daughter removed several large square, tied sheets and untied them. The paintings she uncovered were then placed at the foot of the wall on which she wanted to hang them. She then untied her pride and joy, a piece of art her mother had seen dumped outside a broken house with other objects. She placed the mirror on her bed, leaning it against her headboard. She sat back and admired it before running her fingers around each of the carved symbols.

Deep within the wood, an ancient evil stirred.

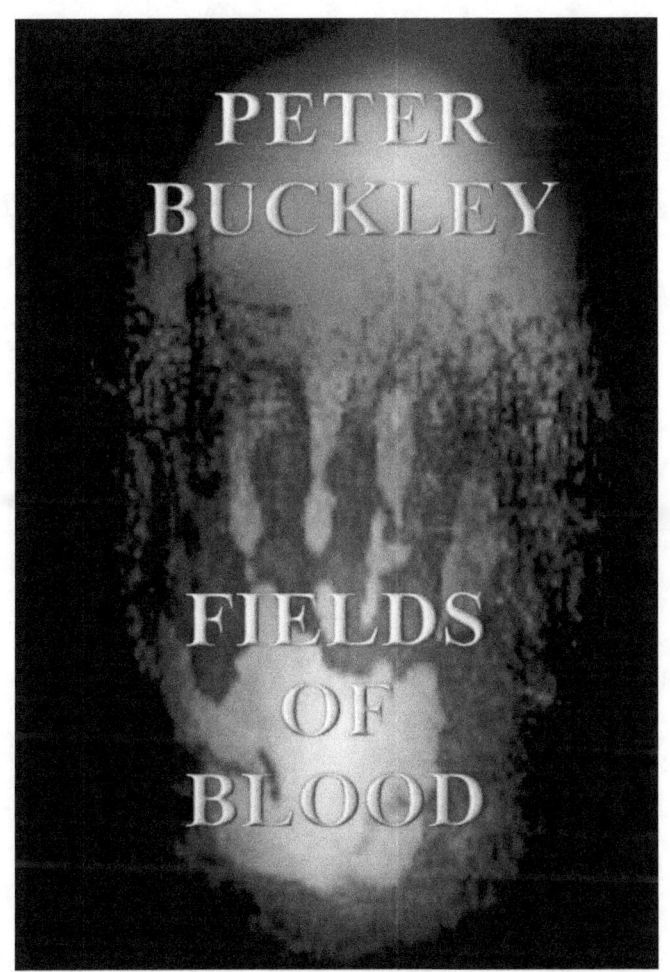

Fields of Blood

By

Peter Buckley

1

The photocopied flyers had been handed out to students in the week building up to Halloween. Truman High School students that had been given a flyer had secretly whispered about the party in classrooms when the teachers weren't present. The moment they had walked into class or back into earshot, all conversation ceased. In a small town like Truman, Pennsylvania everyone knew everyone else's business and what was going on. The high school students wanted the Halloween party to be just for them, without the fear of the adults of the town stopping their fun. Over the years, the farms and farmland that surround the town and its population of 4,608 had struggled with the advancement of technology, and only a handful still produced and sold their crops and cattle for a small living profit. A group of students from the school had found an old derelict barn on the outskirts of town. The farm it had belonged too had been deserted for some time. The fields surrounding it had been bought by another farm owner some miles down the road, and wheat and corn fields surrounded the old, rotten, wooden buildings. They had begun to take bits of equipment and decorations to the barn for the last week. Music would be provided by a battery-powered sound system that could be plugged into one of the teenager's phones that stored music. Kegs of beer had been stolen from delivery trucks or acquired by the older students using fake identification from liquor stores in neighboring towns.

The plan was simple. Get all dressed up and head out as usual as darkness descended to walk the streets during Halloween night where youngsters trick or treated, head over to the barn, party until midnight and then head back. Parents were used to kids playing pranks and hanging out till the early hours on Halloween, especially as it was a Friday night. The local sheriff and his deputies casually patrolled the streets, knowing that the moment they were seen that the groups of youngsters would run and hide, but nothing bad ever happened. There was the occasional egg on a window, burning dog crap left on doorsteps, or toilet paper thrown into trees or over buildings—nothing that couldn't be cleaned up.

Paula and Toby had been dating for the past six months. It was a very innocent relationship. While most seventeen year olds were experimenting and enjoying the investigation of each other's bodies, they were both churchgoing kids. They had met at church, where their parents attended every Sunday. Their parents encouraged them to begin dating, both sets of parents knowing each other and preferring to have some form of control over who their son and daughter dated. Paula had been handed the black and white flyer and had taken it to Toby. She was becoming tired of her ritualistic life of: get up, help with breakfast for her father and brothers, go to school, go home, do homework, and do chores. There was even a time limit on the phone when speaking to Toby. She could only see Toby on Tuesday and Thursday evenings, where they were only allowed downstairs and not allowed to go up to her room. Her parents wanted to make sure nothing unhealthy happened between them. She had craved something different—a little adventure in her life. The Halloween party was it. She had always gone out into the community with the others kids, so she knew she would be allowed to go out with all the others, although dressing up as some unholy beast or ghoul was frowned upon, so she never dressed up. This Halloween was going to be different. She had already begun hiding parts of a vampire costume she had been making.

Toby was reluctant at first to go to the barn on Halloween. He too had never taken part in the dressing up part of the evening. His parents had also not wanted their son to begin to act out some murderous fiend. They had always allowed him to go out with the others, and in the past, he had trick or treated, feeling stupid that while others had run up to doors and collected candy from the different houses, getting words of praise for their costumes, he stood there in his jeans and shirt.

Paula had pestered him for days about the party. He had finally given in and agreed but wasn't going to dress up. If his parents found any form of costume, he didn't want to face trying to explain it to his teary mother. She would burst into tears and tell him that he had disappointed her and broken her heart whenever he did something wrong or had not achieved well enough in school.

Others had spent weeks getting their costumes ready. The party at the barn was going to be the party of the century. If there was a way of capturing the excitement and nervous energy that flowed around the school and from between the different groups of friends that had been invited, it would have lit the town for a week. Locals had noticed the difference: the younger generation were happier, polite and eager to help.

Some of Paula and Toby's classmates had found an old Ouija board game in one of their basements and had taken it over to the barn. They had talked at length about using it at midnight. A couple of them had looked into the town's past to try and find the best place to use it, hoping that if they could find a place where death had occurred then they could try and contact that deceased person through the Ouija board.

James and Frank had taken it on themselves to investigate the best place to go with the board and had found that the very farm they were going to have the party was part of an area where during the American civil war hundreds had been killed in a skirmish between the two sides. There was no mention or evidence to say where those that had died were buried. Frank suggested that those who had been killed would have been buried at the cemetery.

They also found a small newspaper article about a young woman who had been found hanging from a tree in one of the fields. The article stated that suicide was the cause of death. Further down the page was a small piece, highlighting the unknown whereabouts of an eighteen year old male who had been missing for six days.

2

Halloween arrived. School had ended, and every student vacated the premises quicker than normal. As darkness fell, the trick or treaters headed out onto the streets. The youngsters walked the streets with guardians or parents, who guided them from house to house, remaining on the sidewalk as the youngsters skipped their way down the various pathways and up to the doors and either rang the bells or knocked excitedly. The waiting adult escorts waved at the homeowners as they handed out candy to the children.

The older kids of the community roamed around, jumping out on unsuspecting passers-by, they took it in turns to try and frighten each other. Some buried themselves in the piles of dead leaves that had been gathered up on the grass verges. Others jumped up out of garbage cans. Some even went as far as climbing trees and dropping out of them onto friends below.

Paula had told her mother and father that she was going out with a group of her friends to trick or treat and that Toby was going with her. Her mother had looked her up and down, seeing if she could see any signs of costume or excessive makeup. Satisfied, Paula's mother nodded her permission. Toby arrived and rang the doorbell, Paula couldn't get out quick enough, shouting

'See you later' as she closed the door. She dragged Toby down the path and down the sidewalk to where she knew her mother couldn't see her. Paula watched from her vantage point, waiting for her mother's shadow that stood at the window blinds to disappear before sneaking back for the bag and costume she had thrown out of her bedroom window earlier. Toby waited, nervously shaking his head.

They walked hand in hand until they reached the end of the tree-lined street, where an old empty house sat. It had been empty for some time. It was surrounded by a large white wall. The gate had been broken and swung loosely on one hinge. The house had already been the target of the egg-wielding youngsters, seeing it as a haunted house because it was empty and dark. Toilet paper had also been launched into the front garden and hung like streamers from the lonesome tree that stood in the center of the overgrown, grassy front yard. Paula pulled Toby in past the gate and below the tree. A street lamp directly outside the house shone brightly, and a small amount of light broke through the bare branches of the tree down onto the two. Paula dropped the bag on the floor and unzipped it. She pulled out a long black dress and rested it on a nearby branch. Toby looked around nervously as his girlfriend began to undress.

'What are you doing?' he asked, shocked by what he was witnessing.

'I'm going to get changed into my costume,' she answered.

The cold October air attacked her flesh, and goose pimples immediately sprang to life, yet she didn't feel the cold. The excitement kept her warm, or at least kept her mind off the coldness.

Toby stood staring at her. It was the first time he had seen her in nothing but bra and panties. She looked at him. Seeing the excitement in his face, she ran her right forefinger under the left shoulder strap of her bra, slid it off her shoulder and gently pulled her bra down far enough to expose her erect nipple. Toby could feel his heart begin to pound. His stomach felt like it was full of flapping birds. He began to shiver, not from the cold but from the sudden hormonal surge.

Paula gentle squeezed her nipple before moving closer to Toby and kissing him passionately. He found his hand reaching up and cupping her naked breast. A gentle moan escaped his girlfriend's mouth as they kissed. He could feel heat and pain emanating from his groin as his manhood struggled against the resistance of his jeans.

She pulled away from him. Her eyes were closed, but her expression was one of excitement. He kissed her neck and then slowly moved down until he finally found he erect nipple. He teased it with his tongue and then wrapped his mouth over it and gently sucked. She moaned louder as the pleasure ran through her body. Toby moved back up away from her nipple and kissed the flesh of her breast and then began to suck a little harder. Paula could feel him sucking and smiled. She wanted more but then suddenly realized that this wasn't the right time or place.

Paula then pushed him away. 'I think tonight is going to be an exciting night,' she said.

She quickly pulled her bra up and wriggled into the long, slim-fitting dress.

'Oh shit,' Toby said.

'What?' Paula asked, concerned.

Toby put a hand over his face and shook his head. 'I'm sorry, I got carried away.'

Paula looked down and saw the dark mark left by Toby's sucking on her breast.

'Oh my, I just hope I my mum doesn't see it, otherwise we are both in deep trouble.'

Toby stood, his emotions in tatters. He breathed heavily and found himself placing his hands in his jean pockets to try and mask the bulge that had grown there.

He finally understood what the excitement was all about. He had listened to others in the gym locker room boast and share their fumbling sexual experiences and had wondered why they got so childish and silly. Now he knew why.

Paula pulled out a small makeup mirror from her bag and applied some black lipstick she had borrowed from one her friends. She strained her eyes in the low, shadow-filled light below the tree, making sure it was even. She placed her other clothes into the bag and then together they returned to the sidewalk.

They walked down the street until they finally met up with some of the others from their class. Toby was the only one not in some kind of costume. The others knew not to ask; he had never worn a costume. When they saw Paula dressed in her thrown-together female vampire costume, they joyfully congratulated her on it. For the first time in her life she felt a strong sense of belonging and acceptance. She finally fit in.

The group walked around, growing in number until finally it was time to head out of town and to the barn and the party. To avoid raising suspicion, the large group split into smaller groups and headed in different directions. There were enough younger teenagers still on the streets for the older ones to disappear without being noticed.

They stood in front of the candle and said a quiet prayer. They had done the same thing each and every Halloween for the past nineteen years. In other households in town, couples lit a candle before placing carved pumpkins out on the doorsteps with the others that their sons and daughters had carved. They then returned to the front rooms, sat down and read passages from the bible.

Baron had been off school the last two days. He had been advised to avoid others due to him having been diagnosed with a virus. He moaned and argued with his parents about not being allowed out for Halloween. They had stood firm—doctor's orders. Staying in enabled him to see the strange behavior of his parents. They began by lighting a single candle, saying prayers and then carving a pumpkin. He noticed that they had begun to act very strange. As long as he could remember, his mother had always been the stronger, more outspoken of the two, but tonight she was very quiet. His father moved around the house and checked each and every window and locked all the doors. When they sat down and began to read, Baron asked why they had lit the candle and locked all the doors and windows.

His mother spoke quietly; this in itself made him feel uneasy.

'We light the candle because it represents all that is good on this, the darkest of nights. It helps ward off any evil spirits.'

Baron looked at them in disbelief, grunted and headed up to his bedroom, slamming the door just to make them aware of his unhappiness of not being allowed out.

He sat on his bed and stared at the window—doctor's orders or not, he was seventeen and wanted to go to the party. He grabbed his leather jacket and slowly opened the window. He moved through it slowly so as not to make a sound. Once out on the sloping roof above the front door, he turned and slid the window shut. He climbed down the wooden supports of the porch and slipped out into the night.

Paula, Toby and the four others that they walked with had decided to cut through the old church yard. 'It's Halloween after all,' one of them said. They moved amongst the old gravestones, Toby trying his hardest to avoid stepping on any grave. Paula followed his path. She too didn't want to disrespect the dead by stepping on their graves. The others didn't care; they danced around the headstones, making ghostly calls as they moved. Once clear of the church graveyard, they walked along the deserted, unlit road that headed out of town towards the farm. Whenever they saw a set of car headlights, they ducked down behind the overgrown tall grass that lined the side of the road. When all was clear, they once again continued their journey towards the old deserted farm and the party.

Two groups had reached the barn and had begun to organize the drinks and food onto the small tables that they found in the old house and some that they had made from planks of old wood resting on bricks.

James and Frank stood outside looking at the old tree in the distance. It was there that they would go and use the Ouija board. They walked out, shining their flashlights down at the ground in front of them. The last thing they wanted to do was shine it too far ahead, just in case someone saw the light and came to investigate. They walked down a down a dirt path that was surrounded on both sides by old dying corn crops. Though they were dying, they still stood over six feet tall. They were no longer bright green but brown and yellow. For some reason they had not been harvested. A light breeze blew towards them, making the crops rustle gently. Initially, the sound of the crops moving made the two feel nervous. The light wind would head towards them; they could hear it getting closer as the crops ahead of them rustled and, like a wave got closer, the sound of the dead and dry corn leaves getting louder.

When they reached the old tree, they found that it was surrounded by a circular clearing. There was not even any sign of grass or weed; nothing sprouted from the earth. It was empty and lifeless apart from the tree.

They stared up at the dark shape that loomed over them. The gentle breeze that flowed amongst the smallest branches gave it a sense of life. Branches reached out over them like arms, the smaller twigs looking like and moving like fingers. They looked at each other and smiled. This was a great place to do the Ouija board session, especially if this was the tree that the young girl had hanged herself from. They began drawing a large pentagram in the dry bare soil with their shoes. Once done, they then quickly returned to the barn, chatting excitedly as they went.

The group that Paula and Toby had been walking with bumped into another group that was making its way to the farm. They merged as they left the road and began crossing a large field. The further they got from the road the louder they chatted. Toby walked on his own at the back. He was the only one not dressed up. He followed just behind Paula, who was chatting excitedly with two other girls. For the first time, she was accepted and happy to chat with others without the fear of being ridiculed for what she was wearing. She looked back at Toby several times as they moved through the tall grass of the field. She smiled at him and he smiled back. His mind was still back in the garden of the empty house.

They reached the farm and the old barn. The old wooden barn walls allowed green and blue light to escape its cracks as the two lights pulsed in time to the muffled music. The leader of the group pulled on the barn door. The music grew louder and clearer, and the lights burst from the opening and illuminated the group in green and blue. Paula couldn't control her excitement. She grabbed Toby by the hand and pulled him towards the door. Once inside, she paused, her eyes wide, taking in the flashing lights and the group of monsters and vampires dancing in the center. She squeezed Toby's hand tighter as she took in the sights and sounds of her first party. No one seemed to care about how the music sounded tinny; they were all here to have a good time.

Maisey, one of Paula's classmates walked over to her and handed her a large plastic cup.

'Here, drink up,' she said to Paula, touching her cup with the one she held in her other hand.

Paula looked at the dark-colored cup. The flashing green and blue lights made it difficult to make out the actual color of the cup. She raised the cup up to her nose and sniffed. It wasn't the nicest smell she had ever experienced, but she had experienced it before. She took a large sip. The cold liquid that flowed down her throat had a strange taste. It seemed to match the smell, one that was hard to place. She grew up watching her father come home drunk, smelling of what she was now holding. She had seen him sit and drink while watching the Sunday game on TV and always wondered what he was drinking that made him act funny. He hadn't had a drink for three years, well not that she had seen him, but then again, his demeanor was a happier one. She took another mouthful of the liquid. As it moved through her body, it made her shiver.

She handed the cup to Toby, who looked at it and then at the others in the barn who were drinking from the same kind of cups. He took it from her and, in an attempt to impress her, drank it all down quickly as if a can of soda. The taste didn't register until he had dropped the cup empty to his side. The aftertaste made him shiver and screw his face up in disgust. Paula watched with wide eyes and then giggled when he reacted to its taste. She then grabbed him and kissed him passionately before pulling him over to one of the makeshift tables that held the plastic cups full of liquid. She picked up two and handed Toby one. Together they then walked over to where the others were gathered, dancing, and began to move, both a little conscious of how they have never danced in front of others before and worried how they looked to others. After a couple of uneasy songs and finishing off their drink, they began to lose their inhibitions and melted into the crowd, dancing away.

The crowd of alcohol-fuelled teenagers danced happily until the first fight broke out. Two boys from the football team began to push each other on the dance floor. Initially it was fun, but then one shoved the other too hard and he fell to the floor. He returned to the other, who stood laughing, and swung a wild punch. They rolled on the floor trying to hit each other until three of the older students pulled them apart. For some, the evening had been ruined, and they didn't want to be part of any incidents and decided to leave. Toby had seen the two boys rolling on the floor and pulled Paula out of the way. The alcohol in his system had begun to make him feel funny. Paula too had begun to feel the effects of the alcohol. She felt disorientated but happy and excitable at the same time.

Frank took the opportunity while the two drunk fighting friends were being dealt with to stop the music and address the crowd.

343

'For all of those that want to ultimate Halloween experience, James and I will be conducting an Ouija board session. We have done some research into the area and have found that a young girl hung herself not far from here. Everyone is welcome to join us and see if we can communicate with the other side,' he announced.

There were a few shouts of excitement and a few shouts of, 'Boring get the music back on.' As he walked over to James, who stood by the door, a group began to follow him. Paula had grabbed Toby's hand and asked if they should go. He had been told of the dangers of playing with anything that can communicate with the dead, but he was feeling strong. He was beginning to enjoy himself and wanted to prove to Paula that he was a man.

'Let's go and see what happens,' he said, pulling Paula with him over to the door and the small group of people waiting by it.

5

The group followed James and Frank down the narrow dirt path towards the tree. The alcohol-fuelled teens chattered away and shone their flashlights in all directions. They no longer cared about being seen. The rustling dead corn leaves made some of the group feel uneasy. Shining their lights at the wall of brown leaves, the shadows cast by the moving leaves against the shaking lights made several question whether there was someone in the cornfield.

When they reached the clearing and the tree, the group spread out, amazed by the sudden emptiness and the size of the tree. They walked around the outside of the marked-out pentagram. Frank and James walked to the center of it and placed the Ouija board on the floor. They called the others to gather round and use their flashlights to help illuminate it.

After a few attempts at scaring the others with forced movements to say various people's names from the group, they asked if there was any young girl present who had killed herself. Frank looked at James and winked. The glass pointer began to slide across to yes, directed by Frank. It stopped suddenly and seemed to vibrate. Frank's face changed, and he looked at his friend, who looked at him with the same 'Is that you' look. They both let go at the same time and then gasped, as did all that were watching.

The glass pointer began to move slowly away from yes and settled over the no. Everyone sat back and watched the pointer carefully for any more movement, but it didn't move. Frank moved closer and picked up the pointer and looked at it closely. He then lowered his hand down to the board. He felt the cold breeze brush against his hand and smiled.

'It was the wind,' he said with a sense of relief.

The group once again moved closer and chattered with nervous relief. Frank placed the pointer back on the board and asked another question.

'Can you show yourself to us?'

Members of the group giggled and then looked around themselves with their flashlights. Nothing, there was no sign of anything, and then they heard a faint scrapping sound as the pointer began to move once more.

'It's alright, it's only the wind,' one of the group said as others began to back away again.

They watched as the pointer stopped over the letter 'B.' It then moved again, not in a straight line but following the arc of letters written out in alphabetical order.

It paused briefly on 'L' before moving to the 'O.' it again paused and then dropped below the letters, only to return to the 'O.' The pointer then moved its way back along the letters and stopped over the 'D.'

'Blood?' Frank said, confused. The fear of something making the pointer move was lost to fascination and intrigue. Even some of the others who had backed away had returned to watch the pointer move on its own. Paula and Toby were two of the group who had initially pushed themselves away from the board the moment it moved but had returned, fascinated by what was happening.

'Does anyone want to provide the blood?' Frank asked, half joking and half being serious. He wanted to know what would happen.

There was a lot of shaking of heads when he asked for a volunteer. So he asked a further question.

'Why do you need blood?'

The pointer began to move. This time it shifted around the board quicker. Two of the group quickly stood and began to walk away; what was happening, whether a trick pulled by the two who had organized it, was too much.

James spelled out what was being pointed out. This time there was more than a single word.

'We... have... been... told... that... we... cannot... leave... until... blood... has... been... shed,' James said.

'We?' Frank said, looking up at his friend, who shrugged his shoulders.

There was a low thud and then a muffled series of bangs. Everyone looked up at the dark field from where the sounds had begun to grow from. The pointer on the board began to move again.

'She… wants… revenge,' Frank said as he followed the pointer.

'What?' one of the group asked. 'We? She? Who is this?'

The pointer flew from the board and hit James above the eye. He fell backwards holding his face, and everyone jumped back. Those who were standing began jogging away. Those who had been sitting stood quickly. James removed his hands and looked down at them. He could see a dark liquid covering his hands. Frank shone his flash light at him and gasped.

'Holy shit!'

'Is it bad?' James asked, covering his head again with his hand.

A couple of the others came over to him and looked at him, concern and worry evident in their voices.

A stream of blood escaped the barrier that his hand had made and ran down his nose. It pooled at the end until finally, with the gathering mass of liquid aided by gravity, it fell from the fleshy surface of James's nose and fell to the dark earth.

The moment the droplet made contact with the floor, the dead corn field began to sing with a low buzzing sound as a strong wind began to flow through it. Even those who had begun to head back to the barn stopped as the noise grew louder. The thudding and banging sounds increased in number and were joined by distant shouts and screams.

The group beneath the tree began to look around themselves. The noises seemed to be surrounding them. The wind picked up some of the dry dirt at their feet and drove it into their faces. They protected their faces with their hands, trying hard to see from beneath their shielding, saluting-style hands. There was a scream as one of the girls pointed to the darkness of the tree's canopy.

'Oh my God!' she shouted after the scream had died.

The others looked to where her finger pointed. When the others managed to squint through the swirling dirt, they could see a woman in white hanging from one of the thicker branched arms. She was then gone; she disappeared in front of them.

Paula and Toby had both seen the woman and immediately began to run back towards the barn. Others ran past them. Some fell over, the alcohol in their system making running in a straight line difficult. Even the adrenalin rush from fear didn't help as they fell into each other. Those trying to get back to their feet became barriers for others to fall over. At one point there were four people lying on top of each other, each trying desperately to get to their feet. Those who had already made it to the dirt road that led back to the barn suddenly froze as a dense fog burst from the corn field on either side of them, colliding like two waves down the center of the dirt road. Shadows moved within the fog, and voices filled the air. The bangs and thudding sounds echoed around them. They were joined by shouts and screams.

The fog flowed out and across the barren earth that surrounded the tree. James got to his feet and stood with Frank. The two others who had come to his aid moved closer to the two organizers. They all turned back to back as shadows began to move around them from within the fog.

Toby looked down at his feet, trying to see if he could see the dirt road. He was sure he could get back to the barn if he followed it. He strained his eyes, but the flashlight he held just caused a white smoky glare. When he turned it off, he still couldn't see his feet.

'Come on, let's try and get back,' he said to Paula, gripping her hand tighter.

The group that had fallen over each other in their attempt to get away from the woman and the tree stood motionless, their breathing heavy and quick. The noises that echoed around them got closer until a dark shape began to get closer. They expected to see one of the others who had been with them. They all screamed and began running when the figure emerged from the fog. A

350

skeletal face peered at them from beneath a small grey cap. It moaned as its jaw dropped open, and it raised a bony hand towards them.

The four scared and drunk teenagers ran into the field of dead crops. Two of them ran straight into one of the tall dry stalks and fell to the floor. In their panic, they rolled over onto their backs and began crab walking along the floor, looking back towards where they had come from.

Paula gripped Toby's arm. The sudden heavy rustle of leaves coming from the cornfield made her hair stand up on the back of her neck. The sensation of electricity ran down her spine and into her anus as fear gripped her even tighter. Toby began walking slowly in the direction he believed to be the way back to the barn but stopped the moment a large dark shadow began moving towards him. Out if the dense fog, two of the people who had left earlier ran into him and Paula, knocking them over. The two who had just run into them fell too but scrambled quickly to their feet and kept moving. Toby lay on his back. He still held Paula's hand, who moaned and groaned next to him. He sat up and saw several shadows move past them. The fog that hid them swirled, and for a brief moment, a gap revealed a torn pair of trousers surrounding a bony foot. He held his breath and froze before slowly moving to Paula and getting close enough to see her bloody face; her nose was flowing freely. Even in the cloudy darkness Toby could see its wetness on her face. She could feel the metallic taste of the blood and began to panic. Aware that whatever had walked past

351

them may hear her cries, he quickly covered her mouth. Her eyes widened in terror, not knowing why her boyfriend was holding her head and covering her mouth.

'Shhh,' he hissed, looking around him at the dense wall of fog.

One of the girls who had run into the cornfield ran down the narrow dirt path that ran between the crops. She had been lucky enough to avoid running into one of the tough stalks, but the dry dead leaves scratched at her face. She looked back over her shoulder and into the dark swirling fog and then tripped on something. She fell forward. Her scream was brief as it was suddenly turned into a gasping as she fell, unable to judge the distance to the floor. Her outstretched arms reacted poorly and she found the hardness of the ground attacking her chest. All the air in her lungs exploded from her all at once. She struggled to get air into her lungs and instinctively rolled over, where the pressure on her body was less and it was easier to take in the oxygen she required. She opened her eyes wide as she attempted to breathe. A dark shape loomed over her. The fog hid its upper body, but she could see the baggy torn trousers flapping against the thin legs of the person standing over her. Just as she managed to get a lung full of air into her body she saw the long, thin object appear from the fog and enter into her chest. She felt the hollow barrel of the musket enter her. A cracking sound followed as the object was moved back and forth, creating a large cavity that oozed with a dark liquid. Initially, she could feel nothing apart from the sucking and tugging of the gun barrel in her chest, but then it grew, getting bigger and bigger. The pain engulfed her senses, yet she could not let out a scream. There was no air in her lungs for her to use. The musket barrel was pulled sharply from its bloody hole. It hovered over her, and her blood dripped from it and back into the hole it had come from. The last sight her eyes saw was the skeletal face of her attacker as it looked at her during her last moments.

There were screams from the corn field as another student ran into two of the skeletal soldiers who stalked the field. He had fallen, his face sliding along the dirt. Small stones tore at his flesh and buried themselves within the wound. He pushed himself to his knees and raised his hands, pleading with the two skeletal figures. He saw something move through the air and heard the swooshing sound as it travelled towards him. He then felt whatever was moving through the air hit his wrist, it felt like he had been hit by a stick, the dull thud of the impact knocking his right hand down to his side. When he returned it to its original position in front of him. His eyes widened and his mouth dropped open with an almost winded breathless sound escaping. He knelt at the feet of the two dead soldiers, staring at a bloody stump that was once his hand. Blood squirted from the stump where his hand should have been. One of the soldiers stood with a saber. Blood covered its old rusty blade. His skeletal jaw made him look like he was smiling a toothy smile. The other soldier then pushed the barrel of a musket into the eye of the boy and pulled the trigger. The muffled bang and puff of light as the hammer ignited the powder on the side of musket stock illuminated the two skeletal soldiers briefly. The young teenager's body fell forward into the dirt, the back of his head gone. A dark black hole remained of what was once well-groomed hair. The dead corn stalks that surrounded them were now covered in bits of fragmented bone, brain matter and blood.

6

Those that had stayed in the barn and had continued to dance to the tinny sounding music carried on, unable to hear the screams of those outside. One of the older students stood surrounded by younger girls. He enjoyed being the center of attention. The girls tried their hardest to impress him, each one in turn trying to get his attention by outdoing the others with their experience and stories. He laughed at each one in turn, stroking the hair and touching each girl in turn, just to keep their attention on him. He smiled at one of the girls and then something caught his attention—something behind them over by the barn wall. He moved his head and peered past the girls, who in turn looked behind them trying to see what had taken his attention from them.

A grey fog had begun to seep through the cracks and holes of the old barn wall. It flowed through and began to reach out across the floor. The boy looked at it and swore that a strange blue glow was pulsing within it. He looked over to the door and noticed the fog squeeze through the gaps between the door and its frame.

Others in the barn stopped dancing and looked down at the sea of fog as it engulfed the floor around them. Some of the students were too drunk to notice and continued to dance like marionettes, kicking up the fog, making it swirl and lift.

The student who was in charge of the music searched the dimly-lit barn and then noticed a strange figure standing in the center. The long, dark hair and clothing told him that it was a woman. She stood motionless in the center. The fog pulsed with a strange blue color at her feet. Her head moved slowly, turning left and then right. She stared at the youngsters around her.

She had waited for a long time to be freed from the dark and lonely place she had been trapped, her spirit full of hate and vengeance, unwilling to move on. Tonight she had been freed and she was going to make those that killed her pay.

One of the drunken teenagers who continued to dance, oblivious to the fog, was within reach of the strange woman. She reached out and grabbed his sweaty shoulder length hair. He immediately stopped dancing and swatted at the hand that held his hair. The woman grinned at him as his partly limp body moved beneath her grip. The DJ watched, his eyes wide as he saw the woman raise her free hand and then bring it across the face of the dancer in a slapping motion. The body of the boy collapsed into the fog at her feet.

She began to move towards a group of girls who stood around the single male student. The fog that hung around her mid-thigh made it look like she was gliding towards the group.

A couple of others continued to dance and moved towards the center, pumping their fists in the air and jumping up and down. All of a sudden one of them disappeared into the fog. His head reappeared, a look of shock and confusion etched on his face. He could feel something underneath him. He reached his hand up to the others, who helped him up. One of them gasped and pointed to his right arm. The shirt he was wearing had a dark-colored stain on it. He touched it and rubbed the thick liquid between his forefinger and thumb. He then reached down and grabbed the thing at his feet that he had fallen over. He could feel the material in his hands. He pulled, and a wrist and hand appeared out of the fog. The small group gasped and he let go, his eyes wide.

'Who's that?' one of the girls asked.

The boy shrugged his shoulder.

'Do you think he's alright?' another of the girls asked.

The boy looked at his friend and motioned to help pick up the person on the floor. His friend paused momentarily and looked at the fog and then his friend before moving. They reached into the fog and fumbled around for the armpits of the person below them. When found, they hooked their arms under and pulled. The person's chest came up first. Both were expecting to see a limp drunk looking face. They both withdrew the arms quickly and stumbled back away from it the moment both had seen the dark, wet, torn flesh of the boy's throat area. The two girls looked at their dates with wide fear-engulfed eyes as they clung to each other.

The DJ saw the boy's reaction and jumped down from his elevated position. He ran over to where he thought the body was but was looking too far ahead. He caught his foot against the heavy lifeless sack of flesh and fell over the body below the fog. He scrambled along the floor, feeling for it. When he touched it, he pulled at it. When he saw the dark open wound and lifeless eyes of the boy, he dropped the body back into the fog.

The group of girls continued in their attempt to get the older boys attention. He was still looking past them at the woman who slowly approached. The girls didn't notice her presence, even when she stood right behind them. The boy stared at her, trying to see the face underneath the dark, un-kept hair that hung like curtains over her face and down the front of her white dress. He strained his eyes in the gloom, fixated by the woman. The other girls saw his attention was somewhere else and one by one paused. Before they could look around at where he was looking, the woman had wrapped her hands around the nearest girl's throat and began to squeeze. None of the group could move. The boy stared blankly at the woman, as if hypnotized. The other girls could only look wide eyed as the girl being choked gasped for air.

The girl's gasping soon turned to a wheeze as the woman's grip tightened. Her eyes, once wide, began to roll back, revealing an ever-increasing whiteness.

The boy suddenly woke from the trance that had kept him staring. He lunged past the terrified girls and grabbed the woman's hands. He immediately noticed their coldness and bony texture. No matter how much he pulled, he could not loosen the woman's grip. Finally, the young girl gave in and slumped. The woman let her grip go and the girl disappeared into the fog that surrounded them. The group of girls managed to catch their breath and in unison screamed.

Others in the barn stopped their drunken dancing or chat and stared at the group. A few initially laughed but then the high-pitched, terror-infested scream began to eat at their happiness. These screams were different; they were not attention seeking, joking screams. These screams sent shock waves through their bodies. It chilled their bones; it caused the hair on the back of their necks to stand up.

They all saw the woman in white. She stood out amongst the group, her white dress reflecting the strange glow that pulsed within the fog. She flickered, momentarily vanishing from view before reappearing. The boy who had tried to save the girl blinked and stepped back. He couldn't quite believe what he had just seen. She flickered once more and then she was gone. Those that had seen her vanish suddenly found the need to leave. The screaming group of girls began pushing and clawing at each other as they tried to get to the barn door.

There were some in the barn that were still lost in their own alcoholic and drug-fuelled world and continued dancing. The music had stopped; the disc that had been playing reached its end. Even this didn't stop them bopping their bodies rhythmically in time to a tune that played only in their heads.

The woman reappeared in front of the barn door, and several of the teenagers slid to a halt. The moisture that had built up from the fog on the straw-covered wood made it slick. A few ran into those that had stopped and pushed them forward. A blonde-haired boy dressed in a skeleton all-in-one Lycra suit fell and landed at the woman's feet, his white-painted face coming to rest against her cold bony shins. He took a deep breath in and was overcome by a strong, sickening smell. He pushed himself up, quickly appearing out of the fog, coughing and retching as he did.

The woman looked down at him, tilted her head from side to side and smiled. She reached down and put her hands on either side of his head. She then began pushing her fingers into his skull. He grabbed at her hands and tried to stop the fingers probing deeper into his skull. The fingers continued to push deeper, and the sound of his skull giving way filled his head. He didn't feel the pain, just the pop as the fingers pushed past the bone barrier and began pushing into the soft tissue of the brain below. She then curled her fingers around the bone and pulled sharply.

The others who had stopped their advancement to the door watched on in horror as the woman pulled sharply up. The boy's skull separated from the rest of his head. The sudden injection of pain and fear forced his heart to buckle and cease to beat. Blood sprayed those who were at the front. Screams filled the fog-filled barn as girls and some of the younger teenagers reacted to the horror they had just witnessed. Two of the older boys decided it would be easier to rush her at the same time. They agreed while watching their friend being killed that she surely couldn't take on two of them at the same time. They ran forward and tucked their heads into their shoulder as they prepared to shoulder barge her. Just as they were about to hit her, she vanished. Their momentum kept them going until they hit the solid wall of wood of the barn. They missed the door, which would have possibly given way, allowing them to escape. Instead, they bounced backwards and into the fog. They both got to their feet quickly and came face to face with the woman, who grabbed their throats and began to squeeze. They looked at her with wide eyes and tried to pull her fingers from their throats. She just continued to smile at them, her eyes black like polished marbles.

Others had begun to look for an alternative way out of the barn and had noticed the small group pulling at part of the barn wall where the fog was seeping through. They ran over to them and began pulling and clawing at the wooden beams.

The fog continued to flow through the gap in the wall. One of the boys who had joined the original four suddenly let out a gasp and froze. The others looked at him in alarm and stopped pulling at the wooden wall. The boy looked down and saw a large dark object slowly slide from his chest. The others saw the object begin to retract from the boy and slowly backed away from the wall. Once the pointed object had left the chest of the boy and disappeared back behind the wall, the boy slowly turned to them, his hands covering a dark stain on his white sheet he had used to dress himself as a ghost. He looked at them through tear-filled eyes before collapsing into the fog.

The others looked at each other and then at the wall just as several pointed objects began jabbing through the gaps in the barn wall.

***

The woman squeezed tighter and tighter until she felt the two boys' bodies go limp and then let them go. Their bodies fell into the depths of the swirling pulsing light of the fog. She then looked at the group of remaining teenagers who had stood frozen with fear. She sniffed the stale air and moved her head like a snake tasting the air around it. She suddenly stopped. She had found what she was looking for. She vanished once more and reappeared amongst the group that had watched her kill the three boys. The sudden appearance shocked them from their trance and they all scattered in different directions.

One of the girls ran towards where the DJ had stood, elevated above everyone else. As she ran, she tripped over the body that lay in the middle of what was the dance floor. She picked herself up quickly and continued her run to the elevated area above the fog. She focused on the wooden table stacked on the old dry hay bail until the woman in white appeared in front of her and caught her by the throat. The girl's legs shot forward and hit the woman, who held her tight and didn't flinch or move even after the collision. The girl squirmed, and tears flowed freely down her face.

The woman looked at her carefully and then smiled. The girls head became filled with voices. A young child like voice asked if she was one, and a reply came from a much older female voice.

'Yes, she is one of them.'

The girl shook her head, hoping to shake the voices out, but the female voice spoke to her.

'You are one of them. I can sense it in you. Your mother will pay for what she did to me.'

The woman then pushed her little finger into the girl's stomach. It melted the clothing that covered the girl. She could feel the finger pushing against her skin. It was cold, yet it burned. The finger sank deep into her and then began moving slowly down. The clothing that she wore melted away as the finger travelled down her stomach.

The girl gasped as the pain attacked her senses. She could not scream; nothing came out of her mouth. All she could do was take in short bursts of air. Her eyes became glazed by tears that flowed like a waterfall.

The finger was withdrawn and the woman let go of the girl, who stood motionless, still gasping for air. Her hands naturally moved to her stomach and felt the warm wetness of the fluid that was draining from her body. She too then collapsed into the fog.

7

Outside in the fog-filled field, teenagers wandered around, jumping every time they heard a scream, gunshot sound or clash of steel. A small number had stayed with Frank and James near the Ouija board. The tree that towered over them began to creak as a cold breeze flowed around them and the finger-like branches above them.

There was a scraping sound, and the fog began to recede. It moved back to the edge of the clearing and stopped. Like a wall, it surrounded them. The sound that they could hear was the Ouija board glass pointer. It was on the move again, darting from letter to letter. The group approached it carefully, looking down at it and back at the wall of fog.

'What's it saying?' one of the girls asked.

Frank looked at it and tried to make sense of its darting movements between the letters.

'I'm not sure; it doesn't make sense,' he replied.

'What do you mean?' the girl's boyfriend asked angrily.

Frank looked at the girl's boyfriend and then at James.

'It's repeating the same message, or messages. It's almost like there are several people trying to speak at the same time.'

'For fucks sake, what are they saying?' the boyfriend snapped.

James grabbed him by his shirt and glared at him from underneath his bloody compress.

'Leave no survivors. Find and punish the guilty. Let us rest. Cursed earth,' Frank said.

James looked at him.

'It keeps repeating itself,' Frank added.

The girl screamed and pointed at the wall of fog. The others looked to where she was pointing, straining their eyes against the darkness and the fog. Flashes of blue light pulsed from within it, and dark shadows moved around within the thick fog bank. Occasionally a musket barrel or sword tip poked out of it and into the clearing.

'What's going on?' the girl stuttered.

Frank and James looked at each other. Fear filled their eyes and they had no answer.

The scraping of the Ouija pointer suddenly stopped, and an eerie silence caught their attention. They slowly returned their gaze to the board on the floor.

There was a sound of someone stepping on gravel followed by several more heavy footsteps. The group looked up and saw five skeletal figures standing in front of them. The fog no longer hid them. Their clothes were torn and dirty and were old civil war uniforms. They held muskets with bayonets fitted; their empty eye sockets seemed to glow with the same blue that pulsed within the fog.

The group backed away. Frank looked around; the fog still surrounded them like a wall. He looked up at the tree and then shouted to them to climb the tree. They turned and ran the short distance to the tree. Frank helped the girl up to the first branch that was too high for them to reach by standing. When she had moved herself further up the tree via the ever-increasing number of branches, Frank took a step back, used the distance to step in and up onto the tree trunk, using the extra height to push himself high enough to reach the branch. He hauled himself up and then held his hand out for James to reach up. Once their hands were securely linked, Frank pulled James up until he could pull himself up and into the safety of the tree.

The soldiers moved forward, their muskets lowered, the points of the bayonets ready to be embedded into flesh.

The girl's boyfriend looked back. He could feel the fear and panic increase as the soldiers got closer. Frank held out his hand. The initial linking of hands failed, the thick film of nervous sweat causing them to lose grip of each other. The boyfriend jumped up again, desperation in his jump causing him to misjudge the hand being held out to him. Once again he fell. He quickly got himself ready for another attempt, but it was too late. Five bayonets plunged into his back. Frank looked down in horror at the look of terror in the boy's eyes and then watched from above as the soldiers continued to stab the lifeless body.

The girl screamed and then began climbing down from her position high in the tree. Hysteria had overtaken her; she had only one desire and need, and that was to get to her boyfriend. Frank saw her climbing down towards him and grabbed her and pinned her to the thick tree trunk. He tried to calm her by talking into her ear as she fought against him. He closed his eyes tight. He was scared and didn't know what to do, but at that moment in time he didn't want to see another person die.

The soldiers finally stopped stabbing the now squelching body at their feet and backed away from the tree. They looked up at the three students cowering amongst its branches, their skeletal faces grinning as they looked at them. They then turned and returned to the wall of fog and slowly disappeared back into its swirling pulsing depths.

Out on a branch, a piece of old worn rope laid wrapped around it. The tree had continued its growth and the rope had become part of its growing process, embedding itself in the bark of the branch, overgrown with moss and weather-beaten. The rope began to move;

it moved like a snake unknotting itself and sliding along the branch. It began to grow in length as it moved.

8

The woman in white stood and looked around the room at the panicking teenagers who scattered themselves around the barn. Some clawed at the walls where they found small holes, others hid themselves behind bales of hay and other objects that lay around the old barn. Her evil smile suddenly changed. Something had caught her attention. Her head tilted from side to side and then the smile returned. She flickered and then disappeared.

The group who had been pulling at the gap in the wall moved together; they stayed close to each other. One of the girls who had been watching the woman in white throughout became aware that she was nowhere to be seen and had not been seen for several minutes.

'She's gone,' she shouted.

Others in the small group looked at her and then around the room. This was their chance to escape. They all ran towards the barn door. Others in the barn saw the sudden movement of the group and immediately joined them.

They pulled at the door, their hands grabbing a space on its edge, and yanked at it. The door moved a little. Soon the group had a rhythm going. The door warped with every push and pull until finally it gave way. It shot open, and those pulling at it fell backwards onto the floor.

Even with the door open, no one moved. They stood frozen to the spot staring at the wall of fog that pulsed with a strange blue light.

The fog had stopped entering the barn; it just hung as if being held back by a piece of glass.

One of the older boys of the escaping group, moved towards the wall of fog and pushed his hand into it. He expected his hand to touch something solid but it disappeared into the swirling fog. He could feel the difference in temperature as soon as his hand entered it, the sharp coldness biting at his skin. He withdrew it and looked at it. He then looked back at the scared crowd of teenagers and shrugged his shoulders. Before he could say anything, he disappeared into the fog, pulled by some force that yanked him off his feet. There were screams from the girls and shouts of panic from the boys, but all had tears of fear running down their faces.

'Shut the door,' one of the older boys shouted before running over to it and straining to close it. Whatever force had held it shut was now trying to keep it open. He was joined by the boy who had been the center of attention to the group of girls, and together they managed to close it, sliding the wooden lock across to secure it. They both leaned against the door in relief.

They breathed heavily, their chests rising and falling in unison, and then the older of the two, who had been the first to try and close the door, gasped. His chest continued to rise. The other boy watched wide eyed as a bayonet appeared from his chest, the blade covered in thick liquid. The blade disappeared and then quickly burst from his chest again. The other boy pushed away from the door and joined the others who watched in horror as the boy slid down the door. A trail of blood marked his descent into the fog that still hung around their legs.

Frank felt the girl slump and stop fighting. He let her go and helped her back up into the safety of the tree. She sat, head bowed and eyes closed. Even with them closed they still couldn't stop the tears from flowing. Frank then moved over to where James sat and began trying to figure out what was going on and how they could stop it.

The rope continued its snaking movement towards the girl until it finally reached her. Like a cobra rising up, ready to strike, it too rose up and watched the sobbing young girl.

The woman in white appeared out on the branch where the rope had begun its journey. She smiled at the girl and blinked her black eyes. The rope shot forward and wrapped itself around her throat. It then pulled her back along the branch until finally she fell. The rope snapped tight, snapping her neck as she swung beneath the branch.

The two boys heard the struggle and watched helplessly as the girl fell.

The woman in white flickered and disappeared, reappearing in front of the hanging body of the girl. The woman seemed to be hovering in mid-air, her hair and white dress flowing around her as if she were under water. She pushed her hand into the girl's stomach, the popping sound of her flesh giving way to the probing hand echoing around the tree. She then pulled at the intestines that began to unravel as they left her body. The woman in white looked over at the two boys and was gone.

Frank and James sat, unable to speak. They both looked at the girl, who continued to swing back and forth by the rope around her neck, her intestines hanging from the open wound all the way to the ground below.

A scream awoke them from their trance. They looked over at the wall of fog and saw Paula and Toby.

Toby had grabbed Paula and dragged her with him, trying to get away from the shadows and skeletal soldiers that moved within the fog. They had burst free of the fog only to find themselves back at the tree where they had started, only this time they were greeted by a girl hanging with her intestines hanging from her. Toby pulled Paula into his chest to avoid her seeing too much of the girl hanging there. He noticed the two boys cowering in the tree. He wasn't sure if they had done this or were victims of whatever was going on.

373

Frank waved at the couple and called to them to get off the ground and up into the tree. He tried to hold back on making too much sound, fearing he would bring attention to their location.

'Please get up here; they are everywhere.'

Toby paused and looked at the wall of fog and then at the tree. He then began guiding Paula towards the tree trunk, making sure he was shielding her from seeing the girl.

Frank and James moved down to where they could offer a hand and pulled Paula up into the tree with them. They then helped Toby up. They sat on the opposite side of the tree from the hanging girl and discussed what was happening and if they could stop it.

'Obviously the Ouija board was the key to starting this,' Toby said sharply. 'You opened up a door, so you need to close it.'

James held his injured head and shook it. 'We thought it would be fun; we don't believe in this stuff.'

'We did a bit of research, but the first bit of the message was us trying to scare everyone,' Frank said.

Toby looked at Paula, who sat clutching her knees to her chest. He reached over to her and stroked her leg gently. She looked up at him through tear-filled eyes and smiled.

'What history?' he asked.

'This whole area was a civil war battleground; thousands died here,' Frank began. 'I guess we woke them?'

Toby looked at the two boys. 'So who is the woman?'

James looked at Frank and answered with what information he knew.

'She was found hanging from this tree by five of her school friends. The newspaper reports said that she had fallen out with her boyfriend who left town just before she was found hanging here.'

There was a cold breeze that moved through the tree, making the branches creak. Out on the branch that the girl hung from, the woman reappeared.

Paula suddenly sat up and began speaking—but not in her own voice.

'The truth, the truth they hide the truth.'

All three of the boys turned and looked at her with wide eyes.

'Paula, what are you talking about?' Toby asked.

'They stood and watched,' she growled.

Paula then began to shake. Her eyes rolled back, revealing only the whites of her eyes.

'She's having a seizure!' Frank said.

Paula suddenly stood up, her eyes still white over and her body shaking.

Toby stood up on the thick branch he was sat on with the two others and went to grab her before she fell, but he was too late. She shot from the branch she was standing on and out amongst the smaller branches. They scratched at her already bloody face as she moved through them like a rag doll. She came to a stop next to the girl who continued to sway gently from her noose. Paula hung in the air, her head bowed and motionless.

The three boys quickly moved to the other side of the tree where they could see her. Toby felt an electric shock run through his body the moment he saw Paula floating mid-air with the woman in white floating opposite her. Frank and James froze, their eyes fixed on the woman.

Toby quickly climbed down from the tree and ran over to where Paula floated. He jumped up and grabbed at her legs, hoping to pull her down from whatever was holding her there but he just ended up swinging back and forth from her. He let go and turned his attention to the woman. He jumped at her and grabbed her legs. The moment he touched her, he was knocked flying by an invisible force. He landed heavily in the dark dirt below him, all the air in his lungs escaping. He choked as his lungs tried to fill once more, the now dusty air making him cough.

The woman looked at Paula, her eyes widening as the evil smile grew on her face. She raised her hand to

Paula's stomach and began to push into her. The woman suddenly stopped, flickered and then disappeared. Paula fell to the ground, her legs buckling underneath her as she collapsed into herself on the floor. Toby rolled and then crawled the small distance to her and hugged her, his tears joining the blood and cuts of her face. She remained unconscious.

9

A set of car headlights approached the barn and the thick wall of fog that surrounded it. Its driver had done the same journey every year for the past six years, ever since Maggie Jackson had been appointed sheriff. She would always drive up and leave a single flower by the tree out in the field.

She had never encountered fog like this before. It seemed to start at the entrance to the field. It had a strange blue glow to it, and in places she swore she had seen dark shapes moving as she drove up the track. She put her fog lamps on, but the reflected light from the fog made it difficult to see so she shut them off and leaned forward, straining to see the edge of the dirt track.

There was a loud, high-pitched scraping sound along the passenger side of the police car. She cursed, wondering if she had strayed from the track and driven into the barbed wire fence that separated the track and the field. She stopped the car and stepped out. She turned her flashlight on and shone it into the fog. The beam did little to penetrate the thick wall of smoke. She walked around to the side of the car and inspected it. She noticed she was nowhere near the edge of the path, yet there was a long deep scratch that started by the headlight all the way along the side of the car to the tail light.

She felt a cold breeze against her neck, almost like someone had breathed on her. She turned and pointed the flashlight back into the fog, moving it side to side but nothing was there. She felt uneasy, like she was being watched. She placed her hand on her side firearm and slowly moved back around the car to the open driver's side door. She sat into the car seat and reached out to pull the door shut, and that's when she heard the screams. She paused, not sure if she was imagining it, but they came again, along with dull thuds and what seemed like muffled gunshots. She pulled hard on the door slamming it shut, put the car into gear and began accelerating. She turned on the police lights and drove purposely ahead. She knew that at the end of the track was a large barn. That is where she always parked her car and walked the last bit to the tree, but the now swirling and bluish pulsing fog masked all trace of the large building.

Sheriff Jackson slowed her approach. She was sure that she was near the barn, but the lack of visual stimulus made the distance she had driven seem longer than she really had. She stopped the car and pressed the button for the door window to lower. As soon as the window left its seal, she could hear the screams of teenagers and muffled gun shots. She grabbed the radio and called in her location.

'Judy are you receiving me?' she said into the CB radio microphone.

There was a moment of silence and then a response.

'Yes Sheriff Jackson, receiving you,' the voice answered.

'Do we have any other reports of fireworks or gunfire out on the farm road area?'

'That's a negative sheriff, although we have had several calls from worried parents about their teenage sons and daughters not being home,' the dispatcher's voice said.

The sheriff leaned forward and peered into the fog once more and then spoke into the radio once again.

'Yeah well, I'm over at the old farm, and it sounds like the so-called missing teenagers are over here, doing what I have no idea.'

'Roger that sheriff, do you need back up?' the voice asked.

'Erm, no. Keep all cars on the streets to stop any vandalism,' Sheriff Jackson replied.

Sheriff Jackson returned the door window back to its original up position and prepared to get out of the car. Something caught her eye in the rear view mirror. She did a double take and gasped. She recognized the face of the dark-haired woman sitting in her back seat. The sheriff fumbled for the door handle, panic and fear causing her to lose grip and then snatch at the handle before finally levering it open. She stumbled out of the car, drawing her gun as she stumbled to the floor, she stood and pointed it at the car; she could still see the woman sitting in the back seat. She moved around to the front of the car, the headlights of the car casting her shadow against the thick wall of fog behind her.

'Do you think this is some kind of joke?' she shouted, her gun shaking in her hands.

'Get the fuck out of the car, now!'

The woman dully obliged by disappearing. The sudden vanishing caused her to gasp and step back. She felt something behind her and froze. She slowly looked over her shoulder, her gun still pointing at the car. When she saw the woman standing behind her, she lurched forward. She spun and landed on the hood of the car. She pointed the gun at the woman and pulled the trigger. In that moment of panic and fear, she was still aware of the strange muffled sound that her gun made as it fired. It was as if she were firing under water. The two bullets she fired hit the woman, but she didn't flinch, she just stood staring with her black eyes and the sinister smile etched across her face. Both bullets had hit her in the body, but no marks were left on the perfect white dress.

Sheriff Jackson continued to lean against the car, and the gun in her hands shook violently. Her eyes were wide and beginning to fill with tears. She couldn't move; fear had rooted her to the spot. She felt heavy—too heavy to move herself. The woman in white moved towards her and then stopped as two skeletal civil war soldiers appeared from the fog. They looked at the woman in the white dress and then at the other leaning against the car. Their jaw bones twitched as they looked back and forth at the two women. One of them raised his musket up to the woman in white and pulled the trigger. She opened her mouth as if to scream but no sound came out. The skeletal figures began to shake, dropping their weapons before beginning to crumble into fine dust that joined the fog around them.

Sheriff Jackson remained frozen against the car throughout the brief spectral exchange. She was so paralyzed by fear she didn't even notice the warm wetness of her leg and trousers as she lost control of her bodily functions and peed herself.

The woman in white then bridged the gap between them and pushed her body against the sheriff's. She sniffed the face of the lawwoman before placing her hands around her throat.

'I'm sorry. I'm so sorry,' Sheriff Jackson whispered.

Her head then began to buzz before a voice, a voice she remembered, filled her head.

'You are one of them; you did this to me.'

The sheriff answered back through a broken emotional voice. 'It was Jenny; I was just there.'

The voice filled her head again.

'You hounded me, you beat me: you are all to blame for what you did.'

The woman in white then began to squeeze the sheriff's throat. She squeezed until she could feel her body becoming limp and then released her grip. Sheriff Jackson began to cough and gasp, trying to get as much oxygen into her lungs as possible.

The woman then placed her open hand against the sheriff's stomach and pushed. The hand disappeared into the sheriff. She moaned as she felt the burning sensation as it drove through her skin and deep into her stomach. Her eyes widened and she looked down to see the arm sticking out of a wound that pulsed with blood. The woman in white closed her hand around the intestines and pulled back. She held the bloody hand and intestines in front of the sheriff so she could see before dropping them to the floor. The sheriff slid down the front of the car, sitting in her own intestines and blood until finally her heart gave in and she slumped sideways to the dirt road.

10

Out in the field, skeletal soldiers continued their battle, trapped in a constant loop of killing and fighting, occasionally finding cowering teenagers and killing them, not able to differentiate them from oppositional spies and runaway soldiers. They did what they had been told to do: leave no survivors.

The teenagers in the barn continued to cower and hide amongst the objects scattered around the old barn. A small group huddled together trying to figure out a way to escape. They had decided their best option was to try and wait it out until daylight. Someone had asked why then and received the classic response.

'Well you don't see ghosts and undead in the daytime.'

Several of the group nodded.

'But what about that woman,' one of the girls asked.

They all looked around the room; they hadn't seen her for some time.

'Let's stay together and keep away from the walls,' one of the boys said confidently.

Just as he said that, the barn door flew open. The wooden lock could no longer hold back the supernatural energy that pushed against it. The fog no longer stood behind its invisible wall; it cascaded into the barn, quickly filling the room. The teenagers screamed and began running around in blind panic, not being helped by the increasing fog and the bodies that lay on the floor tripping them up. Even some of the small group who had huddled together ran away. One girl ran, looking over her shoulder. She ran straight onto the old rusty spikes of a farm machine, the spikes running straight through her, pinning her to the rusted machine.

Deep within the fog, the skeletal soldiers moved around the barn. Screams, moans and muffled gunshots echoed around the fog-filled wooden structure as one after another teenagers succumbed to bayonets and musket shots. The small group that had stayed together in the center of the barn moved in unison. They pushed their backs against each other, watching for any sign of movement in the fog.

They began moving back towards where they believed the open door was, the fog now so dense that it was hard to see more than a few feet in front of them, especially in the poor light cast by the flashing light and the dim spot lights that had been placed around the barn. Two of the group jumped with fright as a dark shadow moved towards them. Out of the fog, the older teenager fell, bumping into them. Behind him, holding his hand, was one of the girls who had spent so long trying to impress him. No one said a word; they all just continued to move in the direction of the door.

When they finally reached the open doorway, finding it made easier by the blast of cold air blowing through it, they pushed and pulled each other through. The fog continued to blanket everything.

The group stayed together and they continued their huddled movement across the dirt tracks. The older teenager broke away from them and dragged his female companion behind him into the fog. He didn't know where he was going, but anywhere was better than in the barn. The girl he held onto gripped his hand tight. He could hear her sniffling as she continued to cry.

The girl suddenly became heavy to pull along, her grip no longer tight but limp. He stopped and looked at her. She stood looking at him with a blank expression. She then fell forward past him and disappeared into the fog below him. He still held her hand. Where she had stood was a skeletal soldier, his toothy grin chattering away as if laughing. Its musket and bayonet that had been plunged into the girl pointed at him, and a dark liquid dripped from its end.

In a fear-fuelled rage, he knocked the musket out of the way and ran his forearm into the soldiers face. The head of the skeletal figure popped off its connective attachment and disappeared into the fog. The body stood motionless, frozen in the same position. The teenager backed away. Tears filled his eyes, his breathing heavy, causing his chest to rise and fall rapidly.

The bayonet then shot forward and into his face. The blade entered through the boy's eye socket and exited through the back of his skull with a crack.

The small group of huddled friends moved through the fog, pausing whenever they heard the sound of a footprint or saw a shadow move within the fog. A faint sound caught the attention of one of the boys, who held out his arms and stopped the group.

'Can you hear that?' he asked, whispering just enough to be heard. His friend looked at him with concern and then listened.

There was a strange crackling sound and then a voice spoke before the crackling sound began again.

They looked at each other, realizing that what they were hearing was a radio CB. They began moving the group towards the crackling static and voice until they saw the two beams of light and then the car itself, although they could only make out the headlights and everything above. The fog seemed to be even thicker below their knees. The driver's side door was open, allowing them to hear the person on the other end call for a response.

'Hey the cops are here,' one of the girls said with an element of relief in her voice.

One of the girls decided to stand in the light. She moved to the front of the car and kicked something at her feet. She looked down and noticed she wasn't touching the car. She kicked out her leg again. Whatever it was it had a strange soft texture to it.

'Mike, can you come here please,' she called.

The boy who had first heard the car radio looked up at her from peering into the car through the open door. He walked over to her and asked what was wrong. She explained that there was something at her feet in front of the car that felt a little strange. He looked down as she told him, unable to see anything. He reached down and put his hand into the thick swirling fog. His hand touched what the girl had been kicking against and could feel some kind of fur. He wrapped his hand around it and pulled. It was heavy, so he grabbed it with his other hand and pulled harder. The face and wide eyes of the sheriff appeared from the thick river of fog. He let go straight away.

The radio crackled again. 'Sheriff come in.'

Mike moved back to the open door and picked up the radio mic, squeezed the side button and spoke into it.

'Hello.'

The voice responded immediately.

'Who is this?'

'My name is Mike Tanner, we need help. Please send help.'

'Ok Mike, where is the sheriff?' the voice on the other end asked.

After a brief pause, he answered. 'She's dead.'

The others in the group who had gathered around the open door all looked at him.

'What do you mean dead?' the voice shouted back.

'She has been killed.' He began to cry.

'By whom?' the voice asked. He could tell the other person was struggling to keep their emotions under control.

'We don't know. We need help,' he said in response.

The voice answered quickly telling him that there were other officers on their way and not to move from the car. The group of teenagers looked around them at the thick fog, the headlights throwing up a wall of light that encased them, the beams of light unable to penetrate the dense wall. One by one they pushed themselves into the safety of the car and shut the doors.=

11

Toby held Paula tight. He didn't care about what was moving around in the fog, the screams or the woman in white. She could appear and try and take Paula, but he was willing to give his life in protecting her.

'Hey, get back up here,' Frank called from the tree.

Toby ignored him.

Paula's eyes flickered and then slowly opened. Toby took a sharp intake of breath. His eyes widened and a smile broke onto his dirty face.

'Oh baby, its ok I'm here,' he said gently.

She looked up at him. For a moment, she stared into his smiling face and then her expression changed to one of horror.

'What? What's wrong?' Toby asked, his smile fading and being replaced by concern.

'She won't stop until she has had her revenge.'

Toby looked at her. 'What do you mean?'

'She showed me what they did to her,' Paula said before beginning to cry.

'Who?' Toby asked sharply.

In between her sobs she answered, the words sending a shiver down his spine.

'Our parents, our parents were the ones who killed her.'

Toby pulled her close and hugged her until he heard the two boys in the tree call to him to move. He looked at them and then in the direction they were pointing.

He looked at the figure standing in the clearing. It wasn't a skeletal soldier or the woman in white but a pale-looking male figure in a leather jacket. He looked harder and recognized Baron. He lived a few houses down from him.

'What the fuck is going on?' he asked aggressively.

'I got lost on the way up here, but have seen some strange shit! Dead people and skeletons walking around and, oh my god who is that?' he said, looking at the disemboweled girl hanging from the tree.

'Get away from the fog,' James called.

Baron looked back at the wall of fog and moved quickly over to Toby and Paula.

As he walked across the dirt, he noticed the Ouija board on the floor, the glass pointer spinning in its center.

'Who brought this over here?' he said, pointing at it.

'Erm, we did,' Frank said sheepishly.

'You dumb shits!' Baron returned. 'You've opened a gateway for all those that have been trapped here to walk on the earth again.'

Toby looked up at Baron and raised an eyebrow. 'What, seriously?'

Baron looked a down at him, 'Think about it, it's Halloween and everyone knows about all the death that happened around here during the civil war.'

'But what about the woman?' Frank asked.

Baron paused and looked at him confused. 'What woman?'

Paula then began talking, telling her the visions that she saw when the woman in white had taken control over her.

12

Tina walked to school on her own every day. She was the outcast. She dressed different to all the others in her class, partly due to the lack of money to buy the latest fashionable clothing and her liking of heavy metal music. She was used to being the new student. This was the fifth school and town she and her mother had moved to in the last twelve months. Her abusive father always seemed to find them, forcing them to leave in the dead of night and run to the next town.

She was stared at constantly, remarks were made endlessly, small groups of girls whispered as she got changed in the changing rooms for phys. ed., comments on her scars and burn marks on her upper thighs from where her father had put his cigarettes out to teach her a lesson.

One group of girls was worse than all the others; the cheerleaders were the cruelest of all the groups, often hiding her clothes or putting them in the shower to get soaked, only to laugh at her and comment on how they needed to be washed.

They had locked her in rooms, barged past her, knocking her books to the floor several times and written notes about her and passed them around classes. She endured the sniggers, finger-pointing and rumors for several weeks.

Even though the other kids didn't like her and school was hard, she was glad that she and her mother had stopped looking over their shoulders after her father had been arrested for assaulting a woman who had refused his advances at a bar some twenty miles away.

One afternoon, she was on the end of another malicious bullying attack by the cheerleaders, being pushed around the corridor as she tried to walk past. Other students stopped and laughed as she was sent crashing to the floor. After the lead cheerleader stuck her leg out and tripped her over. Her books flying everywhere; some were kicked further down the corridor by one of the group who had always been the quieter, less-bullying girl.

The bell rang for the start of the next lesson and the corridor soon became deserted. The gang of girls walked past Tina, who lay on her back looking up at them.

'Don't stay down there, you are making the place look untidy, bitch,' Mandy, the lead cheerleader said, looking down at Tina before moving on with the others who looked at her and laughed.

Tina lay there asking herself what she had done to them to make them treat her like that. She sat up and looked around at her books scattered on the corridor floor. She heard footsteps and turned to see a boy dressed in jeans, a white T-Shirt and denim shirt bend down and pick up two of her books before crouching down next to her.

'Hey, are you ok?' he said softly.

She sat just looking at him. She was prepared for him to say something hurtful or throw the books he had picked up further down the corridor because that's what everyone else in the school would have done. But he didn't, and that amazed her.

'Let me help you,' he said, placing her books in one hand and holding out his free hand. She took it and he pulled her up onto her feet. He then continued to pick her books up. She stood and just watched. This was the nicest thing anyone had ever done. He returned with all her books tucked under his arm.

'I'm sorry about what the girl's did,' he said.

She shyly shrugged her shoulders and bowed her head. She could feel the nervousness building in her stomach.

'What lesson you got now?' he asked.

'Chemistry,' she replied quietly.

'Come on, I'm going to that part of the building. I'll walk you there,' he said.

They walked down the corridor together, the boy introducing himself as Thomas, 'T' to his friends. She told him her name and he smiled.

'I guess I'll call you T as well.'

She smiled, for the first time since arriving in town she felt a sense of happiness.

Over the next few weeks, the girls continued to berate her and bully her. Some of the boys had begun to get into the act until Thomas stopped them. He was, after all, the school star quarterback. He wasn't like the other jocks; he was intelligent and wanted to go on to study medicine.

The girls had seen them together, talking, Tina laughing and flirtingly stoking his arm. Mandy's anger grew within her. She had been trying to get his attention for the last year and believed that being the top cheerleader, she should be the only one that the school quarterback should date. Whenever she tried to flirt or get his attention by cornering him at his locker, he politely smiled and made an excuse before moving on. The other girls in her little gang agreed with her that they should be dating and went out of their way to try and get them alone, with many of the other girls also dating football players.

The grief Tina got from the girls became something she could block out. She began to look forward to coming to school, just to see Thomas. It made all the hurtful things and bullying mean nothing.

Thomas had begun to spend more and more time with Tina, often going over to hers to study together, walking her home if she missed the school bus and even spending Saturdays at the ice cream parlor in town.

They had been seen by a few of the cheerleaders who had told Mandy straight away. Mandy sat at home, jealousy burning within her, her hate for Tina becoming overpowering.

Over the following weeks, things began to change for Tina. The cheerleaders began to ease off her. They even began to smile at her when they saw her in the corridors. She thought that Thomas had said something to them.

In reality, Mandy was conducting her great plan. She was not going to lose the boy she wanted to the new girl; she was going to make Tina pay for taking him away from her.

Life both in and out of school was easier. The cheerleaders seemed to want to get to know her. The pain and fear of going to school had begun to disappear as she finally felt accepted. Her mother had secured a job at an out of town diner; she was finally happy. Tina was also happily in love with Thomas. The friendly hug had soon become a kiss on the cheek and then the romantic film cliché of staring into each other's eyes, smiling at each other as their lips met. This had progressed to fondling each other and then, one Saturday afternoon, while her mother was out, her first sexual experience.

The cheerleaders began slowly including Tina in their conversations when they all got changed for and after phys. ed. lessons.

'What you think Tina?' Mandy asked her as she put her new bra on, cupping her breasts and smiling at her.

Tina looked up from re-lacing her boots and just nodded.

The group of girls looked at each other and smiled.

'Hey Tina, do you have any other clothes that aren't black or grey?' one of the cheerleaders asked.

Tina looked up again and shook her head.

'When's your birthday Tina?' another of the girls asked.

'Next month,' she replied quietly.

'Oh really, when? We should do something,' Mandy said excitedly. The excitement wasn't because of Tina's birthday but for what she had already planned.

Tina looked up at the group of girls, all of whom seemed to be excited and discussing what they should all go and do.

Today was a bad day. She had spent the last few weeks worrying, even to the point that she had called off dates with Thomas, saying she wasn't well.

As her birthday approached, she began to revert to her shy lonely self. Thomas had tried to persuade her to tell him what was wrong, but she kept saying nothing. He spoke to the cheerleaders, warning them to leave her alone, but they just said that they were all friends and planning to go out for her birthday.

He walked her home after one of his football practices, happy that she had decided to stay and watch. They walked, Tina hugging her books close to her chest. He asked what was wrong. She stopped looked up at him and sighed, tears beginning to run down her face.

Mandy had noticed the distance between Tina and Thomas and laughed; they had split up or were not talking. This was her chance. She had her plan in place. Saturday morning she was going to trick Thomas to the old farm and force herself on him. It would be easier now that Tina was out of the picture. Then all the girls were going to take Tina out and build her up with a false sense of security before taking her over to the farm and telling what had happened between her and Thomas. She had even brought a length of rope as a joke that she was going to fashion into a noose and place it around her neck. They were going to make Tina's birthday one she'd never forget. Just thinking about it made Mandy smile more.

Thomas received a letter, slipped through the side of his locker door. He looked at the light blue envelope carefully. He looked around him at the other students who passed him in the corridor or stood in small groups chatting.

He smiled briefly. 'Tina,' he said to himself before moving his head further into his locker and sniffing the envelope. It didn't smell like the perfume that Tina wore: the one he had become used to and the one he identified with her. But he had no reason to think that the envelope he held in his hand was from anyone else. He opened the envelope and unfolded the piece of paper inside. He expected to see Tina's handwriting but was met by a typed letter. He began reading it, occasionally looking behind him to make sure that none of his friends were standing behind him reading it over his shoulder.

Dear sweetest Thomas,

I know things have been difficult recently but I do love you and want to see you this Saturday. You are the only birthday present that I want.

I know you were planning to go out with your friends Saturday night, after all it is Halloween. I would love to see you during the afternoon.

I want to make my special day even more special by spending part of it with you.

Meet me at the old farm on the outskirts of town at 1pm.

Love you.

Tina

xxxxxx

Thomas smiled as her read the letter, since they had last seen each other and she had told him she no longer wanted to see him, he had felt so helpless. He really didn't care about going out with rest of the football team Halloween night. All they ever did was throw toilet paper over the police station and dress up the town's statues. He wanted to spend Saturday with Tina. One thing that played on his mind was the location of the meeting: the old farm. Why not his or her house?

He hadn't seen her for the last few days and worried about her. He had called round, but no one answered. He read the note again before replacing it in the envelope with a smile. He placed it in the back of his locker and paused, looking at it briefly before the bell rang out to signal the need for all students to begin moving to their next lesson.

From down the corridor, the group of cheerleaders huddled together. Each took it in turns to watch his reaction and feedback to Mandy, who stood with her back against the wall. When one had begun reporting what she had seen, another began looking.

Mandy had already shared with the group what she had brought for Tina. She had found an old white dress in a charity shop in town.

'The bitch is cheap and nasty, so she deserves cheap shit clothing,' she said to the others with venom in her voice.

The group of girls had arranged to meet Tina at the ice cream parlor at three Saturday afternoon before moving on to implement the rest of Mandy's plan.

Tina had avoided Thomas. She had not attended school in the last few days because she had been feeling unwell. Her mother had noticed that Thomas, who she had liked, had not been around recently and attested her daughter's illness to her falling out with him.

She sat in her room on her bed and rubbed her stomach, her mind full of questions. She didn't want to tell her mother, she couldn't tell Thomas and her birthday was only two days away and she was meant to be meeting the group of girls she had become friends with. Maybe she could talk to them? But then her head quickly threw that idea away; memories of how they treated her because she was different raced back into her head.

13

Saturday morning Thomas woke excited. Today was the day he got to meet with Tina. He spent longer than normal in the bathroom, causing his mother to knock on the door to see if he was alright.

He had showered, played with his hair, trying different styles. He wanted to make an impression. Today meant the world to him. He sat in his room watching the clock, every second feeling like a minute, every minute an hour, every hour dragging its heels.

He decided to leave early and walk slowly to the farm. He ran through in his head what he wanted to say and at times found that he was talking to himself.

He walked up the dirt path, the chill in the air forcing him to pull his leather jacket tighter and zip it higher. He reached the large old barn. The fields that surrounded him were full of old dead corn. He looked at the brown dead stalks and remembered the stories around town about the field of corn that never tasted right because of all the death that happened in the fields during the civil war.

He stood outside the barn and looked around. He checked his silver Casio digital watch. The grey and black digital display showed 12:56 pm. He then heard a door open. He turned around and saw Mandy standing in the old barn doorway in just her underwear, her white bra and panties standing out against the darkness of the interior of the barn.

'Hey Thomas, glad you came,' she said provocatively.

Thomas stood staring at her, confusion etched on his face.

'What's going on? Where's Tina?' he asked.

The cold air bit into Mandy, her skin mottled with different shades of red, pink, light blue and whites from the cold. It made her skin dimple with goose bumps but she felt only the heat of her excitement.

When he mentioned Tina, anger began to build within her.

'You don't want that cheap weirdo,' she answered back.

Thomas' face began to show more anger. He was angry that he had been fooled.

'Everyone knows that the head cheerleader and the school star football player should be dating,' Mandy said.

'I don't want you! You are everything that I don't like about school sport. Tina is different. She's smart and not false like you,' Thomas said.

The words that he said cut deep into Mandy. The anger that she felt for Tina was now unbearable, and she could feel hate for him. She looked down at herself. Suddenly she felt the cold.

'I've come here to show you that we are meant to be together, I'll give you whatever you want. You can take me now,' Mandy said, her voice showing signs of anger.

Thomas shook his head and turned away. He began walking away. Mandy's eyes widened as he turned his back on her. She looked around and saw a large stone not far from where she was standing. She moved to it picked it up and ran towards Thomas. He didn't hear her approaching but felt a sudden dull impact on the back of his head. His vision wobbled. He tried to refocus but found everything appearing fuzzy. He turned and saw Mandy, her hand was raised above her head. She held something in it but he couldn't make out what it was. She brought the stone down on his head once again. Her anger grew; it never subsided. She continued to hit him across the head even after he had fallen to the floor. She straddled him and pounded the stone into his face. Even the spray of blood and the feel of the warm liquid running down her arms didn't stop her.

When she did finally stop, her heavy breathing clouding in the cold air, his face was a dark, bloody cavernous mess. His legs twitched as his nervous system continued to fire. She dropped the stone and stood, the anger on her face almost becoming an evil grin.

She looked around and walked calmly back to the barn and put on her clothes. She looked around the barn and noticed an old shovel in the dim light. Once dressed, she returned to Thomas and began dragging his body past the barn and into the corn field. She cursed as he got caught against some of the stalks. She cursed more and kicked his body. When exhausted, she stopped and realized she was covered in sweat.

'I offer my body to you and you turn me down, and now you're making me get dirty and sweaty,' she said angrily.

She returned to the barn and grabbed the shovel. She dragged it behind her, its rusted blade chinking as it slid over the rocks in the loose dusty soil.

She dug a hole and dragged his body into it. She looked at his watch to check the time and smiled. She still had time to get back, get changed and meet the others. Her anger was now excitement. She was excited because of the thought of Tina suffering. She felt no remorse for what she had just done; she felt empowered.

Tina walked slowly into town. She didn't want to stay in any longer, but she was also really not up for socializing with the giggling group of girls. She knew if she blew off the girls it would mean going back to them giving her grief, so she was willing to endure the afternoon.

She saw the others sitting next to the window. They were deep in conversation. When they saw her they waved. She smiled and entered. They all moved up so she could get onto the large red single seat that wrapped round the table. They clapped and sang happy birthday, and Mandy handed her a small present wrapped in paper that had jack-o-lanterns on it.

'Sorry about the paper, but it is also Halloween,' Mandy said.

They urged her to open the present, which she did. For that brief moment, she had forgotten about her problems. When she removed the white dress, her secret crashed back to the forefront of her mind.

'What's the matter? Don't you like it?' Mandy asked.

'Er no, it's nice,' Tina responded.

Two of the girls grabbed her hands and pulled her off the seat.

'Come on let's go and try it on,' the one said, wrapping her arm around Tina's.

Tina looked at her with surprise. 'Where?' she asked.

'In the restroom, you got to put it on,' the other said, wrapping her arm around Tina's other arm and walking her into the restroom. They stood and watched as she took off her faded black jeans and Iron Maiden T-shirt and then pulled on the dress.

Back at the table, Mandy recalled to the others how she had seduced Thomas, letting him do whatever he wanted. The other girls asked for details to which Mandy was happy to give.

'He bent me over a hay bale in the old barn and took me from behind. It was so nice,' she said, her imagination creating the images for her, playing them in her mind like a movie.

In the restroom, one of the girls gathered up her clothes and walked out back to the others. The remaining cheerleader helped Tina do up the small zip on the back of the dress and then led her back to the table, where she was met with claps and whistles.

Tina sat down. She had not worn a dress since she was six and felt a little uncomfortable.

They all sat chatting away, the cheerleaders looking at each other, smiling and laughing every now and then. For some unknown reason that bewildered Tina.

Once they had finished the ice creams, the group of girls led Tina out of the parlor and up out of town. Tina had asked where they were going several times and was told not to worry; it was her second present.

They arrived at the dirt road that led up to the old farm. Tina looked at the dead stalks and felt a chill run through her.

'Why are we here?' she asked the group, but they didn't answer.

They walked up to the barn. Mandy made sure she avoided walking near the damp slightly red dirt where she had beaten Thomas earlier.

They walked over to the barn door and Mandy opened it. They walked in one by one, the cheerleaders giggling to each other as they entered.

Tina stepped into the dimly lit space and looked at the group of girls who now stood in a curved line in front of her.

'So?' Tina said, shrugging her shoulders.

Mandy laughed, followed by the other girls.

'Well you see tramp,' Mandy began, 'earlier today, me and your boyfriend met in this very place.'

Tina could feel her heart sink. Her stomach suddenly made her feel sick.

'What you saying?' Tina asked.

'He couldn't keep his hands off me. He made love to me in here,' Mandy continued, enjoying seeing Tina become uncomfortable.

Tina turned and moved towards the open door but felt her hair being yanked back. She reached up and clawed at the hands that had clamped around her hair. She recognized the voice as it cursed. Mandy had grabbed her and was pulling her back deeper into the barn. Tina lost her balance and fell backwards onto her backside; the hands that grabbed her never let go. She found herself being dragged across the floor. When Mandy did let go of Tina's hair, she walked around her as she lay on the floor, giving details of what Thomas had done to her. The other girls gathered around and laughed at her.

The tears poured from her face. She watched as Mandy prowled around. Once she had finished telling her story of her and Thomas, she then began shouting insults at her.

'You think you can come to this town and take the best looking boy from me?' Mandy shouted before bending down and pulling Tina's hair back.

Tina was forced to look into the face of Mandy, who moved in nose to nose with her and shouted at Tina. Mandy let go quickly of Tina's hair, causing her head to fall forward. Mandy slapped Tina hard across the face. The other girls all laughed and began kicking dirt and hay that lay on the barn floor over Tina.

Mandy slapped Tina again and again. Tina's face became red to purple in color. Soon, the dirt-kicking girls began kicking Tina, first in the legs and then in her back. Each time Tina tried to crawl away from the attacking crowd, she was yanked back by the hair.

Mandy moved past the group of kicking girls and walked over to a bag that had been sitting on an old wooden crate. She reached behind it and pulled out a length of rope and returned to Tina.

One of the girls saw Mandy with the rope and stopped the kicking.

'What are you doing?' she asked Mandy.

Mandy looked at the smaller blonde cheerleader and sneered at her.

'You are either with us or against us. If you want to join the bitch on the floor then fine,' Mandy snapped.

The young girl looked at Mandy, shock and fear etched on her face. She didn't want to be on the wrong side of Mandy and the others.

Mandy pulled the noose over Tina and pulled the rope tight. The other girls stopped their onslaught. Mandy then began dragging Tina back towards the door. Some of the girls laughed and began barking.

'That's it bitch, go for a walk,' one of the others shouted.

Mandy dragged Tina along the floor until she finally managed to get to her feet and relieve some of the pressure from the rope. Mandy continued to pull Tina out of the barn and down a small dirt road surrounded by the dead corn until they reached a large tree. Tina fell to the floor again, coughing and gasping for air. Mandy looked at the other girls and smiled.

'I'm going to make sure she gets the message. You lot start heading back; I will catch you up,' Mandy said.

The other girls nodded and began walking away.

Mandy turned her attention back on Tina. She grabbed the rope and threw the one end over a large overhanging branch. She threw it over again and then began to pull. The rope tightened again around Tina's throat. Mandy could feel the excitement of watching her suffer and soon she was winching Tina off the floor. Tina's legs began kicking thin air as she struggled against the rope. She could feel her life ebbing away.

Mandy pulled again on the rope and Tina's body jerked higher. Mandy watched until Tina had stopped kicking and then let go. Tina began falling to the floor, but the rope suddenly snagged on a small protrusion on the branch it was wrapped around. Tina's descent to the floor jerked to a halt, and her legs collapsed below her. Mandy looked at her body, limp and swaying gently, Tina's legs acting like an anchor. She walked over to Tina, knelt down and whispered into her ear.

'Thomas never did anything. He didn't want me. He wanted you, you dirty bitch, so I killed him because if I can't have him no one will.'

Those were the last words that Tina heard before her life ended.

Mandy ran and caught up with the others. She ran towards them shouting.

'She's killed herself. She's killed herself.'

The others stopped and looked at Mandy,

'She became crazy and hung herself, I tried to stop her but she climbed the tree, wrapped the rope around a branch and jumped.' Mandy said with tears running down her face.

The group of girls ran back up the path to the tree and saw Tina hanging, her legs limp underneath her.

'Oh my god what do we do?' one of the girls shouted.

Mandy looked at all the girls and began to explain what they should all say. If they told the same story then they would never be accused.

They nodded and began their journey back to town. When they came across a phone booth, they called the police, who met them up at the farm. They stood by the barn and gave their statements, each one identical. They had come over as a Halloween dare after celebrating their friend's birthday in town, Tina had recently been dumped by her boyfriend who had left town.

The town's sheriff and his deputy's looked around and found nothing else. The story that the girls had given seemed rock solid. It was an unfortunate love-sick suicide. They looked into Tina's and her Mothers past when they delivered the news to her mother. She blamed herself, especially when the autopsy found she was pregnant. The local newspaper ran the story of a heartbroken teenage girl, pregnant and abandoned by her boyfriend, committing suicide.

When the other girls read the article and saw that Tina was pregnant, all but one felt sick and guilty. Mandy just smiled, when she was asked about when she saw Thomas last, she just kept up the pretense of having sex with him that morning and that was the last she saw of him.

Tina's body was taken back to where she was born and buried next to her grandparents. Her mother never returned to the town.

The cheerleaders never left town. They dated and married other local boys and football players, becoming well to do stay at home mothers, all except one who chased a dream of becoming a police officer. When she did, she worked her way up the ladder until finally she became the town sheriff. Even though she knew what punishment and cruelty she and the others had done to Tina all those years ago, she was still afraid of Mandy.

They met regularly, Mandy organizing drinks and evenings together. She bossed her husband around something rotten. Some of the others couldn't believe how she treated him. She kept her daughter under a tight leash. They all attended church on Sundays with Mandy being one of the church leaders. It was the power she liked; being part of the church gave her certain powers over the townsfolk. She was well known for reciting scripture and verse freely when she needed to control a situation. The others attended church, some not really wanting, to but that was also an order from Mandy.

A few of the other ex-cheerleaders lit a candle each year in memory of a girl who committed suicide on her birthday. All but Mandy felt the guilt of that day. The sheriff still drove over each Halloween and placed flowers by the tree.

14

Mandy had ordered her husband to call the police and tell them that their daughter had not returned home. When he put the phone down and told his wife that the officer had said that several others had also called worried about their sons and daughters whereabouts and that she was sure that they were all fine and to call again in an hour if she had not turned up, Mandy released a torrent of abuse at him. She picked up the phone and called the police station. Her husband sat down quietly and listened to her shout at the person on the other end.

'I don't care about anybody else's sons or daughters, I want mine found and brought back home now. You get on the radio and tell the sheriff that Mandy wants her to find her daughter,' she shouted down the phone before slamming it down.

She stood by the window and stared out into the dark streets, the street lamps illuminating small areas along the sidewalk. The much larger trees cast darker shadows, reducing the lamps' effectiveness.

She heard a siren break the calmness of the night and then saw the red and blue flashing bounce from house front to house front as the car approached and then sped past, followed by another. Mandy could feel something was not right. There was something eating at her; this wasn't normal. She ordered her husband to get in the car. She placed the key in the ignition, pulled the gear stick into drive and then slammed her foot down on the accelerator. The car shot off the drive and turned sharply to follow the two police cars disappearing in the distance. Her husband sat in the passenger seat gripping the handle above the door with both hands, his knuckles white with pressure as he held on. He looked at his wife's face. Her expression of anger told him not to speak. He had seen this look several times before, and when he had tried to speak to her, she had become so angry she had attacked him, punching him in the face, on occasions leaving him with a black eye.

Baron's parents heard the screeching of tires and sirens and watched as the two police cars drove past. They looked at each other and then heard another car, its engine screaming from the acceleration. They watched as Mandy's car flew past.

Baron's mother looked over her shoulder at the single candle burning on the mantelpiece. She gasped as it suddenly went out. She ran to the stairs, her husband close behind. She reached Baron's room and barged the door open. She fumbled along the wall for the light switch. When the light came on and she saw the room was empty, she screamed.

Her husband managed to catch her as she collapsed. He pulled her to their bedroom and placed her up onto the bed. She lay in a fetal position, crying hysterically. He left her and ran down the stairs, grabbing the car keys that hung on the hook by the side of the front door and began unlocking it. Once free from the numerous locks, which his wife had insisted on he, pulled open the door and ran to the car. He yanked the door open and dropped into the seat. He then pushed the key into the ignition and quickly turned the key and held it there until the old Volvo started. He reversed at speed off the drive, the tires screeching as he hit the brakes, put the car into drive and accelerated off in pursuit of the other cars.

He was in such a rush and panic he didn't even notice he was driving with no headlights on.

All four of the cars raced out of town and towards the old farm.

The teenagers hiding in the police car lay motionless. Even those who were being sat on had no desire to try and move to be in a more comfortable position. They jumped whenever they saw a shadow move past the car. Even the girls who had been crying uncontrollably had managed to stop, or at least had stopped the sounds of their crying; tears still flowed down their cheeks.

Mike Tanner lifted the radio to his mouth and quietly spoke into it.

'This is Mike Tanner, are the others on the way?

The radio was silent for a few seconds and then the voice on the other end replied, breaking the eerie silence of the car so much that the others began telling it to shush. Mike pulled the mic into his chest to muffle the sound.

'Officers are on the way. Do not move from your present location.'

There was a clanging sound and then a sharp, high-pitched screech as a bayonet was dragged along the side of the police car, followed by another on the other side. The occupants of the car fidgeted nervously and then the windows exploded in. Skeletal hands grabbed at the youngsters, who kicked out at them trying to beat them away.

One by one they were pulled from the car until only one was left. Mike pushed himself into the foot well of the passenger seat. The others continued to fight their bony abductors, their screams filling the cold night air. They were dragged deep into the swirling fog. The skeletal soldiers took it in turns to run their bayonets into the teenagers they had dragged from the car. Two of the girls found themselves looking into each other's eyes as several rusty bayonets plunged into their backs. Their wide eyes looked deep into the other as their life escaped them. One of the boys kicked out at the hand that held onto his ankle. He felt the floor change from rocky to leaf filled dirt; he realized he was being dragged into the corn fields and kicked harder. The soldier stopped, looked down at the kicking leg and raised his free arm. The saber he held in his hand came down and sank into the bone of the boys shin. He screamed, feeling the dull thud and then searing pain in his leg. The soldier raised the weapon again and hacked down again and again until the ankle he held came away from the rest of the leg. The soldier then walked to the boy's upper body and hacked at his head until it split in half diagonally from his left temple to the right side of his chin. Other screams filled the air until suddenly they stopped. All that was left was the thuds and bangs of gunfire.

Mike remained curled up, staring at the seat in front of him, his breathing more of a gasp.

15

Baron looked at Toby and then the two boys still sitting in the tree. Paula had finished telling them the visions that had filled her head, placed there by the woman when she had taken control over her.

'So what do we do?' Toby asked Baron.

Baron shrugged his shoulders and then looked back at the Ouija board and its pointer that continued to spin in the center.

'The board is the key. If we destroy the board then maybe that will close the gateway,' Baron said.

Frank and James looked at each other and nodded. They then looked back down at the three students below them and out at the board.

'Who's going to get it?' Frank asked nervously. He wasn't going to volunteer.

Baron looked at Toby and Paula and then up at the other two in the tree.

'I will help Toby get Paula up on her feet and support her,' he began. 'Who has a lighter?' he then asked.

Frank felt his heart sink; he knew he had the lighter in his pocket.

'I do,' he said disappointedly.

James began moving down the tree until he was able to hang low enough from a branch to drop down to the soil below. He looked at Frank and waved him down. Frank sighed and began moving himself onto the same branch that James had used to hang from. He lowered himself until he was hanging and then let go. He misjudged the distance and ended landing on the side of his right foot. His body weight forced his ankle to buckle and roll underneath him. Amongst the dull thuds and bangs of gun fire echoing around them, the sound of his groan as he tore the ligaments of his ankle made the others all look over at him. He collapsed in a heap on the dusty floor, clutching his ankle. He rolled back and forth, cursing between gasping for air and moans of pain.

'Can you not do anything right?' Baron said.

James bent down, his head still throbbing. Bending down to his friend added to the pressure and dull ache. He put his arm under Frank's armpit and hauled him up onto his one leg. He leaned against his friend, hopped a few times and wiped away the tears that had filled his eyes.

'You wait by the tree. I will go get the board,' James said to Frank, who nodded and hopped over to the tree trunk and leaned against it.

Baron watched as James slowly walked towards the Ouija board. He quickly looked away when he felt Paula become heavy and collapse. Still holding onto her, he and Toby dragged her over to the tree, where Frank stood, and sat her against the trunk.

James looked at the wall of fog, his slow walk stuttering each time he saw a shadow glide past within it. He reached the board and its spinning glass pointer and crouched down to pick it up. He didn't take his eyes off the wall of fog until he realized he was feeling around in the dirt and not feeling the board. He quickly looked down and grabbed the edges. He didn't want to touch the spinning pointer and picked up the board, keeping it flat, allowing the pointer to continue its spinning motion. He turned and began his slow walk back towards the tree and the others. He no longer cared about the fog; his attention was firmly fixed on the spinning glass pointer.

He managed to get within twenty feet of the tree and his friends when a dull thud sounded behind him. He felt like someone had poked him with a finger in the back, the sensation made him raise his eyebrows and look up from the board and at his friends. His legs suddenly buckled and he began to fall forward, a sudden searing pain raced from where he had felt the strange sensation on his back to his eyes. As he fell, he threw the board forward. The glass pointer never left the board as it flew several feet forward; it continued its spinning motion.

James fell heavily into the dirt, his arms slowing him down enough to stop his face crashing into the earth.

Frank saw his friend fall and for a moment all his pain had gone. He pushed away from the tree and steeped towards his friend but fell to the floor, pain filling his head as his swollen injured ankle gave way and he fell to the floor. He looked up from where he lay and saw a skeletal soldier walk from the wall of fog and towards James.

The soldier walked up to the injured boy, his back covered with a dark moist stain, grabbed his ankle and began dragging him back towards the fog. James could do nothing. He could not feel his legs and he was losing his strength to try and pull away from his abductor. He looked at his friends, tears filling his eyes as he was finally pulled into the wall of blue-tinged fog.

Frank lay in the dirt, tears streaming from his fear-filled wide eyes. Baron looked at Toby and then left them and ran to the Ouija board that lay on the floor, its pointer still spinning. He brought it back to where they sat under the tree, placed it down on the dirt and then helped Frank back up.

'Where's the lighter?' He asked.

Frank fumbled around in his pockets, not sure which one he had put it in. He reached into a small inside breast pocket and pulled it out. Baron snatched it from his hand, flipped the silver hood off the flint and lighter part and thumbed down hard on the circular part that caused the flint to spark. The flame jumped into life. Baron held it there for a second and looked at the Ouija board on the ground.

'We need something to help it catch alight,' he said, releasing his thumb from the lighter, extinguishing the flame.

Frank looked at him and then at Toby, who looked up from kissing Paula's forehead.

They both shrugged their shoulders. Baron then looked down at his T-shirt and began tearing off a section from where the seam began. He pulled the material until he had a long length of T-Shirt hanging from his hand. He reignited the lighter and held it under the dangling material, it began to burn with growing yellow flames. He then draped the burning material on to the board.

The flames flickered in the small breeze that swirled around them, the board began to darken where the flames ate into the surface. They watched as the Ouija board began to catch fire on the corner. The board hissed as it began to burn. Frank looked up at the wall of fog, hoping to see it disappear now that the board was burning, but it continued to swirl and pulse with the strange blue hue.

16

The police cars skidded into the dirt road of the farm. The officers stared wide eyed at the wall of fog ahead of them. They slowed their approach and put on the side searchlight, hoping to pick out anything that may be hidden within the dense swirling fog. The rear police car suddenly jerked forward, the officer being thrown forward. His seat belt snapping tight. He stopped the car and radioed to his colleague in front that he had just been hit by something and that he was going to check it out. The radio crackled and then a voice responded.

'Ten four, you need back up?'

The officer looked in is rear view mirror and could see the bright spots of light from another car.

'Just don't go anywhere; looks like someone has driven into me,' he answered.

The lead police car stopped, its brake lights casting a red glow in the thick smoky fog that surrounded it.

The police officer who had been hit grabbed his flashlight from the passenger seat and pushed the door open. He walked, gun drawn and the flashlight held over the wrist of his pistol carrying hand towards the headlights of the car that had hit him.

When he arrived at the driver's side door, he called for the driver to step out slowly. The door didn't move. The window made a whirring noise as it began to lower. The officer moved back slightly and pushed his gun out further towards the driver's side door.

'I said, step out of the car,' he said more assertively.

The door still didn't open but the window finished its descent.

'Why have you stopped?' a voice barked.

For a split second he was stunned. Who had spoken to him like that? Then he recognized the voice as it continued to shout at him from inside the car.

'Why have you stopped? We need to find my daughter!'

The officer lowered his gun and approached the open window.

'Listen, you shouldn't be here. You need to go back home,' he said.

'Don't you dare tell me what to do. I supported you in getting your job, now I want you to do what I pay you for and that's find my daughter,' Mandy barked.

The officer looked at her angry twisted face and then saw her husband sat in the passenger seat, staring straight ahead.

The window then began its journey back up before he could even say another word. He had felt the rage of the woman once before when someone had hit her car. All the evidence suggested she was at fault. When he suggested that she was, he found himself being reprimanded by the sheriff for accusing the woman of being in the wrong and lying about what had happened. She had so much power in the town that no one dared cross her.

He returned to his car and radioed to the other officer in front.

'I'm ok, but we got company. The wicked witch of the west just ran into my car. She's looking for her daughter.'

The radio buzzed and then a reply came.

'Oh shit, that's all we need.'

The officer took his foot off the brake and continued his slow drive along the dirt road until he reached the sheriff's car.

He radioed to the officer behind that he had just found the car and that it had its windows smashed. The other officer stopped when he saw the red lights of the car in front and then got out and joined his fellow officer who stood, gun drawn behind the driver door.

Mandy saw the brake lights and quickly stopped. She shut the engine off and got out quickly, running forward until she was standing behind the two officers.

'Ma'am you need to get back in your car. Please go back and stay with your husband,' the officer told her.

Again she angrily stared at him and told him that she wanted them to find her daughter and she had every right to be there to make sure they did their job correctly.

Mandy's husband sat in the car. He didn't want to step outside into the strange fog but knew if he didn't join his wife he would pay the consequences later. He pushed his door open and walked to where he could hear his wife's voice. When he arrived by the car, he could see she was berating the police officers, pointing her finger at them and then out in front. He could hear her demanding that they go find her daughter. He drew level with her. The officer who was taking the verbal abuse saw him.

'Sir, could you please take your wife back to the safety of your car?' the officer asked.

Mandy's husband sighed and put his hand on her shoulder and quietly told her to come back to the car. She turned and looked at him, her anger boiling over.

He tried again to get her to go back to the car with him by putting his arm around her and trying to guide her back with him. She snarled at him and then punched him in the face. His nose exploded with a popping and thudding sound. He fell backwards and disappeared into the thick fog. The police officers stood stunned; they couldn't believe what they had just seen. Groans came from within the fog and then Mandy's husband reappeared. He stood and looked at them through tear-filled eyes, blood smeared all over his face. He turned and walked away, disappearing back into the fog.

'What the,' one of the officers said, still shocked at what had just happened.

Mandy looked at the two officers and snarled. Her clenched fist waved at them.

'You boys had better find my daughter or else you'll never get another job in this town or state again once you've been fired from this one for incompetence.'

They looked at each other and knew that she had the connections and power in the town to make life difficult for them.

The two officers walked slowly towards the sheriff's car. They each took a side and began inspecting the interior through the broken windows, their torch beams crossing as they both shone into the rear seats. They moved further along. The officer on the driver's side peered in and could see nothing. The other officer shone his torch in through the passenger window and saw something move in the foot well. His immediate reaction was to step back and raise his gun. His partner saw him react and also took evasive action, backing away from the car with gun drawn.

The officer on the passenger side took a deep breath and stepped towards the door. He held the flashlight between his shoulder and ear and gingerly, keeping his gun pointing at the cars open window, reached forward and pulled on the handle. The moment the door began to swing open he grabbed the flashlight from its temporary support and shone it at whatever he saw move in the foot well.

He saw the tear-smeared face of a boy, his eyes staring lifeless at the seat. The officer motioned to his colleague, who moved quickly around the front of the car, ready to assist him. He managed to get to the hood of the car and then tripped over something. He fell forward, disappearing into the thick fog that surrounded their feet. He sat up and looked back but could see nothing. He reached his hand into the swirling dense fog and grabbed what felt like hair. He pulled at the object, raising it enough for it to appear out of the fog. The deathly stare of the sheriff caused him to let go of the hand full of hair.

'Jesus,' he shouted, crab-walking away.

The other officer who was quietly talking to the traumatized boy looked up when he heard his partner shout. All he saw was the faint outline of the police officer's head bobbing up and down as he moved away from the car.

'What's wrong?' he asked.

'I found the sheriff,' he said in between large gasps of air.

Mandy had heard the commotion and ran towards where the officer was talking to the boy. She pushed him aside and looked into the car.

'Paula?' she asked.

When she realized that it was not her daughter, she groaned angrily and walked off into the fog in search of her daughter, cursing as she went. The officer who she had pushed past watched as she disappeared. The other officer, who was back on his feet, also watched as she marched past him.

The boy stayed firmly wedged in the foot well of the car. The only movement he made was the constant shaking of his body and quivering of his lips. The officer tried once more to get the boy's attention but realized that whatever had happened was so traumatic that he was in no state to be moved. He removed his radio from his belt and spoke into it. The other officer joined him, looked into the car at the boy and then shone his torch into the fog. He was sure he had seen something move within it.

'This is Officer Walker, up at the farm, we need paramedics and forensics up here right away,' he said before pausing. 'Better wake the county medical examiner as well.'

The voice on the other end responded, the usual calm voice was now broken and emotional.

'Copy that, we are getting calls about missing teenagers. What's going on up there?'

The officers looked at each other and shrugged their shoulders, neither wanted to venture any further.

'We don't know. We've located the boy; something is not right up here,' he responded.

Mandy's husband stood by the passenger side door of their car. He wiped his blooded, tear-filled face with his T-Shirt. He had accepted numerous beatings at the hands of his wife throughout the years, blaming himself for her anger and pain. He had stopped loving her years ago. He had thought about walking out on several occasions, but not only did he fear that if he left he would never see his daughter again; he was sure she would kill him.

He stood against the car and wept. He then heard the sound of a car approaching, its engine screaming.

Baron's father had lost sight of the other cars and had driven past the dirt road to the farm. When he could not see the police cars' flashing lights or the taillights of the other car in the distance on the straight road, he pushed hard on the brakes; the car skidded to a halt. He turned the car around and headed back the way he came. As he drove back along the road, he searched the dark fields for any sign of where the cars had gone. He looked out at the fields and noticed a wall of fog. He stopped the car and looked at it, amazed that it seemed to be trapped within the confines of the barbed wire of the boundary of the field.

He began moving slowly down the road until he came to the dirt road that led into the fog. It was then he saw a strange pulse of blue. He hit the brakes and looked into the fog. A second pulse of blue appeared and then another and another. His brain shouted to him that it must be the police cars and pushed hard on the accelerator pedal. He was a man obsessed. He still had no headlights on and was speeding up as he travelled up the dirt road. The fact that he couldn't see what was in front of him didn't matter. His son was all that mattered.

He didn't see the other car until he hit it. The car ploughed into the rear of the stationary car. Baron's father gasped as his car launched into the air and began to rotate. The car managed a complete three hundred and sixty degree roll before cashing back to earth. The connection between the front of the car and the corn field soil acted like a massive brake, the force of the impact throwing Baron's father into the windshield. His head exploded as it was forced against the glass barrier, the impact causing the windscreen to become a blooded spider's web of cracks.

Mandy's Husband saw only a glimpse of the car as it hit, its rising trajectory causing the front bumper to hit the side of his head just below his ear, decapitating him.

The officers heard the explosion of sound coming from behind them and automatically ducked. The officer who had stumbled over the sheriff's body was hit in the chest by an object, knocking him backwards back beneath the thickest blanket of fog. Whatever it was had come to rest in his arms as they instinctively wrapped themselves around whatever had hit him. He sat up and looked at what he was holding. He screamed when he saw the head of the Mandy's husband. He threw it to the side and stood up quickly. He could feel the wetness of the head's blood on his jacket as he brushed his hands on his front trying to get any remnants of the head off him. They heard the sound of the car land but did not see it.

17

The Ouija board began to burn with a green flame, Frank gasping as it did. Baron however, didn't seem bothered by the bright, odd-colored flame.

'Don't get too excited; the color of the flame is probably because of the chemicals used on it,' he said confidently.

The board began to warp under the heat; it began to bubble and then spit, launching small embers through the air and landing on the dirt floor. The glass pointer continued its crazy spin in its center.

Frank looked up from the board and gasped, the cold night air flooding his lungs. He moved back towards the tree, his eyes wide and fixed on something ahead of him. Baron looked at him and then in the direction he was looking. Standing on the edge of the clearing stood the woman in the white dress.

Toby looked at Frank and then to the woman.

'Shit,' he exclaimed.

The woman flickered and then disappeared. Baron moved slowly towards Toby and Paula.

'Is that the mystery woman?' he said as he got closer to Toby.

Before he could answer, the woman reappeared, standing in front of Baron. He felt the lightning bolt of shock and fear shoot through his spine.

The woman stared at him with lifeless black eyes and an evil grin etched on her face. She flickered again and he found that when she stopped flickering in and out of his vision, she had her hand around his throat. He could feel her bony cold grip beginning to tighten. He tried to pry her hands away but found her strength unearthly.

The Ouija board continued to burn just behind the woman, the flames growing larger and brighter. There was a bright flash that caused all of them except the woman to blink, followed by a strong blast of air.

The wall of fog pulsed quicker and quicker, the blue light becoming a rapid beat. The fog itself began to slowly lower until finally it exploded up into the air. It momentarily hung and then began to fall back to earth as a blue-tinged fine rain.

The soft thuds and bangs of gunfire ceased, as did the cries and shouts of battle that filled the fields.

***

The police officers began to take a deep breath when the felt and saw the fog that surrounded them begin to

437

pulse and then explode around them. When the fine rain had fallen and settled, revealing the large barn in front of them, they sighed. They looked down at their feet with their flashlights and saw the body of the sheriff and the head of man who had accompanied his wife. They looked at the field where they had heard the car crash to the ground and saw the mangled remains of the car. Smoke and steam rose from its engine.

Mandy had continued her march, not sure where she was going, noticing dark shadows move around her. Each time she saw one, she called her daughter's name. When the fog began to pulse blue and rise around her, she still continued her march. Nothing was going to stop her. When the blue fine rain fell, clearing her ability to see, she found that she was on the old dirt path that led to the large old tree.

***

Frank found a surge of strength. The fog had gone, and he could not see any soldier. The only spectral thing left was the woman. He launched himself at her, ignoring the pain from his ankle.

She flickered as Frank's body got close, and disappeared, his momentum carrying him past Baron, who began gasping and fell down into the dirt. He moaned as he hit the floor.

The woman reappeared in front of Baron, her hand returning to his throat. He began struggling for air once more.

The woman's grip grew tighter and tighter. He could feel the sensation of sleep creeping in; he knew his time was nearly done. The vision of the woman became more and more blurred as he began to lose the fight to live.

He suddenly felt his throat fill with cold air and then his lungs begin to work hard to replace the oxygen they had been starved of. His vision slowly improved, and he noticed she was gone.

'Paula!' Mandy shouted, her voice piercing the night's silence.

She listened carefully and then called again—nothing. She then continued her march up the dirt path towards the old tree.

She called again, but this time she got a response.

'Over here,' a voice whispered.

Mandy stopped and looked around her. The voice continued to repeat itself. Its chilling whisper seemed to be coming from different places. Each time she heard it, she turned quickly to where it had come from.

'Who is that?' she shouted.

'You know,' the voice answered back.

'Show yourself,' Mandy demanded.

She then heard another voice; this voice, however, had a sense of panic to it.

'Up here,' it said, loud and high pitched.

She looked around her once more, seeing nothing. She continued her march up the small incline of the dirt road to where the last voice had come from.

18

The police officers made their way over to the smoking wreckage of the car. The now blood-stained officer shone his flashlight at it. He paused when he saw the bloody mass sticking out of the windshield. The other officer turned away quickly when he caught sight of the man with his flashlight beam.

'What the fuck is going on here?'

The blood-stained officer shrugged his shoulders and began walking back to the car where the boy still cowered.

The red and blue lights of approaching police cars and the larger ambulance made them both sigh with relief.

The cars pulled up, the drivers quickly getting out and joining their colleagues. The EMTs rushed up to them carrying their bags of medical equipment and were pointed to the sheriff's car. The two paramedics looked at the car then the officers and then back to the car before moving quickly to its open doors and the boy.

'What's going on?' one of the new arriving officers asked.

The two original attending officers looked at each other and began to recount what they had seen. As they gave their account, two of the other officers broke away from the conversation and headed over to the old barn. They drew their weapons and slowly stepped through the open door into the darkness of the barn's interior. The beams of light from their flashlights danced around the barn's interior; nothing moved within.

As they moved forward deeper into the darkness, they both caught their feet against something—and then again as they continued moving forward. When they pointed their flashlights to the floor, they both gasped and retreated quickly back to the open door. Once back outside, one of the officers grabbed his radio and began speaking into it, his voice broken and disjointed with panic.

19

Mandy reached the top of the small incline and saw the large old tree. Beneath it she could see a number of people. She increased her pace. When she saw her daughter sitting against the tree with Toby crouched next to her, she broke into a run. She ignored the girl who hung from the tree and the two boys who were kneeling in the dirt trying to help each other, the one coughing as if he had been choked.

She reached her daughter and grabbed Toby by the shoulder of his jacket.

'What have you done to her,' she shouted at him angrily.

Toby stuttered and raised his hands in a defensive pose.

'Nothing, I haven't done anything. It was the woman,' he said.

Mandy snarled at him and then let him go. She then knelt down by her daughter and began to shake her, hoping to wake her from her semi-unconscious state. Paula's eyes fluttered and then opened, her mother's face gradually coming into focus.

'Why did you do it?' were the first words out of her mouth.

Mandy looked at her, confusion stretched across her face.

'Do what?' she replied while stroking her daughter's hair.

'Tina. Why did you do it?' Paula continued.

Mandy stopped stroking her daughter's hair and stood up.

'What you talking about? That bitch killed herself,' Mandy snapped.

Toby looked at Mandy and then at Paula.

'What's she talking about?' he asked.

It was at that point that the two boys who were helping each other shouted in unison.

'She's there.'

Mandy looked behind her and saw the woman in white standing by the body of the young girl who had been hanging from the tree. She stroked the rope that held the girl's body and it began to move. It uncoiled itself from its noose, the body of the girl finally falling to the damp, blood-soaked earth. The intestines that had hung from the opening in her stomach now surrounded her face.

The rope moved back up into the branches of the tree and began to snake its way towards the five people gathered by its large ancient trunk.

Frank looked at Baron. 'Why hasn't she gone?' he asked.

Baron looked at the now charred Ouija board and noticed the glass pointer still spinning.

'The pointer,' he said in response.

Mandy looked at the woman, memories flooding back, as did the anger of that day.

'You slut! You dare try and hurt my daughter,' she shouted and began walking towards her.

Tina flickered and disappeared. Not even seeing her disappear stopped Mandy, her anger so powerful she felt no fear of the spirit that had returned. Mandy walked several steps and then felt something wrap itself around her throat. The rope had snaked its way to a large branch just above where Mandy was standing. It reared up like a cobra about to strike and then launched itself at her. Mandy reached up and pulled at it. The rope began to tighten, causing her to gasp for air amongst her cursing.

Paula screamed. She tried to get to her but collapsed back against the tree. Toby pushed himself up and ran to Mandy, attempting to try and remove the rope as it began to tighten.

Tina flickered into view. She stood in front of Mandy and smiled. Mandy let go of the rope around her throat and swung wildly at Tina, who stood just out of reach. Toby let go of the rope and lunged at the woman. Just like she had done with Frank. Just as he was about to hit her, she vanished, sending him to the floor before reappearing. Toby tried to get back up but found that an invisible force held him down against the dirt.

The rope fell from the tree and began moving its way like a winding snake across the floor towards the dead corn field. Mandy felt the pull of the rope; she tried to fight against it, but it continued its relentless pull. She fell on her back and began to be dragged across the dirt floor. Tina watched as Mandy passed by. She then looked up at the dark figure standing within the boundary of the corn.

Baron watched as Mandy struggled against the snaking rope on her journey towards the corn field. He caught a glimpse of a dark outline of a man standing amongst the dead corn. He then refocused his attention on the Ouija board and the spinning glass pointer and made a move towards it.

This was the key, he was sure of it. If he broke the glass then the doorway that had allowed the woman in white into this world would be broken and she would be sent back. That was the only way she could still be here. He brought his heavy boot down onto the burnt board and the spinning glass pointer. He had a sense of relief when he heard the cracking of the glass below his boot.

He ground his foot down, making sure that the glass was crunched into thousands of little pieces and watched the woman in white.

Something was wrong. He pushed on the broken glass harder, but she was still there, walking alongside the woman being pulled by the serpentine rope towards the cornfield.

Paula sat, unable to move against the tree. Tears streamed down her face as she watched her mother disappear into and amongst the corn. Frank sat, mouth open unable to move or speak. Toby still struggled against the invisible force that held him down in the dirt. Baron stopped twisting his foot into the board, glass and dirt.

20

Mandy struggled, trying to pry the rope away from her throat. It was tight enough to restrict her intake of air and stop her from getting her fingers around it. She occasionally reached out and grabbed an old corn stalk, hoping to stop whatever was pulling her. Tina walked past her and began walking alongside the dark figure.

Tina and the figure walked into a small clearing in the field and paused in its center. The rope continued its journey until Mandy had also reached the small clearing and the feet of the two figures standing in its center.

Mandy lay, staring up at the star-filled night sky, and the tightness of the rope released. Two faces came into sight: one being Tina, whose black eyes and evil smile stared down at her. The other face looking down at her, also with black, lifeless eyes, was that of Thomas. Mandy gasped with fear.

Thomas reached down and picked her up by her hair. For the first time in her life Mandy was frozen with fear. Voices began to fill her head: the voices of her two victims, the voices of the two who were going to exact their revenge this cold Halloween night.

'We've waited so long for you,' Thomas's voice echoed.

'You took my life, my love and my baby,' the second voice screamed.

'You are going to endure pain like you never have,' Thomas's voice added.

Mandy could not move; she was paralyzed. She could do nothing as Thomas dug his fingers into the flesh of her perfect face, his dark pointed nails sliding between her skin and muscle. Tina began pushing her hand into Mandy's stomach. The burning sensation as it penetrated beneath her soft skin caused her to urinate herself. The warm wet sensation as it ran down her leg and soaked her trousers made her feel dirty and worthless.

Thomas began to peel back her skin, strip by strip from her perfectly formed face. She could feel the tearing and pulling as her skin was removed but could do nothing but endure the pain as it flooded her senses.

Tina pushed deeper into Mandy's stomach, wrapping her hand around the soft, silky feeling intestine and then pulling sharply back. Tina enjoying showing Mandy her own intestine in the moonlight.

Thomas pulled the last piece of skin off the left side of Mandy's face. He then stepped back along with Tina. He looked at her as she stood, slightly swaying. They smiled and embraced. A bright light encased them. Its brightness grew and grew until finally it exploded out in all directions. When it faded and the darkness of the night returned, Tina and Thomas were gone.

Mandy collapsed to the dirty floor where her life slowly drained from her. Her blood soaked into the dirt of the clearing and soon her life was gone.

21

More police cars arrived. Word had got out of the strange macabre findings up at the old farm. As the sun began to rise, several officers found four teenagers up by an old tree. The boy would not leave the side of his girlfriend. When they had tried to separate them, he had begun to scream, only stopping when he was allowed to hold his girlfriend's hand. The girl herself was nonresponsive. She was stuck in some form of trance. Incidentally, her father had been killed when a car had crashed into his vehicle in the fog, decapitating him. Another boy had a broken ankle and was speaking gibberish about soldiers and ghosts. A third teenager spoke of gateways and spirits. When he was told his father had died in a car crash not far from where he stood, he had to be sedated after becoming hysterical.

The biggest and strangest scene was in the large old barn, where protruding out of the solid dirt floor, hands reached up. The FBI were called, and after a thorough investigation it was determined that the large number of teenagers that had been found buried in the barn were part of some strange religious cult suicide.

A body of a woman was found in a small clearing in one of the fields. She had been identified as a local power-mongering religious council member. It seemed like she had ripped off half of her own face and somehow managed to disembowel herself. Even stranger was that when they removed her body, they found a shallow grave directly below where she was laying. The bones in the grave suggested that a teenage male had been killed via several blows to his head, based on the damage to the skull.

None of this made it into the national papers or even the local papers. The only reference to the large number of disappearances of teenagers in the town was a bus crash—a crash that never happened.

The surviving teenagers were placed into a psychiatric hospital and soon forgotten about and all records of what happened that night strangely disappeared.

PETER BUCKLEY

THE MANSION

The
Mansion

By

Peter
Buckley

1

They had tried for five years to get permission to do a paranormal investigation at Hallstorn Manor. The stories of its hauntings were legendary in the Cornish area of the UK. Headless maids, ghost children, and a vengeful wife had all been documented throughout its two-hundred-year-old history.

The Southern Paranormal Investigator Society finally got the go ahead to spend the night in the old mansion. The five members of the society were excited; as soon as they received the clearance, they arranged an emergency meeting and decided to conduct their investigation on December the thirteenth, the date when the Mansion had held its last party and where, as legend had it, all the guests disappeared.

Tony Mortan, the lead investigator and founder of the Southern Paranormal Investigator Society, had been obsessed with the mansion. He had collected every bit of information he could find about the building at its hauntings. His obsession had cost him his marriage, his long-suffering wife walking out on him and moving in with another man she had met over the internet. Tony hadn't even noticed she had gone until he realized that there were no clean plates to eat from. He had searched his house calling out his wife's name when he found the hand-written letter on the mantel piece. He had walked past it several times but had never taken much notice of it until then. He read it and then crumpled it up and threw it in the open fireplace. He grumbled to himself and reassured himself she had never understood him and his passion.

He had agreed to allow only a small group of people join his society. Only those that shared his belief in the paranormal and who could bring equipment and technical knowledge to his ghost hunts were allowed.

Michael Hall and John Peterson were the first two to join; they brought a knowledge of video cameras and computer setup. On their first ghost hunt together, they had introduced Tony to the joys of thermal cameras and computer recording camera setups so that they could capture what was happening in each of the rooms even if the three were investigating somewhere else in a house. They had captured several "orbs" as they called them. Some would argue that the small balls appearing and moving across the camera were actual dust particles, but they were convinced they had captured paranormal energy.

Phoebe Richards was the only female in the group. Tony initially didn't want a woman in the team. He didn't trust them, especially after his wife had left him. Phoebe brought a knowledge of electronic voice phenomenon, EVP for short. She captured several voices and sounds that she convinced the others were responses to her questions.

The final member of the group was a newbie; Jeremy Sanderson was a religious education teacher and brought a large knowledge of religious beliefs and theories as well as a book about exorcism.

The group began to meet more and more as the mansion investigation date approached. Tony had purchased several pieces of equipment in preparation: new thermal cameras, static electricity monitors, and temperature gauges. Hotels were booked for a couple of days prior to and after the investigation. The team members had all booked their holiday time with their respected jobs and counted down the days until they left for the mansion.

The two minivans travelled down the long and winding road that led to the mansion. The team of paranormal investigators had spent the past two days and nights staying in a hotel in the local village, using the time to check equipment and speak with locals about what they had heard about the history of the mansion.

Tony Mortan, the team leader, had slept very little. This was his holy grail—the one he had been dreaming of since he first started investigating paranormal activity.

They drove down the leafless tree-lined road with no other vehicles around, and all five of the team took the opportunity to enjoy their picturesque surroundings. Statues occasionally appeared amongst the old trees; their strange disfigured faces caused the team members to look at each other with surprise.

They pulled up outside the large wooden front door, and a man dressed in blue dirty overalls and mudded boots waited in front. Tony exited the van and approached the man. He extended his hand but was greeted with a gruff, 'Morning' as the other man placed his hands into the pockets of his dirty overalls. Tony lowered his hand, thinking how rude the man was not to reciprocate the handshake.

'Do you want to tell the others to join us?' the man said, nodding towards the two minivans and their occupants. 'I don't want to spend too much time here. I got other things to attend to.'

Tony looked at the man with raised eyebrows and then looked back at the others and waved them to join him.

The man waited until the whole team was gathered by the door and then unlocked it. He pushed the large door open, the hallway beyond seemed to be covered in dust. The man in overalls stepped in, his footsteps echoing around the high-ceilinged hallway. The team followed him in. Phoebe, the last person, closed the door behind her, shutting out the only light source.

'Don't move,' the man said.

They heard his footsteps walk away, and then the small chandeliers above them burst into life. He stood at the far end of the hallway and beckoned them towards him. As they approached him, they looked up at the strange macabre paintings that adorned the walls. Two of the larger paintings depicted hangings and sacrifices.

'Come on, I don't want to spend more time than I have to here,' the man said, getting inpatient with the group of fascinated paranormal investigators.

He began walking through the mansion, room by room, giving a brief history of its décor and use. Several times he paused and took a deep breath before entering. One of these pauses was before he pushed a pair of great oak doors into a large dining room. A long, dark, wood table stood in its center, and in the middle of it a strange art sculpture stood. It was made from hundreds of deer antlers, and it spiraled and twisted until it reached the ceiling. Phoebe stared at it wide eyed; there was something about it that grabbed her attention. Both Michael and John called to her as they moved to the large fireplace at the far end of the room, but she seemed to be in a trance. It was only when Jeremy tapped her on the shoulder that she snapped back into the moment.

'This room has a long dark history of death,' the man began. 'Two children of the first owner were found poisoned sitting at this very table.' He pointed at two chairs, one at either end of the table.

'Most recently, the current owner's grandson was found dead lying in this fireplace.' Again, he pointed a dirty finger at the place where the body was found.

'What was the cause of death?' Tony asked.

The man in overalls looked at him and shrugged his shoulders. 'No one knows. "Natural causes," is what was entered on the death certificate.'

As they left, Phoebe took one last look at the sculpture. They moved through to a small kitchen, and as soon as the door was opened, they could all feel the drop in temperature.

'Is there a door open or a window?' John asked.

The man turned, looked at him, and shook his head. 'It's always cold in here. Some say it's the restless spirits; others say it's just the position of the room in relation to the building.'

'Restless spirits?' John asked.

'There are stories that a large number of people were murdered in here,' the man said before quickly moving to the next door and into the adjoining room.

They were shown several other rooms that all had strange macabre pictures on the walls before they reached the large, marble, curved staircase.

'Well, that's all I got time to show you,' the man said, gently tapping two fingers on the large banister.

Tony looked up the stairs and then back at the man. He pointed up the stairs and was about to ask about being shown the next level, but the man cut him short.

'I don't go up there; no one goes up stairs,' he said.

'But we need to know what rooms are the best to set up our equipment in,' Michael said.

The man shook his head. 'You can set up in any of those room, it makes no difference; something bad happened in each of them.'

'What like?' Tony asked eagerly.

The old man looked at each of the investigators and again shook his head.

'You people are crazy. If you really want to know what happened upstairs, there is a book on the small table over there,' he said, pointing at the small round table next to a black wooden coat stand and a large door.

A cold breeze flowed down the stairs and engulfed the group standing at its bottom. They all shivered and looked back up the stairs. The old man took a step backwards towards the large door.

'Right, that's all I have time to show you. I have a very busy day, and there is meant to be a dumping of snow later today,' he said.

He walked the group back to the front door and stood outside and looked up at the grey, cloudy sky. 'There's snow on its way, and I think it's going to be here sooner than the bloody weather man said.'

The others looked up at the clouds and then at each other. The temperature had dropped, yet it still felt warmer than the icy chill they got from the breeze that came down the stairs.

'You better hurry up and get your stuff out of your vans; I don't want to be here any longer than I have to.' The old man said, still looking up at the clouds.

The team of investigators looked at each other and fell into their well-rehearsed routine of gathering equipment from the van and moving it inside. They carried the equipment into the dining room and placed it against the wall. Phoebe stayed and began setting up the laptop and arranging the cameras, placing them on the large table. Normal cameras, night-vision cameras, and thermal cameras were each labeled with the name of a member of the group. She then began unpacking the stands and the multiple lengths of cable that were going to be run around the house to connect all the fixed cameras and scientific data recorders to the laptop and recorders.

The others returned several times with other bags and crates full of cables and equipment until she was finally joined by Michael and John, who began busily setting up screens and recorders, connecting cables, and talking in a language that even Phoebe didn't understand: numbers and words that referred to lengths and power outputs of cables and resolutions of cameras and screens.

Tony and Jeremy made sure that the vans were empty and locked before turning to the old man, who impatiently looked at his watch.

'Ok, that looks like everything,' Tony said.

'You sure you want locking in?' The old man asked, confusion etched on his face.

'Yes please, it's just to make sure there is no outside interference. You can return in the morning and unlock the doors,' Tony replied.

'Ok, but you are all crazy if you ask me,' the old man said, shaking his head.

Tony and Jeremy walked in through the front door and turned to see the old man close the door. They waited until they heard the key in the lock turn and click, signifying that it had locked before joining the others in the dining room.

The old man walked to his old muddy Landrover, and he pulled on the door. It creaked as it opened, and the chassis also gave a groan when he got in. he sat motionless and stared at the house. He shook his head once more and started up the engine. He turned the car around in the wide gravel driveway and headed down the long, tree-lined road leading back to the main road.

3

Once all the monitors were up and running in the dining room, Tony, Michael, and Jeremy took a number of cameras each and headed to different rooms, setting up the cameras in positions where they could observe the largest part of the room. They each contacted Phoebe via the handheld radios they all carried, each responding to her directions by moving the cameras left or right to get the best picture. The three men all met at the bottom of the stairs. They looked at each other, Michael radioing their position and saying that they were about to head upstairs to set up the cameras. Phoebe told them to stay where they were until John had joined them. He had been working on a special electrical charge detector that sounded an alarm and flashed when a static charge passed over it.

Once he had joined them, they all headed up the large winding staircase. As they reached the top, a strong, cold breeze crashed against them, it's cold bite making the hairs on their necks rise; they could see their own breath as they exhaled. They all automatically slowed and looked at each other.

They moved down the corridor, its dark wallpaper and red carpet making it feel dark and mysterious. They passed several paintings, all depicting women and men being tortured in different ways. Jeremy decided to head back to the top of the stairs and place a night vision camera pointing down the corridor. He then jogged back down to the others, who continued to inspect the paintings.

'This is some sick shit!' Michael said.

The others looked at him and nodded.

As they reached the other end of the corridor, Tony turned and directed the others. 'Right, there are six rooms. We'll set up a camera in each, and John, if you place your static charge monitor in the middle of the corridor when we head back that should cover everything. We can look at the book of incidents when we get back to the dining room.'

The others nodded and then they all entered the rooms.

Tony pushed the door open and was met by a strong beam of light. A large window that stretched from floor to ceiling bathed the room in the grey light from outside. A large four-poster bed sat proud in the center of the room, dark, wooden cabinets and wardrobes stood in sharp contrast against the faded cream wallpaper. He looked closer at the wallpaper and could see a faint print on it. He found it hard to see what the pattern actually was, so he ran his hand over it and could feel the raised outlines of the lines and circles that made up the pattern. He stood back and turned on his digital camera. He had placed an infrared filter on its lens and took several pictures of the largest un-obscured wall. When he was done, he set up the night-vision camera he had on a retractable tripod and positioned it in the corner of the room, focusing on the bed and cabinets. He radioed down to Phoebe to check that she was receiving the picture but was met with static. He tried again and was met with a static-filled voice telling him all was ok with the picture. He looked down at the receiver in his hand. *Maybe it's the batteries*, he thought to himself. Just as he left the room and pulled the door behind him, he heard a thump coming from the room and froze. His radio bust into life, making him jump.

'Tony, did you knock the camera over?' Phoebe asked.

He looked at the radio receiver in his hand before replying. 'Erm no, I'm no longer in the room. I just closed the door and heard a thump.'

He turned the handle, pushed the door open, and stepped back into the room. The camera was on its side, the tripod legs still in their fixed triangular position. He walked over to it and picked it up and inspected it carefully. He wobbled it but it didn't fall over; it was in a secure place and position. He stood in front of it and radioed down to Phoebe.

'Can you see me?'

The radio again fed back static before clearing.

Phoebe stared at the screen and Tony crouching, his face in frame. She was about to reply when she saw a dark shadow move across the room behind him. She gasped and shouted into the radio.

'Behind you, I just saw something move behind you!'

Tony quickly stood up and turned around. He could not see anything. He moved to the large window and peered out. All was still outside until he heard the faint call of a crow. He looked at the trees and finally found the lonesome bird that was calling. He turned again and carefully scoured the room. He raised the radio to his mouth and spoke slowly into it as he turned again and looked outside at the grey sky.

'You must have seen a shadow cast by a passing bird or something because there's nothing here.'

'No it wasn't a bird's shadow; it was behind you and then moved away out of shot,' Phoebe said.

'When I get done here we'll check the footage,' Tony replied.

The others then began responding, asking if Tony was ok. He replied quickly, telling them to continue with their jobs of placing cameras in the other rooms. Tony once again left the room and moved on to another room, passing John, who was standing outside the door to another room.

'You ok?' he asked.

'I pushed open the door and then it closed suddenly, now I can't seem to open it,' John replied.

Tony stopped and watched as John struggled to open the door. He then offered to try. He placed his hand on the round door handle and turned it. When it had reached its furthest point, he pushed. The door slowly opened; he even let go of the handle and the door continued to open with a creak.

He looked at John who looked at him in astonishment.

'Are you messing with me or something?' he said to John.

John just stood, mouth open, shaking his head. Tony sighed and moved on to the next room.

Michael had entered his room, its walls covered in a dark red paper. The ceiling was covered in small irregular-shaped mirrors, creating a mosaic pattern.

The bed, a four-poster, rested against a wall. Above the headboard was a painting of several skeletons sitting at a table. A large grime-stained window let in the grey light of the outside world. He stood at it and looked out. The mansion's gardens stretched out in front of him. A small gathering of trees stood in the center of the lawn, and he looked at them. Their leafless limbs began to sway gently. He was about to turn away and begin positioning the camera he held in his hand when out of the corner of his eye he saw a dark outline of a figure standing at the tree's base. He stopped and refocused but saw nothing. He shook his head and began setting up the tripod and camera facing the bed, contacting Phoebe to check position and reception. When he got the all clear, he left and headed to the last room.

Jeremy walked into a large room covered with wallpaper that depicted a carnival scene. The room itself consisted of four small beds and a large gathering of dolls and cuddly toys piled in a corner: there were teddy bears in various types of clothes, and dolls sat and stared blankly at him, some with clothes, and others sat naked; a few had limbs missing. He shivered as a cold breeze surrounded him. He never liked dolls; there was something sinister about them, especially their eyes, which seemed to follow you wherever you went. He moved from bed to bed, noticing the old faded and stained sheets. He took several pictures with his digital camera of each bed and the pile of toys, and he then began to set up the camera and tripod. A large bang made him jump back from the camera. He spun around, searching for whatever had made the noise. He radioed to the others, asking if any of them had heard the loud bang. Each in turn responded with a 'No' or a 'Negative.' He walked around the room, pushing his feet hard down into the carpet to see if there was a loose floorboard that may have returned to its normal place after he had stepped on it, but nothing felt loose. He opened the small wardrobe that rested against a wall but found it empty. It was then that he noticed the wallpaper in detail. The carnival scene he had initially noticed was a complete scene, starting by the door and depicting different rides and animal

470

attractions all around the room until it reached the door again, only breaking where the large window separated the design. He looked closer and saw that the people depicted in the design were all headless. He then heard another loud bang that shattered the silence of the room. He turned quickly and pushed his back against the wall. This time he knew where it had emanated from.

'Did you hear that one?' he called into the radio.

Again the others responded with 'No.' The door opened, and he gasped. He relaxed and sighed when he saw Michael walk in.

'What's going on in here?' he asked Jeremy.

Jeremy pointed to the window and explained that he had heard two loud bangs. They both slowly moved over to the window and peered out. The window overlooked the garden that Michael had seen from the room he had just set up. Unlike the room he had just been in, this window led onto a small balcony. They both looked down at the balcony floor and saw what had caused the two loud bangs. On the floor of the balcony lay two large crows.

'Crazy birds have just flown into the window and killed themselves,' Michael said.

At that moment, another crow came out of nowhere and crashed into the window. The two investigators fell backwards, their hearts racing from the sudden jumpstart.

They sat on the floor, looking at each other and then at the window.

'Get set up and let's get out of here,' Jeremy said. Michael nodded and helped his friend quickly set up the camera, they decided to set it up so they could see the beds and window as well as the mountain of dolls and toys.

John slowly entered the room he had been struggling to open the door too. He was greeted by a musty smell and an icy blast of air that made him shiver. Mold covered the light green wallpaper, the carpet had several dark stairs on it, and the four-poster bed that stood in the center of the room had no bed covers, just an old, stained mattress. There were several gouges cut into each of the bed posts. The windows that let in the light were thick with grime, letting in very little natural light. He looked for a light switch and found one in the middle of the wall that the door belonged to. He flicked it, and the small crystal chandelier came to life, bathing the room in a strange low light. The walls danced with spots and shapes cast from the small crystals of the light fixture. He took several pictures of the room before setting up his camera. He called down to Phoebe while standing in the camera's view and waving. Phoebe responded by telling him he was silly. He felt another icy blast of air and then the door he had struggled to open slammed shut. He stood bolt upright and looked at the door. He quickly walked over to the door and tried to open it, but again it didn't move. He radioed to the others but was met with static. He looked around him at the room. The small light spots and glints cast onto the wall from the light began to move quicker and quicker. He looked up at the chandelier, expecting it to be swaying, but it was still. He then heard a quiet, sinister laugh. He felt a cold electric shock shoot up his spine to his head. His heart began to pound as he heard a low voice speak. He quickly grabbed his voice recorder from his pocket and pressed record.

'What is your name?' he asked.

The voice continued to speak, but in a language he didn't understand. There was a click as the door opened. The voice ceased at that very moment. He quickly exited and walked into Jeremy. They looked at each other, and they didn't have to say anything; they both knew that they had just experienced more in the last few minutes than all the other investigations they had ever done.

Tony opened the door to one of the last two remaining rooms in the corridor. He stepped in and found the room to be very dark; only a small amount of natural light illuminated the room. There was only one window in the room, which ran along the length of the skirting board of one of the walls and was no more than a foot in height. The walls of the room were painted black. Nothing else was in the room except for a large crystal chandelier that hung down from the ceiling; its point finished just inches from the wooden floor. He found a light switch that had been painted black also and pushed his finger down on it. The chandelier burst into life. The walls that were black now showed pictures of mutilated corpses. The large chandelier was in fact a form of cinema projector, projecting the pictures that were caught and stored within the crystals. He looked at each one: bodies with their chests skinless and showing the ribs, headless bodies, female bodies with their breasts removed, and several men hanging with their feet and hands tied together. He quickly set up a night vision camera and left the room, turning the light off as he left.

He was met in the corridor by Jeremy and Michael, who were standing by the final door. John was placing his static charge detector in the middle of the corridor and turned it on. The others all entered the final room, which was the largest of all of them. The four-poster bed sat on top of a raised wooden platform in the center of the room. The walls were covered in black and white photographs and painted pictures. They separated and looked at the pictures: photographs of children sitting together in pretty dresses and shirts and trousers. There were several pictures of a family, the man standing proud behind a chair, and his wife sitting, looking pale and non-expressional. The children, all of whom looked to be a similar age, stood around the chair either side of him, none of them smiling.

Other pictures showed the dining room filled with people. All sat, looking down the table towards whoever was taking the picture. The table itself was full of food: roasted pig, what looked like pheasants still feathered, and a head of a stag, its antlers adorned with ribbons. Michael looked at a painting and noticed that it was of the mansion, but in front of it were several small fires with people standing around them. He looked closer and saw that within the fires were partly painted shapes of people.

'What kind of people lived here?' he asked out loud.

The others all turned and stared at him. They all shook their heads and shrugged their shoulders.

Tony set up the tripod while Jeremy fixed the camera on top of it. Tony then radioed down to Phoebe to check that she was receiving a picture before sighing heavily and telling the others it was time to head back to the dining room, which had become their base camp to plan for the evening's walk through.

While the investigators were setting up the cameras, Phoebe had felt the temperature in the room drop. The large sculpture that rose from the table cast a strange shadow, and she was sure that she had seen the shadows move. When she looked up from the TV monitors, she could see nothing. Just as she received the message from Tony that they were heading back, she heard what sounded like a child laughing. She looked around the room but saw nothing. Then she heard it again, this time coming from above her. She looked up at the ceiling but saw nothing but the small chandeliers that filled the room with light. She looked back at the monitors and saw a figure run past the camera in the kitchen. She grabbed the radio off the table and began asking where the others were and if they were trying to scare her. She heard a buzzing and then the others walked into the room.

'Did you hear that?' she asked.

'Hear what?' John asked. She explained about the laughter and the figure moving past the camera.

She rewound the recording but could see nothing. The others then asked her to run the footage back so they could try and explain their experiences, but nothing was found on the recordings.

Even the brief EVP session that John had taken showed no evidence of what he had heard.

On the way down the stairs, Tony had picked up the book that contained information about each of the rooms. He sat down at the large dining room table and began reading, filling the others in with what was written as they continued to check recordings and prepare their recording equipment ready for the night's investigation.

'The master bedroom, the one with the bed on the platform, is apparently where there has been sightings of a man and woman. They stand at the end of the bed and pull the sheets off the bed if anyone sleeps in it. It doesn't say who they are. The children's room is where people have heard child laughter, and some of the toys have moved. People who have tried to stay the night in the other rooms have reported they have been attacked, leaving them with scratches and bruises. Figures have been seen in most of the rooms.'

'What about that weird blacked out room you told us about?' Jeremy asked Tony.

He looked through the pages for further information about the room and found only one small paragraph. He began to read it out.

'The projector room is one of the most sinister and macabre rooms of the upper level. Its large crystal chandelier is the only one known in existence. The pictures imbedded within the crystals are believed to be of drifters and trespassers caught hiding amongst the trees of the property grounds. Who did the killing and mutilations no one knows.'

'Jesus, this place is not right,' Phoebe said.

Tony placed the book down on the table and sighed. He'd wanted to investigate the mansion for so long and now he finally had his chance; he didn't want to make any mistakes or miss any possible evidence of the existence of the paranormal. He was already excited after what he and the team had witnessed so far.

'I've made sure that all the wooden outdoor window shutters have been closed and locked. All the doors to the outside are locked so there can be no interference from anyone,' he said.

Phoebe and Jeremy looked at him. They both had an uneasy feeling about being locked in with no escape in case things went wrong. Recently, another paranormal investigation group had been locked into an old building when it caught fire, killing the team inside.

Tony set out the evening schedule: who was going to what room and what experiments they would undertake. John and Michael were to head to the kitchen and use a thermal camera as they conducted an electronic voice phenomenon session. At the same time, Phoebe and Jeremy would conduct EVP sessions and thermal camera sessions in the dining room.

'So many have died in here we should be able to capture something with all our equipment. I will head into some of the other rooms and conduct EVP and night vision sessions,' he said.

There was a slight pause, and then Jeremy asked the main question that was on everyone's mind.

'When are we doing the upper floors?'

Tony looked at the team and responded, 'The early hours.'

Just as he said that, an icy blast of air descended into the room. They could all feel the cold breeze move down from their heads to their feet. They all looked up at the large sculpture. The antlers that it was made out of seemed to glisten in the light.

'Where's that cold air coming from?' John asked.

Tony shook his head; it didn't feel like a normal winter's breeze; it had a strange thickness to it—it felt heavy.

Outside it began to snow.

'Right, before we get started, I need to visit the ladies room,' Phoebe said.

The others looked at her and rolled their eyes. Every time they were about to start an investigation, she needed to go to the toilet. She had noticed a door just off to the side of the kitchen that said 'Toilet' when they had had their walk through with the old man, she had not seen any other toilet or bathroom.

'Did any of you notice any bathrooms upstairs?' she asked.

The four men looked at each other, their brows low as they concentrated on remembering whether they had seen one or not. They then all shook their heads.

'So apart from the one off the kitchen—well I hope it is one—there are no other toilets or bathrooms?' she questioned.

4

Phoebe made her way through the small adjoining rooms and entered the kitchen. The coldness of the room made her skin pimple. She saw the white door in the corner; the small sign plate on it reading 'Toilet' made her sigh with relief. She walked over to it and pulled the handle. It opened to reveal an old white porcelain toilet with a handle hanging from a long silver chain from the tank which was situated about seven feet above the toilet seat. She looked at the wall and saw the light switch, which she flicked straight away. A dull, yellowish light sprang from the bulb in the center of the ceiling. She then looked to see if there was any toilet paper, and she smiled when she noticed a full roll. She quickly stepped in and closed the door behind her. A sigh of relief escaped her as she pulled down her jeans and knickers just in time for her to begin to relieve her full bladder. Phoebe stared at the wooden door in front of her as she sat on the toilet seat. There was something strange about the grain of wood and the numerous circular knots clearly visible beneath the coat of white paint. She pulled a couple of sheets of toilet paper from the roll and wiped herself. Then she stood and pulled her knickers and jeans back up, still looking at the door as she fastened her buttons. It was then that she noticed what was so strange about the door. Rather than made up of several long panels of wood, the door seemed to be made from one piece. She ran her fingers across it and could not feel any joins only the raised areas where the knots lay.

She slid the little bolt across that locked the door and pushed, but the door didn't move. She tried again, but once more it didn't move. She paused, thinking back to when she entered and whether she pulled it or pushed it. There wasn't enough room for the door to open inwards, and she clearly remembered pulling it shut.

She pushed one more time, but yet again it didn't budge. She stood back and looked around the frame of the door to see if there was some form of catch that had locked the door, but there was nothing.

The paint on the door began to bubble as if it were liquid boiling in a pot. More and more bubbles rose and popped. She looked at the walls and noticed that they too were bubbling. She could feel her heart pounding against her chest as she began to panic. She turned and looked at the toilet and noticed the water in it was bubbling away and rising up until it began to flow over the top of the bowl, cascading to the floor and surrounding her boots. She spun around to face the door again and its bubbling surface. It was then that she saw something begin to grow from its center. The outline began to take a definite shape, and soon she could make out the nose and brow of a face, its mouth open in a strange smile. It turned left and right as it got closer to her. She backed away until she could feel the toilet seat against the back of her knees. The water that continued to flow over its lip burned into her skin. She screamed, calling out the names of the others, hoping they could hear her and get to her in time.

Jeremy was the first to hear Phoebe's cries for help. He didn't move first time, not sure of what he was hearing. When he heard the second scream, he bolted from his position, shouting to the others who were deep in conversation to follow him. They ran into the kitchen and heard Phoebe's screams full of fear and panic. They ran over to the toilet door and yanked at it. It shot open; there was no resistance. Standing on the toilet seat with her hands covering her eyes, screaming, was Phoebe. Jeremy called her name and grabbed her by the arms. She looked up from her hands and saw the others all stood in the toilet doorway, concern etched on their faces.

'What's wrong?' Jeremy asked her, his eyes wide with confusion.

'It wouldn't let me go, I couldn't open the door. The water wouldn't stop; it was burning me,' she said in panic-stricken gasps.

'What wouldn't and what water?' Tony asked.

She looked down at the toilet and the floor. There was no sign of the hot boiling water that had begun to burn her feet and legs as she tried to get away from the face pushing through the door.

She stepped down from the toilet seat and explained what had happened, tears flowing down her face. Jeremy put his arm around her and helped her back to the dining room. The others looked at the toilet, trying the door to see if it had somehow locked itself.

They returned to the dining room, where Phoebe was sipping on a small cup of tea, poured from Jeremy's thermos flask.

'Phoebe, we need you to explain everything that happened again, in detail. We need to record everything that has happened,' Tony said, placing a Dictaphone in front of her and pressing the record button.

She looked at him, and then the small recorder, sighed, and began telling her story once more. The others listened carefully, their mouths slowly opening when she recalled the face appearing from the bubbling door.

Once she had finished, Tony then began telling his experiences whilst in the bedrooms, and he encouraged the others to share their experiences. Each one spoke in turn into the recorder, and as they did, each one began to realize that the investigation they were about to undertake would be a very memorable one, one like none they had ever done before.

After they had eaten the food that they had stored away in cooler bags, they began their investigation.

John and Michael headed to the kitchen. The thermal camera held by John leading the way, they both stared at the little monitor that showed what was ahead of them. They opened the door to the kitchen and stepped in. The screen went a blank and then began showing the outlines of all the tables, chairs, and other kitchen implements in different shades of blue.

'Man it's cold in here,' Michael said.

John moved the camera around, sweeping the kitchen. 'Mike, can you walk in front to show a comparison?' he asked.

Michael stepped out in front of the camera and began walking over to the large table that sat in the center of the room, a large rack of pots and pans hung over it. In the center sat a rack full of knives. The moment he walked into frame the screen showed his body's outline in reds, greens, and whites where his body was hottest.

Michael took out his recorder, pressed the record button, and placed it on the table. He then began asking the normal set of questions that he had used in each of the previous investigations.

'Is there anyone here with us at the moment?' He paused before asking the next question. 'If there is someone here, can you make yourself known to us by making a noise?' he paused again.

They both felt a cold blast of air rush past them, and the pots and pans hanging above the table swayed and clashed gently against each other, making gentle clanging noises.

'Is there anyone here with us at the moment?' John asked.

A little red light on the recorder began flashing against the darkness of the room, catching the two investigators' attention. The recorder stopped flashing just as another icy blast of air rocked the pots and pans again.

John panned the thermal camera around the room. Apart from the heat from Michael, everything showed up in the cold blue color. He lowered the camera and looked ahead of him towards Michael, but something in the screen caught his attention—a different color. He raised the screen back up to his eye so he could focus on what the camera was pointing at and saw a light blue outline of a hand. His gasp alerted Michael, who looked through the darkness towards the face of his friend that was slightly lit by the cameras detachable screen.

'What is it?' he asked.

'You got to look at this,' John said excitedly.

Michael moved over to him and looked into the screen, he too gasped when he saw the light blue outline of the body that was being caught on the camera. John began to raise the camera and noticed another hand, then a leg, and then a head all bathed in a light blue against the coldness of the dark blue of their surroundings. They began moving back towards the door that they had walked through, still looking into the camera's monitor. Michael pulled his radio from his belt and radioed to base camp to see if the others were picking up anything on the night vision camera positioned in the corner of the room.

'That's a negative. But we can see you moving towards the door,' Phoebe replied.

Tony looked at the TV monitor carefully that showed the kitchen before radioing to Michael.

'What are you experiencing?'

'We are picking up what seems like bodies on the thermal camera. They are covering the floor; it's as if they have been dumped on top of each other. The room is covered in them,' Michael responded.

Neither of the two investigators could feel anything but the hard floor beneath their feet but, yet when they moved the camera to where their feet were, they could see the reds and whites of their feet standing on the light blues of the bodies.

Another icy blast or air rushed past them, and this time it brought a strange metallic smell with it that engulfed the two men's senses. Out in the darkness of the room, the little red light on the recorder began to flash again.

'Shit,' Michael said, seeing the light flash.

'Just leave it. This is getting real weird. Let's get out of here; we got enough footage,' John said. He was no longer enjoying being in the room.

They moved to the door, and Michael pulled it but it didn't move. He pushed it, but again it didn't move.

'Stop messing around,' John said quickly, looking up from the screen at his partner struggling with the door.

'I'm not messing around. The door won't budge,' he replied.

He raised his radio and called base camp, panic making his voice wobble as he spoke.

'Tony, we can't get out; the door is locked.'

Tony looked at Phoebe; her eyes were beginning to well up, the memory of being locked in the toilet and the face in the door flooding her mind. He looked back at the monitor and could see nothing but the two investigators standing by the door, John pointing the camera towards the room while Michael faced the door and continued to pull at it.

'I'm on my way,' Tony said.

Michael stopped pulling and pushing the door and turned to look into the darkness and the camera monitor. From their position, they could see the floor covered in bodies, their light blue outlines clear against the black and dark blue of the room's walls and objects. They both gasped and felt an electric shock shoot up from their anus to their heads when pairs of bright white dots flicked open on every one of the bodies on the thermal camera's screen. The bright white eyes stared up from the floor towards the dark ceiling.

'Oh my god,' John said, panic clearly evident in his voice.

Michael turned quickly and began to bang on the door, shouting Tony's name.

John backed into him, pushing Michael against the door causing him to stop shouting and turn back towards his friend and the room. They heard a click and a slight whirring sound and then another click.

'What was that?' Michael asked.

'I don't know,' John said, still staring at the camera's monitor and the bodies with white eyes.

From within the darkness, the sound of Michael's voice spoke. The recorder was playing back his set of questions. The two men looked at each other and then out into the darkness. In between the standard questions there was nothing but silence until a low, gravelly voice broke through.

'You are welcome to join us,' it said.

Several other voices joined in, both male and female, all calling at the same time.

'Join us! Stay with us!'

More and more voices joined in, all calling for the two men to join them.

Michael called base camp on the radio, asking where Tony was and if they were receiving what they were hearing.

Phoebe responded, her voice full of tears and terror. 'Tony should be there. I can only hear you.'

The voices continued, more and more joining in. John pointed the thermal camera at the table where the recorder was playing, Michael joined his partner in staring through the monitor at the bodies that covered the floor, their white eyes blinking in unison.

Another cold blast of air rushed around the two investigators; the strong metallic smell that they had noticed earlier was getting stronger. The pots and pans began to clang in the darkness, and then the voices stopped.

For a moment, all was silent; the only sound that the two investigators could hear was their own breathing. They looked up from the little monitor and into the darkness, both straining to make out the shape of the table. When they returned their gaze to the monitor, they both screamed and jumped backwards. The bodies that covered the floor were now standing, the white glowing eyes trained on them. John dropped the camera and monitor, and the sound of the heavy equipment crashing against the cold hard tiled floor echoed around the room. Michael joined him in pounding against the door, shouting for help and for Tony.

On the other side of the kitchen door, Tony pulled and shoulder barged at the large wooden barrier that separated him from his two friends. He called to them, shouting for them to pull. The louder their screams and shouts got, the more frantic Tony became. He was soon joined by Jeremy, who began kicking at the middle of the door just to the left of the handle. They were soon hitting the door with a constant rhythm.

Michael and John both began clawing at the door handle, occasionally looking over their shoulders. It didn't matter that they could not see anything but blackness; their minds had painted the picture of all the bodies standing watching them, and they could feel the all the eyes locked on to them.

'Where the fuck are Tony and the others,' John shouted.

There was no answer from Michael, only a whimper as tears began to flow from his eyes and an intense feeling of fear took hold of him.

Tony and Jeremy heard John's shout and responded by hitting their fists against the door and shouting that they were there. Michael and John heard nothing.

There was another icy blast, and John felt a cold hand grab his shoulder, followed by another and another. Soon he could feel the cold hands grabbing his legs, arms, and body. He let out a loud scream and vanished into the darkness. Michael also screamed and collapsed to the cold floor. He could hear the moans of his partner moving away from him and the sound of his body being dragged along the floor.

Phoebe watched with wide, tear-filled eyes as on the monitor she saw John sliding along the floor, his arms and legs flailing around at an invisible force. He moved past the view of the night-vision camera that had captured his abduction.

John could feel the hands pulling him along the floor. He kicked and punched out, but there was no resistance to strike against. He hit his head against something solid and realized he was being pulled past the large table. He tried to reach out and take hold of it in an attempt to stop whatever was pulling away from his friend and the door. His fingers momentarily wrapped around a leg, but the invisible hands that dragged him along were too strong, and his fingers gave up the fight. A bright light flashed above him; a white light so powerful it stung his eyes. He shut them tight, but the light still attacked his sight through his eyelids.

It then went all black.

The kitchen door burst open, Tony and Jeremy flew forward with it, and the heavy door collided with the kneeling, sobbing body of Michael, knocking him over onto the cold, tiled floor. The two rescuing investigators fell over Michael and rolled across the floor. Tony was the first to get to his feet, helping Jeremy up, the little light cast from the small light bulb enabling him to see his two colleagues.

They both helped up Michael and began dragging him back towards base camp, where they were met with an empty room. Phoebe was missing.

Phoebe's mind raced with all the visions of what she had seen in the last few hours. The visions all fought each other to be at the front of her mind: the face, the water, and the sight of John sliding across the floor, kicking and swinging wildly. Her whole body shook with fear, her chest began to get tighter, and she fought against the rising feeling of panic and distress.

She heard a giggle and turned from staring at the TV monitor to look at the table and its large sculpture. Impaled on the sharp antlers looking down at her were three children: two girls and a boy. The clothes that they wore were the same style as some of the people that she had seen in some of the photos that were placed on the fireplace from the early 1900s. The clothes were heavily stained with red where the antlers protruded from their bodies. They giggled at Phoebe and held out their arms towards her.

Her already fear-ravaged body and mind could take no more. She pushed herself from the chair she was sitting in and ran from the room, down a corridor, and through an old library, her eyes searching for a way out. But each time she saw a window, it was covered by the large wooden shutters that covered the outside windows. She ran to the front door and tugged at it, but it too didn't move.

She heard another giggle and turned quickly to see one of the young girls that she had seen on the sculpture standing in front of her hugging a doll. The doll was headless and wore a dress that matched the young girl who hugged her.

'Please don't leave us,' the girl said before disappearing, and her giggle continued to reverberate around the hallway.

Phoebe ran back down the hallway, trying each door she passed but finding them locked. She soon found herself standing at the bottom of the staircase. A cold wind wrapped itself around her, and she could feel its rotating icy fingers against her face and her hair being pushed into her eyes. Deep in her psyche, a battle raged. Part of her told her to go back to the dining room and the others, while another fear-fed voice screamed at her to head upstairs and escape her torture via the only way out: the windows.

Tony and Jeremy dragged the shivering, sniveling Michael over to the chairs that sat in front of the TV monitors and dropped him on one. They then leaned on the tap and stared at the monitors and the multiple small screens that fed back what each of the night vision cameras were seeing. They searched each one for any sign of Phoebe. Jeremy was the first to spot her standing motionless at the foot of the staircase. His attention was then caught but something flashing on one of the small screens. The static electricity monitor that John had designed and had placed in the middle of hallway at the top of the stairs was flashing. Tony turned to Michael and grabbed his arms and shook him.

'Get a grip,' he shouted as he slapped Michaels face. 'We need you to help us.'

The slap woke Michael from his sniveling blank staring into space. He looked up at Tony, his eyes wide and blinking wildly, his face a mixture of tears and snot.

'I need you to get in touch with Mr. Bannister, the old man who showed us around, and tell him to come and let us out right away. If you can't get in touch with him, call the police,' Tony said to Michael.

Michael nodded as Tony handed him his mobile phone. Michael then turned to Jeremy, and the two of them left the room.

Phoebe heard a giggle and turned around to see the three children standing behind her, their arms outstretched towards her.

'Please don't leave us,' all three of them said in unison.

Phoebe turned and ran up the staircase. As she climbed the marble steps, she heard the three voices.

'Don't leave us.'

'They always leave us.'

'She is not allowed to leave.'

Phoebe kept moving. She reached the top of the stairs and headed down the hallway, and her attention was fixed on each of the doors. She tried each one as she came to them, but they didn't open. She didn't even notice the bright red, blue, and green flashes of the little device that had been placed on the floor.

She tried another door and it flew open. She moved quickly into the dark room, shut the door, and pressed herself against the door and stared into the darkness, her heart pounded against her chest. Her whole body shook with fear and adrenaline. There was a small line of light ahead of her that separated the darkness like a crack. As her eyes became more accustomed to the darkness around her, she could make out four small beds. She ran her hand along the walls on either side of the door, feeling for a light switch but couldn't find one, she pushed herself off the door and moved towards where the light was coming from and found soft curtains. She fumbled with the material until she found the opening and pulled them open. The grey light of the clouds in the night sky and the snow that covered the ground outside created a strange glow that bathed the room with a soft, grey light. She stood staring out into the white gardens, and a cold breeze woke her from her momentary trance. Then the voices began again. This time, however, there were more of them, and they were all asking her to play.

She looked around her and noticed the pile of dolls and stuffed toys. Their eyes seemed to move and look at her. She returned her attention to the window and searched its frame for a handle or latch that would enable her to open it, but she could find nothing.

***

Michael searched the phone's previous calls until he found the name Bannister next to a number. He pressed the screen, put it to his ear, and waited while it rang. When he heard the ring stop and someone breathe on the other end, Michael quickly began telling Mr. Bannister that they needed help and the door unlocked. He then waited for a response.

The heavy breathing on the other end continued for a few seconds and then a low gravelly voice spoke: 'Come join us. Be our guest.'

Michael moved the phone away from his ear and looked at it; it then burst into flames. He automatically dropped the phone to the floor and stood up from the chair he had been sitting on. The moment the phone hit the floor, the flames disappeared.

He looked at the monitors and scoured them to see where his partners were. He finally saw them running down the hallway upstairs; the small detector continued to flash wildly as they went from door to door. He then heard a thud—and then another and another. It sounded like someone was jumping up and down in the room above him. He stared at the ceiling as more and more heavy banging sounds erupted. He then heard a voice—a voice that called out to him—a voice he knew well. It was the voice of his friend John.

'Where are you?' Michael called, spinning round as he looked up at the ceiling.

'Help me,' John's voice called again.

Michael looked at the monitors and saw that Tony and Jeremy were still in the hallway upstairs banging on the doors. He heard John's cry for help once more and decided to join the other investigators upstairs searching the rooms. He wasn't bothered about Phoebe; he wanted to find his best friend.

***

Tony and Jeremy tried the first door and found it to be locked. Tony beat his fist against it and called Phoebe's name, but no answer came. The sensor that was flashing began to beep rapidly, causing Jeremy to pause as he tried the next door.

What was it that John said? He thought to himself. *The stronger the static charge near or around the sensor, the quicker the flashes and the louder the alarm will beep.*

The beeping increased in time with the pulsing lights and began to increase in level.

Jeremy tried the door and it sprang open. For a moment everything was still and quiet, and then something pulled him into the room. The door slammed behind him. Tony saw his fellow investigator suddenly disappear out the corner of his eye. He turned and ran to the door, shoulder-barging it as hard as he could, and there was no resistance; the door gave way, and he fell into the room, crashing against the large crystal chandelier projector. The walls were awash with the grim pictures that were encased within it, and a strong cold wind blew around the room, making the crystals gently jingle as they moved. The pictures on the wall also moved, but not because of the wind blowing the chandelier. The pictures on the wall were alive. It was like watching a number of small movies on a cinema screen, only this one showed how the people that he had seen earlier were mutilated and killed. Hooded figures tortured the people with knives, spears, and burning torches.

He forced himself to look away, searching the room for his friend. Tony saw a leg and then another. He crawled along the floor until he found Jeremy, who was sitting up against one of the walls. His arms were stretched out straight against the wall and his eyes were wide and didn't blink; they looked like they had been glued open. They streamed with tears as the wind brushed against them and flung dust and dirt into them.

Tony grabbed Jeremy by the jumper and pulled, but he didn't move. He grabbed the jumper with his other hand and pulled again, and this time there was a little movement. He tugged again, and slowly Jeremy began to peel from the wall. Once he was free from whatever force had stuck him to the wall, Tony dragged him back to the opening of the room and back through the open door into the hallway. The moment they had cleared the door frame, the door slammed shut.

Michael stopped his run when he saw the other two crawl out of the room. The beeping from the sensor was now a high-pitched wail.

'I heard John calling for help,' he shouted.

The other two lay on their backs, staring up at him, mouthing and gesticulating that they couldn't hear him.

Michael stepped over them and ran to the sensor. He paused and then stamped his foot down as hard as he could. He repeated the stamping until all was silent. He ran back to the other two men, who were now sitting up, and repeated his message. They looked at each other and then stood quickly.

'I'll check the rooms on the right, and you and Jeremy search the rooms on the other side,' Tony said quickly.

***

Phoebe put her hands against the glass window of the children's bedroom. The sharp, cold feeling momentarily stopped all other feelings until the numerous voices once again filled her head.

'Stay with us,' they said collectively.

She turned around and saw several faint children's figures dance around the room in front of her. It was like watching a sped up movie, where the person being shot is blurred by the speed of the film. She could tell that there were several because of the different colored dresses or shirts that they wore in their blurred appearance. She felt the strong biting wind that she felt at the bottom of the staircase wrap its coldness around her like a blanket. The next feeling she had was that of small hands holding her arms and legs. They began to pull her away from the window towards the pile of toys. Phoebe fought against the force that was pulling her. She grabbed the window frame with her fingertips and pulled. The adrenaline that surged around her body fought back against the fear and the hands that pulled at her.

'Don't go, we want you to stay,' the voices chanted in unison.

For a moment, the hands let go. Phoebe re-established her place in front of the window and began pounding her hands against the pane. Outside, a crow flew past idly, its blackness dirtying the light grey clouds and whiteness of the untouched snow. Its eyes catching glimpsed a woman banging against a window, but there was no sound.

The cold wind increased in strength—as did the voices. They no longer called for her to stay; they now screamed at her in anger that she wanted to leave.

Phoebe felt the hands grab her body once more. This time they pinched at her skin and pulled at her hair. She screamed as she continued to fight against the invisible force, once again clinging to the frame of the window by her fingers. The voices got louder and louder, shouting and screaming at her.

'You are like the others!'

'You will stay here forever! You will not leave us!'

Amongst the young childlike voices were a few deeper, older ones. These shouted at her and bullied her senses.

'You whore, we won't let you leave.'

'You are going to suffer like all the others, you bitch.'

Tears flowed freely down her face as she fought to hold onto the window frame. She managed to scream and shout for help before using her remaining energy and fight to pull against the hands that tugged at her.

Out of the corner of her tear-filled eye, she noticed a bright light begin to grow. She didn't want to look, but she couldn't help herself. From within the pile of toys, a bright white light began to shine. The toys surrounding it all held out their hands towards her as if it was they who were pulling her towards them. The light grew in size and brightness, and she could make out several figures standing on either side of the mountain of toys: boys and girls all laughing at her. She turned her face and looked to the window and her fingers. Standing in front of her was a young girl, her hair not being disturbed by the strong wind that circled the room, her dress, white with embroidered red roses, had a red stain around its neck. As Phoebe stared into the young girl's pale face, she could see the long red open wound running around her throat. The young girl smiled at Phoebe and then began prying her fingers from the window frame. Each time the girl pulled a finger from it, Phoebe could feel the iciness of the girls touch. When the strength of the pulling hands over came the last two of her resisting fingers, Phoebe was pulled towards the light and the pile of toys. Phoebe's wide eyes stared at the young girl, who waved at her. She tried to let out a final scream, but nothing escaped her mouth before her body was pulled into the space between the toys created by the bright white light.

Phoebes' last vision of the outside world before all went black was several children's faces peering into the hole she was being sucked into and smiling.

The moment the light died, the door burst open. Tony stood at the doorway breathing heavily. He had been wrestling with the door for a few minutes, fighting against either a strong wind that pushed the door closed each time he attempted to open it or an invisible force that teased him by allowing him to open the door slightly only to push it shut again.

Tony's eyes scoured the room. For the briefest of seconds, he saw the figure of a young girl standing by the window. He did a double take, but what or whoever he saw was gone. He walked over to the window and peered out. The snow covered landscape encapsulated him. Even though it was night, the light from the snow clouds and snow on the ground enabled him to see most of the garden. His moment of solace was broken by the giggles and laughter of children and the echoing cry for help from Phoebe.

He called her name and waited, and her cry for help came again. He found it hard to pinpoint where her cry had come from due to the reverberation. He ran out of the room, into the corridor, and on to the next room.

Jeremy and Michael paused outside the next bedroom door. They both put an ear to it and listened. When they heard nothing, they smiled to each other and removed their ears before Jeremy turned the handle and pushed the door open. The large four-poster bed with the stained mattress sat in the darkness of the room, its outline just visible. Jeremy slid his hand along the wall. The last thing he wanted was to enter the room completely until there was enough light to see everything in there.

The chandelier burst into life, the small spots of light covering the walls and floor. A strong cold breeze moved around the room, causing the crystals of the light fixture to sway, the lights that they cast danced around the room, and the light chinking sound of them colliding added to the effect. The four-poster bed and its stained mattress stood somewhat proud in the center of the room. A strong damp smell attacked their senses. The smell was so strong that it also had a taste. They stepped into the room together and moved slowly towards the bed. They were so close together that to an outsider looking in they would have thought they were joined at the hip. As they moved around the room, they could hear the carpet beneath them give off squelching noises. They both paused looked down and saw that they were standing on a large dark stain. As they pushed down with their weight, thick red liquid spurted up over their shoes.

'What the hell is that? Please don't tell me that is blood,' Michael said.

Jeremy moved his feet around, displacing more of the liquid, and shrugged his shoulders before moving over to the bed. Michael stayed where he was and just stared at his feet. The cold breeze that had made the crystals move on the chandelier began to build in strength, its iciness making the two investigators shiver. The crystals began to chime louder and louder as they crashed together, causing the dancing lights to become blurred lines and circles as some began to rotate. Michael quickly moved towards Jeremy; he didn't want to be on his own even if by a few meters. A red liquid began to seep from the large stains on the walls, and it flowed down to the floor and began to pool on the carpet.

'Let's get out of here,' Michael shouted against the now strong wind blowing around the room. He looked back at the door, and it was still open.

'Ok there's nothing in here anyway,' Jeremy shouted back.

They both turned and began moving to the open door. They had made only two steps each towards it when it slammed shut, and a deep voice began laughing.

They looked at each other, tears beginning to well up in Michael's eyes again. It had always been fun, sharing the odd scare here and there on ghost hunting nights with John; they were the ones who always had an answer to whatever happened; they were Tony's debunkers. Never in his wildest dreams would he have thought he would have to deal with anything like this.

Jeremy turned and pulled at the door handle. He may have been the more religious one of the group, but this was way above his expertise.

They both began shouting for help, and the swirling cold wind that raced around the room forced them to shout as loud as they could.

'You are my guests! Let me entertain you,' the voice said. It was as if the cold wind were speaking to them because the voice was clear and unhindered by the wind's noise.

There was a cracking sound, and a heartbeat later, Jeremy sank to his knees. He screwed his face in agony. There was another cracking sound, and he screamed in pain once again. He arched his back as bloody slits appeared on his brown jumper.

Michael stared at his colleague, mesmerized by the bloody whip marks appearing before his eyes.

'Stop it,' he screamed.

The voice laughed once more.

The wind began to die, and the clanging of the chandelier eased. The lights cast by the crystals returned to slow, swaying dots. The door opened slightly, forcing Michael to jump. He pulled at it, flinging it open until it crashed against the wall. Michael grabbed Jeremy by the armpits and dragged him into the corridor. Once clear of the room, the door slammed shut once more. Michael quickly moved to where he could see Jeremy's back and the bloody cuts he had witnessed in the room. Jeremy remained on all fours, his breathing heavy.

'What the?' Michael said within a gasp through tear-filled eyes.

'What is it? How bad is it? It stings and burns; what's happened to me?' Jeremy asked. There was a sense of exhaustion in his voice.

'Nothing,' Michael replied. 'There's nothing wrong with you. The cuts and blood that I saw happening right in front of me are no longer there. There's nothing wrong with your back.'

'What do you mean? Nothing? I feel like I've been whipped,' Jeremy said.

Michael put his hand on Jeremy's back just in case the angle he was standing was hiding the cuts.

'There's nothing wrong with you,' he said again.

Michael sat down next to Jeremy, who turned over and sat motionless too. They both looked at the next door and then at each other.

'You sure you heard him up here?' Jeremy asked Michael.

'His voice came from above me,' Michael responded.

They both looked at each other again and then stood and moved towards the last door on the left side of the hallway.

***

Tony turned the handle of the bedroom door and pushed. The door swung open slowly with a creak. He paused before stepping in. the door creaked as it closed slowly behind him. He turned and watched it close. When he heard the click of the lock, he returned his gaze back to the room. The grimy window let in a strange light cast from the reflection of the snow. He looked up at the mosaic mirror that covered the ceiling. His body was stationary, but his eyes were searching it. His eyes widened and his mouth dropped open as he watched his reflection walk from his position over to the bed and smile at him. He quickly looked down at the bed but saw nothing. He returned his gaze to the ceiling, seeing his reflection now joined by a naked Phoebe. She sat next to the reflection of Tony, who then pushed her back onto the bed and buried his face into her naked breasts. Tony looked up and began shaking his head. Phoebe wrapped her legs around the waist of Tony and began moaning as she writhed around. The reflection of Tony then raised his hands above his head, and a long blade glistened in the low light. The blade was brought down quickly and with force into Phoebe's chest. He shouted out as he watched blood spray from her chest and red splatter fly from the blade each time the reflection withdrew the blade only to plunge it in again.

Tony forced himself to look at the bed and saw nothing. His chest began to feel tight, and he was struggling for breath. He stumbled towards the bed and collapsed onto it, burying his face into the cold covers. He turned his head to try and take in as much as air as possible. As he gulped large amounts of stale-tasting air, he noticed the painting. The skeletons that sat at the table were all gone. He could feel the tightness begin to lift and sat up, staring at the picture. A cold wind blasted from beneath the bed, lifting the sheets that hung over the gap between the floor and frame. He felt something grab his ankles and pull. Tony flew forward off the bed, crashing face first to the floor. He spread his hands out, trying to grip the smooth wooden floor but could feel whatever was pulling him was winning as he began to move towards the bed. He turned his head to see what was pulling him and shrieked when he saw four skulls grinning back at him, their bony fingers wrapped around his ankles and calves. He tried to kick but couldn't create enough space or momentum to knock the skeletal hands off him.

The skeletons dragged him beneath the bed, and he reached up in a last-ditch attempt to stop from being pulled completely under. He rolled onto his back and gripped the bed sheets, and there was a moment when he felt the sheets give way and then the weight of them, combined with the tightness of the tucked in corners, anchored him where he was. He could feel the skeletal hands begin to claw at the flesh on his legs. He grimaced as he felt the grating of bony fingers against his shin bone.

There was then a huge sense of relief when the hands ceased clawing at him. He quickly kicked his legs, using them to push himself clear of the bed, and he stood quickly. First he checked the bed and then his legs; he couldn't see any marks or tears in his jeans. He moved to the door and pulled at it, but it didn't move. Whatever was in the room hadn't finished with him yet; he could sense it. He quickly moved to the window and looked out. The blanket of snow cast an eerie light across the gardens; even the darkness of the gathered trees were lit by the pureness of the snow.

A fox ran from beneath the trees and paused as it looked at the house and the man standing in the window. It then darted away as if it had seen a predator. Tony watched as dark, shadowy figures began appearing from beneath the trees. There was a strange humanness to the shapes, even though their form constantly changed. For a moment, he wasn't concerned by the fact that the wind had begun to swirl around him in the room or that moments earlier he had been attacked by skeletal figures; he was mesmerized by the shapeless figures as they glided across the snow towards the house. He was so transfixed by the black figures that continued to move from within the trees that he didn't even notice the growing white light that had begun to emanate from beneath the bed.

The figures gathered on the snow-covered garden beneath the window that Tony stared out of. They then began to float up into the cold night air until they came level with the window. Tony continued to stare, his mouth hanging open, his eyes wide in amazement. His body seemed to be unable to move from the spot he was standing. A voice in his head screamed at him to get away from the window and escape the room, but his body refused. The dark figures hung in front of him, their numbers growing until they began to melt together, creating a black blanket that covered his view of the whiteness of the garden. All of a sudden the black canvass in front of him came alive with hundreds of white eyes flickering open. His paralysis was broken with a sudden injection of terror at seeing all the eyes open, and he stumbled backwards. At last he felt the coldness of the wind against his face and the glow of the light beneath the bed. His heart pounded, his mind raced, and he turned to the door and pulled at it, but it still resisted. He looked up at the mirrored ceiling and saw hundreds of bright white eyes blinking at him. He looked at the white light beneath the bed and saw the skeletons who had attempted to drag him beneath it waving at him. He struggled to breathe as his heart raced faster and faster, and his lungs struggled to draw in enough air against the strong wind that blew around the room. Tony turned back to the door and began shouting and banging on the door. He tugged at it again and again.

'You are going to join us,' a deep voice sniggered.

The door sprung open, catching Tony off guard. He fell backwards, his gaze looking up at the hundreds of white eyes staring at him. He rolled himself up onto his hands and knees and quickly scuttled out. The moment he crossed the threshold of the door, it slammed shut. He collapsed onto his back, gasping for air, and for the first time, he noticed the warm dampness on his upper leg. He lifted his head and looked at his leg and the damp patch where his bladder had given up trying to repress its contents against the terror and fear that surged through his body.

Jeremy and Michael pushed open the bedroom door. It opened slightly and then stopped. They exchanged glances, and Jeremy pushed the door a little harder. It began to move again, revealing the large four-poster bed in the center of the room bathed in a strange grey light. They slowly entered, moving quickly past the bed and to the large window. They stood starring out into the snow-covered front garden and driveway. They both looked down at the snow-covered vans that they had parked out front and then along the fine outline of the driveway border. Michael then grabbed Jeremy's arm.

'What you doing?' Jeremy asked, pulling his arm away.

'Look!' Michael gasped before pointing out towards the statues that lined the long drive way.

Jeremy focused hard on the sculptures and then gasped himself.

Out in the snow-covered driveway, the strange contorted sculptures moved in swirling movements as if swaying to a silent piece of music. As they swayed in unison, a slight green hue surrounded them, making the sight even more sinister and scary.

Behind the two men staring out of the window, the door slowly closed, and the faint lines on the wallpaper began to emanate a bright red light,

The click of the door closing caught the men's attention. They turned quickly and stared wide-eyed at the glowing red outline of several large pentagrams. The segments of the star had small symbols within them. The outer triangles of the star housed symbols that represented earth, wind, fire, water, and a circle with a hand print in the center. The large wardrobe began to vibrate, its doors rattling as if someone were trapped inside and was trying to get out. Michael grabbed Jeremy's arm again, who was so overwhelmed by what he was seeing he didn't notice his friend's hand grip tighter and tighter.

The doors of the wardrobe suddenly burst open, and the two men were knocked to the floor by the sudden force of wind that escaped from it. The wind swirled around them. It had a thickness to it that made it feel like a snake was wrapping itself around their bodies. The intensity of the pentagram lines began to increase, before pulsing like a police car's emergency lights. With each pulse came a wave of air that blasted the two men as they sat on the floor. Michael was the first to try and get up but found that he couldn't. The sheer weight and density of the wind that flew around them had pinned him down. Jeremy tried, straining against the invisible force. He managed to move onto his knees when he felt a cold hand grab his shoulder. He looked back, expecting to see Michael holding him but was met by a large black shadow. He looked up to where the head and face should be but was met with a dark space with two bright white circles where his eyes should have been. Jeremy naturally drew in a lung full of stale, air ready to scream, when the shadowy figure plunged its free black hand into his open mouth. He could feel his airway begin to struggle against the smoky obstruction. He swatted at the shadow figure, but his arm passed straight through it. With every second, he could feel his life and fight begin to drain away.

Michael sat motionless as his friend fought against the large dark figure. The wind continued to swirl around him, pushing him back each time he attempted to move. He began to shout at the dark shape, cursing at it and pleading for it to stop and leave them alone.

The figure's bright white eyes looked down on the man struggling for air beneath it and blinked.

The wind suddenly disappeared, the shadow was gone, and the walls were once again bathed in a strange grey light.

Jeremy began to gasp for air and cough. The sudden release from the invisible restraint forced Michael to shoot forward, almost head butting his own bent knee.

The bedroom door clicked and opened slowly. The two men looked up at it and quickly got to their feet and exited the room. They pushed themselves through the door into the hallway to find Tony sitting up with a large wet patch on his trousers. For a moment they did nothing but stare at each other.

It was then that they heard the laughter and music.

The three men looked at the first door in the hallway. It had been locked when they had tried it earlier but now it was open. Children's laughter escaped the room, and a warm yellow glow shone from the small crack of the open door.

There was more laughter and music coming from downstairs, unlike the laughter in the bedroom, the several voices laughed out loud in deep, strong tones.

'What do we do?' Jeremy asked, looking at Tony for an answer.

Tony shrugged his shoulders and then looked back at his two friends.

'We need to find the other two, which means going in there,' he said, nodding towards the open door of the bedroom.

He stood up and pulled his damp trousers away from his skin. The damp patch returned quickly to its original position, sending an unpleasant cold, wet feeling to Tony's brain and causing him to shiver.

The three men slowly approached the open door, listening to the laughter and voices as they chattered away. Tony pushed the door, and it gently creaked open, revealing the room with a large four-poster and all the photos and paintings on the walls. They began to enter cautiously when Jeremy stopped them.

'Wait, I'm not getting locked in this room.' He quickly moved to the electrical charge detection machine that sat smashed in the middle of the hallway. He returned to the door and placed it against the door frame.

'If the door tries to close, this will keep it open,' he said.

The other two looked at it wedged against the door frame and then Jeremy nodded and proceeded into the room.

Laughter echoed around them, and the light from the small crystal chandelier cast a strange yellow hue onto the picture-covered walls. The light seemed to have a texture—a movement about it. It was this that intrigued Jeremy, who walked over to the wall that was covered in photographs and leaned into it, getting as close as her could without touching it. His eyes focused on the thin streamer-like lines that gently oscillated. He turned and looked at the chandelier and then back to the wall. *What is making this movement?* He thought to himself.

The other two walked around the large four-poster bed, watching as the sheets gently rose and fell as if someone were breathing from within the mattress, causing the sheets to rise in the form of a hill and then fall quickly as if being sucked back. They looked at each other. Michael continued to shake. Tony could see his fellow investigators hands and arms vibrating rapidly. He looked down at his own hands and lifted them slightly and noticed their tremor.

The laughter grew louder, and more and more voices joined in: chatter and then laughter, chatter and laughter.

'What do you want?' Michael shouted. He could no longer take any more; his mind was overcome by fear and panic. He began to cry uncontrollably. Jeremy moved over to him and put a hand on Michael's shoulder. He could feel his friend flinch the moment his hand touched him.

'What do you want? Where are they?' he shouted again, through snot and tear-filled lips.

The laughter and chatter died. In that moment, all was silent, causing all three of the men to look at each other nervously. They could feel the tension in the air building. There was a sound like someone drawing in a breath, and then the answer came, with multiple voices responding in unison.

'We want you to stay, join us. Yes, join us.'

At the same time that the voices answered, a strong blast of air engulfed the room. The bed sheet blew off the bed, momentarily covering Michael and Jeremy. In his hysterical and panic-stricken frame of mind, Michael began thrusting his arms out, trying to get the sheet off his head. He was so focused on removing the sheet he didn't feel his hand collide with a heavy object.

Jeremy began pulling at the sheet. Just as it slid from his head, he was hit hard in the mouth and then in the nose by the flailing Michael. He fell backwards, falling like a felled tree, and the back of his head bounced off the wooden floor with a loud thud.

Tony moved quickly over to Jeremy, crouching next to him and lifting his head, calling his name. He could feel dampness on one of his hands; he removed it and saw it was covered in blood.

Michael began shouting and screaming for the voices to stop. Tony looked up and saw his friend spinning around. His hands covered his ears as he shouted at the invisible force and the voices. He finally stopped and ran towards the door. Just as he reached it, it began to close. Initially it was slow, but as he closed in, it picked up speed.

He looked at the broken electrical charge detector that was placed against the door frame and smiled to himself internally. The door slammed against the obstruction and began retreating a few inches before once again slamming into it. Michael reached the door and grabbed at it. He pulled with every last ounce of strength, trying to open it far enough for him to escape the room. The invisible force that continued to slam the door eased enough for Michael to open it and squeeze through.

He made it into the hallway, his right hand gripping the door frame to help steady himself while he fought to pass through the small gap. The door swung open and then smashed against the obstruction at the foot of the frame. What was left of the machine shattered, and the door slammed into its correct position.

Tony watched with horror as he saw his friend's fingers fall to the floor on his side of the door and heard a blood curdling scream from outside. Then the voices began laughing once more.

Jeremy slowly opened his eyes. The blurred vision that greeted him was of his friend and group leader, Tony. The sudden throbbing feeling from the back of his head forced him to close his eyes again and reach back to where he felt a hand. When he opened his eyes again and brought his hand into view, he could see the crimson liquid that had escaped the large gash on the back of his head.

'Oh Jesus,' he said.

'Come on,' Tony exclaimed, getting to his feet and pulling his friend up with him. Bloody handprints covered the light brown jumper that Jeremy wore from where Tony had pulled at him; a larger, darker stain covered the neckline of the back of the jumper.

The laughter continued, and more and more voices joined in as they moved slowly towards the door. The strange waves of color on the walls began to build up speed, as did the wind that continued to swirl around them.

Jeremy found his eyesight finally begin to focus on what was around him as he and Tony closed in on the door. The photos and paintings that covered the walls were alive; all the faces were laughing. The people danced and jigged, and even the paintings seemed to move in a robotic fashion within the confines of their frames.

Tony grasped the door handle and pulled at it. The door resisted and stuck firm in its frame. He tugged again and again, but there was no movement. Jeremy looked around the room, trying to see if there was anything that they could use to pry open the door. Next to the artistic, boarded-up fireplace sat an old water jug with three iron poker looking implement handles. He ran over to the jug and pulled at one of the handles. He held up what he had grabbed and saw a blackened shovel-shaped end. He threw it to the floor and pulled the next handle. Again he inspected its end and saw the thick bristles of a fireplace brush. He threw that down next to the shovel and yanked at the last handle in the in the jug. He watched as a blackened, thick, pointed end of a poker came free of its dark home. He ran back to the door, pushing Tony aside and ramming the pointed end into the small gap between the door and the frame. He withdrew it several times and returned it sharply back into the same area of wood. The frame began to splinter and crack. As soon as there was enough of a hole, he forced the poker into it and began levering the door open. With each stab at the wood, the voices began to scream, pleading with the two men not to leave but join them.

The door opened with a crack. The force that had been holding it shut had given up. The door flew open, and the two investigators quickly exited. Tony even took time to pick up the three fingers that had fallen to the floor.

As soon as they were safely back in the hallway, the door slammed shut. They looked back down to the far end of it but could see no sign of Michael, only a pool of blood outside the door and then drops of the red liquid disappearing back towards the stairs. The sound of music still filled the air, as did the adult-toned laughter. Tony looked the three fingers he held in his hand and dropped them, disgusted with the fact that he had picked them up in the first place.

6

It was the sound of the door slamming shut and the sight of his hand being in its way that registered first; the pain was secondary, but when it came, it attacked him violently. He watched with tear-filled wide eyes as blood pumped from the three short red and purple stumps that were his fingers. The pain he felt somehow felt like it was coming from the ends of his fingers the ones that were no longer there. Amongst the pain he was feeling, his ears picked out another sound: a childish snigger echoed around him. He pushed his bloody hand into his opposite bicep and held the injured appendage by the elbow, he hoped that this self-cradling arm position would help stop the flow of blood. He ran down the remaining hallway and back down the stairs, which were now illuminated by the large chandeliers that traced their way down the stairway. His subconscious noted that there was something different about the stairs as he descended them, but he was too busy running back to the dining room that had been the group's base camp to take any notice.

He burst into the room expecting to see the bags, cases and monitors that he had helped set up, but all of that was gone. The room was filled with laughter, a bright orange glow of a fire, and smells of food. The laughter was coming from the men and women who were sitting at the table. Their conversations ceased as they all looked at him. A broad-shouldered man who sat at the far end of the table stood and raised his glass towards the injured investigator.

'I am so glad you have decided to join us,' he said.

The others in the room joined him by raising their glasses before taking a sip.

Michael stood frozen, and sweat began flowing down his already moist face. He looked at all the faces staring at him and noticed their pale complexions. There was a strange blue tint to their skin. His attention was then caught by something in his periphery. He looked at the food laid out on the table. His eyes widened so much they could have fallen out of their sockets, and he began to struggle for breath. His chin once again began to tremble, signaling the start of another flood of tears.

The people at the table returned their attention to the food and conversation, apart from the man at the head of the table, who continued to stand and stare at Michael with an evil smile across his face. The guests began pulling at the cooked flesh of the now headless and garnished body of the missing investigator and Michaels best friend, John.

He wanted to run but couldn't move, fear had caused his limbs to refuse any order his brain was telling them. He stood staring at the pale guests ripping pieces of flesh from John's body and impatiently feeding it into their mouths.

'See, not only has your male friend joined us, but your female companion has agreed to entertain us,' the broad-shouldered man said, looking up at the twisted sculpture of deer antlers.

Michael followed the man's gaze and noticed the sculpture begin to move. It rotated like a tornado in slow motion. His cradled arms dropped to his sides when he saw Phoebe appear, her naked, impaled body moving with the rhythmic movement of the antlers. Two antler horns pierced her breasts where her nipples once were, and another seemed to curve round and insert itself into her vagina.

His jaw began to loosely vibrate as if he was trying to say something, but nothing but low quiet moans escaped him. The door opened that led towards the kitchen, and a headless body dressed in a maid's clothing walked in. The body carried a large silver dome-covered serving tray. She moved around the table, placed it in a small space amongst all the other food, and lifted the cover.

Michael screamed when he saw his friends head. Johns face was covered in blisters and charred skin where he had been cooked, and the skin had cracked and hardened like a roast chickens. His mouth was open with his tongue stretched out over his lower lip and chin.

He could take no more. Michael's last vision was a blurred, almost melted collage of color as he collapsed onto the small pool of blood that had escaped his swollen, stumped fingers.

7

Tony and Jeremy could hear the laughter coming from downstairs. They looked at each other with exhausted eyes.

'After you,' Jeremy said with a sigh.

Tony closed his eyes and listened to the inner voice that continued to tell him, *This is what you've been looking for! Real proof! It's going to make you famous.*

He opened them again and began moving towards the stairs, noticing the brightness cast from what he had thought were just decorative, no-longer-working chandeliers. They both pressed their backs against the wall and slowly descended, their eyes searching what was below and along the side of the staircase.

A cold blast of air engulfed them as they reached the midway point in their descent. They both stopped and pressed themselves harder against the wall.

'You beginning to see the pattern here?' Jeremy said.

Tony looked up at him and nodded. It was clear to both of them that the cold wind that seemed to materialize from nowhere was the dark spirits' calling card.

Jeremy tapped Tony on the shoulder and motioned with his head to continue. Tony began moving once more, almost side-stepping down each of the marble steps of the staircase. He stopped again when he saw the three children appear at the bottom. The two girls each held a patchwork doll, and their blond hair was tightly curled like little springs. The boy stood behind them. He looked much older, his dark hair slicked back on his scalp. They all had pale complexions and dark, sinister eyes.

Three voices filled the heads of the two investigators, who stood motionless on the staircase. They both stared at the three children but could not see their mouths move, yet their voices were strong and loud.

'Come join us. Come join the party,' the voices called.

The three children began to slowly fade as if made of dust, and the cold wind that blew around them blew them away grain by grain.

When they had disappeared completely, the two men continued their slow descent of the staircase. There was a sudden blast of cold air that seemed to wrap itself around them, and then the three children suddenly reappeared, standing on the same steps as the two men.

They both felt the sudden electric shock of fear and surprise shoot through their bodies. Their fight or flight response shifted into overdrive, and the two men began launching themselves down the stairs, bounding down the steps and missing one here two there. Finally, Jeremy could no longer keep up with what his legs were doing. His right foot slipped off the edge of one of the lower steps, which made him lose his balance and begin to fall forwards. He reached out his hands and found the back of Tony pushing him forward just as he had reached the final step. Tony felt the heavy shove of his colleague and began to buckle under the strain of momentum and weight. Tony crashed face first onto the cold floor, the bridge of his nose and chin splitting open on impact. Jeremy had the unfortunate luck of having his left hand slip from the back of his friend and smash into the floor at an awkward angle. The sound of his arm breaking and the searing pain resonated in his head.

'Get off me!' Tony shouted, spitting blood onto the floor beneath his face.

Jeremy moaned and rolled onto his back, cradling his arm that hung limp under the support of his strong arm.

The cold wind began to rotate around them. Dust and dirt from the floor began to lift up and show the spinning vortex of the wind.

Tony pushed himself up onto his knees and looked around, wiping his nose and chin with his sleeve. His eyes widened when he saw the large amount of blood smeared on the material. He looked at his friend, who continued to moan while lying on his back and holding his arm. Tony then looked back up the staircase, expecting to see the three children, but they were gone.

He spat a mouthful of blood that had drained from his nose through his nasal cavity onto the floor.

'Come on, we got to get out of here,' he said to Jeremy.

He knelt next to his friend and began to aid him, first into a sitting position and then, once he himself had gotten to his feet, he helped Jeremy into a position where he could get his feet underneath him and allow Tony to pull him up by the armpits. Once they were both standing, they slowly began to walk towards the lights and sounds of the dining room, pushing through the invisible barrier of spinning dust and dirt.

As they entered the dining room, all the laughter stopped. The broad-shouldered man at the head of the table stood and smiled at them as he beckoned them in.

'You have finally made it,' he said.

The two remaining investigators froze. They then felt cold hands push them into the room. They both looked around and saw several young children. The girls all had large white dresses while the boys wore black bow ties on their white shirts. They all pushed the two men further into the room. Both Jeremy and Tony tried to stop their momentum by leaning back and pushing against the cold force, but their legs kept moving forward. Soon they found themselves being pushed onto a chair that had been pulled from the table by a couple of men, who bowed and, as they sat, they then returned to their own chairs. The children then moved around the room, each one standing behind a person sitting on a chair.

'I am so glad you could join us at this special time,' the man at the head of the table said.

Tony looked at all the faces of the people sitting at the table and noticed their pale complexions. Their clothing and hairstyles were of an early Victorian time. He then noticed the partly eaten body of a man, its side and stomach open and revealing a cavernous void where its intestines should have been.

Jeremy gasped and gagged as if he were about vomit. He had seen the head of his friend and fellow investigator, John. The top of his head had been removed and a large silver handle protruded from it. Tony heard his friends gagging sound, and it distracted him from staring at the cooked flesh on the body. He looked at Jeremy and then followed his gaze until he saw the head. Tony could do nothing more than stare. There was no thought or emotion present at that moment—just the vision of the head.

'As you can see, your friends have agreed to join us on this special night—a night when we will all become one—one with each other and one with this great house,' the man said.

His words slowly began to fill the emotionless and empty void of Tony. For a moment there was no sound, and then his inquisitive inner voice began to ask what the man meant.

'I can answer that for you my friend,' the man said, smiling at him.

Tony began shaking his head. He was sure he had not said anything out loud.

'In this house, all voices can be heard. All thoughts can be seen, and all fears and desires can become a reality,' the man continued.

Tony again shook his head and looked nervously at Jeremy, whose pale skin had an almost green hue to it. Jeremy swayed lightly back and forth as the pain from his arm engulfed his body.

'What we believe is that once the body has expired, its spirit or energy can be utilized to help us stay here in our own paradise. This house has been passed down from generation to generation—its secrets and rituals handed on to the next member of the family. The family lineage died out, but we found a way to live on. Sacrifice of the innocent, the taking of the will of someone feeds us—it feeds the house and all that are tied to it through blood.'

Tony looked at all the people sitting at the table. They all smiled and nodded. He then noticed the sculpture of antlers begin to move. It swayed gently as if being blown by a gentle breeze. It then began to rotate.

The man looked up at the sculpture and then at Tony and Jeremy and continued.

'We can give you all that you desire. All you have to do is to give in to us. Your friends have allowed us to share their spirit and energy in exchange for their deepest desires. As you can see,' he said, pointing up at the sculpture.

Jeremy looked up at the two bodies that slowly moved with each other as the sculpture moved, their nakedness and contorted position looking like a page from the Kama sutra, except that in several places antlers protruded from them. He then began to throw up on the table space in front of him.

'What...have...you...done?' Tony stuttered.

'The man desired the woman, and the woman had deep feelings for him, so they received their gift. Each other,' the man said, smiling.

Jeremy suddenly shot to his feet and kicked back the chair. He turned and ran to the open doorway. The children in the room all looked at him as he left, their faces momentarily disfigured. Tony saw their faces and gasped, their real identity revealed: blackened, cracked skulls.

Jeremy ran through the corridor and reached the front door. Even with his arm still being cradled by his un-injured limb, he still managed to launch a heavy kick at them. The loud bang as his foot crashed against the solid oak door echoed around the open hallway. He could feel the cold wind begin to swirl around him, signaling the arrival of a spirit or spirits. He ran back up the stairs, bounding two at a time, until he reached the hallway with all the bedroom doors. He paused, briefly noticing they were all open, and looked back over his shoulder and noticed a spinning vortex of dust and dirt ascending the stairs. He ran along the hallway until he found the room with the large window. The strange grey light from the snow outside still cast an eerie luminance in the room. He ran to the window and kicked at it. The window vibrated, and he stepped back and kicked it again. Still it didn't give in. He looked it up and down, searching for any signs of weakness. He then peered out through it and stepped back quickly. Gathered on the snow-covered lawns were hundreds of black, misty shapes. Bright white eyes blinked at him. A sudden blast of cold air made him shudder, and he turned quickly to see two boys standing at the door, their faces full of anger. He heard a giggle and saw two girls lying on the bed, their lower legs being kicked alternatively in a playful manner as they rested their chins on their interlocked fingers. There was a flicker of black against the grey light, and two more children appeared, a young boy and girl holding hands, their blank, expressionless faces staring at him. He could feel his heart pounding against his chest. His mind was full of a strange, loud nothingness, and he couldn't think straight. He could hear only white noise as his brain and emotions exploded within him.

'You are not allowed to leave.' The sudden sound of several children's voices filled his head.

His whole body shook; he was finding it hard to breathe. Through complete fear, he turned and threw his whole body at the large window. The sudden shattering sound of glass pierced the grey night sky. He stumbled briefly before falling. He felt a moment of peace settle over him, and time slowed down; he felt like he was falling for an age. He had time to hope that the fall would end his torment. He waited for the ground to arrive, but it never did.

As Jeremy burst through the window, the dark shadowy figures quickly began to swarm around him, their dark energy swallowing him up.

8

Tony sat motionless in his seat, his mind full of questions. Even in a state of terror, he could still find himself questioning everything.

'You want to know about your friend on the table? He wanted to be desired and have women enjoy his body,' the man said, laughing.

Tony managed to force out a question, his voice broken by fear.

'Why are you doing this?'

The man sat back down in his chair and lifted his glass of wine.

'Tonight is a special night. The moon is full, and the house is alive with energy. A celestial alignment has allowed us to roam free,' he said.

Tony sat shaking his head, his eyes fixed on the twisting sculpture. Each time the two entwined bodies of his investigating friends appeared, his eyes widened.

'We've been waiting for you for a long time,' the man at the head of the table said.

Tony looked at him with confusion.

'What do you mean?'

'The world beyond the one you live in is full of opportunity. There is no such thing as distance or time. You can travel and hear everyone and everything. We heard your prayers of wanting to visit here. Our living relatives allowed you to be here on this night,' the man said with a grin.

Tony shook his head harder and faster.

'I don't believe you. You're just trying to get into my head,' Tony shouted.

The man began laughing. He placed his wine glass on the table and stood once more. He then began speaking out aloud in Latin.

Tony could do nothing but sit in the chair. He told himself over and over again to move, but his body refused. The man's voice grew louder, Tony could feel the air in the room become thicker, and then it began to crackle with energy. Little sparks exploded all around the room.

An ice-cold wind began to circle the room, picking up the sparks as they exploded and joining them together until a ring of blue light throbbed above the heads of the guests sat at the table. The children moved closer to the guests who sat in front of them. Tony watched as the young girls and boys faces began to darken. Their flesh began to disappear until all that was left was burnt and charred skulls. They brought their hands around to the front of the guests, each child holding a rusty knife. The guests lifted their heads back as if offering their throats to the blades that hung a few inches from their skin.

Tony looked back down at the man who had his arms raised, his hands disappearing into the pulsing blue cloud of energy. The blue ring became more and more intense as he his voice grew louder. The sculpture in the center of the table spun faster and faster until it became almost tornado-like.

The man at the head of the table suddenly stopped his chanting and removed his hands from the ring of energy. When he opened his eyes, they were a shiny black color.

Tony watched as the children drew their rusty blades across the throats of the men and women sitting at the table. No blood escaped the open wounds, only a dark haze that flowed like smoke up into the ring of energy. Once the last of the black smoke of their spirit had escaped the bodies of the guests, they fell forward, their faces smashing into the plates and food that lay in front of them.

Tony could feel his heart pounding against his chest. The anxiety and fear that had welled up inside of him as he sat and watched the spectral deaths of the guests blocked any rational thought. He could feel his spirit fighting against whatever force was keeping him in the seat. Suddenly he was free. The sudden release caused him to shoot to his feet. The children all looked at him and began to shriek, their high-pitched wails forcing him to cover his ears as he bolted to the door.

'There is no escape my friend,' the man at the head of the table shouted just before he faded away.

As Tony reached the door, he had an urge to turn and look back. The sight of the room changed before him like a reseeding tide; half the room was still dressed in all it's splendor and brightly lit and still decorated, while the other half was returning to the darker old room that the team had used as a base camp for their monitors and equipment. On both sides of the room the children still stood, their charred and burned skulls screaming at him.

He ran through to the front door and charged at it. He tucked his head down in preparation for the impact of his shoulder against the door and closed his eyes. The heavy thick-set door didn't even budge. He found himself rebounding and sliding along the floor.

A blast of cold air alerted him to another presence. He didn't want to wait to find out whom or what was going to appear; he just wanted out. He pushed himself to his feet, not even noticing the little pool of blood left by the open gash in his chin, reopened the moment he crashed into the door.

He ran back towards the dining room and almost fell over his team's equipment and monitors. There were no other people or any sign of the ring of blue energy that had hung above the table moments earlier. He quickly looked up at the sculpture and noticed it was back to its darkened, empty self. He moved through the adjacent door and down a small corridor and burst into the kitchen, the darkness of the room causing him to come to a complete stop just inside. He could not see or hear anything; he backed up until he was standing next to the open door. He ran his right hand up and down and along the wall, feeling for a light switch. His eyes searched the darkened room ahead of him, and he made several passes of where he thought the switch would be before looking at the wall in the dim light and seeing the little round-tipped switch. He quickly flicked it down and returned his gaze to the room.

The room sat empty; the pots and pans that hung above the large table slowly began to move. He then felt the cold air begin to swirl around his legs before increasing in intensity and height. The clanging of the pots and pans caused a sudden electric charge to run up his back. He spun around, searching the room as the cold wind continued to increase in speed.

'You can't escape what you always wanted. You asked to join us,' several voices said in unison.

Tony ran across the kitchen towards the door in the corner. Pots escaped their hooks and flew from the rack towards the investigator as he raced across the room. He ducked and dodged the metal cooking pans, hearing them crash against the floor or wall. He reached the door and pulled on the handle, half expecting it to resist against his effort, but it flew open, forcing him to stumble backwards. He felt the coldness of the floor tiles on his hands and his backside through his trousers as he hit the floor. He quickly pushed himself up as the voices began to laugh. The sound of the laughter surrounded him as if it were coming from within the swirling wind. He ran through the door and into a corridor. He continued down towards the large oak door at the far end of the corridor that led through to the library. He looked over his shoulder several times, seeing nothing but sensing the energy and coldness of the wind that followed him. Several voices continued to laugh and call to him as he ran towards the door, a door that seemed to be moving away. His eyes widened as he watched it pull away from him. He found himself running faster, his chest burning as his lungs struggled to take in oxygen. The laughter got louder, and he could feel the cold air pushing against the sweat on his neck. He couldn't run any more, and his body began to buckle, his legs giving way, forcing him to begin to stumble forward. Just as he gave in to his exhaustion and prepared himself to fall to the floor, the large oak door appeared, and he smashed his already bloodied face into the dark-stained wood, his nose shattering on impact.

Tony's body lay at the foot of the large oak door motionless. Blood pouring from his now disfigured and splintered nose. The laughter became hysterical, until the man who had sat at the head of the table materialized from the swirling wind that surrounded the unconscious investigator. The man looked down at him and grinned; he then disappeared. The wind began to speed up and tighten its rotation around Tony's body. A white glow began grew above him, its light becoming brighter and brighter until finally it exploded like a firework, silver glitter like sparks falling around him. When the last spark extinguished itself on the floor, all was dark in the corridor. The body of the investigator had disappeared, leaving only a bloody stain on the wooden floor.

9

Voices spoke from within the darkness. Young children and adults were having a number of conversations, but he could see no one. It was so dark that he lifted his hand up to where his face was but could not see it. He brought it closer until he felt his fingers touch his nose. His nose felt normal, and he ran his fingers down over his lip until he reached his chin. Again there was no pain, and all he could feel was the thick prickle of the stubble that had grown over the last four days.

The voices suddenly stopped, and only one spoke. It spoke direct at him, calling him by name;

'Tony, welcome. We are glad you have decided to join us,' the deep voice of a man said.

He recognized it as the man who had sat at the head of the table in the dining room.

'Where am I?' he called out.

A number of voices began to laugh, and then the man spoke again.

'You are everywhere. You are about to become part of the house. You will live forever between the living world and the next, able to travel wherever you want—to listen to all the people in the living world if you desire too.'

Tony could feel his anger inside him begin to grow. He no longer felt fear, only anger. They had taken him away from where he wanted to be. He didn't want to stop living.

'I don't want to be here with you!' he shouted.

There was more laughter, and then the voices began to attack his mind. They shouted and they screamed at him.

He lifted his hands to his head and covered his ears, but the voices were relentless. They were passing the barrier his hands had made and still invading his head. The pain from his face suddenly returned, and he could no longer see his nose. The pain caused him to screw his eyes tight.

He screamed, squeezing his eyes shut. He suddenly felt a sharp coldness on his skin that forced him to stop and open his eyes.

He could see the light grey clouds above him. Snow lay on the ground and lightly dusted the branches of the trees. He tried to move but found himself unable to, his arms were tied back behind him around something. His fingers quickly began feeling whatever he was attached to. He could feel rope fibers and the rough texture of tree bark. He looked down at his feet and saw a pile of wood stacked up against the base of what he was tied to. He looked around him and saw four piles of wood. A body hung limp from a thick wooden stump in the center of each. He recognized each of the bodies as his fellow investigators. His attention was then drawn to the dark shapes that stood just beyond the pyres. A cold blast of air swirled around him and then the man and several children slowly appeared. The children all giggled, and the man smiled at him.

'The mansion keeps us all alive, able to cheat death and enjoy the wonders of the world beyond,' the man said.

'But you are dead!' Tony shouted.

The man was about to speak when the voices of the children began talking in unison.

'Our bodies may have died but our spirits live on. The adults look after us as we play. The mansion allows us to return to this world providing we give it what it needs.'

Tony looked at them as they grinned at him. 'What does it need?'

The children began to laugh.

'It needs a sacrifice—a sacrifice to allow us to continue to live,' they responded.

Tony's attention suddenly shifted from the children to his four friends. A figure walked between each, touching the piles of wood with a burning torch. The figure stood back as if to admire his work once the wood beneath John had been lit. The light from the fires highlighted his features. The old man who had shown them around when they first arrived stood holding the burning torch.

'What are you doing?' Tony screamed at him, the damage to his nose causing him to shout with a lisp.

The man stared at him and smiled.

The four investigators suddenly came to life and began screaming. They struggled against the ropes that held them back, finally looking up to the cloudy sky and letting out a final blood-curdling scream.

Tears ran down Tony's face, running around the bone splinters that protruded from his flattened nose.

The children moved closer to him and began to speak to him in an eerie, comforting tone.

'Don't cry, we want you to join us.'

He managed to gather enough saliva and spittle in his dry mouth to be able to spit at the children out of defiance before once again all went dark.

10

When he opened his eyes, he found himself lying on his back, staring up at a ceiling. A red pentagram stood out against the black. He tried to sit up but found his wrists and ankles bound and tied to the floor. He looked at his wrists, and his attention was suddenly taken away from the rope that held him down and to the walls of the room. Skeletal remains were stacked up along the walls. The bodies of children and adults, some were clothed, others still had hair attached to the dry, green-colored skin of the skulls.

He lifted his head and looked towards his feet, seeing that the same kind of rope that tied his wrists bound around his ankles. He craned his neck so he could look behind him and noticed that there was no door set into any of the walls—just human remains.

He turned his head to the side, his cheek coming to rest on the cold, smooth floor, a floor that was white and stone. His eyes then focused on a green line that scored the white stone. He raised his head and followed the line as it curved around him. The straight lines that ran underneath him told him that he was lying on a pentagram, one that mirrored the one above him in red. He yanked at the rope that held his wrists and found them to be set within the stone and fixed so that he was unable to create space for him to slip his hand out.

He felt the coldness of a breeze race over his face. It made his nose sting, which was the first time he noticed the numbness of his smashed nose. It hadn't even registered that he had stopped breathing in through it.

The breeze got stronger and stronger until the dust that covered the skeletal remains began to rotate above him. The skeletons didn't move; they remained in their fixed and intertwined positions.

Tony could feel his heart begin to pound against his chest as the wind increased and tightened until a spinning vortex of dust spun above his chest, the top of it connecting to the center of the red pentagram. The tightest part of the tornado began to push into his solar plexus; the pressure as it pushed down made the investigator take short deep breaths.

The red pentagram began to glow brighter, the spinning winds turning red as if the color were being sucked from the ceiling and becoming part of the tornado. Tony struggled again against the ropes that held his wrists. He began to fight back against the probing, spinning winds that pushed harder into him. He looked at his left wrist, hoping that by looking at it he could see some kind of difference. What he did see forced his eyes to bulge.

The green pentagram he was lying on was glowing, its bright rays of light slowly reaching up like a sail being hoisted up into place.

A number of voices began to laugh, and a mixture of adults and children's voices began to speak.

'Join us, become one with the house.'

The tornado that pushed down on him began ripping his clothes from his body, the fabric disintegrating and joining the now red and green spinning winds.

Tony watched with his eyes wide as his flesh began to burn as the friction of the winds and debris cut into him. The twister pushed further and further into him until it finally penetrated his layers of skin and fat. Blood began to spin from his body up around the swirling winds until it engulfed the mini tornado. The now red fluid spinning vortex pushed deeper into his body.

Then he could feel the probing finger-like end of the tornado; he took one final deep breath and let out a scream.

Deep within the walls of the snow covered mansion, within a windowless and door less room at the heart of the building, a scream pierced the silence.

11

The sun rose slowly, the thick grey clouds cloaking its bright rays. A man began to unlock the doors of the mansion and entered. He moved straight through to the dining room, where he began to unplug and remove the equipment that had been placed there by the paranormal team. He loaded it back into the vehicles that the team had arrived in before taking them one by one to a large lake on the estate that was hidden by a barrier of thick conifer trees. He drove them down the small dirt path until he reached a steep slope above the lake. He placed them in neutral, released the handbrake, and let them roll into the cold waters. The light frost that had turned the lake to ice gave way easily and the vans slowly sank beneath the surface, joining the several other vehicles that lay on the bottom, cars and vans that spanned different generations of design. The old man then walked back to the house and removed any other evidence of the group's presence. The four piles of burnt wood and chard bones were cleared from the back garden, the remains of the four paranormal investigators were taken to one of the statues that lined the long driveway and buried beneath them, joining the several other skeletal remains that had been placed there over the years.

He returned to the dining room one last time, bowing towards the large deer antler sculpture. As he left the house, he paused at the bottom of the stairs and looked up. Standing on the staircase were three children. They smiled at him and waved.

'Thank you for bring us someone to play with,' one of the girls said without moving her lips.

The man smiled back and then left the house, locking the doors once more. He walked slowly to his car. Before getting in, he looked up at the windows of the bedrooms; a face looked down at him.

The face looking out at the man standing by his car was that of the lead investigator, his spirit now trapped within the walls of the mansion.

About Peter Buckley

Peter Buckley is a British Horror writer who has wowed readers across the globe with his visual and descriptive writing, something he is quickly being recognised for. He enjoys painting a vivid picture for the reader and jabs at their emotions throughout his stories that build and build until their climatic finale. With several more titles due for release he is busy writing not just novels but also several film scripts. When not writing he often spends time painting, or playing guitar. These creative activities often helping him create ideas and visions for his next story.

For further information about up and coming releases, visit:

www.peterbuckley.info

Follow him on twitter:

http://twitter.com/@PBuckleyBoH

Instagram:

http://instagram.com/pbuckleyhorror

Peter has also designed several fun and attractive horror themed T-Shirts available from PBuckley Horror Store. Head over to www.peterbuckleystore.info to get yours.

www.ingramcontent.com/pod-product-compliance
Lightning Source LLC
Chambersburg PA
CBHW072008020726
47501CB00006B/1736